This special signed
edition is limited to
750 numbered copies.

This is copy 655.

The Reader's Bloch, Volume Two

•

Skeleton
in the Closet
and Other Stories

•

The Reader's Bloch, Volume Two

• • •

Skeleton in the Closet and Other Stories

• •

Robert Bloch

•

edited by
Stefan R. Dziemianowicz

Subterranean Press • 2008

ISBN: 978-1-59606-122-4

Subterranean Press
PO Box 190106
Burton, MI 48519

www.subterraneanpress.com

Contents

● ●

● ● ●

Tooth or Consequences

Doctor King rose to his feet abruptly. His lonely vigil as night physician in the clinic was interrupted by a curious sound. A very curious sound. A *clicking* sound.

Harry Spencer stood in the doorway. He was the young dentist from the office down the hall. King knew him well, but now he stared curiously, wondering if Spencer had a pair of dice in his hand.

No dice. But Spencer moved slowly into the office, a look of dismay on his usually cheerful face.

"Do you hear that noise, Doctor?"

"Yes," said King. "Sort of a clicking, isn't it?"

"Clicking, hell!" gasped Harry Spencer. "That's my teeth chattering!"

"A dentist with chattering teeth," chuckled King. "That's a novelty." But his eyes held no smile as he scrutinized the agitated Spencer.

"Sit down—I'll get you a drink," he promised. And he did. Spencer gulped the whiskey gratefully. His teeth now clicked only against the glass.

"Better?"

"Much better, thank you. But Doctor—I didn't come in here for a drink. I need your help."

"Suppose you tell me the story," King suggested.

Spencer shrugged. "You may think I'm crazy. I wonder myself. But—you asked for it."

King sat back as the young dentist began to speak.

"I had only one patient tonight. He came in about an hour ago. I'd dozed off in my chair, and when I looked around, this stranger was standing in front of me, smiling. He was a tall, dark man."

"Mae West type, eh?"

"You wouldn't joke about this guy if you saw him, Doctor. Or heard him talk. He looked—funny to me. Oh, nothing I could put my finger on. Just that he made me nervous, because he was so calm, so deliberate, so *cold*.

"He said his name was Vonier. Claimed to be a mill-worker. He was off the job at night, and he heard about the clinic so he came here to get some cavities filled."

"What's wrong with that?" asked King.

"Nothing. But he had a few ideas on how he wanted to be treated. He refused to fill out a patient's card with his name and address. He said that if he could come to me twice a week with no questions asked, he'd pay double for my work."

"Just an eccentric," King commented.

"Perhaps. But that no questions asked idea—that's bad. I realized that the minute I got him into the chair and took a look at his mouth. Then I wanted to ask questions."

Spencer shuddered.

"I wanted to ask him why his teeth were so large. So abnormally developed. Particularly the *biting* teeth."

Spencer shuddered.

King smiled. "Little Red Riding Hood and her grandmother?" he suggested.

"I told you it sounds crazy," Spencer murmured. "But there was nothing funny about that stranger's teeth. Like the fangs of a wolf, or a dog. That's what they were, I tell you! Fangs. Fangs in the throat of a stranger with cold, deep eyes."

"Have you been having trouble with your nerves recently?" asked King, smoothly.

"No—but I will have from now on. You see, I haven't told you the worst part yet. The part that made my own teeth misbehave.

"After I took my first inspection I got my hand-mirror to examine a bicuspid. I thrust it into his mouth for a back view."

"Go on."

"I put it into his mouth to see the reflection—*and there was nothing there!*"

"Nothing?"

"No reflection at all! It may sound foolish, but have you any idea of how horrible it was at the time? You do the natural thing and get the unnatural. Like—like turning on your cold water faucet having a snake wriggle out.

"I backed away from the chair and told him to go away. Told him to come back tomorrow night—I wasn't feeling well. He just smiled and left, because he could see it was true. I wasn't feeling well at all. That's why I ran down the hall to you."

Doctor King grunted. Then he went to work.

"Hallucinations, eh?" he mumbled, as he helped remove Spencer's shirt. "Dizzy spells," he commented, busying himself with a stethoscope. "Delusions," he chanted, applying armbands.

Then—"Aha, just as I thought! Nothing wrong with you at all Spencer, except perhaps a little high blood pressure. Here—take these. Three a day, one after every meal. Ought to fix you up perfectly."

"What are they?"

"Garlic pills. Perfectly harmless. Now, don't worry. Come in again at the end of the week. You ought to come around nicely if you'll just forget this little incident."

Spencer thanked him, pocketed his pills, and left the office. King had given him back his courage, and his pills were easy to swallow. His advice, though—that wasn't easy to swallow.

Spencer did his best to forget, but that night he had a dream. It was a dream about a stranger with deep dark eyes, and long, pointed teeth. The teeth chattered, and Spencer woke up and listened to the clicking in his own mouth.

* * *

Harry Spencer breezed into Doctor King's office with a hearty, "Hello, Doc!"

"Well, how's it going?"

"Swell. No trouble at all."

"Glad to hear it. No more—spells."

"Not at all. This Vonier fellow came in again this evening. I examined his teeth with the mirror."

"Reflection O.K.?"

"Of course. Say, Doc, I must have sounded like a fool when I came babbling in the other night."

"Nonsense. I appreciate your little problem. Now, perhaps, you can help me with one of mine."

"Certainly—what's up?"

"Nothing much. But maybe you could help me. It seems something has happened to our blood plasma stores."

"Your what?"

"You know we keep canned blood for transfusions here at the clinic. In case of factory accidents at the mill. Well, during the last week they tell me some of the cans have been disappearing."

"Stolen?"

"Apparently. And at night. There's plenty of staff people on duty all day, but in the evenings there's no one here in the clinic but you and myself. The refrigerator is down in the annex corridor. Haven't noticed anyone prowling around, have you?"

Spencer shook his head.

"No. But that's funny. Stealing cans of blood. Could it be a practical joke?"

King turned to his desk as he spoke. "No—I don't think so. You see, I found one of the cans outside in the alley last night. It had been ripped open. Here, take a look. Tell me what you think."

He held out the gleaming metal container to Spencer.

Spencer stared at the corrugated edges of the can for a long moment.

"Somebody has been feeding wolfhounds," he said. "There are toothmarks on this can."

"Thought so," said King. "Well, there's nothing to worry about. I'm putting a new lock on the refrigerator."

"No," said Spencer, edging out of the office. "Nothing to worry about at all."

But on the way home he worried, just the same.

During the last week, blood had disappeared.

During the last week, Vonier had come to the clinic.

The long arm of coincidence?

Granted. The long arm of coincidence might sweep away a few cans of blood. But the long arm of coincidence didn't have any teeth in it. Teeth, biting into can tops. Long, pointed teeth, like the ones in Vonier's mouth.

The following evening Spencer took a look at those long, pointed teeth again.

Vonier came in quietly, sat down in the chair. Spencer tried to smile professionally as he produced his mirror and made his inspection.

Then he gulped.

The mirror thrust in Vonier's mouth showed nothing, again. Nothing at all.

He went dizzy, for a moment, because he remembered there was a new lock on the refrigerator down the hall. And now there was no reflection in the mirror.

Vampires have no reflections.

After drinking blood, after absorbing the *humanity* of blood, they might become normally visible in mirrors for a short time. Vonier, sneaking in and ripping open cans with his teeth; drinking deep. Then coming into the office for dental work. Once before he had missed, somehow, and there had been no reflection. Now the refrigerator was locked, and again there was no reflection.

* * *

Spencer stared down into the thin, pale face in the chair. His mind whirled as he stepped back. He nicked his thumb accidentally as one hand brushed the instruments on his table.

"You'll—you'll have to excuse me," he murmured. "Another spell, I'm afraid. You'd better come in again tomorrow."

The tall, dark man smiled, shrugged, arose from the chair.

Spencer couldn't help it. He sat down, closed his eyes. He heard Vonier's footsteps across the floor. His eyelids flickered momentarily—but he saw.

He saw Vonier bending over the white tile table, his head darting like a serpent's to the spot where the tiny red jet lay. His tongue lapped—and then Vonier grimaced with a look of curious pain.

Spencer sat, there, trying to control his shudderings as Vonier left the room.

Now it couldn't be denied.

The dark stranger with the long teeth, the bad teeth, was a vampire.

Abnormal teeth because of an abnormal diet. Why not?

It explained the decay, too. There was another explanation for the decay—an explanation involving sleeping all day in a terrible way. In a coffin, packed in grave-earth, hidden somewhere in the city.

Vonier, who came only at night. Who drank blood from cans. Whose reflection vanished when he had no nourishment.

"The blood is the life."

Of course he wouldn't allow his teeth to be pulled! A toothless vampire?

Naturally he wouldn't give his address. If Spencer tracked him down by day he knew what he'd find.

Certainly he had to grimace when he encountered the spot of Spencer's blood. Spencer was taking garlic pills, and vampires cannot endure garlic. Some authorities—Spencer shuddered when he thought of a demonolatrist as an *authority!*—said that garlic killed vampires. Why should it have such an effect?

Well, why is an allergy?

So there it was.

Spencer didn't sleep that night. Early in the morning he went down to the public library. He wanted to read certain books.

About silver bullets and stakes through hearts, and crucifixes and holy water.

About bodies that decay not in the tomb, and rest not.

About things that never die, that walk by night and drink deep from the throats of men.

About sunset to sunrise and pointed fangs and the legends of all nations in all times.

Early that evening he went in to Doctor King's office. He didn't have the courage to speak. King would accuse him of madness, in the stupid, melodramatic way in which people actually do accuse others of madness. The police would do nothing, and Spencer must keep still, keep the lock on the refrigerator door, keep thinking.

Doctor King gave him something to think about, all right.

"I'm out of those garlic pills right now, Spencer. Get another batch in Monday, I expect. It won't hurt you to wait a few days, I guess."

He guessed.

No garlic pills. No garlic in the bloodstream. And a *hungry* vampire!

Spencer backed out of the office, hurried clown to his own quarters. "I must keep that refrigerator locked," he whispered. "I must. What if there's an accident and they need blood in a hurry and it's gone?"

Yes. But—*what if Vonier is hungry and goes for your neck?*

There was a solution to this problem, Spencer realized. He could run like hell.

He opened his office door with that resolve.

And the vampire walked in.

* * *

Vonier was tall, dark, thin.

That's the way vampires are supposed to be—but so are a good third of all normal males.

Vonier was a foreigner with an accent. But there are many such in a mill town.

Vonier was pale. But Spencer was even paler, just now.

Now, it wasn't height, weight, complexion or accent that marked the vampire for what he was. It wasn't even the teeth, or the peculiar *faded* quality of his dark suit.

It was something about his lips. Lips that were thin, yet full. A paradox, unless you saw it. Lips that were used too much in partaking of nourishment, and became overly developed.

And of course, Vonier's eyes remained. Remained, staring sightlessly in death for twelve hours out of every twenty-four. Staring sightlessly at—what? No wonder they were dark and deep and knowing. No wonder they glared in hunger greater than human hunger. How long had they stared and hungered? How old was this creature?

Vampires are ageless and deathless until stake or silver strike their hearts into corruption. How many throats had been ripped before this thing discovered the blood transfusion cans in the refrigerator? How many would be ripped again, now that the cans were protected by a stout lock? And how soon?

Very soon, Spencer thought, unless he could act. For Mr. Vonier was quite pallid tonight. He was slow in his movements, almost drunkenly deliberate. Only his eyes were quick. Quick and hot, as they gazed at the dentist's throat with a desire he had never seen in human eyes before. An unimaginable desire.

"You're—late," Spencer choked out.

"I was held up," Vonier answered, with a little smile. "I had to do some shopping."

Shopping. That's what you do when you're *hungry*.

"Well, let's get started."

Vonier slid into the chair.

"What must you do tonight, Doctor?"

Spencer's voice trembled. He had to put this over. He had to.

"I'm afraid, Mr. Vonier, that some of those teeth must come out. If you'll let me make a cast of your mouth now—just a wax impression—I can tell you in a jiffy where the trouble is."

"Please, no. I am very sensitive. I do not wish for you to place any-thing in my mouth."

What? No nice little plaster of paris cast that Spencer had worked on? No nice little plaster of paris cast, treated with liquid air, to harden im-mediately in the vampire's mouth and clamp his teeth together forever?

That *was* a disappointment.

But there was plan number two. Spencer's voice mastered a tremor. "Still, you'll have to have a few extractions. Those lower left molars are pretty bad."

"I do not wish—"

"I'm the Doctor! I'll give you gas, so it won't bother you. Those teeth are probably dead, anyway."

Dead.

Vonier smiled, but Spencer didn't like it. He got the gas going, fumbled with the tube and cone.

"Breathe deeply."

Do dead men breathe?

The gates of Hell closed. Eyelids fluttered down over them.

He—it—was sleeping.

Now! Spencer was stern. Sure, they'd call it murder. But he must chance it.

* * *

H e fumbled with the drill. Put in the new head. The long steel bit he'd bought specially. The steel bit that was like a sharp splinter. Sharp as a stake. A stake to drive into the heart.

The drill buzzed. Spencer fed more gas into the creature that lay all white and still under the cold blue light; lay like a slick and glassy corpse in the morgue. Fill it with gas, and then drive that drill home into the heart—

Pulses pounding, he guided the drill towards the rotten chest. One swift stab, now.

"Just a moment."

The eyes flickered. Lightning. More lightning in the steel clutch of the long, cold hands.

"My teeth are not there, Doctor. You know that."

"You know a lot more, too. Don't you, Doctor?"

Tooth or Consequences

"I—"

Vonier sat up. The smile was full now, the long fangs exposed.

"You know why the blood was stolen, don't you? You know about my teeth, too. You know why your garlic kept me off last night. Isn't that so, Doctor?"

"Y—yes." Spencer said it the way men used to when the Inquisitors tightened the rack.

"Ah. Then don't you know that one of—us—cannot be killed by poison, or bullet, or sword? That fire does not consume us when we walk, nor gas drug our senses?"

Spencer realized the truth too late. Much too late.

"Who has locked the refrigerator?" A soft voice. Soft as the clinging caress of a serpent. And as cold.

"I don't know. The clinic doctors must have the key."

"Get it for me tomorrow. You know why. I will have it or you will provide me with nourishment."

"Garlic—" Spencer began. It took courage to say anything without screaming.

The vampire smiled. "I think not. Something has happened to your supply of garlic, hasn't it?"

"How do you know?"

Mr. Vonier's answer was quite dreadful. "The *carnivorae*, my dear Doctor, have a very acute sense of smell."

The black-clad figure slid from the chair, moved towards the door. Then Vonier turned. Spencer looked into a haggard white face. There was hunger there—but for the first time he read something inherent in all starvation. A kind of pathos.

"I don't like this," Mr. Vonier said, softly. "You must believe that, Doctor. I was—normal—once. It's what psychiatrists might call a compulsion, you know. A compulsion. Something driving you.

"But that's beside the point, isn't it? You are not interested in the long years. The long nights. The longer days—"

Spencer stared, but Vonier regained his composure swiftly.

"I tried to fight it. I took blood from the cans, instead of in my *regular* way. But when you are denied food too long, you get hungry.

"Remember that. Give me the key tomorrow night—or I shall force my way to nourishment with my teeth. They are very sharp teeth, aren't they, Doctor? Good night."

The door closed.

Spencer didn't follow. He could have taken that last chance, trailed the vampire to its lair somewhere in the city, waited until daylight and entered with a stake.

But human beings are human beings. Sometimes they faint. Spencer did when the door closed.

* * *

It was dawn when he came to. Dawn—of the last day.

Spencer didn't waver. If it wasn't his neck tonight, it would be somebody else's neck. He had to protect the blood supply, for he had seen the injured workmen roll in, their families clustering about them in moaning groups. They could not be denied. There was no way out unless he could find it himself.

The priest couldn't help him. It was noon when Spencer went to Father Donnelly and gave him the refrigerator key to keep. He wanted to confess, but at the last moment he knew it would be no use. He just told Father Donnelly to keep the key for him.

He took a crucifix, too.

That might hold *it* off for a little while. The crucifix could not destroy, but like garlic, the shape held an allergy.

Then Spencer went home, tools out his revolver, and began to mould a silver bullet.

The stake had failed. Garlic had failed. Gas had failed. Poison and fire wouldn't work. He couldn't pull the teeth or trap the mouth.

So mould a silver bullet.

Why should silver affect *them?* Perhaps it was the contact of silver with the blood stream. The blood circulates in 46 seconds. That is, in normal men. The physiology of vampires must be strange enough. Silver poisoned, silver might disturb elements of dead blood mingled with living blood.

The physiology of vampires…

Spencer believed in the silver bullet. He had to. It was the last resource of vampire legends and it had to work.

But it didn't.

Evidently legend was legend—legend from a day of rough pistols and muzzle-loaders. It was already dusk when Spencer realized he was beaten by ballistics. Mould and file as he would, the bullet wouldn't fit for firing.

Tooth or Consequences

And he had melted down the silver crucifix for the bullet!

It was the old story. Science against the Powers of Darkness, that sort of thing. And this time science had failed. Spencer smiled wryly. He wished he had the crucifix now. But with it or without it, he had his rendezvous to keep.

How he walked to the clinic he never knew. Every step was a battle. But Vonier would be there, and if he didn't show up, Vonier would stalk abroad. Stalk abroad and drink—

Spencer hurried in. No weapons now. He knew what this meant. He was walking the Last Mile when he went down the hall to his office.

He sat there counting the minutes. Silver bullets shooting into Time. Silver bullets and a silver key and a silver crucifix. 46 seconds, and the physiology of a vampire...

The door opened.

Vonier.

He didn't say anything. He didn't need to. Spencer read it in his eyes, read the hunger blazing there.

The smile in the pale face, the ageless face, was sardonic.

"I have two cavities to fill tonight, Doctor. One in my teeth and one in my stomach."

Spencer almost laughed. There was a jest—with teeth in it.

"Before we proceed, please, will you take a look at this one here? It's very painful."

Harry Spencer's most difficult patient climbed into the chair, and like an ordinary mortal, indicated a yellow fang. His tong, talon-like finger fumbled in his mouth.

"*Zhiz un eer.*"

Just another patient, indicating the source of his pain. Just another—

Spencer looked at the infected incisor. Enamel decay. Cavity. Against the roots, deep.

Fill the teeth of the creature that was to kill him? Anything! Just to stall, stall for time, stall against the question of where the key was. Perhaps the creature thought he had brought the key. Perhaps these last few moments might suggest a way out.

Harry Spencer was, after all, a professional man. He gave his patient's teeth a professional examination. He would give this tooth a professional filling.

"Lose the fear in routine. It's just another patient."

17

Spencer's brain mumbled to him, then shivered in fear as he looked into the deep eyes of Vonier, saw what waited there, what lurked in hunger.

* * *

His fingers didn't tremble as he drilled. How he longed to plunge that drill down the red throat—into the lungs from which welled an odour of unspeakable corruption! But it would do no good. Vampires do not die by steel.

His fingers didn't tremble as he turned away and compounded the filling.

But they did tremble as he packed it into the enlarged cavity. For a moment his pick slipped, and he cut a tiny nick in the gum of the creature as he finished the job. A little gout of blood welled, and Vonier winced in pain. But the filling was in place.

Vonier sat up. "There, now." His voice was hoarse with a hunger no longer concealed. "And now, Doctor—if you'll just hand over that key?"

He read the answer in Spencer's eyes, read it in Spencer's beaded forehead.

The vampire rose swiftly.

Arms wound about Spencer's body, tight as the grip of shrouds. Fingers like white worms writhed into Spencer's throat, bending him back.

Clothes smelling of grave-earth, a breath of carrion, and through it all the white face burning bright, bending closer. Spencer saw the yellow fangs gleam, saw the teeth descend to his neck.

He fought desperately—but Vonier held him as though he were a puppet with flailing arms. Vonier held him and the teeth descended.

Even at this last moment he could think about how long they were, and how sharp, and how they could sink into a throat and tear the life away.

The vampire ripped his head backwards, stabbed that mouth down into Spencer's neck—

And fell.

Spencer went down, too, when the grip was released. The creature was somewhere beneath him, groaning. Or was he? Groans died away, and Spencer stared at a litter on the rug.

Less than a minute since it had risen from the chair and gripped him. Less than a minute, and it was gone. Even the rotted clothing...

And it was less than a minute later that Doctor King walked into the room.

"Hello, Spencer. Just closed up the office for the night. Thought I'd drop in and see how you felt."

Spencer was busily engaged with a broom, sweeping up a little pile of powdery dust on the floor.

"Had a patient tonight?" King asked.

Spencer nodded. "He's gone though. Filled a tooth for him."

He stooped and picked something gleaming from the dust at his feet.

"Funny thing—the filling seems to have dropped out when he left. Careless of me."

"You're a bad dentist, eh?" King chuckled.

"No," said Spencer. He stared for a long moment at the tiny silver filling he held amidst the dust in his hand.

"No—I'd say I'm a damned good dentist, at that!"

The Curse of the House

"Did you ever hear of a haunted house?"

I nodded slowly.

"Well, this case is different. I'm not afraid of a haunted house. My problem is that there's a house haunting *me*."

I sat silent for a long moment, staring at Will Banks blankly. He in turn regarded me calmly, his long, thin face impassive, and his gray eyes shining quite rationally as they focussed at random on various objects about my office.

But a slight, almost imperceptible twitching of the lips indicated the undoubtedly hyper-neurasthenic tendencies which his calm exterior hid. Nevertheless, I mused, the man had courage. Victims of hallucination and obsession are usually quite unstrung, and their schizoid tendencies generally are uncontrollably manifested. But Will Banks had guts. This thought came quickly, then was overmastered by curiosity regarding his statement: "There's a house haunting *me*."

He had said it so matter-of-factly, so calmly. Too calmly. If he had been hysterical about it, or melodramatic, then it would indicate that he realized his plight as a victim of an obsession and was trying to fight it. But this acceptance implied implicit faith in his delusion. A bad sign.

"Perhaps you'd better tell me the story from the beginning," I said, a bit nervous myself. "There is a story, I presume?"

Banks' face, all at once, displayed genuine agitation. One hand rose unconsciously to brush back his blond, straight hair from the perspiring forehead. His mouth twitched more perceptibly.

"There is a story, Doctor," he said. "It isn't an easy story for me to tell and it won't be an easy story for you to—to believe. But it's true.

21

Good God," he burst out, "don't you understand? That's what makes it so awful. It's true."

* * *

I adopted a professional suavity as I ignored his emotion and offered him a cigarette. He held it in nervous fingers, without lighting it. His eyes sought mine imploringly.

"You aren't laughing at me, are you, Doctor? In your capacity—" (he could not bring himself to say "psychiatrist") "you must listen to a lot of things that sound peculiar. You do, don't you?"

I nodded, offering him a light. The first puff braced him.

"And Doctor, another thing. You fellows have some kind of medical oath, don't you? About violating confidences, and all that sort of thing? Because there are certain—"

"Tell your story, Mr. Banks," I said, briskly. "I promise you that I'll do what I can to help, but in order to help you I must have absolute sincerity from you."

Will Banks spoke.

"I told you that I'm haunted by a house. Well, that's true, strange as it may sound. But the circumstances are stranger still. To begin with, I'm going to ask you to believe in witchcraft. Get that, Doctor? I'm going to ask you to believe. I'm not arguing with you to convince you, although I think that can be done. I'm merely asking you. That in itself should convince you of my sincerity and my sanity, Unless I miss my guess, the sure indication of a psychotic personality is when the deluded puts up a long, fantastic argument to convince his hearer. Am I right?"

I nodded. It was true.

"Well, I'm merely asking you to believe in witchcraft for the duration of my tale. Just as I believed, years ago, when I went to Edinburgh. I had been a student of the lost sciences men choose to call the Black Arts. I was interested in the use ancient sorcerers made of mathematical symbols in their ceremonies—surmising that perhaps they were unconsciously employing geometric patterns which hold keys to the outer cosmos, even the Fourth Dimension recognized by modern-day scientists.

"I spent years in the fascinating pursuit of olden devil-worship, traveling to Naples, Prague, Budapest, Cologne. I shall not say what I came to believe, nor shall I do more than hint at the survival of

22

demon-worship in the modern world. Enough that after a time I established connections with the vast underground system controlling hidden cults. I learned codes, signals, mysteries. I was accepted. And material for my monograph was being piled up.

"Then I went to Edinburgh—Edinburgh, where once *all* men believed in witchcraft. Talk about New England witch-baiters! That's childish stuff compared to the Scottish town where not twenty or thirty old. hags, but thirty thousand witches and sorcerers once lived and lurked. Think of it; three hundred years ago there were thirty thousand of them, meeting in old houses, creeping through underground tunnels in which lay buried the black secrets of their blood cults. *Macbeth* and *Tam O'Shanter* hint of it, but vaguely.

"Here in ancient Edinburgh I hoped to find the final corroboration for my theories. Here in the veritable witches' cauldron of wizardry I settled and began to investigate. My underground connections served me, and after a time I was admitted to certain houses. In them I met people who still live a secret life of their own under the very surface of a quiet, modern Scottish city. Some of those dwellings are many hundreds of years old—still in use—some in use *from below*. No, I won't explain that.

"Then I met Brian Droome. 'Black Brian' Droome he was called, and in the coven he had another name. He was a gigantic man, bearded and swarthy. When we met I was reminded of descriptions concerning Gilles de Rais—reminded in more ways that one. Indeed, he did have French blood, though his ancestors had settled in Edinburgh hundreds of years ago. They had built Brian's house, and it was this house that I particularly wanted to see.

"For Brian Droome's ancestors had been sorcerers. I knew that. In the infamous secret history of European cults, the clan of Droome occupied a detestable eminence. During the great witchcraft craze of three hundred years ago, when the king's soldiers came seeking the burrows in which the wizards lay hidden, Droome House was one of the first to be ransacked.

"For the Droomes presided over a truly terrible cult, and in their great cellars fully thirty members of the family died before the muskets of the outraged militia. And yet the house itself had survived. While thousands of ransacked dwellings had burned in those terrible nights, Droome House had been left gaunt and deserted, but untouched. Some of the Droomes escaped.

"Those surviving Droomes returned. The worship went on, but in secret now; the Droomes were a devout race, not easily moved to abandon their religious tenets. The house stood, and the Faith stood. Until this day.

"But now only Brian Droome remained, of all the line. He lived alone in the old house, a reputed student of sorcery who seldom attended the gatherings out on the hills where surviving believers still invoked the Black Father. My connections secured me an introduction, for I was greatly desirous of seeing the ancient dwelling and looking at certain inscriptions and designs which legend said were engraved on the stony walls of the cellars.

"Brian Droome. Swarthy, bearded, burning-eyed! Unforgettable! His personality was as compelling as a serpent's—and as evil. Generations had moulded him into the epitome of a sorcerer, a wizard, a seeker after things forbidden. The heritage of four hundred years had made a wizard of Broome.

* * *

In boyhood he read the black books in his old house; in manhood he walked the shadows of its halls in a palpable atmosphere of witchery. And yet, he was not a silent man, he could talk a blue streak, and was remarkably well-informed and well-educated—in a word, cultured. But he was not *civilized*. Brian Droome was a pagan, and when he spoke of his beliefs he had the trusting manner of a fearless child.

"I met him several times at—gatherings. Then I requested the pleasure of visiting him at his home. I had to wheedle, I admit, because he was damnably reluctant. On the excuse of showing him certain notes of my own, I at last obtained his grudging consent. Others expressed genuine amazement when I told them; it seems that Droome had never allowed strangers in the great house was alone in the sense that he entertained no *human* company.

"So I called on Brian Broome. When I went, as I told you, I believed in witchcraft; believed, that is, that the art had been practiced and had a scientific basis—although I did not concede that its achievements were in any way connected with the supernatural.

"But when I came in sight of the House of Droome, I began to change my mind. I didn't realize the full extent of the change until later, but even at the time the first glimpse of Brian Droome's dwelling filled me—filled me—with horror!"

* * *

The last words seemed to explode out of Will Banks He went on, more softly than before.

"Now you must mark this. The house stood on a hillside against the bleeding sunset sky. It was a two story house, with twin gables on either side of a peaked roof. The house rose out of the hill, like a gigantic head emerging from a grave. The gables were horns against the heavens. Two jutting eaves were ears. The door was wide as a grinning mouth. There was an upper window on each side of the door.

"I won't tell you that the windows were like eyes. They *were* eyes. Through their narrow slits they peered at me, watched me approach. I felt it as I have never felt anything before—that this house, this centuried dwelling, possessed a life of its own; that it was *aware* of me, saw me, heard me coming.

"I walked up the path, nonetheless, because I didn't know what was to come. I walked up and the mouth opened—I mean, the door opened—and Brian let me in. *It* opened, I tell you. Brian didn't open it. That was awful.

"It was just as though I had walked into a monster's head; a thinking monster's head. I could almost feel the brain buzzing about me, pulsing with thoughts as black as the shadows in the long, narrow, throat-like hallway through which we walked.

"Bear with me while I give a few details. There was a long hall, with a stairway at the further end, branching off into side rooms. The first side room to the left was the study Brian took me to. How well I know the geography of that house! Why shouldn't I know it? I see it every night in my dreams.

"We talked. Of course it's important to remember what we talked about, but I really cannot recall. Brian, immensely forceful personality though he was, paled into insignificance beside the weight exerted by that ghastly house. If Brian Droome was the product of twelve generations, then this house was the twelve generations incarnate.

"It was something that had stood for three hundred and eighty years, filled with life all that time. Filled with evil life, filled with weird experiments, mad cries, hoarse prayers, and still hoarser answers. Hundreds of feet had trod its floors, hundreds of visitors had come and departed. Some, many in fact, had not departed. And of those, legend said that some had not been men. Blood had run in a slow, throbbing stream.

"And the house—not Brian Droome but the house—was an aged person who had seen all of birth and life and death and what lay beyond. Here was the real wizard, the true viewer of all secrets. This house had seen it all. It lived, it leered down from the hill.

"While Brian talked and I automatically replied, I kept thinking of the house. This great study, a monstrous room filled with massive bookcases and long tables burdened with excess tomes; this great study with its olden oak furniture, suddenly seemed in my mind's eye to be stripped of all extraneous objects. It became an empty room again—just a vast wooden expanse with huge timbers that formed the rafters overhead.

"I imagined it like that, dusty and deserted, robbed of all signs of visible habitation. Still that damnable impression of life remained. An empty room here was never empty. The thought agitated me.

"It agitated me so much that I had. to talk about it to Brian Droome. He smiled, slowly, as I described my sensations. Then he spoke.

"'It is a much older house than even you imagine,' he said in his deep burring voice: 'I who have dwelt here all my life still do not know what further secrets it may possess. It was built originally by Cornac Droome, in 1561. You may be interested in knowing that at this time the hill on which it stood supported several Druidic stones, originally part of the circle-pattern.

"'Some of these were laid in the foundations. Others still stand in the upper cellar. And another thing my dear Banks—this house was not built, it *accumulated*.

"It was reared upward for two stories, that is true. The gables and eaves and roof were then as they are now, and the second floor remains unchanged. But the house had once only a single cellar. It was not until the Faith prospered that we built again. And we built *downward*.

"'We built downward, I say. Just as a church spire rears toward Heaven, we of the Faith appropriately builded toward our own Kingdom. First a second cellar, and then a third; finally passages under the hill for secret goings-forth when under duress.

"'When Droome House was entered, the King's men never discovered the lower cellars, and that was well, for they would not have liked what they saw, being unbelievers and sacrilegious. Since then we have been wary of visitors, and the covens no longer meet; the lower cellars have fallen into disuse. Still, we have held many private ceremonies, for the Droomes had secret pacts of their own requiring certain regular rites. But in the past three hundred years we and Droome House have lived together in solitude'."

Will Banks paused, drew breath. His lips twitched, he went on:

"I listened eagerly to his admissions concerning the cellars which I so desired to inspect. But something of his discourse puzzled me—his use of the word 'we' interchangeably, so that at times it meant the family, at times himself, and at other times it actually seemed to imply the very house!

"He arose and stood by the wall, and I noted how his fingers softly caressed the ancient wood. It was not the caress of a connoisseur handling a rare tapestry, not the caress a master bestows upon a dog. It was the caress of a lover—the soft stroking motion of understanding and concealed desire.

"'This old house and I understand one another,' Droome burred. His smile held no humor. 'We take care of one another, even though today we are alone. Droome House protects me even as I guard the secrets of Droome House.' He stroked the woodwork gently."

* * *

Banks paused again, swallowed hard before continuing. "By this time a revulsion had set in. Either I was mad, or Brian Droome was. I wanted my information and then I wanted to get out. I wanted to get out, I realized, because I never wanted to see this house again. I never wanted even to think about it again. And it wasn't the well-known fear of enclosed places— It wasn't claustrophobia, Doctor. I just couldn't stand the place, or rather, the unnatural thoughts it aroused. But a stubbornness was in my soul. I did not want to leave without the information I had come for.

"I rather bungled things because of the unreasoning panic I felt, the unreasoning panic that rose in my heart as he lighted candles in the gray room and peopled the house with walking shadows. I asked him almost point-blank if I could visit the cellars. I told him why, told him about inspecting certain symbols on the walls. He was standing by a candelabrum on the wall, lighting the waxen taper. As it flared up, a corresponding flare flamed in his eyes.

"'No, Will Banks,' he said. 'You cannot see the cellars of Droome House.'

"Just that and nothing more. The glare, and the flat refusal. He gave no reason, he did not hint of mysteries I had no right to know, he did not threaten harm should I insist. No, not Brian Droome. But the house—the house did! The house *hinted*. The house *threatened*. The shadows seemed to coalesce on the walls, and a gathering oppression fell upon me, seized me in impalpable tentacles that strangled the soul. I cannot express it save in this melodramatic wise—the house *hated* me.

"I was silent. I did not ask again. Brian Droome tugged at his black beard. His smile signified that the incident was closed.

"'You'll be going soon,' he said. 'Before that, a drink with me to stay your journey.'

"He walked out of the room to prepare the drink. Then a mad impulse seized me. Yet the impulse had reasons behind it. After all, I had come to Edinburgh solely for this end. For years I had studied, and here lay a clue I sorely needed. It was my only chance of obtaining the information I desired, and if the inscriptions were what I fancied, I could jot them down in a notebook in a moment. This was the first reason.

"The second was more complicated. The house—it threatened me. Like a mouse in the grip of a cat, I knew my doom but could not keep still. I had to squirm, wriggle. Once deprived of Droome's company, even for a moment, panic gripped me like that cat, pouncing on the helpless mouse. I felt as though eyes were watching me, invisible claws extending on every hand. I was unable to remain in this room, I had to move. Of course I could have followed Brian Droome, but the other reason impelled me.

"I determined to enter the cellar. I rose quietly, on tiptoe, went down the hall. It was dark and still. Now don't misunderstand. It wasn't *haunted*. This was not a mystery-thriller mansion, with cobwebs and bats and creaking noises. It was merely dark, and the dark was old. Light hadn't shone here for three hundred years, nor sane laughter broken the stillness. It was darkness that should have been dead, but it was alive. And it oppressed and terrified, a thousand times more than the sight of a ghost.

"I found myself trembling when I located the cellar door with the steps below. The candle I had slipped into my pocket before leaving the study came into my hands, wet with sweat from my palms. I lit it and descended the stairs. I left the house's head and entered its heart.

The Curse of the House

"I'll be brief here. The cellar was huge and there were many rooms, yet there was no dust. I won't go any further to describe the signs of life. There was a chapel and long walls with the symbols I sought, and an altar that undoubtedly must have been one of the Druid stones Brian referred to.

"But I didn't notice that. I never did see what I came to see. Because in the second chapel room I kept looking at the rafters. The long brown beams overhead against the cellar roof. The long brown beams with the great hooks on them. The great steel hooks. The great steel hooks that held dangling things! White, dangling things! Human skeletons!

* * *

"Human skeletons that gleamed as they hung in the breeze from the opened door. Human skeletons still so new as to remain hanging articulated. New skeletons on hooks on the long brown rafters.

"There was blood on the floor and strips of flesh, and on the altar a thing still lay—not cleanly stripped—yet. There was a vacant hook waiting, but the thing lay there on the altar before the black statue of Satan.

"And I thought of Brian Droome's mention of *private rites* still carried on by his family. I thought of his reticence concerning guests, and his refusal to allow me entrance to the cellar. I thought of the further cellars that lay below; if this were the heart of the house what might lie beyond in the *soul?*

"Then I looked back at the dancing skeletons that trod the air with bony feet and swung their gleaming arms as they grinned down on me in mockery. They hung on the rafters of the House of Droome, and the House of Droome guarded them as one guards a secret.

"The House of Droome was with me in the cellar, watching me, waiting for my reaction. I dared not show it. I stood there, in fancy feeling forces quiver about me. Forces radiating from the bloodstained walls. Forces bursting from the outlandish designs cut in the stones. Forces rising from the floor, from depths still further below.

"Then I felt human eyes. Brian Droome stood in the doorway."

* * *

Banks was now on his feet. His eyes were staring. He was reliving the scene.

29

"I threw the candle and struck him in the face with the burning end. Then I snatched up the unmentionable basin from the altar top and I hurled it at his head. He went down. I was upon him then, desperately tearing at his throat. I had to act first, because when he had stood there in the doorway I had seen the knife in his hand. A cutting-knife, a sawing-knife. And I remembered the thing still lying on the altar. That was why I moved first, and now I was wrestling with him on the stone floor, trying to wrest the knife away. I was no match for him.

"He was a giant and he picked me up and carried me to the center of the room, carried me toward the vacant hook that gleamed in the line of skeletons. Its steel barb projected outward, and I knew he meant to hang me there. My hands fought for that knife as he forced me down that grinning line of eyeless watchers. He lifted me high, until my head was on a level with his own madly distorted face.

"Then my hands found his wrist. Desperation gave me strength. I drove his wrenched arm back, upward. The knife entered his belly in one great thrust. The force spun him around and he fell back. His own neck caught against the steel hook hanging from the rafter. As his great arms released me he was pinioned. Blood gushed from his corded throat as I plunged the knife home again and again.

"He died there, on the hook, and he mumbled, 'The Curse of my House upon you.' I heard the curse through red hazes of madness. It was not dramatically impressed on my mind—then. Instead, there was only the gnawing horror of our struggle and his death; the fear which caused me to race up those steps without turning back, grope through darkness to the study—and set fire to the house.

"Yes, I burned Droome House, as one burns a witch or warlock; as they destroyed wizards in the olden days. I burned Droome House so that fire might purify and flame consume the evil that leaped at me as I ran out of the blazing dwelling. I swear the flames nearly trapped me as I ran, although they had only risen a moment before. I swear I clawed at the door as though it were a living thing that grappled with me, seeking to hold me back.

"Only when I stood below the hill and watched the red glow arise did I remember Brian's words. 'The Curse of my House upon you.' I thought of them as the door broke into a gash of scarlet flame, and when the people came and clustered about I still remained, heedless of danger, until I saw the walls of that accursed mansion crumble into glowing ash, and the place of evil destroyed forever. Then I knew peace, for a while.

"But now—Doctor—I'm haunted."

Will Banks' voice became a whisper.

"I left Edinburgh at once, dropped my studies. I had to, of course. Fortunately I was not incriminated in the affair, but my nerves had been shattered. I was on the verge of a true psychotic condition. I was advised to travel, regain my health and strength to fortify my mental outlook. So I traveled.

"In England I saw it first. I was spending a week with friends at Manchester; they had a country place just outside the industrial town. We rode about the estate one afternoon and I lagged behind to rest my horse. It was about sunset when I rounded a bend and saw the hill. The sky was red above it.

"I saw the hill first. And then, something *grew* on it. It *grew*. You've read about ghosts, Doctor? About how they manifest themselves with ectoplasm? They say it's like watching a picture come out in the solution in which a print is developed. It comes gradually, takes shape. The colors fill in.

"It was the house that did that! Droome House! Slowly, wavering lines grew solid as I recognized the damnable head that leered out of the hillside. The window-eyes were red with slanted sunlight, and they looked straight at me. 'Come in Will Banks,' they invited. I stared for a full minute, blinking and hoping with all my heart that the vision would go away. It didn't.

"Then I spurred my horse to a gallop and fled down the road to my friends, never looking back.

"'Who lives on the hill?' I gasped. Jessens, the banker friend I was staying with, gave me a look. Even before he spoke, I knew. 'No one,' he said. 'Trying to pull my leg, are you?'

"I kept still. But I left the next day. Went to the Alps. No, I didn't see the Droome House on the Matterhorn. I had a good solid six months of peace. But on the train back to Marseilles I looked out of the window at sunset and—there it was. 'Come in, Will Banks,' the eyes invited. I turned away. That same night I went to Naples.

"After that it was a race. For six months, eight months at a time I seemed safe. But if sunset found me near a hillside, be it in Norway or Burma, the damned vision reoccurred. I've put it all down. Twenty-one times in the past ten years.

"I grew clever enough about it all. After the third or fourth manifestation I realized that this combination of sunset and hillside was necessary to produce the image—for ghost I would not admit it was. I avoided being out in the open after dusk began. But in the last year or so, I've grown more hopeless.

"Travel has proved fruitless. I cannot escape it. Naturally, the story has remained with me alone. I dared not tell anyone, and several occasions served to convince me that nobody saw the apparition save myself. What has frightened me is the later developments of the thing.

"Now, when I force myself to gaze steadily at the house, I see it for a longer and longer time. And each time—this in the last three years, I have finally computed—that house appears nearer and nearer to the spot where I am standing.

"Don't you understand what it means? Sooner or later I shall be before the house, at the very door! And one sunset I may find myself inside! Inside, under the long brown rafters with the hooks, and Brian all bloody and the house waiting for me. Nearer and nearer. Yet God knows I'm always on the road when I see it up there on the hill. But I get closer to it every time, and if I enter that place of ghosts I know *something* waits for me; the spirit of that house—"

* * *

Will Banks did not stop of his own accord—I stopped him.

"Shut up!" I rapped sharply.

"What?"

"Shut up!" I repeated. "Now listen to me, Will Banks. I've listened to you, and I haven't commented; I expect the same courtesy in return."

He calmed down at once, as I knew he would—I was not a psychiatrist for nothing, and psychiatrists know when to let their patients talk and when to shut them up.

"I've listened to you," I said, "without any gibes about witchcraft or fantasies. Now suppose you listen to my theories with the same respect. To begin with, you're suffering from a common obsession. Nothing serious, just a common, everyday obsession—a cousin to the one that makes a habitual drunkard see pink elephants even when not actually suffering from *delirium tremens*."

Banks bridled. I stared him down.

The Curse of the House

"It's undoubtedly a symptom of a guilt-complex," I said matter of factly., "You killed a man named Brian Droome. Don't bother to deny it. We'll admit it. We won't go into the motives, we won't even examine justification. You killed Brian Droome under very peculiar circumstances. Something about the house in which the deed occurred was strongly impressed upon your susceptible subconscious mind. In a state of tension following the killing, you fired the house. In your subconscious, the destruction of the house loomed as a greater crime than the destruction of the man. Right?"

"It did, Doctor—it did!" Banks wailed. "The house had a life of its own, a concentrated life that was greater than that of a single person. That house was Brian Droome, and all his wizard ancestors. It was Evil, and I destroyed it. Now it seeks vengeance."

"Wait a minute," I drawled. "Wait—a—minute. You're not telling me, I'm telling *you*. All right. In consequence of your guilty feelings this complex has arisen. This hallucination is a mental projection of your own guilt; a symptom of the weight you felt while keeping the story a secret.

"Understand? In psychoanalysis we have come to refer to confession as a *cathartic method* whereby the patient is often relieved of mental difficulties by merely telling frankly the story of his troubles. Confession is good for the soul.

"It may be that all of your problem has been solved by simply unburdening yourself to me here. If not, I shall endeavor to probe more deeply. There are some things I wish to learn regarding your association with witchcraft cults; I will need to find out certain details of your mental attitude regarding superstitions and the like."

"Don't you see?" Banks muttered.

"You can't understand. This is real. You must know the supernatural as I do—"

"There *is* no supernatural," I stated. "There is merely the natural. If one speaks of *supernatural* one might as well speak of the *subnatural*, a manifest absurdity. Extensions of physical laws I grant, but such things merely occur in a disordered brain."

"I don't care what you believe," Banks said. "Help me, Doctor, only help me. I can't bear it much longer. Believe that. I would never have come to you otherwise. Even drugs won't keep me from dreaming. Wherever I go I see that cursed house rising up out of hills, grinning at me and beckoning. It gets nearer and nearer. Last week I saw it here—in America. Four hundred years ago it rose in Edinburgh; I burnt it ten years ago. Last week I saw it. Very close. I was only fifteen feet away from the door, and the door was open. Help me, Doctor—you must!"

"I will. Pack your things, Banks. You and I are going fishing."

"What?"

"You heard me. Be ready at noon tomorrow. I'll bring the car around. I have a little lodge up in the Berkshires, and we can put in a week or so of loafing around. Meanwhile I'll get a slant at you. You'll have to co-operate, of course—but we'll discuss those details later. Here now, just do as I say. And I think if you try a tablespoonful of this in some brandy tonight before you go to bed you won't have any more house-parties in your dreams. Noon tomorrow, then. Good-by."

* * *

It was noon the next day. Banks wore a gray suit and a nervous frown. He didn't feel like talking, that was evident. I chatted gayly, laughed a lot at my own stories, and swung the car up through the hills all afternoon.

I had it all planned out in my own mind, of course. The first notes on the case were down. I'd handle him easily the first few days, watch him for betraying signs, and then really get to work from the analytical side. Today I could afford to put him at ease.

We drove on, Banks sitting silent until the shadows came.

"Stop the car."

"Eh?"

"Stop it—it's getting toward sunset."

I drove on, unheeding. He shouted. He threatened. I hummed. The redness deepened in the west. Then he began to plead.

"Please stop. I don't want to see it. Go back. Go back—there's a town we just passed. Let's stay there. Please. I can't bear to see it again. Close! Doctor, for God's sake—"

"We'll arrive in half an hour," I said. "Don't be a child. I'm with you."

I piloted the car between the green borders of the encircling hills. We headed west against the fading sun. It shone redly on our faces, but Banks was white as a sheet beneath its glare as he cowered in the seat beside me. He mumbled under his breath. All at once his body tensed and his fingers dug into my shoulder with maniacal strength.

"Stop the car!" he screamed.

The Curse of the House

I applied the brakes. He was cracking.

"There it is!" he yelled, with something that was almost triumph in his voice. Something masochistic, as though he welcomed the ordeal to come. "There's the house, on that hill. Do you see it? There!"

Of course it was just a bare hillside, some fifty feet back from the road.

"It's grinning!" he cried. "Droome is watching me. Look at the windows. They wait for me."

* * *

I watched him closely as he moved out of the car. Should I stop him? No, of course not. Perhaps if he went through with it this time he'd throw off his obsession. At any rate, if I could observe the incident I might get the clues necessary to unraveling the threads of his twisted personality. Let him go.

It was awful to watch, I admit it. He was screaming about the "House of Droome" and the "Curse" as he went up the hillside. Then I noticed that he was sleep-walking. Self-hypnotized.

In other words, Banks didn't know he was moving. He thought he was still in the car. That explained his story of how each time the imaginary house seemed closer. He unconsciously approached the focal point of his hallucination, that was all. Like an automaton he strained up the green grade.

"I'm at the door," he shouted. "It's close—God, Doctor—it's close. The damned thing is creeping toward me, and the door is open. What shall I do?"

"Go inside," I called. I wasn't sure he could hear me in his state, but he did. I counted on such an action to break the thread for him; watched his reactions carefully.

His tall form was silhouetted against the sunset as he walked. And now one hand reached out, his feet rose as though crossing an actual threshold. It was—I admit it—horrible to watch. It was the grotesque pantomime beneath a scarlet sky, the mimicry of a madman.

"I'm inside now. Inside!" Bank's voice rose with fear. "I can feel the house all around me. Alive. I can—see it!"

Without knowing it, I too, compelled by a fear I could not name, had left the car. I started for the hill. "Stay with it, Banks," I called. "I'm coming."

"The hall is dusty," Banks mumbled. "Dusty. It would be after ten years of desertion. Ten years ago it burned. The hall is dusty. I must see the study."

As I watched in revulsion, Banks walked precisely along the hilltop, turned as though in a doorway, and entered—yes, I said entered—something that wasn't there.

"I'm here," he muttered. "It's the same. But it's dark. It's too dark. And I can feel the house. I want to get out." He turned again and made an exit.

"It won't let me go!"

That scream sent me scrambling up the hillside.

"I can't find the door now. I can't find it, I tell you! It's locked me in! I can't get out—the House won't let me. I must see the cellar first, it says. It says I must see the cellar:"

* * *

He turned and walked precisely, sickeningly. Around a bend. A hand opened an imaginary door. And then—did you ever see a man walk down non-existent stairs? I did. It halted me on my charge up the hillside. Will Banks stood on the hill at sunset walking down cellar stairs that were not there. And then he began to shriek.

"I'm here in the cellar, and the long brown beams are still overhead. *They* are here, too. *They* are hanging, grinning. And why—it's you, Brian. On the hook. On the hook where you died. You're still bleeding, Brian Droome, after all these years. Still bleeding on the floor. Mustn't step in the blood. Blood. Why are you smiling at me, Brian? You *are* smiling, aren't you? But then—you must be alive. You can't be. I killed you. I burned this house. You can't be alive and—the house can't be alive. What are you going to do?"

I had to get up the hill, I couldn't stand hearing him shriek such things into empty air. I had to stop him, now!

"Brian!" he shrieked. "You're getting down off the hook! No—the beam is falling. The house—I must run—where are the cellar steps? Where are they? Don't touch me, Brian—the beam fell down and you're free, but keep away from me. I must find the steps. Where are they? The house is moving. No—it's crumbling!"

I made the top of the hill, panting. Banks screamed on, and then his hands went out.

The Curse of the House

"God! The house is falling—it's falling on me. Help! Let me out! The things on the brown beams are holding me—let me out! The beams are falling—help—let me out!"

Suddenly, just before my outstretched hands could reach him, Banks flung up his arms as though to ward off an impending blow, then crumpled to the grass.

I knelt at his side. Of course I did not enter a house to do it. It was under the dying sun that I gazed into his pain-contorted face and saw that he was dead. It was under a dying sun that I lifted the body of Will Banks and saw—*that his chest had been crushed as though by a falling beam.*

Never Trust a Demon

"**I** guess I'm just no good as a carpenter," said Mr. Snartch, as he sawed the woman in half.

"Look at this sloppy stroke!" he muttered, as he hacked through the lady's hips.

Of course, Mr. Snartch muttered all this under his breath, because an audience isn't supposed to hear such comments from a stage magician. And Mr. Snartch was a stage magician, traveling under the name of Jeffrey the Great.

As Jeffrey the Great, he had to saw a woman in half every night, and twice a week at matinees, and he was getting pretty sick of it. The first few times were fun, but now it was just plain drudgery. Sometimes he hardly had the ambition to put the lady back together again at the end of the show. And of course, such a thing would be bad. If it kept happening, he would not only get a poor reputation as a magician, but he would also lose a lot of partners.

So tonight he hurried through his act, sawing away like mad, and then put the pieces together in record time.

Mr. Snartch wanted to finish the show and get back to his magic.

That was Jeffrey Snartch's salvation. His only hobby—magic. Not stage magic, but *real* magic. Black magic. Not the hocus-pocus variety, but the genuine article. Sorcery. Necromancy.

Tonight he was particularly anxious to get away from the theatre because he had just discovered a swell new formula for conjuring up a demon.

Perhaps it wasn't a swell new formula, exactly. It was more of a swell *old* formula, and Jeffrey Snartch discovered it in a very ancient book, printed in Latin.

So he finished his performance in a hurry and ran out of the theatre and over to his hotel room where he had the book hidden under the mattress.

He had translated the particular spell he was interested in, and written it out on a piece of hotel stationery, along with a list of things he had to use in order to make the incantation work.

"Let me see," said Mr. Snartch. "I will need some toad's blood and some sacramental wine and some chalk to draw a pentagon with and five black candles and mandrake roots to burn."

So he put on his hat and coat and went out on a shopping trip. Half an hour later he was back in his room with the bundles. He spread everything out on the bed and pulled down the shades.

"Of course, I didn't manage to get *exactly* the right things," he confessed to himself. "But I guess they are just as good."

Instead of toads, Mr. Snartch had to buy some frogs at a pet shop. Naturally, he couldn't buy sacramental wine, but he figured on using a little grape juice instead. He had the chalk, though, and the candles. Of course, the candles weren't black ones. They were birthday candles—but it was all the store had. And Mr. Snartch didn't even know what mandrake roots look like—so he just stepped into a vacant lot and pulled up a handful of weeds.

"But I guess it will be all right," Mr. Snartch kept reassuring himself.

* * *

So he took his translation of instructions and began to do what the book told him. He drew a pentagon and lighted the candles and mixed up some frog's blood and grape juice and set fire to his weeds in a tray. Of course, there were a lot of technical things he had to do with all this, but the important thing is—in half an hour he had his room in one hell of a mess.

Then he turned out the lights and began to chant his formula out loud by the light of the candles.

It was very dark and frightening in the hotel room, and the birthday candles cast some very unusual shadows. The air was filled with the smell of the burning weeds.

But Mr. Snartch didn't worry. He was an old hand at wizard's work, and he just read his Latin, rolling out the syllables, and hoped for the best.

Never Trust a Demon

He got the worst.

When he finished with the Latin—cheating a bit now and then, where he didn't understand how to pronounce the words—he started to make the necessary passes in the air. And that's when it happened.

Suddenly the curtains began to blow. This was unusual, because the windows were all closed.

Then the shadow appeared on the wall. Some one else was in the room! This was unusual, because all the doors were locked.

Mr. Snartch looked at the shadow. Then he blinked. He looked again and saw what cast the shadow. Then he yelled.

"Eeeeowie!"yelled Mr. Snartch.

"Not bad at all," said a voice. "The last man who saw me didn't yell at all. He merely jumped out of the window."

"Candidly, that's what I'd like to do," chattered Snartch. "The only trouble is, the windows are locked. And my knees are trembling too hard for me to jump."

"So I notice," said the voice. "Hold on now, I'm coming out into the light."

Mr. Snartch watched the figure coming forth against the candle light. That is, he started to watch it from where he stood. But he ended up by peering at it from under the bed. He crawled there in a hurry when he got a good look at what he had conjured up.

For a minute he could hardly speak.

"Bless my soul," he whispered. "Bless my soul!"

"Sorry," said the voice. "That's not exactly in my department. Maybe I'd better go."

"I didn't mean to offend you," said Mr. Snartch, hastily, as he came out from under the bed and stood up. "It's only that you sort of over-whelmed me."

"Did I really?" said the voice, with a pleased chuckle. "Well, well."

"You're pretty awful, you know," said Snartch.

"Am I?" cooed the voice. "Am I ghastly?"

"Frightful!" exclaimed Mr. Snartch.

"Oh, you're just trying to flatter me," simpered the voice.

"Not at all," Snartch insisted. "You're really and truly hideous."

The demon *was* hideous.

* * *

He squatted there in the center of the floor. His body was lean, mean, green, obscene. A vast bulk, toadlike, with slick reptilian skin. He had webbed feet and claws, fringed with moss at the cuticle. He looked as though he had been pickled a long, long time ago.

His face, as faces go, just didn't. Imagine a green skull with yellow eyes and you get the idea. You can have it.

Mr. Snartch felt the same way. The more he looked, the less he liked his visitor.

The demon crouched forward, extending his grinning face on a stalk-like neck. A forked tongue licked forth between fretted lips. He looked as though he were crouching to spring.

Mr. Snartch stepped hastily back inside the pentagon, which was to protect him from the demon.

"You can't cross the line of chalk or go between the candles," he whispered. "Stop looking at me that way!"

"What way?" whined the demon. "All I wanted was a glass of water. Can't you see my tongue is hanging out? I've had a long, hard trip."

"Try some of this," Snartch suggested, pointing to the bowl of frog blood and grape juice.

"Ah!" said the demon. "That's more like it."

"Vitamins," said Snartch.

"Yes, it was a terrible journey," the demon sighed, between gulps. "Whirling across space that way. And then wriggling between dimensions. It's not easy when you get to be my age."

"I can imagine," sighed Mr. Snartch, sympathetically.

"Besides, I haven't been getting any calls now for a long time," the demon confessed. "I'm out of practise."

"Really?" said Mr. Snartch.

"Yes. You know what's happened to sorcery in the last few centuries. It's fallen off terribly. Nobody even practises witchcraft. Say, by the way, how did *you* happen to run across my address?"

"In this book," Mr. Snartch explained, pulling the volume out of his pocket. "Ever see it?"

The demon cocked his head thoughtfully.

"Of course. It used to get me a lot of trade several hundred years ago. Now nobody seems to read it any more. This modern age!"

He sighed, like an air-raid warning.

"Mind if I sit down?" he asked. "I'm tired out from the trip."

Never Trust a Demon

"Go ahead," said Mr. Snartch, hospitably. "You *are* pretty old, aren't you?"

"Just look at me," groaned the demon.

* * *

Mr. Snartch didn't want to look at the demon, but he managed to stand the sight for several minutes. He noted the wrinkles in the demon's face, the flabby pouches on his arms and legs where muscles had once flexed. Varicose veins stood out prominently.

"'Ook 'ere," rasped the demon. "'Ook af my teef. Mof of 'em are miffing."

Sure enough, only a few big yellow stumps remained in the demon's mouth.

"Too bad," Mr. Snartch sympathized.

"Yes. I can hardly eat a thing any more," the demon confided. "I just nibble at an arm or leg now and then."

"You do," wheezed Snartch, turning pale. "Just—nibble—you say."

"Nibble," repeated the demon.

Mr. Snartch suddenly dropped all notions of becoming friendly with his guest from Gehenna. He trembled anew and hugged the safety of the pentagon.

"Well," he said. "This is all very interesting, but it isn't getting us anywhere. Pretty soon the candles will burn down—they're only birthday candles, you notice—and then you can step across and. get me. In order to avoid that, I think we'd better get our business out of the way right now."

"To be sure," said the demon. "Of course." He squatted on his haunches and rubbed his hands together thoughtfully. "What can I do for you, sir?" he inquired.

Mr. Snartch cleared his throat nervously.

Here it was! It was all true, then. Mr. Snartch could actually get what the old books promised! He had a genuine dead-alive demon at his command. What *did* he want?

"Money," said Snartch. "I want a lot of money."

"A wise choice," said the demon. "I'll just put you down for say— a million dollars?"

"*And* the income tax," Jeffrey Snartch added, hastily.

"And the income tax. Very well."

43

"In return, of course, you'll want something?" said Mr. Snartch.

"Naturally." The demon's eyes sparkled. "Let's have a look at you now. Hmmm. You're nice and plump. I think I would enjoy you."

"Enjoy me?"

"Enjoy eating you, I should say."

"I should say not!" Mr. Snartch turned pale. His eyes narrowed. "I have hardening of the arteries," he said. This was a lie.

But the demon paused. Mr. Snartch quickly followed up his advantage.

"Besides, I am a heavy smoker," he remarked. "And you know what the cannibals of New Guinea say."

"No, I don't. What do they say?"

"That smokers have an unpleasant tobacco taste."

"I see."

"Also," added Snartch, " I wouldn't like to hurt those teeth of yours. You aren't so young any more. You might have trouble with bones." He shook his head. "Really, as your friend, I'd feel very guilty about letting you eat me."

"Well, if you put it that way—"

"Why not take my soul?" suggested Mr. Snartch. "Give me my million, plus taxes, and six months. Then take my soul. It's a better deal, I think."

"All right," said the demon. "I'll buy that. Would you mind signing here, please?"

* * *

A little black book appeared in the demon's claws. He tossed it across the pentagon. Mr. Snartch took out his pen.

"Blood, please," insisted the demon. "Let's make this thing legal."

Mr. Snartch pricked his finger and wrote his name. Then he tossed the book back.

"Thank you," said the demon. "See you later with that million."

He disappeared. Mr. Snartch sighed.

Suddenly the demon's head glimmered in the air before him.

"How do you want the money?" he inquired.

"Oh, any way at all," Snartch told him. "Large bills will do. Just so I get it soon."

"To hear is to obey," hissed the demon. The head disappeared.

Never Trust a Demon

Mr. Snartch breathed a sigh of mingled relief and regret. Then he set about re-arranging the room. It took him quite a while to clean up and restore order. By that time it was very late. He lay down on the bed and went to sleep.

When he woke up it was daylight.

"Oh oh!" thought Mr. Snartch. "I'll be late for the show at the theater today."

He'd forgotten about the matinee.

Dressing hastily, he ran out of the hotel lobby in a frenzy and hailed a passing cab.

"Grand Theatre!" he yelled.

The show had already started when he arrived. Myra, his assistant —the lady he sawed in half—was anxiously awaiting him.

"Oh, Jeffrey!" she wailed. "What happened to you?"

Jeffrey Snartch shrugged feebly. He wasn't exactly pleased by her solicitude. A very determined type of woman, Myra. And apparently she had determined to marry him. He avoided her whenever possible, never talking to her. Their only intimate contact came when he sawed her up.

Snartch put on his dress clothes and emerged again as the magician. *Jeffrey the Great.*

The band was playing for the opening of his act. Quickly he arranged props with Myra. Then he strode out on the stage.

During all this time he had no chance to remember the events of last night. He was too busy, too rushed. Once on the stage, the audience claimed his attention.

* * *

Jeffrey Snartch started out with a few card tricks and a couple of handkerchief bits. As he went through the business and reeled out the patter, his thoughts blurred. He followed through his paces as a matter of routine

Absent-mindedly, he waved his arms, feeling for the gimmicks which controlled a rabbit, flowers, and a boiled dinner which would be produced from his sleeve.

He made a few passes and let the first object slide into his hand.

"I have here a rabbit," he said.

The audience laughed.

"I have here a—what the—"

Snartch stared at his hands. There was no rabbit in his palm. Instead, his fingers clutched a wad of yellow bills. Thousand dollar bills!

Again, automatically, he gestured. "A rabbit!" he muttered.

No rabbit. Another package of bills. The audience howled.

"All right," said Snartch, desperately. "No rabbit. But I *have* got a lot of lettuce!"

The laugh that followed won the audience once more. Desperately Snartch wriggled around. What in blazes had happened to that rabbit?

He patted his coat. Another wad of bills flew out. And then another. He scarcely noticed.

Again he clutched at his shirt, seeking for the elusive bunny. Money showered on the stage.

Desperately now, he wondered if the rabbit had wandered into his trousers. He shook his trouser-legs.

There was a furious clanking, and a flood of gold pieces dropped from his trousers. The audience hooted and screamed.

So did Snatch.

As he attempted to bow, greenbacks burst from his waist, cascaded from under his vest, poured from his pockets. He stood knee-deep in currency as the curtains fell.

Indignant voices rose around him. The stage manager ran out, cursing.

"What the hell's the big idea?" demanded that worthy.

Then he stared at the money.

"Jeez, it's real!" he gasped.

Snartch grinned. Suddenly he realized what had happened. The demon's promise—one million dollars! He'd chosen a unique way to deliver it.

"Of course it's real," Snartch chuckled, scooping up bills like mad. "And so is this."

"What?"

Snartch tweaked the stage manager's nose.

"My resignation," he said. "As of today. Now. I quit. I retire."

Leaving the manager goggling, Snartch strode off the stage, carrying his cash.

Myra waited for him in the wings.

"What's this?" she sobbed. "You can't really mean you're through?"

"But I do mean it," Snartch said, trying not to be unkind. "I don't know just how to tell you this, Myra, but I have sawed you in half for the last time."

"What will I do?" whispered the girl. "Without you around to saw me, I'll just go to pieces."

"Maybe you can find somebody else to saw you," Snartch consoled her. "A nice young girl like you. Anybody would be proud to slice you up."

She sobbed after him as he collected his belongings.

"It won't be the same," she moaned. "No matter what happens, I'll always be thinking of you and how you dismembered me."

"Take this, kid," said Snartch, pressing a handful of gold pieces into her palm.

"Where are you going?"

"To my country estate," Snartch told her.

"Country estate? You haven't got a country estate."

"I will have," Snartch grinned. "Soon."

And he did.

* * *

Snartch went to the realtor's office. From there he proceeded to a haberdasher's, and ordered one hundred suits, to be delivered at the address of his new country estate. On a sudden impulse he went out and bought a yacht. Not that he needed one—he just felt like it. Besides, one of his suits was a white tropical that went well with a yacht.

After that, he invested in a limousine, a roadster, a diamond-studded wrist watch, and five hundred cases of Scotch whiskey.

All of which was to be sent C.O.D. to his new address. He felt very pleased by his day's work, and decided to relax in a night club.

He relaxed very pleasantly there. Anybody who tips waiters with twenty-dollar gold pieces can get excellent service.

Jeffrey Snartch woke up the next morning with a definite hangover. He was in bed at his new estate, and he wanted to stay there.

But the doorbell began to buzz at nine o'clock, and kept buzzing all day. Delivery men and drivers began to arrive with his new possessions, and Snartch stood at the door paying off in cash. All in all, he managed to get rid of a lot of money. The men came to sign over the house, and somebody else arrived to report that his yacht was ready in the lagoon.

Snartch paid with a smile, though his head buzzed. Finally the tumult and the shouting died. He lay down on the sofa to enjoy what remained of his hangover.

And then the doorbell rang again.

Snartch answered it.

A pugnacious-looking truck driver greeted him with a truculent sneer.

"What is it?" asked Snartch.

The truck driver scowled. "I was here earlier today," he growled. "Brought yez that there Scotch."

"What about it? I paid you, didn't I?"

"Yeah. Yez paid me, all right. In marked bills."

"Marked bills?"

"Sure. Look." A grimy hand held out yellow currency. Mr. Snartch examined it. Yes, it was marked, all right.

"Where'd yez steal it?" muttered the truck driver.

"Steal it?" gasped Mr. Snartch. "I didn't steal anything."

"This dough is stolen!" barked the truck driver. "Take it back."

"Wait a minute," Snartch gulped. "The phone is ringing."

It was. He trotted down the hall and answered. The voice on the other end of the wire belonged to the man who had sold him the yacht.

"Mr. Snartch?"

"Speaking."

"You bought a yacht from us for $200,000? Remember?"

"That's right."

"You paid cash."

"Why not?"

"Mr. Snartch, where did you get that money? We've just checked the currency and found it marked."

"I—I—"

"Mr. Snartch, did you know that it is necessary for us to report such bills to the Federal authorities? They plan to call on you this afternoon regarding this matter."

"Fine," said Mr. Snartch. "Swell. I'll expect them. I'll bake them a cake."

* * *

Never Trust a Demon

He hung up. Down the hall he saw the truck driver muttering over his money.

Mr. Snartch shrugged and sighed. He couldn't explain this. Something was wrong. But he didn't want to explain it, or find out what was wrong. All he wanted was out.

Mr. Snartch tiptoed into the library and got out, through the window.

He sneaked into his limousine and drove down the drive. Then he tore hell-for-leather into town.

He registered at the hotel where he had conjured up the demon. Then he went out and bought some supplies.

Promptly at midnight that night he evoked his supernatural side-kick.

The demon crouched outside the chalk pentagon in the gloom and sighed wearily. But Mr. Snartch did not show any pity. He did not invite the demon to sit down. He didn't even offer a drink. He just stared and tapped his foot accusingly.

"You sent for me?" rasped the demon, at length.

"You know I did," Snartch snapped.

"What do you desire? Is there anything wrong?"

"You know what's wrong."

The demon blushed a deeper green. "Oh. About that money, I suppose? I can explain that. You see, I—"

"Never mind," said Mr. Snartch, bitterly. "The deal's off. Breach of contract. You know I'm in the right."

The demon squinted at him. A difficult thing to do, for the demon had no eyelids.

"Wait a minute," he said, softly. "Wait a minute. Money isn't everything, you know. We could work something out."

"What?" said Mr: Snartch.

"Power," purred the demon. "You want power, perhaps? A lot of men are eager for power these days. Take that fellow Hitler," he hinted.

Mr. Snartch made a face. "Not for me," he said abruptly. "Power like that wouldn't interest me a bit."

"How about—women?"

"Women?"

"I could get you the most beautiful women of history," the demon coaxed. "Think of it! Helen of Troy. Cleopatra. Du Barry. Madame Pompadour. Josephine."

"You could?" said Mr. Snartch. He was thinking of Myra. Anything would be a relief after Myra.

"How would you like to be a great lover?" hinted the demon. He was on the right track now, and he smelled a sale. He hurried to close the deal.

"Gorgeous girls," he chanted. "Fond blondes. Brunette pets. Redheads galore."

"Yes," said Mr. Snartch, suddenly. "Yes. I'd like that."

"Of course," said the demon, glibly, "this is a special deal, and it will mean that your time is shortened. Instead of a six-month contract I must reduce my offer to three months."

Mr. Snartch smiled.

"That will be all right," he said. "Take back your money and bring on the girls."

The demon nodded.

"No more tricks, though," warned Jeffrey Snartch.

"Cute tricks," giggled the demon. Then he disappeared. Only the giggle remained.

Snartch cleaned up the mess thoughtfully and went to bed.

* * *

As a result of his hangover and unusual exertions, he slept more soundly than usual. To tell the truth, when he awoke it was night once again. Mx. Snartch had slept the clock around.

He rose, blinked, and went into the bathroom to shave. After shaving he bathed, leisurely. By the time he was dressed it was almost nine o'clock. He stepped back into his hotel room.

Then he reeled back into the bathroom.

Sitting on Mr. Snartch's bed, chair, and bureau, were six girls. Two blondes, two brunettes, and two redheads.

All were of different types. Short, tall, fat, lean, frail, husky. But all had one thing in common. A costume consisting of rhinestones. A few here, a few there. But the costumes were similar.

So were the scowls on the faces of the girls.

Mr. Snartch staggered in the doorway. They looked up at him.

"All right," demanded a tall redhead, in a husky voice. "What's the big idea, mister?"

"Why, don't you know what the big idea is?" asked Mr. Snartch.

Never Trust a Demon

"No, we don't," insisted the redhead. "Here we are, sitting in our dressing room getting ready for the first floor show, when this guy shows up with a gun—"

"What guy?"

"How should I know? He wore a mask. Besides, he didn't give us a chance to look at him. Just made us go out the back door and climb into a taxi. Then he drove us here, took us up the freight elevator, and smuggled us into your room. He locked the door from the outside."

"Kidnaper," screeched a little blonde. "That's what he was. A kidnaper."

"Taking us from the night club," complained a plump brunette. "Dragging us here at the point of a gun. And I suppose you're a white slaver."

Mr. Snartch received these revelations in dismay.

"Girls, please!" he said. "Let me explain—"

"Nuts to your explanations! Let us out of here!"

The redhead rose and faced him.

"But—" said Mr. Snartch.

It was the wrong word.

The redhead lowered her head and butted him.

"Come on, girls!" yelled the blonde. "We'll show this big bully!"

* * *

What happened then was very painful. Six women went for Mr. Snartch in a big way—but not the way he had anticipated. They went for him with hair-brushes and mirrors and pitchers and picture frames and other loose articles. They went for him with their teeth and nails.

They left Mr. Snartch lying on the floor with a Gideon Bible on his chest. And he was almost ready for it.

He recovered nearly an hour later. The girls had left, taking the door from its hinges *en route*.

Mr. Snartch had barely the strength to totter downstairs and buy fresh candles, frogs, and grape juice. He could scarcely manage to tear up some more roots and draw his chalk pentagon. His voice was hoarse as he chanted the Latin invocation.

But he made it.

And the demon appeared.

51

It squatted malignly before him, and Mr. Snartch thought he detected a mocking gleam in his eyes.

Gleam or no gleam, Snartch was too angry to hesitate.

"Now you've done it," he grated. "Those women—come clean now, where did you get them?"

"What's the matter?" asked the demon.

"You know very well!" yelled Mr. Snartch. "Famous beauties of history—bah! You stole a bunch of chorus girls from a night club, didn't you?"

"Well—"

"Damned right you did!" screamed Mr. Snartch. "Just a common kidnaper, that's what you are."

"But you asked for women—"

"Another thing," Snartch continued, ignoring the demon's words. "I've just figured out about that money, too. It's all here in this morning's paper. About the bank that was held up. No wonder the currency was marked. Hot money, that's what you gave me."

The demon hung his head.

"Why?" groaned Mr. Snartch. "Why? That's all I want to know."

* * *

The demon faced him, his skull-like features contorted.

"Because I'm old, that's why. Because I'm old, and out of practice. I haven't got the stuff any more."

"The stuff?"

"The power. Everything passes with age, you know."

The demon sighed, heavily. Windows rattled.

"I used to be omnipotent, almost. Like the book says. I could do anything, bring you anything, grant any wish. But now I'm all through.

"I did my best for you, though. I couldn't produce wealth for you as I used to, so I went out and stole it. And I couldn't evoke beautiful women for you, so I stole them. Thought you wouldn't find out. But you did."

"Yes, I did." Mr. Snartch was stern. "Of course, you realize this makes our agreement null and void."

The demon sat up.

His claws scraped restlessly against the floor. His lips drew back in a bony grin. He hunched closer across the flickering shadows.

"Oh no," he droned. "Not at all."

"You mean?"

"In three months you die. You give me your soul."

"Now listen here—"

"You listen to me." The demon crept closer. "I kept my part of the bargain. I brought you a million dollars, didn't I? I didn't say where it would come from or who it might belong to. You got your money."

"Still—"

"Keep still!" The demon grinned wickedly. "You changed your mind. You wanted women. Blondes, brunettes, redheads. I gave you blondes, brunettes, redheads. I didn't specify that they would like you. But I brought them. And so, Mr. Jeffrey Snartch, I am holding you to your bargain. In three months I will claim your soul."

Mr. Snartch drew himself erect. He shrugged.

"Very well, demon," he sighed. "You asked for it, I suppose."

"What?"

"I had hoped to spare you this final humiliation for a while," said Mr. Snartch. "Out of consideration for your age."

"What do you mean?"

"You are very old, demon. Otherwise you wouldn't make such a mistake when you signed the contract with me. You would have looked my name up first. But you didn't. You wanted my soul and tried to cheat me. Instead, I cheated you. You don't get my soul after all."

"Why not?"

"Because," said Mr. Snartch, slowly, "I sold my soul to the Devil two years ago!"

Pink Elephants

Screwballs don't bounce. Otherwise, Gregory Mitre might have sailed up to the ceiling every time he took a step. As it was, he was flopping around the room like a badly chloroformed baboon.

It really wasn't funny, though—it was just too pathetic to deal with seriously. Greg Mitre was a great guy once, before he started traveling; rather close friend of mine, as a matter of fact. And now he was a professional grape-squeezer.

Of course, he'd invited us all to the home-coming party; there were at least a dozen of us in his apartment that evening, and we fully intended to do well by the liquid hospitality we expected. Nevertheless, everyone was a bit put out to walk in and find mine host loaded to the gills in advance. What made it worse, Greg Mitre appeared to be more than ordinary bottle-dizzy. He was mawkishly, almost helplessly drunk.

Foster and I arrived first, at about the same time. We had to wait several minutes before Mitre answered the bell, and when he opened the door he almost fell on top of us. Once inside, when we got a good look at that red, sweating face with the unnaturally rolling eyes, we were both a little shocked, I think.

Of course, neither of us showed it, though Mitre's quite incoherently mumbled greetings further distressed us. He waved us to chairs and indicated the refreshments by walking up to the table and clawing out a bottle from the imposing array thereon. He gulped his drink from the neck and urged us to partake. We did so, silently. I know Foster's thoughts were my own.

* * *

What the devil had happened to Mitre? He never had been a heavy drinker, before his trip. Two years is a good stretch, but granted he had picked up dipsomania in that time, the fact remains that in two years a man should also mature by that much. And Mitre apparently had lived a dozen since we last saw him. He was thinner, and his hair was graying. He'd tanned, but there were unpleasant lines about his eyes and mouth. And his smile was forced, maudlin. We took quick glances at him, and I caught Foster's eye.

Mitre never appeared to notice. He just lapped up the gravy, shot after shot. In ten minutes we saw him put down a swig of rye, two highballs, a straight Scotch and a brandy. During that time he said scarcely a word. I began to grope for an opening question.

The doorbell began to ring. From then on it kept ringing steadily throughout the evening. The apartment filled up. I. watched my fellow guests. All of them seemed genuinely puzzled by Mitre's obvious in-toxication; no one, apparently, knew any more than we did.

Mitre didn't explain. He kept on drinking. Somewhat embar-rassed, the others joined in, though naturally at a much slower pace, which rendered Mitre's own antics less conspicuous. But I kept my eye on him alone, wondering as the hours passed how any man could put away what he did without passing out.

It worried me; that and his silence. He laughed a lot, gabbled to the boys, but never once referred to his trip. Naturally they threw him a few friendly questions, but he ignored them. That wasn't like Greg Mitre. I felt a little put out because of his attitude. After all, we had been friends. Now he'd made a toy ship of his interests and put it in a bottle.

I kept my eye on Mitre, and I was watching him when the doorbell rang, at about eleven. Mitre stumbled through the laughing, chattering crowd to answer the door and I saw him open it.

A dapper, black-haired man with a Latin face stood in the hallway, and when he saw Mitre he bowed and smiled, showing his even white teeth, which stood out in startling contrast to the pallor of his face.

I was watching Mitre, and I almost fancied I saw a look of curious recognition in his drink-bleared eyes. Through the buzz of conversa-tion about me I caught a few words of the quick exchange.

"So sorry to disturb, but I thought that perhaps you might wish to part with the object now."

The stranger spoke with a peculiar accent, in a hissing voice that annoyed me.

Pink Elephants

But Mitre's sudden angry response disturbed me more.

"No, no, I tell you! I gave you my final answer on the ship, and that still stands. You can't frighten me out of it, you can't do that! No use of phoning any more, either."

The man smiled, unperturbed, though there was a flaring in his deep, dark eyes.

"But I thought perhaps my last message might have made you change your mind."

"You mean that call yesterday afternoon?"

"No." There was mockery in the hissing voice. "I mean the message last night. Last night after you went to bed. Last night when you wanted to sleep, Mitre. Surely you remember the message you heard— the playing, and what followed?"

"No!" Mitre's shout rose to quiet the room. "No! There was nothing, nothing. You can't devil me that way!"

"My message will come *every* night, Mitre. It will come stronger and stronger. I do not wish to be harsh, but if my message fails I shall soon have to send a stronger one. A more persuasive one. I shall have *it* deliver that last message, Mitre."

Mitre got apoplectic. *"Get out!"* he screamed. *"Get out!"*

The smiling stranger made a single gesture. I seemed to catch a glint of silver flashing from his sleeve, as though he were pulling out a dagger—no, a steel rod of some kind. At the sight, Mitre lashed out with his hands, wildly, and the stranger ducked, then turned and hastened down the hall.

We all stood stock-still now, staring at the open door and the retreating figure of the man. Mitre was trembling, purple-faced, in the doorway; he seemed quite unconscious of our presence, and he was gasping for breath in a desperate sort of way.

And then, in the stillness, we heard a sound from down the hall. It was unmistakable; we all heard it.

A thin, wailing whistle rose on the air—a reedy piping from afar, as though played by eerie flutes. Mitre heard it, too.

"The Dance!" he muttered in shocked voice.

The wailing rose, and abruptly a vision came to me wherein the stranger was pulling something long and silvery from his sleeve. Had it been a pipe, a flute of some kind? And was this the "message" those two had spoken of so mysteriously?

The music reached a horrid pitch, an inhuman shrillness that brought the puzzled guests to their feet. We stood staring at each other like fools, and then the music seemed to touch a responsive chord in all of us—a chord of stark fear. It was as though cold air had blown through the room from some outer gulf of space. The music bit into my brain as it faded away down the hall, still rising, rising, rising.

Mitre's gasps brought us to our senses. He turned and stared wild eyed at his guests. And then speech came to him.

"You'd better go," he mumbled. "Quickly. Can't explain. Just go—clear this all up later. Get out, all of you—for God's sake, get out !"

* * *

Foster started toward the distraught figure of our host.

"What's the matter, old man?" he began.

"Don't touch me! Go—go, for the love of mercy, go! I must get back, get back and look at *it* to see if the music has stirred it again. It mustn't be left alone when the music plays. It has to be watched, because if it ever—"

Mitre checked himself hastily, on the verge of hysteria. He pulled himself erect with a tremendous effort that did not deceive me, though the others may have been deluded.

"I'm sorry about this," he said, speaking very precisely. "I'm not well—touch of nerves, I guess. Nothing to worry about. And I've been drinking a bit too much. Won't you all accept my apologies? And forget what just happened here tonight? I'll explain all this—matter of fact, I'll drop in and see you, Bob, tomorrow." He nodded at me. "But if you'll be kind enough to leave now, I'd be obliged."

This was better. At least he was rational now. The crowd donned outergarments and departed. Conversation was subdued and there were wondering glances, but on the whole things were clearing up. I lingered behind. Mitre stood in the doorway, bidding farewells in a nervous manner.

"You'll be in my office, Greg?" I murmured to him.

"Yes, I meant what I said about explaining. I'll see you tomorrow."

"Would you like some company tonight?" I ventured, trying to seem casual about it. After all, I was not only his friend but his doctor, and thus had a double responsibility, so to speak.

Fear flamed in his face. "No—no, not tonight!"

I abruptly changed my tack. "Could I prescribe a sedative, then?"

Pink Elephants

"No. It wouldn't help—God, I know! I'll see you tomorrow—explain it then—"

He pushed me out and closed the door. Going out, I looked around quickly but saw no sign of the stranger and his pipes....

The next morning. "Got a drink, Doc?"

I had, and I gave it to him despite any scruples to the contrary. Mitre looked as though he needed a drink, and damned badly. He put it down and stopped shaking a bit. Then he looked at me and apparently thought about smiling, but gave it up.

"Listen, Doc. Got to help me! I've got 'em bad."

"Got what?" I considered looking surprised and gave that up, too.

"D.Ts. Hallucinations. Something, I don't quite know what. But I *see* things."

"What sort of things, Mitre?"

"What do you suppose? Pink elephants, mostly."

Now right then is where I should have suspected a gag. I've had *delirium tremens* cases before, but in all my experience the only time such patients see pink elephants is in the funny papers. The devil of it was, Mitre was obviously serious.

"Go on," I prompted; but that was entirely unnecessary, because Mitre had already started. His jaw was hanging loose, and his eyes were half closed as he mumbled in the flat, monotonous drone characteristic of hysteria.

"I see them at night. Every night they march into my room—out of Ganesha they come, and march around the bed. When the light is on they go away, but then it's worse because I *hear* them. Nobody else sees them and hears them, but I do. That's why I know they're not real, those little pink elephants.

"But even if I know it's a dream, why do I fear them so? I can't stand to see them walking around with their tiny red eyes staring at me and their gleaming yellow tusks raised, and then they trumpet at me and come closer and closer and I can't sleep, or they'd get on top of me!

"They come out of Ganesha, I tell you—every night they come— and I have to drink and drink until I fall asleep. Then I don't hear them any more with their little shrill trumpetings in the dark, just as I did that first time in the temple. No, I know what you'll say, and it's not true. They *aren't* fantasies of alcoholic origin! I wasn't drinking when I went into the temple that day, and I heard them then. I heard them when I pinched the idol—the Ganesha idol."

59

Mitre shuddered. "I was all alone in the big dark room with the awful stone frescoes on the walls. The silly priest had gone out to ring the bells, and I was alone, and here was this little statue in the niche. I didn't take it for its value; it had none. It wasn't like stealing a jewel from an idol's eye and then having a curse set on you—none of that stage melodrama stuff. I wanted the dirty little statue for a souvenir, and that was that.

"Put it in my sun-helmet, I did, and carried it out in my hand. But when I copped it, I heard the trumpeting, and I've heard it ever since. I've seen them marching around in my room, at night. They come out of Ganesha and march and their red eyes stare, and—"

* * *

He began to tremble again, and I gave him another drink.

"Let's go over and have a look at your statue," I suggested. I wanted to look over his room, look over the figurine. The Hindus are great ones for hypnosis and I've seen some damnable tricks; statues with polished surfaces that reflect light so that, when stared at, they induce self-hypnotic states. Mitre might have been the victim of some similar device; hence my suggestion.

On the way over I questioned him. I got more details of the story. Mitre had stolen a statue of Ganesha, Hindu elephant-god, from a little temple in Seringapatam. The fantasies began then, and his drinking mounted apace. No priest had shouted hysterical curses, no little dark men with knives followed him about. It was just that the temple had given him the creeps, and the statue seemed so evil, so *malign* that he believed his theft had invoked a curse on him.

The little pink elephants running around—I tried to trace the image. The temple had housed several live, sacred white elephants. They are really pink in color rather than white. I could see that the hallucinations might have arisen there. That and the fact that Ganesha is the patron god of the elephant. Moreover, Mitre said that after his "haunting" began, he read up on Hindu mythology. Potent imaginative forces involved here, obviously. Oh, he had the D.Ts. very properly, poor Mitre did. I wanted to see his room now.

I did. Ordinary enough, surely. I looked at the statue, and it was black and dull. There was no reflecting surface, no jewel. The statue was scarcely eight inches in height, carved out of basalt, and the execution was crude but effective. I didn't realize how effective until I had handled and stared at it for some minutes. Then it hit me full force.

* * *

The figure was that of a seated man with much too many arms. The figure was of a man, but the head that of an elephant. Grotesque? Yes; and frightening, too. The thing had eyes that almost peered from the stone, and its trunk was not motionless—it was *poised!* Simple as it was, the effect was not that of an inanimate representation, but rather of a creature whose arms and legs might move at any second. Watching it, I began to *wait* for it to move.

Then I understood Mitre's case. He'd watched it, too; watched it with many bottles before him, and waited for that movement so diabolically captured in stone. And fantasies had come to haunt him; guilt-complex had arisen. Now the elephants indeed marched. Pink elephants, in all truth.

"But why didn't you get rid of it?" I asked, at length. It was a logical enough question.

"I was afraid," Mitre answered simply. It was a quite logical reply. The more I looked at the thing, the more sensible the reply became. I'd be afraid, too—I confess it quite frankly. I wouldn't throw the staring statue into the sea, or break it, or lock it away; not unless I could destroy completely the evilness inherent in it. Mitre had borne his cross with him halfway around the world; and seeing it, I understood. But something had to be done, logic or no logic.

We stood there in his bedroom staring at that horrid little black idol with its man-body, its extra arms with the detestably exquisite fine work that made even the tiny fingers real; stood staring at the horrid elephant trunk and the sharp, pointed tusks; staring at the little hoofs on the ivory-inlaid feet. The little, dark eyes seemed to stare back in return, to flash as though with sardonic life. In the dusk the dully gleaming statue unnerved me, and I began to wait for it to move—

And then, from the window, came the sound. It trickled in, as though from the courtyard below, and I recognized it with a chill prickling of my spine.

It was the music—the eerie flute music that had played in the hallway last night after Mitre had repulsed the stranger. It was the high, shrill, hysterical music that seemed to flicker from indefinable, alien worlds, bringing a message of some unhuman madness. I recognized it with a fear I could not name, could not hide.

Mitre recognized it, too. He blanched, faced me wildly.

"The music," he whispered, "Again! It's the *Dance of Ganesha!*"

The words broke the spell. He had said something during that mysterious conversation last night—something about a "Dance." This was it, then?

I seized his trembling shoulders and looked straight into his eyes.

"Tell me the truth, man," I said. "Out with it. Who was that stranger, and exactly what does he want of you?"

Mitre shook all over. "I'll tell you—but make him stop playing— make him stop before it—*before it's too late!*"

I flung open the window and peered down into the courtyard. As I did so the music abruptly ceased! My eyes swept the opening below. I fancied I saw a figure moving quickly away through the shadows close to the building, but I could not be sure. Did the dying sun glimmer on a silver reed?

No, there was nothing there! Nothing but the last haunting echo of that strangely ceased music. I turned to Mitre again. He sighed deeply with relief.

"It's gone. And it didn't do what he threatened. Thank God for that!"

* * *

My patience snapped. "Who is that fellow—and what is this all about, anyway? The truth, Mitre—if you really want my help?"

Mitre looked away and spoke rapidly. "I didn't tell you everything, Doc. But. you might as well know now. I *was* followed from that temple, have been—ever since. At first, I hadn't realized it; the man was dressed like a European, talked like one. He didn't wear a melodramatic beard-and-turban get-up, and he didn't come yipping to me with threats or curses.

"On the boat he sidled up to me one day and asked if I'd picked up any curios in the East. We fell to talking, and I took him down to the cabin and showed him some vases, other knickknacks I had purchased. When we finished he said nothing, but smiled. And then he asked me to show him the statue of Ganesha.

Pink Elephants

·   "I got excited; asked him how he knew of it. He didn't say anything—just told me that he'd heard. And he would like very much to
buy it. Offered me a thousand, there, sight unseen, in spot cash. I refused, showed him curtly to the door. He just smiled again and said
I'd hear from him."

Mitre mopped his face. "In Paris, on the way back, he came to my
hotel. How he found me, I don't know. Offered me ten thousand this
time. Again I refused. By now I was getting worried. How did he know
of the theft? If he knew, who else knew? Who might send agents after
me in vengeance?

"On the boat here it began all over again. He showed up; I almost
expected him to. I asked the steward and the purser about him—they
could tell me nothing. They withheld his name but said he came from
India. Then I realized—he was the agent sent by the temple!"

Mitre's eyes seemed haunted. "He didn't flash a knife or send co-
bras through my transom, or even threaten me, like such people are
supposed to. He just smiled, showed up in unexpected places, and offered me money. Sometimes he just showed up—and that alone got on
my nerves, I can tell you! Wherever I went he was standing off at the
side, smiling, watching me. I began to drink then and there.

"And the second night out for New York, he came and whispered
outside my stateroom; whispered because I wouldn't let him in. He
made his only threat then. He said that if I didn't return the statue, he
would make the statue come to him!"

I could see the sweat on his face now. "That was sheer madness. I
asked him whether he was a priest; point-blank. And he said 'yes,' he
had been in the temple when I stole the idol, and. he was a priest who
knew many mysteries and had powers over the elephant-god. Power
enough to make the statue come when he called, if need be."

Mitre paused, stared at me with haggard eyes.

"Doc, it's crazy, and it's wild—but it's true! He said he could play
the Dance of Ganesha on his pipes—play the sacred music used in secret temple rites, and make the idol come alive. He said they did that in
the temple, that the stone held the spirit of the god incarnate—and that
the spirit could be released by playing sacred music. Or am I mad?"

"No, Greg," I said softly. "Go on."

"Well, I scoffed. And so he played. Played softly, shrilly. The music
sounded into my room. And that's when I first saw the things—those
damned pink elephants, coming like—like little pale ghosts from the

statue! They were pink, misty things, but they marched around the room at my feet and trumpeted shrilly in reply to that wailing music. I almost fancied I saw the idol moving, its malignant little eyes staring at me—and I began to scream and scream—"

I could see Mitre shudder. "So he went away quietly then, before anyone was aroused. And I took a drink and went to bed and had dreams. Dreams of Ganesha.

"The next morning some fool stubbornness kept me from going to him. I couldn't confess that I was afraid—I *couldn't* confess that he had these powers, don't you see? If it were true, then this world is a monstrous, unthinkable place, and we walk unheeding amidst unimagined terrors. I could not believe that and remain sane!"

Mitre shrugged helplessly. "So I guarded the statue, thinking he might steal it. But he would never stoop to such a petty trick. He played again, though, that same night. And I drank and drank, and the elephants marched around me, and the statue nearly moved. I think it did, I mean…."

"Then we landed. I hid out in a hotel for three days, and I thought I'd slipped him off my trail. So I came home to the apartment. I had to; it was getting so that I'd sit in front of this damnable idol all day and stare at it, and take another drink whenever my head cleared. I threw the party last night to get people here; to take my mind off this horrible elephant-creature."

The man's eyes were bitter. "You saw what happened, Doc. He showed up. And he made those threats. Said that he'd play again—this was the *last chance* I had to sell! He wants to take the thing back to the temple for rites soon to be performed. He said it was angry now, and if it came alive it would harm me before going to him. And it will come alive if he plays again—*I know it!* It might have happened today if you hadn't been here."

I faced him then. "Greg, keep still."

"What—"

"I said, be quiet. Listen to me, now. At first I thought you were being hypnotized by the statue. Your drinking and continual staring might have given you hallucinations."

"That's not true!" Mitre flared. Anger—an encouraging sign!

"I know it. It's *not* the statue that has hypnotized you—it's that unearthly music."

Mitre gaped at me. "The music?"

64

Pink Elephants

"Yes, those pipes. I've heard them—they *are* insidious, Greg. They hold certain tones that appeal to primal instincts; paralyze certain nerve-centers and in some way deaden the brain, as an opiate does. And so you imagine pink elephants marching out of the statue, imagine the thing is about to move. There's absolutely nothing in the statue. Do you follow me, Greg? It isn't hollow—it's solid. I could smash it, of course. But I won't. You're going to fight this thing like a man, and I'll fight with you. Here's my plan, Greg. This man must be stopped. And stopped now."

* * *

Mitre began to shake. "No—don't harm him! He's a priest, he has powers—"

I shook my head. "No powers, Greg—he's simply a dangerous fanatic. Now, I'm going to post myself down the street. In the drugstore. I'll wait. When you hear the music, I'll come back. And Mr. Fluteplayer won't get away this time. Believe me, Greg—this is the only way to stop this morbidness of yours. Breaking the statue won't help your mental state any. We must have that man. He's the source behind all your troubles."

Mitre still wasn't entirely convinced. "Yes, but the danger—If he plays again, the statue moves."

"Nonsense! You must keep a grip on yourself, man. Do as I say now. Stay here; the Hindu will be back, I know. Then call me at once. And don't worry. We'll lick this guy yet!"

I gripped his shoulder, turned and departed. Mitre was still shaking, but he managed to pull himself together a bit, grinning weakly in farewell. I went down the stairs and crossed into the drugstore; arranged with the clerk that when my call came, he was to turn around immediately and phone the police, sending them right up to Mitre's.

Then I sat down to dinner in the booth. It was dark in that corner of the store, and as I stared into the shadows an image rose, unbidden, to my brain.

The staring elephant face of Ganesha emerged blackly and grinned, and the trunk began to wave and wave; the tusks moved forward, the horrid hoofs pranced evilly.

Stifling fear, I ate. That cursed idol, that cunning music was getting me, too.

Night fell, and though the drugstore radio played reedy jazz my brain was listening to other music—strange, eerie music from afar, that crept through my senses and clawed away at my sanity. I heard the awful music rise as in a daze and then—

Then came the sharp tinkling of the phone!

The booth was black as I lifted the receiver in a trembling hand. And over the wires, Mitre's voice screamed in high hysteria.

"Doc! He's here—in the courtyard! I've shut the window, and still the music comes, louder and louder. It's dark here in the bedroom, and yet I can see the statue! It's glaring at me, and the eyes are moving— *stop the music, Doc!"*

"Greg, control yourself !" I snapped.

"Doc, hurry—it's beginning to wave its trunk—in time with the music! Listen, Doc, you can hear the music—They're coming out of the statue now! I see them glistening in the light—Doc, come on—the music is louder, closer—"

"Greg, for God's sake!"

"Doc—it's getting down off the pedestal—it's coming for me— I see the tusks—it's crawling—up—now—*Doc!"*

There was an indescribable scream, an echo of pure madness. And then over the buzzing phone I heard that damnable, that accursed, that soul-chilling flute music, rising and rising in bubbling waves of horror.

I dropped the phone and scrambled out. My feet thudded down the street, into the lobby, up the stairs. Greg's key was in my hand and I yanked the door open upon harsh blackness. Through the parlor I raced, as the music burst out on me from all sides—triumphant, cackling notes that seemed to mock and scream defiance.

Then I was in the bedroom. Mitre lay on the floor, and I snapped up a lamp. Still the music shrieked in the air about me, and I glanced wildly at the pedestal. It was—*empty!*

My eyes went to the door with a dread I dare not name, and the music screeched in horrid glee. I didn't see pink elephants marching. There were none. There were no beasts with tiny hoofs and gleaming tusks. But over at the window—

* * *

Something crawled blackly into the shadows. Something dark, stony, about eight inches high. Something gleamed in the lamplight and lumbered across the floor, climbing up the window ledge and resting there as though directed by the unearthly music.

From the street a police car squealed, but I scarcely heard it above the infernal music that dinned in my ears. I scarcely heard it, because I could only stare and *see*—

See that unbelievable, grotesque little monster clambering to the window ledge and with one stony arm raise the window to permit an exit. See, in the lamplight, the miniature elephant-head with the bobbing, moving trunk of stone, the little red eyes staring down, the tiny hands clawing, the hoofs of the feet lumbering as it prepared to leap from the window toward the waiting flute player below.

And then the roar of a revolver sounded from the courtyard and the music abruptly ceased....

But another sound came then from within the room. It was not from me, nor from Mitre. It came from I dare not say where—but it was a *tiny, shrill trumpeting!*

Abruptly the thing leaped. Just as the shot died away it leaped from the window. A second later it landed with a crash on the stone court below.

I rushed to the window, stared with uncomprehending eyes at the tiny statue that had fallen to the ground, shattered now into a hundred little pieces—fragments of simple stone.

Next to it lay the dark body of a strange man—a man whose dead hands still clutched a silver pipe. And policemen were bending over him; bending over the little broken statue that was, thank God, only stone after all.

I turned with a sob of relief. It had been the music, at that—horrible sounds that hypnotized Mitre and had hypnotized me, too, at the last. The statue must have been on the windowsill all along; it had toppled out. Hallucinations induced by the music had made me see what could not have been.

But how had that statue got to the window?

Had Mitre placed it there and then fallen back on the floor?

Mitre—on the floor. What had this cruel hypnosis done to him, with his maddening obsession of living statues and pink elephants and Hindu vengeance?

I bent over the body of Gregory Mitre—for it was his body, and he lay quite dead.

Robert Bloch

And then I stood up and began to scream and scream, staring at the body of Gregory Mitre—that loathsome, mangled body, *covered all over with the bruises of stony hoofs, and the little red stabs from the goring tusks of a tiny elephant!*

The Last Plea

There was nothing supernatural about the way Clay Clinton got his start.

That part comes later.

In the beginning, there was only Luther Snodgrass, of Crump Creek, Texas.

Nobody paid much attention to Luther Snodgrass at first, including his own mother. She took one look at the squalling brat when he was born, then dumped him in the railway ditch next to the water-tower. Within five hours she took the next freight out of town and vanished into Oblivion (Okla.).

All she bequeathed the infant was his name, scribbled with the stub end of a pencil on the inside of a Sterno label. She christened him with a note pinned to half a pair of panties which she ripped down the middle and wound around his spindle-shanks as he lay cradled in an old orange-crate.

Her message was brief and to the point, if any.

> *To Whoom It may Concern:*
> *Pleese somebody take care of my babey boy*
> *his name is Luther Snodgrass after his fa-*
> *ther the no good sunabich he run out on me*
> *in Waco.*
> *Hoping You Are The Same,*
> *—Joyleen Crutt*

A gandy-dancer named Hank Peavey found Luther—and his letter of introduction to a waiting world—within a matter of minutes after the freight pulled out. He called the sheriff and the sheriff took the baby to the County Hospital, and the County Hospital (after a few desultory efforts to locate either Joyleen Crutt or the no good sunabich she had honored with the paternity of her offspring) passed the infant on to the County Orphanage at Crump Creek.

Luther Snodgrass did a lot of howling when he was a baby, but nobody can lay credit to discovering him then.

In due time he grew up to attend grammar school, where he pledged allegiance to the American flag, broke three windows, learned how to read (*Goofball Comics*) and write (*"Old Ladey Krantz Has Dirtey Pants"*) and do elementary sums (*"Cigarettes—28¢. Muscatel—59¢ a fifth"*).

At the age of sixteen he completed his formal education and his informal education simultaneously—the latter through the kind offices of a young lady named Luletta Switzel. Unfortunately for Luther Snodgrass, Miss Switzel was her father's pride and joy; rivalled in his affections only by the 12-gauge shotgun that he subsequently pointed in Luther's direction.

Luther got out of range in a manner apparently traditional to his family; he hopped the next rattler.

What he did in El Paso we'll probably never know. What he did in Fort Worth was thirty days for vagrancy.

* * *

During the next two years it almost seemed as if the young man were destined to become a writer. At least, he underwent what is apparently the customary apprenticeship for that career—he was a dishwasher in a restaurant, a house-to-house salesman, a fry-cook, and a merchant seaman. Actually, however, he flunked out on this last requirement. Luther Snodgrass never really went to sea; he merely did some work as an itinerant stevedore on the banana boats moored at the docks in New Orleans.

It was there, presumably, that he picked up his talent for the guitar (along with something else which he was fortunately able to get rid of after a few visits to the Public Health Clinic). But the musical affliction persisted; probably some of the local roustabouts encouraged him. He even managed to obtain possession of his own instrument—fortunately, nobody asked to examine the dice during the game—and before long he was playing and passing the hat in the French Quarter.

The Last Plea

The Vieux Carré Association takes a dim view of such activities on Bourbon Street, but he managed to get into a few dives on Decauter and Chartres. He developed a popular repertoire, including such authentic folk-classics as *The Harlot of Jerusalem, Christopher Columbo,* and that plaintive ballad, *The Ring-Dang-Doo.*

The few connoisseurs of folk music who heard him agreed unanimously that Josh White in his prime had never sounded anything like that. Luther Snodgrass was already beginning to develop his distinctive wriggling style; he learned that it was better to writhe and keep moving so as to avoid any missiles aimed his way by listeners who *didn't* appreciate his talent.

It was during this period that Opportunity knocked on young Luther's door. That chance of a life-time appeared.

To be exact, it wasn't really *his* door, but that of Miss Evangeline LaTour, who resided in the Quarter as a young art student (the art being pickpocketing and the old badger-game). And it wasn't really Opportunity knocking, but a gentleman named Jefferson Davis Fink, renowned throughout the sunny Southland as the progenitor, proprietor and sole purveyor of *Finkola.*

* * *

Who has not heard of *Finkola*—that antidote for asthma, banisher of bunions, cure for catarrh, destroyer of dandruff, eradicator of eczema; indeed, of all the alphabetically-arranged ailments the flesh is heir to, including such obscure sub-Masonian-and-Dixonian-Line afflictions as the running trots, the galloping consumption and the creeping miseries?

If there are any amongst you who remain in ignorance of this amazing new scientific discovery, it is not because of any failing on the part of Jefferson Davis Fink. He has spared neither pain nor expense in his effort to spread the glad tidings of *Finkola's* miraculous healing properties throughout the length and breadth of Dixie. Wherever five watts join together in the conspiracy known as a southern radio station, the *Finkola* jingles jangle forth. Wherever a tall pine or a majestic cypress looms along the highway, a *Finkola* billboard obscures it. Wherever the sweet scent of magnolias mingles upon the soft and balmy breeze, it mingles with the joyfully-drawn breath of a *Finkola* user (*37% alcohol, by volume*).

71

"Yeass, honey-chile," said Jefferson Davis Fink to Miss Evangeline LaTour, as he skillfully diverted her caressing fingertips from the neighborhood of his watch-chain, "Ah reckon they ain't hardly nobody nohow who don't guzzle the stuff."

"My aunt Minnie, she used it for a poultice, time she had them boils," Miss LaTour volunteered, eyeing her companions gen-oo-ine 5-carat (slightly yellowish) diamond ring.

"Sure, sugah," Mr. Fink agreed. "It cures most anything, up to and including mastitis. And I hear tell it makes a mighty refreshin' douche, too. *Mighty* refreshin'." Then, "Great bolls o' cotton, what's *that?*"

* * *

That proved to be Luther Snodgrass, returning unexpectedly early from his nightly rounds and roundelays. The sight of the tall, gangling youth who confronted them menacingly, armed with a guitar, served to both annoy and affright Miss LaTour.

"Gah dam'," she exclaimed, with girlish petulance. "Ah *tole* you to knock, afore you come bargin' in heah that away."

"Who is this?" inquired Jefferson Davis Fink, sitting up and reaching for his vest.

"Mah *nevvoo*," Miss LaTour explained. "He's like mah *proto jay.*"

"*Proto jay?* What-all is he a *proto jay* of ?"

"Well, he plays *git*-tar. Ah been soht of boa'din' him heah whilst he studies up on it."

Noting the look of skepticism on Mr. Fink's face, she turned to Luther and waggled a coy cuticle. "You-all play suthin' foe Mistah Fink, hear?"

Luther heard. And Mr. Fink, whether he was thus inclined or not, heard also.

"Purty?" Miss LaTour inquired.

The least that gallantry demanded was a nod. Mr. Fink gave it, and thus precipitated another selection. Luther was all set to launch into a third, when Mr. Fink held up his hand.

The sight of the diamond silenced the young man.

"You right talented, boy," he declared. "Right talented. Evah think of goin' into the show bizness?"

"Show bizness?" Luther's eyes rivalled the diamond. "Ah been aimin' fer it."

The Last Plea

Jefferson Davis Fink cleared his throat, or at least a portion thereof which was not occupied by plug tobacco. "Well, reckon you done hit the mark, son. So happens Ah'm readyin' anothuh ex-strava-ganza. Yessiree, anothuh big *Finkola* Fun Festival is 'bout ready to hit the road."

"Do tell!" Luther's reply was academic; actually it was scarcely necessary to tell him anything about the famous *Finkola* productions. Every year a truckload of top talent trouped through the turpentine swamps and bayous, and into the big tent swarmed every man, woman and woodcolt who possessed the *Finkola* label which entitled the bearer to admission. It was all part of Mr. Fink's advertising campaign, and he spared no expense in mounting his entertainments; raiding every cultural Mecca from Grossinger's to Las Vegas in his quest for top talent. And now—

"Boy, Ah'm gonna give you a chance. Yesiree, that's *exactly* what Ah'm gonna do! You're gonna work for me!"

"You mean, play mah *git*-tar in the show? How *about* that?"

"Wonderful!" Evangeline LaTour beamed fondly on Luther and still more fondly an Jefferson Davis Fink. "Ah do appreciate this. Truly Ah do."

"Think nothin' of it. Always ready to encuh-ge talent when Ah see it." Mr. Fink patted Miss LaTour on the thigh in a fatherly fashion and turned to Luther Snodgrass. "Repoht to mah office at the factory tomorrow mohn'in'."

"Yes, *suh!*"

"Meanwhile, kindly git to hell out'n heah."

"Yes, *suh!*"

* * *

Thus, as every biographer knows, Luther Snodgrass made his professional debut for *Finkola* the following week, in the thriving metropolis of Ague, Louisiana.

What every biographer doesn't know—or carefully neglects to mention—is that the young musician laid a bomb.

A liberal swig of *Finkola* has a tendency to deaden the hearing (indeed, there are some authorities who claim that steady indulgence will eventually deaden the indulger to a point where his only further use for *Finkola* will be as embalming-fluid) and the good people of Ague had sampled enough of the nostrum before Luther appeared so that they were more or less inured to the actual sound of his singing and playing.

However, their olfactory powers remained acute, and before Luther had finished his first number, several of the spectators were glancing under the wooden seats in an effort to detect the whereabouts of a sick polecat.

Some of the men in the audience considered slipping out quietly and summoning an emergency meeting of the Klan.

Jefferson Davis Fink, astute showman that he was, got the message. And right after the first show, he delivered it to Luther Snodgrass.

"Out, boy," he said. "You finished."

"Finished? But Mistah Fink, suh—"

"Don' you-all *Mistah Fink suh* me, hear? Git!"

"Ah thought Ah sounded purty good out theah tonight."

"Good foh what? Lookee heah, boy, Ah'm sellin' medicine to make folks feel bright an' sassy. Then you come on, a membah of mah own company, an' you sound like a hog with it's ham caught in a bob-wire fence. Call that smart advertisin' ? No, son, you gotta go."

"Please, give me anothuh chance."

"Sorry. Powerful sorry."

"But you-all cain't leave me stranded heah. Got no grit-money, got nothin'—"

"Heah." Jefferson Davis Fink held out a five-dollar-bill and a bottle of *Finkola*. "This ought to see you back to town. You-all can drink the bottle on the bus. Compliments of the house."

* * *

And that was all Luther Snodgrass could get out of him.

In the end he trudged away, guitar in one hand, grip in the other. But the bus station was closed, and there would be no transportation available until ten o'clock the next morning, so Luther didn't go Greyhound.

He picked at his grits and some iguana gumbo in Ague's sole culinary establishment; meanwhile squandering another fifty cents in the jukebox to play the latest recordings by Elvis Presley, Jerry Lee Lewis and The Platters.

"Ah kin sing evah-bit as good as they," he muttered. "Louder, even!"

The Last Plea

The thought—as well as the sounds—understandably depressed him. So much so that after he left the restaurant he spent his remaining capital for a bottle of something called *Old Poontang—A Blend: 85% Neutral Spirits, 15% Hostile Spirits*. It was something like that, anyway; he didn't bother to read the label. And he didn't bother to delay in consuming the contents. By the time he'd finished, Luther made up his mind to hitch-hike back to New Orleans. He took the road to the Crescent City, but it was very dark outside, and somehow he seemed to have missed his way.

The next thing he remembered ways wandering down a bayou byway which led deeper and deeper into the swamps. The night was black as pitch and even smelled that way; tarry bubbles oozed from the swamp as Luther trod a path never used even by day, and then only by Voodoo conjure-men. A mist crept out of the trees, and Luther shivered. He emptied the bottle and tossed it away, then stumbled on.

"Ah'm purely lost," he complained, sitting down on an old log and fishing out the other bottle, containing *Finkola*. He uncorked and attacked it, and before long, it was attacking him.

Perhaps the *Finkola* was to blame. I'm not going to attempt to sway your opinion. You'll have to decide for yourself. At any rate, nothing happened to Luther Snodgrass until he began to drink the stuff.

"Lost!" he sighed. "Nowhere, U.S.A.!"

* * *

It suddenly occurred to him that he was addressing his complaints to an exceedingly large alligator which had crawled up out of the bubbling blackness and was perched on the log beside him.

Luther put his arm around the alligator's neck.

"Whassa matter, ole buddy-buddy?" he asked the saurian. "Y'all look purty green around the gills. What you need is a slurp of *Finkola*." He extended the bottle. "Mebbe it'll help you to git rid o' them warts, too!"

The alligator shook its head politely.

"Party-pooper !" muttered Luther, bitterly. He took another swig. His mood changed. "Ah don't blame you. Nobuddy wants to drink with me. Nobuddy wants to heah me sing an' play. Nobuddy loves me. Ah jus' ain't appreciated, nohow. Why for is evvy-buddy agin us artists?"

The alligator shrugged.

"What's Elvis got that Ah ain't got?" Luther demanded. "How come folks make such a fuss ovate a square piano-player like this heah Albert Schweitzer?"

The alligator started to squirm off the log.

"Don' leave me!" Luther wailed. "Ah craves sympathy. You see befo' you a beatdown cat. Ah's sick of tryin' the ha'hd way. A man gits fed up, you know? Right now, Ah'd sell mah soul fo' a little ole hunk of prosperity."

The alligator edged away.

"Git me out'n this swamp," Luther implored, clutching vainly at the departing reptile and falling backwards off the log into the muddy ooze. "Take me to your Leader!"

That's what the man said.

Of course, it was only a current phrase; a commonplace expression, like the one about selling one's soul. And naturally, the alligator was only an alligator.

* * *

You can interpret it that way if you like. On the other hand, you may choose to believe otherwise.

In either case, all I can do is offer the facts in the matter.

Which were, and are, as follows. Luther fell off the log into the mud. When he sat up again the alligator had disappeared—but there, sitting on the stump-end of the fallen tree, was another presence. It seemed to be a man; at least its face was slightly less green and slightly less warty than the alligator's had been.

Luther stared up at the stranger.

"Evenin'," he murmured.

"Good evening, son," the stranger replied. "What seems to be the difficulty?"

"Ah fell."

"Hmm, so I perceive. Well, you're not the only one. I've had some previous acquaintance with the fallen." The stranger smiled benignly. "It behooves us, if you'll pardon the expression, to take consolation at times likes these in that glorious motto—'The South shall rise again!' And now, if you'll permit me to assist you—"

He extended a hand and hauled young Luther up to a seat beside him on the log. Luther blinked at him and beheld his benefactor. The

76

stranger was a plump, white-haired gentleman wearing a hammer-tail coat and a modest five-gallon hat.

"Who mought you be?" Luther inquired.

"I might be Judge Harmer," the stranger told him.

"Judge?"

"An honorary title, of course," his companion assured him. "But I'm a real Harmer, of that you may be sure. Come from a long line of Harmers. Certainly you are familiar with the name?"

"Reckon not," Luther answered. "Ah'm a stranger in these parts. Luther Snodgrass, at yo' service."

"Pleased to meet you." Judge Harmer's eyes twinkled. "But speaking of service, I perceive you have a bottle—"

"He'p yo'self," Luther urged, extending the *Finkola*.

Judge Harmer reached for the bottle, read the label, then hastily drew his hand away. "No, thank you," he muttered. "On second thought—"

"But it's only *Finkola*—"

"I assure you I'm perfectly familiar with the concoction," Judge Harmer replied. "And so again I say, no, thanks."

"You talk awful funny."

"Just plain English."

"Yeah, what I mean. Y'all sound like—pardon the expression—a Yankee." Luther gazed suspiciously at his new acquaintance. "If'n you ain't a real judge, then what are you, anyhow?"

"Call me a talent scout, if you like."

"A talent scout? You mean like for shows and all?"

Judge Harmer nodded.

"Come now!" Luther stood up. "What-all would a talent scout be doin' out heah in this little ole swamp?"

"Why, looking for talent, of course."

"In a bayou—at midnight?"

"I was informed that there might be a possibility of an informal get-together in these purlieus," the judge explained.

"Who-all would hold a sociable in a place like this?" Luther's eyes narrowed. "Hold on—you-all ain't talkin' about one of them Voodoo meetin's, are you?"

* * *

The judge shrugged. "I believe I've heard the term used in that connection, yes."

"But what kind of talent can you git out'n a bunch of conjure men and hexers?"

"Oh, you'd be surprised." The judge smiled. "I understand they sing and dance at such ceremonies. And of course, there are always drummers. There's a great demand for drummers up North, you know. Give a man a set of bongoes instead of a drum and clap a beret on his head and you've got a good non-union Beatnik."

"Nevah figgered it that way befo'," Luther admitted.

"But I fear I was mistaken," the judge continued, consulting his pocket-watch. Luther couldn't imagine how he could possibly see it in the darkness, but apparently the green and glittering eyes searched out successfully. "Here it is, past midnight, and no meeting in evidence." He sighed. "I don't know what's come over folks nowadays, really I don't! Used to be an average of three meetings a week, regular as clockwork, and a human sacrifice on Sundays. Now everybody stays home and watches Oral Roberts on television." He sighed again. "Apparently I'm wasting my time."

"Hold on!" Luther said. "If it's talent you're after, mebbe Ah'm your boy. If'n Ah kin find mah *git*-tar—"

* * *

He stooped and fumbled in the mud at his feet until he located the battered instrument. Raising it, he brushed his fingers lightly across the strings, then turned the guitar and shook it vigorously.

"Dern that toad!" he muttered, then brightened. "Happens that Ah'm a entetainer mah-self. You-all care for an audition?"

"Be delighted." The judge settled himself on the log and Luther, without further preamble, launched into the rendition of a popular ditty entitled *The Hang Down Your Head Tom Dooley Cha-Cha-Cha*.

Several alligators back in the swamp joined in the second chorus, and Luther finished with a brisk obligato which caromed off his left tonsil.

"Well?" he inquired. "What do you think?"

"I think I'll have a drink after all," said the judge, hastily reaching for the *Finkola* bottle.

"You didn't like mah singin'?"

"I never said that," his audience replied. "In fact, I was merely about to propose a toast."

"What about mah playin'?"

"I never heard anything to equal it." The judge took a deep gulp.

"Mebbe you-all'd like to give me a job?"

"My dear boy, I'm no impresario!"

"Is that like an imp, mebbe?"

"In a way." The judge smiled. "Actually, an impresario is a bit worse—he's a man who puts on theatrical performances. Well, as I say, I'm not one of those. I'm merely a sort of talent scout. I only find talent."

"An agent, like?"

"Ah, yes. That would be closer to the truth. I'm an agent."

"Then you could sign me up?"

"Well—"

"Mebbe you ain't convinced. Mebbe Ah ought to sing agin—"

"No!" the judge exclaimed, hurriedly. "No, that won't be necessary at all. I'm quite willing to sign you right now."

"Ten per cent, ain't it?"

"A hundred per cent, if you like."

"That's moughty generous," Luther grinned. "One o' them long-term contracks?"

"Lifetime," the judge assured him. "Better still, in perpetuity."

"Ah was kinda hopin' we could sign right heah."

"Good enough." The judge produced a document—not from his pocket, not from his sleeve, but from somewhere around his person. "Errs—I seem to have mislaid my fountain-pen. But this twig will do. And for ink, let's just prick your finger, here."

"Nothin' doin' !" Luther drew himself proudly erect. "Ah suspicioned you-all was the Devil right along."

"But I'm not the Devil, I swear it—merely an agent!" The judge's tones were unctuous. "Son, this is your big chance. Don't toss it away because of a technicality!"

"Well, Ah ain't signin' anythin' in mah blood." Luther frowned determinedly, then brightened. "Lookee heah, how's about me signin' in some of this *Finkola?*"

"Hmmm—I don't know—it seems highly irregular—"

"Ain't nothin' irregular about it!" Luther protested. "Ah done heah the raddio announcer tell just the opposite. He say there ain't nothin' like *Finkola* for keepin' you *regular.*"

"I'd prefer blood," the judge murmured.

"You-all want me or don't you?". Luther was solemn. "Ah tell you, friend, it ain't every day you git a chance to heah a talent like mine. You better not pass it by."

* * *

The judge sighed. "That's right," he said.

"So what you say?"

The judge sighed again. "Oh, very well. Sign in *Finkola*. After what you've already drunk from the bottle, I'm sure your blood is probably ninety per cent *Finkola* anyway. So there's not much difference."

"You-all want this formal?" Luther inquired. "If so, Ah'll make a capital X."

"Can't you write?" The judge frowned. "Not even your own name?"

"Course Ah kin! It's the spellin' Ah ain't so sure of." Luther scrawled his X on the document, then reached for the bottle.

"We got us a deal," he said. "Mought as well kill this now."

Apparently the *Finkola* had the same idea, because shortly after swallowing it, Luther gazed at his newfound agent with a contented grin, rolled up his eyes and heels, and passed out.

* * *

When he came to, he was in Noiseville, U.S.A.

Now the actual name of the town may be Nashville, or Chattanooga, or even Memphis. All three communities have at times proclaimed—and loudly—their right to be called the music capitals of America.

Call it rock-'n-roll, call it country music, call it hillbilly style, call it something which can't be printed in these pages—the fact remains that these three cities are responsible for more popular entertainment, decibel for decibel, and dollar for dollar, than any other metropolises since Sodom and Gomorrah.

And it was in one of them that Luther Snodgrass awoke.

"Where am Ah?" he wailed.

"Does it matter?" replied Judge Harmer.

"Matter? Ah'll say it does! Must've been drunk as a skunk! Ah do declare, Ah don't even remember mah own name."

"It's Clay Clinton," the, judge told him.

The Last Plea

"Clay Clinton?" The young man blinked suspiciously. "You sure it ain't Luther Snodgrass?"

"Not after last night it isn't. Don't you remember? You auditioned for me, I signed you up as my client?"

"Yeah, reckon so."

"Well, as your agent, I'm taking over your career. And the first thing I'm doing is changing your name. Luther Snodgrass—that's no good for theater marquees. Takes too many lights. And it's too long for TV credit-cards. You're Clay Clinton."

"Ah'm goin' on television?"

"Eventually. After you've had your vocal lessons."

"Ah don't need none. Ah sing okay."

"I'm not referring to singing. You're going to learn English."

"But who kin unnerstan' Elvis or Jerry Lee Lewis—?"

"I'm not referring to the way you deliver the so-called lyrics of your so-called songs. It's just that when you talk, it helps to be intelligible."

"You gonna ruin mah style."

"Trust me. From now on you're Clay Clinton, and you're my boy."

"He's *my* boy!"

For the first time Luther heard the strange voice.

He raised his head (he was lying in bed in Room 666 of the Flabbee Arms Hotel at the time) and instantly regretted his effort. It made his skull ache with a hangover, and worse than that, it afforded him a glimpse of the speaker.

A dear little white-haired old lady stood at the judge's side, smiling lovingly at Luther from behind the neck of a gin-bottle. She gazed at him with tender, bloodshot eyes.

"Son," said the judge. "I want you to meet your mother."

"Mother?" Luther sat up. "Not really?"

"Don't ever let me catch you talking like that again," the judge cautioned him. "From now on, you're Clay Clinton, like I said. And this is your dear mother."

"But—"

"It's time, son, that you learned the Facts of Life. Every young popular singing star has a mother, whom he worships and adores. Not only is it good for reams of publicity, but it can also help to take the heat off if—perish forbid!—he happens to get tangled up with one of those chorus girls in Las Vegas. You understand?"

Luther nodded. "So you hired me a mother, is that it?"

* * *

He stared at the little old lady. "Where'd she park her broomstick?"

"If you must know, it's on the roof," the little old lady told him. "My cat is watching it. She's queer for phallic symbols."

"Then you *are* a witch?" Luther swung his legs over the side of the bed. "Ah was only kiddin'—Ah nevah dreamed—"

"Here, where are you going?" the judge demanded.

"Away!" Luther fumbled for his jeans. "Ah don't aim to mess with no witches—"

"We have a contract," Judge Harmer reminded him. "Besides, she's not a practicing witch. She's retired."

"That's right, buster," cackled the old woman. "The judge hired me right out of the Old Spook's Home."

"But Ah don't need no super-type-natural Mamma."

"No. But you do need an English instructor. And that's something your new mother can do for you. She can teach you how to speak properly. Besides, I want someone around here to keep an eye on you while I'm away."

"You goin' somewheres?"

"Of course. I'm an agent. You're not my only client, you know. I've got people in New York, Miami, Hollywood, who need my help. But ask your mother. She can tell you."

And in the days that followed, she did.

* * *

Mother proved to be an apt instructor. During the next few weeks, the new Clay Clinton stayed in his room with her and she patiently taught him the rudiments of grammar and pronunciation. Using such standard texts as *Downbeat* and *Variety*, he gradually enlarged his vocabulary.

The judge appeared three weeks later.

"Well?" he inquired. "How is it going?"

"Crazy, man!" Luther informed him. "Mom falls up to the pad here, making the scene with the English bit every day, and I'm coming on strong. I mean, it's like a gasser, Dad. You dig?"

The judge beamed. "My boy, I'm proud of you!" he declared. "All that vulgar Southern accent has disappeared—now *anyone* can understand what you're saying. Son, I do believe you're almost ready."

"Almost? Like I'm the most, Daddy-O." Luther paced the floor. "I'm with it, Pops. Solid."

"Not so fast. First we'll have to work on your musical education."

"What's with the music, Clyde? I make with my pipes, I belt it out and they flip. I mean like they'll love it."

The judge shook his head. "You need polish. That's another thing Mother is here to teach you." He turned to the little old lady. "Let him study for another couple of weeks," he commanded. "With the cat."

"The cat? Which cat?"

"My black cat," Mother told him. "She's got just the right *vibrato* for a popular singer these days. Real fish-shaped tones."

So for two weeks, Luther listened to the cat. The cat didn't always feel like howling, but mother belted it regularly with her broomstick and belted herself with the gin-bottle as Luther listened and learned.

When the judge returned he was properly impressed. Luther did a number for him.

"Wonderful," Judge Harmer exclaimed. "Why, you can't hardly tell him and the cat apart!"

"He's a good boy," mother declared. "You know, Judge, I had my doubts when you took me out of straight sorcery and made me get into show biz. I thought you were like putting me down. But this is the greatest! Sticking pins into wax figures, all that jazz—it's funky compared to working with live talent. And when I think of all the harm I can do—"

She cackled and tackled her gin.

"Never mind that now," the judge cautioned, with a warning look in Luther's direction. "We're going to put the finishing touches on his education now. I think we're ready for Eddie."

"Eddie?" Luther echoed. "Who's he?"

"Eddie Puss, at your service—blowing cool and plenty nervous!" A dapper little bald-headed man bounded into the room. "Ah, Mother, good to see you! Share some skin!" He shook hands enthusiastically. "Same old fascinating witch, eh? Have broom, will travel. Righter-ooni?"

"This is Eddie Puss," the judge said. "He writes songs."

"Not my real name, of course," the little man said, grinning at Luther. "They slapped the handle on me because I write a lot of *Mother* numbers. Eddie Puss, like in the complex and all that jazz, dig? Also, because I'm quite a cat."

* * *

"But I don't need a songwriter," Luther objected, in his newfound English. "I'm the most."

"Everybody needs songwriters in this business," the judge told him. "How do you suppose a hit singer operates these days? They all have to write their own numbers in order to get into the Top Ten. And that's where people like Eddie come in handy. They can do the coaching. Teach you the ropes." He turned to the little man. "How about it—what do you think?"

"Well, I don't know." Eddie Puss surveyed Luther with a calculating eye. "He's almost too old, don't you think? I mean, what we need like is young blood. Most big hits, they're written by kids still in high school. Freshmen are best. Me, I've even worked with seniors, but it's hard."

"He's really very childish," the judge reassured him. "I want you to try."

"I can't promise anything—"

"You wouldn't be going back on our agreement, would you?" The judge was suave. "Remember what you were when I met you? Just a frustrated lyric-writer. All you ever were able to do was those four-line poems on the walls of public—"

"Never mind!" Eddie Puss shuddered. "I appreciate what you've done, and like I say, I'll try."

"Then get busy," the judge muttered. "I want this boy in shape for his debut in two weeks. Teach him the popular song business."

So Luther learned the popular song business from yet another teacher.

"Really nothing to it," Eddie reassured him, during the course of their daily lessons. "It's as simple as NBC. All you got to remember is that there are only two kinds of pop hits today. One of 'em is about a couple of high school kids in love, and the other makes even less sense. The main thing is, you have to remember to include certain phrases in each lyric."

"Such as?"

"Well, we got what we call key-words. You know 'em."

"You mean like *heart,* and *tears,* and *embrace?*"

The Last Plea

"Crazy, man! Only you never use 'em that way. You make with the phrase. So it comes out, *this heart of mine,* and *these tears in my eyes,* and *your fond embrace.* Whatever you do, never change a single word. Here's the rest of the list—dig it, because it's all you're gonna need to write dozens of songs. *The touch of your lips. They don't understand. I hold your charms. Each thrilling moment. Of love divine.*" He paused. "And one thing more. The most important bit. Every couple of lines, you got to throw in the word, *baby.*"

Mother was crying. "I always was one to snap my cap over poetry."

Luther himself was equally impressed.

"See how easy it is?" Eddie remarked. "With me helping you on lyrics and the cat here giving you the tunes, we can't miss."

And they didn't.

* * *

Two weeks later, to the day, Judge Harmer appeared in the hotel room.

"Everything in readiness?" he demanded. Mother and Eddie Puss beamed proudly and the cat purred at Luther and nodded.

"Prepare to dig your wig, Big Daddy," Luther said, picking up his guitar. "We've got a smasheroo."

And he launched into the world premiere of the number now universally known as, *If I Had To Do It All Over Again, I'd Do It All Over You.*

For a moment after the last note sickened and died away there was an impressive silence in the little room.

Then the telephone jingled and Judge Harmer picked it up.

"Yes," he said. "Yes, I understand. Right away."

He replaced the phone in its cradle and turned to the gathering with a smile of relief.

"Management is getting complaints on the noise," he said, happily. "We're being evicted."

"Then it registered," Eddie Puss muttered.

"It must have. Come on, let's get started."

"Where are we going?" Luther was puzzled.

"To New York, of course. For your debut. I understand that Hank Corrupta is replacing Terry Coma at the Club Sandwich on Saturday."

"Corrupta? He's with that rival outfit, MCA, isn't he?" Eddie demanded.

"Right. We got to get rid of him. And we will." Judge Harmer grinned. "What he doesn't know is that our boy here will be replacing him."

"But how—?" Luther murmured.

"You'll see." The judge turned. "Start packing, we're off to the big city."

* * *

Mother started for the window.

"Where are you going?" the judge demanded.

"I was just after my broomstick—"

"We're traveling by TWA this time," he told her. "Never mind the expense. Besides, I'll need your services *en route.*"

"What do you want me to do?"

"Get three pounds of wax —no, two will do, Corrupta's pretty skinny. Make me a poppet. And then—"

"With the pins, eh? Give him the old stab-and-jab routine?" Mother cackled.

"No, he wouldn't even feel the needle. He'd just think it was a fast fix. I've got a better idea." And the judge whispered something in her ear.

She cackled again.

And she continued to cackle on the plane, as she sat beside Luther and moulded a wax figurine which took on an eery resemblance to Hank Corrupta.

"Why, it's amazing!" Luther marveled. "Where did you ever learn to model like that?"

"In my younger days I used to work for Disney," the crone confided. "I was a stand-in for *The Reluctant Dragon.* I picked up a lot of techniques from his artists."

"Well, it's certainly a remarkable job," the young man said. "Even those hands are perfect."

"They have to be," the old woman said. "Because of this." She began to mumble over the mannikin and then, suddenly, she reached out and squeezed the waxen right hand.

"You—you *crushed* it!" Luther exclaimed.

"Natch. And I just got you a job!" she predicted.

Luther didn't believe it.

86

The Last Plea

* * *

Not until he arrived in New York and Judge Harmer showed him the announcement in Ed Sullivan's column. Hank Corrupta would not be opening at the Club Sandwich on Saturday night after all.

"Lost his voice?" Luther wondered, aloud.

"Worse than that," the judge declared, smugly. "Read what it says. He can't sing because he hurt his hand and he won't be able to snap his fingers!"

"But I still don't see—"

"Leave everything to me. I'm going down to the Club Sandwich right now and talk to the boys about putting you on."

"You have connections?"

"In this business, you've got to have connections. Why, the Musician's Union and I are just like that." He held up two fingers, then drew them across his throat.

Luther shivered.

He was still shivering after the judge had left.

"What's the matter, boy?" asked Eddie Puss. "What gives?"

"I'm scared," Luther confessed.

"What's to be scared of? You're all set. You've let your sideburns grow, you haven't combed your hair in a month, and if you shiver like that on stage tonight nobody can tell you from Elvis himself."

"It's not that. It's like I never really believed what the judge said before. And I never thought mother was a real witch—"

"Wise up, buster," the old woman said. "How do you think anyone gets ahead in show business these days? It sure enough ain't talent."

"You mean it's all the result of magic?"

"What do you think? You've watched television, haven't you? How else could half of those ham-bones get on in the first place?"

"But I've always thought—"

"Never mind what you thought. This is it, pal. This is the big time!"

And it was.

* * *

That evening, at ten o'clock, Luther Snodgrass, alias Clay Clinton, stepped up to the microphone of the Club Sandwich and brandished the gold guitar which Judge Harmer had slipped into his surprised fingers just before his number was announced.

And he killed the people.

"I did it!" Luther marveled, at the impromptu party following his performance. "I really sent them!" He laughed happily and nudged Eddie Puss in the ribs. "And it was me, singing and playing up there. That's what they dug the most—me. Nobody hoo-dooed them into applauding. And to think I almost fell for that line about witchcraft!"

"Yeah," said Eddie.

"You were ribbing me, weren't you? I mean, you're just a lyric-writer. The judge is a smart agent, but he's only human. Mother gets stoned and thinks she's a witch, but that's for the birds. I see it now—you were all in it together, a real swinging combo, feeding me that jazz so I'd keep up my confidence."

"Yeah," said mother.

"But from now on, we're straight up and flying right. I get the message—you can level with me. Because I'm not scared any more. I know I can punch over a number. So let's forget all that Creepville jazz."

"Yeah," said the cat...

* * *

And Luther Snodgrass forgot witchcraft from then on. In a little while he almost forgot his own name. Because he was Clay Clinton now, and there wasn't time to think about anything else.

Judge Harmer kept him busy.

First of all, there was the recording bit.

"Records," the judge told him. "That's where the big loot is made. I'm going to get you into every juke-box in the country."

"But I'm not even signed with a recording outfit," Luther protested.

"Who needs it?" Eddie Puss demanded. "What we do is, we set up our own waxworks. That way we don't just collect the royalties—we get profit on distribution, the whole package."

"But how can we be sure the records will become popular? How can we get them spinning?"

"Through the dee-jays," Eddie told him. "They can make you or break you."

"Can Judge Harmer get the disc-jockeys to play our waffles?"

Eddie Puss smiled grimly. "Believe me," he said, "some of his best friends are disc-jockeys. When it comes to going after a fast buck, he doesn't care who he associates with or how low he stoops!"

* * *

And so Clay Clinton's gold guitar was matched by his growing collection of gold records. Remember his clever modern adaptation of great classical favorites—*Rock-'n-Roll Of Ages* and *When The Rock-'n-Roll Is Called Up Yonder* and all the rest? Or would you rather forget?

The point is, the public didn't forget. It never had a chance to do so. Clay Clinton was on every radio show. Clay Clinton was in every juke-box. Clay Clinton moved from the Club Sandwich to top spots in Chicago, Detroit, St. Louis, Miami. Clay Clinton appeared in theaters and auditoriums. Clay Clinton guested for his fan-clubs. Clay Clinton did his act on the *U. S. A. Grandstand* television show, and two fourteen-year-old girls tore off his pink shoelaces for souvenirs.

He acquired a wardrobe of sixty suits and a fleet of nine Cadillac convertibles, and eventually reached such heights of success that he was seriously thinking about going to a psychiatrist.

But he just didn't have the time. There was never any time, any more.

Eddie Puss had long since dropped out of sight. "You don't need him," the judge decided. "From now on, you plug standard tunes. Besides, I've got other assignments for him to handle."

That was something Luther had learned; he was indeed far from the only client Judge Harmer dealt with. It seemed, in his travels through the enchanted realms of show business, that the judge had connections everywhere. Although he specialized in teenage talent, it almost appeared as though teen-agers had taken over the bulk of the entertainment outlets in the country. Between rock-'n-roll singers and progressive jazz combos, they dominated the musical end, and there was little else.

* * *

"Of course, there's the movies to be considered," the judge said, thoughtfully. "I've got something working for me out there."

"You mean you're active in Hollywood too?" Luther marveled.

"Why not? Who do you think is responsible for all those pictures about juvenile delinquents? If it wasn't for the how-to-do-it movies, the average kid wouldn't know how to handle a switch-blade or smoke a reefer."

"You're kidding, of course," Luther said.

"And then there's the monster-movies," the judge went on. "That's a pretty important department. You know the kind—*I Was A Teen-Age Supreme Court Justice*, and *Invasion of the Giant Spirochetes?* I've been promoting them pretty heavily, and with fine results. Ten years ago there was a lot of silly talk about motion-picture audiences with a mental age of twelve. Well, we've made a lot of progress since then. I think we've got it down to around seven. Of course, this doesn't include western fans or Mickey Spillane addicts, or the people who think a girl is hiding her talent if she wears a brassiere. If we included them, we'd have the index of intelligence down to about five years of age."

"I doubt it," Luther mused.

"Well, I can dream, can't I?" the judge retorted.

"Look here," said Luther. "You aren't serious, are you? You don't really want to put out all this crud? I mean, in my spare time between shows, I've been doing quite a bit of reading on my own—"

"Reading?" The judge raised his eyebrows. "Mother had strict orders to keep you on *Billboard* and *Mad Comics.*"

"Mother isn't around much," Luther confessed. "When all this loot started pouring in she came to me and hinted about retiring. Said it wasn't so much her idea as it was the cat's. It seems like the cat had always wanted to settle down in a little vine-covered cottage and raise mice for a hobby. And for twenty thousand dollars, mother found just the place—not exactly a cottage, but a lovely old liquor store. She said that with all that wine and stuff around she wouldn't need any vines. So I bought it for her, and she cut out."

"Leaving you to read, eh?" The judge frowned.

"Well, like why not? I mean, I dig education the most. I figure education is one of the best forms of learning, particularly if you want to know something. And like that there."

"It's corrupting your taste, son. Pretty soon it will affect your art."

"I meant to flip my lip about that, too." Luther sighed.

"You know, sometimes I wonder if all this singing I do is really the living end. I get to thinking it's cornball. Now you take this character Boris Pasternak and what he says about the artistic conscience bit—"

The Last Plea

"Look." Judge Harmer put his hand on Luther's shoulder. "You're a singer. I'm your agent. I made you. I have further plans. Your only job is to carry them out."

"But why? I'm making plenty of money now. I could retire on royalties. And you've got other clients, a lot of them."

"It isn't a question of money. It's a question of ethics."

"Ethics?"

"Sure, what else have we been talking about? Ethics—I want to degrade them. I won't rest until the whole world is rocking and rolling."

"But why?"

"Because it's my duty, that's why. Just as it's mother's duty to be a respectable, practicing witch instead of running off to lush it up in a liquor store. Not that I have anything against lushes, understand— they're quite acceptable, in a way. But the major task comes first. To corrupt, and to destroy."

* * *

Luther grinned. "So you're back to that old line again," he said. "Trying to scare me with that phoney superstition talk. Well, it won't work. I've come a long way since you met me in the swamp."

"And you can go right back there if you aren't careful," the judge retorted. "Very well, I have no intention of convincing you that I'm an emissary of infernal powers. Just let me say this, though—when you argue against bad taste, you're arguing against your own bread and butter, to say nothing of the necessities of life, such as caviar and champagne. Forget all this nonsense about self-improvement."

"But I don't want to forget—"

"Then remember this. You and I have a contract. And according to the terms, I'm entitled to plan your itinerary. From now on I'll see to it that you're so busy you won't have time to read or moon around with a lot of egghead ideas, either."

The judge stood up. "Start packing," he said. "I'm taking you right to the Home Office." He frowned grimly.

Luther gulped. "Now, look here," he said. "Don't put me down."

"Put you down? That's a good one." Judge Harmer chuckled gutturally.

"It isn't that I believe you, or anything," Luther quavered. "But you keep talking about the Home Office. I understand that the climate in

Hell is pretty bad."

The judge laughed again. "Who said anything about Hell? Where I'm taking you, the climate is even worse. This is the twentieth century, son, and we move with the times. Our Home Office is in Hollywood!"

* * *

Luther Snodgrass was in Hollywood for exactly three days when he met Mary Jane Hawkins. He happened to be sitting in the outer office of Judge Harmer's agency office on Vermont when the girl walked in.

He watched the little blonde request an interview from the receptionist, and saw her receive the usual brush-off—the *don't-call-us-we'll-call-you* routine. He noted how her shoulders sagged, and noted too how other salient portions of her anatomy remained fascinatingly firm.

Then she turned away, and saw him sitting there, and something happened.

It was hate at first sight.

"Clay Clinton!" the girl exclaimed. "Aaargh!"

"What?" said Luther, rising to his feet.

"Aaargh!" the little blonde repeated. "Also pfaugh!"

"I don't dig you, chick."

Mary Jane moved closer and peered up at him. "You *are* Clay Clinton, aren't you?"

"Well—like yes, I guess so."

"Then blecchhh," she told him. "To say nothing of bracchhh. And, if you'll pardon the expression, *pfui!*"

"Now wait a minute, doll. Listen to me—"

"I *have* listened to you," Mary Jane told him. "Which is precisely what I mean when I say—"

"Let's not go through that routine again," Luther said, hastily. "It hurts me to hear such sounds coming out of a lush thrush like you."

"You're a fine one to talk," the girl retorted. "What about the sounds *you* make?"

"Are you knocking my singing?" Luther demanded.

"Singing!" She sighed dismally. "That's what you call it, eh?"

"Well, I may not be the greatest," Luther admitted, "but it's a living. I mean, I got nine Cadillacs, and—"

"Sure. You've got nine Cadillacs. And meanwhile, a girl like me can't even get an audition from an agent. That's because I have a trained voice and all the public wants to hear nowadays is a lot of screeching. You and your kind are responsible for that."

"Now don't make a federal case out of it," Luther murmured. "Don't hang me, judge!"

"I wish I could. I happen to love music, and when I think of what you've done to ruin singing in this country, I could just scream."

"In what key?"

"Now you're making fun of me." Mary Jane stamped her foot petulantly, and it was Luther who screamed, because she came down on his toes.

"Ohh—I'm sorry—I didn't mean to lose my temper—"

"That's all right," Luther told her.

"I apologize for being so rude."

"You only told the truth."

"*What?*" She stared at him.

"I know I can't sing," Luther said.

"But—"

"Let me explain." He smiled at her. "Kind of a long story, so I won't do a standup routine. How about lunch?"

* * *

Cadillac Number Seven (the pink one, with the purple upholstery) happened to be on the parking lot outside, and he drove her to the Derby. And it was there that he told her the story.

"I can't believe it," she murmured, shaking her head slowly.

"This is Truthville, U.S.A.," Luther insisted.

"But it's fantastic!" Mary Jane wrinkled her forehead. "It's absurd to think of the Devil trying to take over the entertainment and television industry in this town! Besides, he wouldn't have a chance, as long as Desi Arnaz is around."

"I didn't go for the bundle myself, really," Luther confessed. "Not until Judge Harmer brought me out here and I dug what went on around his office. In the past couple of days I've seen him do business with half the weirdies in show biz."

He described some of the no-talent he'd met—the orchestra leaders who couldn't read music and their musicians who couldn't play a note as written—the offbeat young actors from the torn-shirt schools of drama who seemed to have a madness in their Method—the dancers whose movements depended less on choreography than on the tightness of their underwear.

"All right," Mary Jane conceded. "I know a lot of these people are bad. But that doesn't mean they're part of some organized conspiracy. Aren't you exaggerating just a trifle?"

* * *

Luther shook his head earnestly. "Has to be a plot," he insisted. "How else would all those idiot M.C.s get jobs on those daytime give-away shows? Where do all the loudmouthed announcers come from with their pitches for pile remedies?"

"But surely it's not the Devil's work?"

"Oh, no?" Luther stared at her triumphantly. "Who do you think invented the singing commercial?"

"Well—"

The girl was weakening.

"You heard how I got into this racket," Luther continued. "Judge Harmer admitted he was an agent, didn't he? He laid it on me about how he was out to ruin the public's taste. It figures."

"Yes, it figures." Mary Jane nodded at him. "You're a nice person, Clay. I misjudged you."

"Call me Luther," he begged.

"All right—Luther. I'm ashamed of the way I acted when we met. Now that you've told me your story, I think I'm beginning to under-stand the situation. And I'd like to help you."

"You can't help me," Luther said. "I never knew until recently that I was no good, and that the reason I was hired was just because I was so ter-rible. But it's too late to do anything about that now. I'm under contract."

"Contracts can be broken."

"This one is in perpetuity." Luther smiled and shrugged. "When the judge told me that, I thought he was talking about a place. Since then I've done a little reading, you know? I'm up on all this longhair talk."

"Like paranoid delusions, for example?"

"Huh?"

"Like sick-sick-sick," the girl explained, patiently. "Rationalizing your sudden success into a diabolical conspiracy."

"Stop making like a square," Luther begged her. "All I know is, I've got a contract. I'm hooked."

"You really believe this?"

"If I don't, may I drop dead and work for Lawrence Welk. "

Mary Jane bit her lip. "Please—watch your language."

"I'm sorry."

"I'm sorry, too." She gazed at him for a long moment. "Well, if there is something to what you say, then maybe there's a way out."

"Like what?"

"Perhaps you need to be exorcised."

"I get all the exercise I need at the hotel swimming-pool."

"Not exercise—exorcise. That means to cast out demons."

"You mean there's a way to get rid of the Devil?"

"I wouldn't know. But I do know there are a lot of psychic mediums in this town. Some of them claim to be able to communicate with spirits. Suppose you went to one and presented your problem? Maybe something could be done."

"But I wouldn't know where to find a cat like that."

"Let's try the Yellow Pages."

And sure enough, in one of the five phone-books of Greater Los Angeles, they discovered Dunn.

* * *

Medium Dunn turned out to be a little old man who operated a spiritualist parlor on Fairfax, above one of those used-clothing shops which specialized in selling the discarded costumes of motion picture stars. There was a big sale on leopard-skin trusses left over from an old Tarzan movie in the downstairs section, but up above all was quiet.

Little Mr. Dunn listened to Luther's story in silence and seemed not at all surprised at his client's revelations.

"Do you think you can help him?" Mary Jane asked.

"I'm not sure." The little old man cupped his hand to his ear. "Who did you say it was held your contract?"

"Judge Harmer. At least, that's what he calls himself."

"Judge Harmer." The cupped hand trembled perceptibly. "I was afraid I'd heard the name."

"Then you know him?"

"Yes. He's got quite a reputation in certain circles."

"Could you exorcise his influence?"

Medium Dunn shook his head slowly. "Judge Harmer is mighty big in this town," he said. "Mighty big. He's got quite a large and dependent following."

"Then there's nothing you can do?"

"I didn't say that." Medium Dunn peered out of the window at the pink Cadillac. "For a reasonable offering—say a thousand dollars—I can put you in touch with certain parties who have the power to negotiate. Mind you, I couldn't help you break the contract; I can't promise that. All I can do is open the way for a meeting."

"A conference?"

"You might call it that."

"When? Where?"

"Now. And right here. If you happen to have the thousand on you. Or are you one of those people who never carry more than fifty dollars in cash?"

"I never signed for those ads," Luther told him, pulling out an alligator billfold and prying open its jaws. "Here's the loot."

Medium Dunn glanced at the girl. "I'm going to ask you to step outside and wait," he said.

Mary Jane departed for the reception room and settled down with a bundle of old psychic magazines. She buried her nose in a copy of *The Saturday Evening Ghost* and kept it there, even when the smell of burning sulphur issued from behind the closed doors. She could hear the scraping of chalk on the floor and the sound of an eery chant. Then there was silence.

Inside the darkened room, Luther Snodgrass lay on a couch. He too could smell the sulphur, hear the chalk tracing a curious geometrical figure which resembled nothing so much as a pentagram with two pairs of gents. And then he listened to the chanting. His eyes closed, and the chanting rose to a faint and faroff wail. The smoke rose around him in the darkness. And then—

* * *

And then he was rising, not to walk but to swoop through space. He was rising, or was he falling? He didn't know, because all at once there were no directions any more; no *up*, no *down*. But Luther moved, moved through blackness into deeper night. And there was a circle of light which moved with him, supporting his substance until he stood silently before the shadows.

Behind the shadows were stars, and he realized then that he must be in outer space.

"I'm way out," he said.

* * *

The shadows stirred. Stirred and blurred. Blurred and brightened.

Now he could see the enormous outlines of the crouching figures, stare into the gigantic eyes which held all emptiness. There were two figures, four eyes. He faced them, puzzlement overriding panic.

"*Two?*" he muttered to himself. "I always thought there was only one—"

"*There is one,*" came the reply. "*But he is not here. We are but judges.*"

"Judges? What do I need with a judge?"

"*You wish to discuss a contract, is that not so?*"

"Yes."

"*Then it is a matter of law, and judges are required.*"

"I never thought of it that way."

"*We will hear your plea.*"

"Well—"

"*Proceed. There is no time to waste. The Devil will find work for idle hands to do.*" Two pairs of gigantic hands reached towards Luther's neck, and he retreated hastily to the center of the circle of light.

"I get the message," he said, shuddering. "But it's really just a simple bit. You see, there's this deal I have on with Judge Harmer, if you happen to know him—"

"*We know him. He is our brother.*"

"Ullp ! Your brother, eh?" Luther hesitated, then plunged on. "Well, we had this little agreement, dig? Only now I want out. That's all there is to it. I want out."

"*You signed a contract?*"

"Uh—yes."

"*Then you are committed. There is no legal may to free yourself of obligation unless he releases you.*"

"But couldn't you persuade him?"

"*Why should we?*"

"Can't I buy my way out?"

"*With what?*"

"Money. Loot. Moola. Look, I'm loaded. I've got nine Cadillacs—"

"What do we want with your Cadillacs? We do not run a used-car lot. Although, naturally, we do business with. many used-car dealers."

There was faint amusement in the booming voice, but none in Luther's quivering whisper.

"But there must be some way I can lick this thing. If you don't want money, what do you want?"

There was a long pause until the voices came again.

"We do not buy."

"We do not sell."

"But at times we trade."

"Trade what?"

"An eye for an eye. A tooth for a tooth."

"I didn't sell any eyes or teeth."

"We know what you sold."

"So shall we say—a soul for a soul?"

"Another soul in exchange for mine? But whose—"

"There is a girl. One who trusts you."

"Now, hold it—"

"If you were to take her to Judge Harmer, she would go willingly enough. You would tell her you were mistaken about him, that it was all a delusion on your part. You would say that you were using your influence to secure her an opportunity. It could be arranged for the judge to offer her a contract. Once she signs, you are released."

"That would be a fair exchange."

"Like hell it would! Nothing doing!"

"Then your plea is dismissed."

"But—"

"Go."

The huge hands reached forth. And the voices boomed.

"A final warning. Do not attempt to evade your contract. This time you have come to us. But next time we can come to you."

The hands swooped down and Luther moved. He blurred his way through darkness and then he was falling in the endless emptiness beyond the stars. Falling back on the couch in the little room. Yes, he was there once more, and awake. He could smell the sulphur.

* * *

Only it wasn't sulphur, now. It was something else. Something like brimstone—

"How'd you make out?" Medium Dunn inquired.

Luther blinked and sat up. "You mean you don't know?" he asked. "You didn't see them, or hear them?"

"I noted nothing," the little old man said. "You appeared to be in a deep trance. Quite similar to that of a hypnotic subject." He brightened. "I happen to be a competent hypnotist, too," he continued. "In case you are ever in need of such services—"

"Never mind," Luther said, rising.

"I am adept at Reichian psychotherapy," Dunn said. "Orgone treatments day or night, by appointment."

"Not interested."

"Tea leaf readings?" Medium Dunn grasped his arm as he hastened towards the door. "How about a high colonic—"

"Let's get out of here," Luther gasped, pulling Mary Jane to her feet and leading her over to the stairway.

"You might stop downstairs," Medium Dunn called hopefully. "Tell them I sent you and get a ten per cent discount. I understand they have something special in Jayne Mansfield's old bras—"

* * *

The smog was reddening into sunset as they reached the street. Luther opened the door of the Caddy and helped the girl to enter.

"How did it go?" she asked. "What happened?"

"Wait," he said. "I don't want to talk here."

They drove in silence up through the hills. In spite of what the TV comics say, it is possible to find a certain serenity in the darkness on Mulholland Drive. And it was there, gazing down across the neon nonentity that is the city, that Luther told Mary Jane of his experience.

"Or was it a dream?" he concluded. "I don't know."

"In any case, you protected me," the girl said. "I'm proud of you."

"I'm not proud," Luther answered. "I'm scared. If it *was* just a cooky dream, then I'm flipping. And if it happens to be real, well—"

"Forget it," Mary Jane commanded.

"How?"

She showed him. Nice girl or no, Mulholland Drive has a magic all its own. And as she entered his arms, Luther murmured, "Don't worry, baby. I won't let anybody hurt you. And I'm going to get out of this deal, wait and see—"

Suddenly he froze. For there was no need to wait and see. He was seeing, right now.

He was seeing the neon lights blotted out, obscured by the huge talons which descended from the sky, shoving aside the stars as they scrabbled towards him.

"Honey, what's the matter ?" Mary Jane whimpered.

The claws came closer. Luther shuddered.

"They're here," he whispered. "They're watching. They know they can't have you—and they won't let me touch you, either."

"You're imagining these things," the girl reassured him. "I don't see anything."

"I do."

"Look." She sat upright, faced him, grasped his hands. "You're not well. You ought to get out of here, go away from all this. I'll come with you."

"But—"

"Let me take care of you. I want to."

"We'd be poor." Luther glanced up at the sky nervously.

"Who cares?"

"But you don't know what a raunchy character I was when I was poor. Strictly a no-goodnik. Anything for kicks. I was willing to sell my soul—"

"You're not like that any more. We'd get along, I'm sure we would."

"No." Luther was watching something outside the car. He didn't look at her.

"You don't love me, is that it?"

He looked at her then. "Of course I do. Can't you understand? I *want* to go. But they won't let me. They have a contract. They have plans for me. Me and my lousy voice."

"All right." Mary Jane turned away. "I guess I *do* understand, after all. There's no need to hand me a line about how you hate what you're doing, or dream up any more stories about the Devil. I can take a hint. When it comes to a choice between me and nine Cadillacs—"

"It's not that at all," he protested. "There isn't a Cadillac made that can compare with you. Why, I'd trade them all in for just one—"

"I'm not an automobile dealer," she sniffed. "Just take me home, please."

The Last Plea

"But—"

"Please," she repeated; kicking him politely in the shins.

Luther drove her home in silence.

And all the way, the shadowy hands followed him across the sky, and somewhere between the stars the eyes blazed down...

* * *

Judge Harmer was waiting for him beside the swimming pool at the Beverly Hills Hotel.

"Where have you been," son?" he demanded. "What have you been up to?"

"I—" Luther hesitated, gulping.

"Don't tell me, I already, know." Harmer raised a pudgy hand and smiled. "Well, it doesn't matter. I'm sure you've learned your lesson. Now we can just let bygones be bygones and get down to business."

"Business?"

The judge nodded. "I didn't bring you out here for a rest cure," he said. "Though speaking for myself, I could certainly use a black sabbatical. It's time to go to work. I've just been talking to the Boss."

"The Boss?"

"Who else? He's out here, too. Just got in from Las Vegas. And he's a little worried about the opposition."

"What opposition?"

"There are certain signs of good taste creeping into the field, and he doesn't like it. You know, things like Playhouse 90, some of those Sunday egghead shows. And movies are improving, too. We've got to hit, and hit hard. That's where you come in. At midnight, Monday, in my office. He wants to meet you then."

"Supposing I refuse?"

Judge Harmer glanced up at the sky.

"Nice clear weather we're having. I'd hate to see a storm come up over the week end."

* * *

Luther sighed. "What does he have in mind for me?"

"First of all, we're lining up a regular television show for you. A full thirty-nine-week series, every hour staged like a spectacular.

You know the bit—lots of guest stars for you to insult and call by their first names, plenty of novelty acts with chimpanzees. You've seen those dance-numbers they stage where three creeps in tights come out and swish around the singer? Well, money is no object—we're going to hire *six* creeps for your show! Already lined up a sponsor; he's one of the biggest laxative manufacturers in the business. We're going to have singing commercials, too. Remember all these cigarette programs where big burly guys go around puffing on cigarettes as soon as they've finished wrestling an alligator or jumping from a plane without a parachute? The ones where everybody has a tattoo on the back of his hand? Well, the sponsor came up with a great gimmick. Our guys are going to be tattooed on—hey, what's the matter, son?"

Luther groaned.

"Sounds like hard work, eh? Don't worry. You'll have writers. The best. We'll hire five of 'em just to turn out ad-libs for you. The same guys who make up all the jokes about how Ed Sullivan looks like an undertaker, or an undertaker's customer. And that's not all."

"More, yet?"

"Certainly! Boss wants you to make a movie. He's doing the script himself. It's called *I Was A Teen-Age Chicken-Plucker For The—*"

"No!" Luther gasped. "No, not that!"

The judge glanced at the sky again and gestured with his cigar. Something brushed Luther's cheek, and a gigantic shadow blurred past him. There was a great splash in the swimming pool and the water suddenly began to steam.

"Hold it," Judge Harmer said, grasping Luther's collar. "I'd hate to see you fall into that pool. Looks to me like it's full of crocodiles, too—you see?"

Luther took one glance, then turned away. "Monday at midnight, you said?" His voice was dull.

"Right! In my office, remember. That gives you the whole weekend to rest up." Harmer nodded briskly and stepped away. "Well, if you'll excuse me, I have an engagement at Forest Lawn."

"At this hour?"

"The young lady prefers it." Judge Harmer chuckled. "Perhaps you'd care to join us? I'm sure we could dig up a date for you."

Luther shook his head and ran down the path towards his guest-house.

The Last Plea

"See you Monday night, then," the judge called. "Meanwhile, take care of your voice. We're counting on you."

Luther took care of his voice. He used it immediately, to call Mary Jane.

"I'm sorry," he said, over the phone. "I know you're making with the mad bit at me, and this is no time to bother you. But I'm really in trouble, and I've got to talk to someone. Unless you can help me—"

"I'll be right over," said Mary Jane Hawkins.

"Good." Luther glanced out of the window. "I was hoping you'd say that. Somehow, I don't care to go out at night myself. Not right now."

"Stay where you are. I understand."

She came over, just as she promised, and Luther told her the story.

* * *

And then, I think, is when Mary Jane came up with her idea. I say I *think*, but I'm not sure.

You see, I hadn't made the scene yet. In fact, I hadn't even met Luther Snodgrass.

I didn't meet him until Monday night.

That's when he walked into Judge Harmer's office and saw me, sitting all alone behind the big desk.

He stared at me as I checked my watch. It was midnight, right on the head.

His eyes bulged. "You're the boss?" he murmured. *"You?"*

I smiled. "Why not?"

"But—"

"What did you expect, a long red tail?" I laughed and brushed the cigarette ashes from my sports-jacket.

"You're just a man, aren't you?" He was utterly deflated. "And here, all along, I've been thinking—"

"I know what you've been thinking." I shrugged. "That's what comes of too much reading, my boy. You've been digging the *Faust* bit, haven't you? And *Damn Yankees,* and *Will Success Spoil Rock Hunter?* and all that jazz. You've got the idea that anyone can sell his soul for talent. Let's face it, *you're* not talented."

* * *

Luther nodded at me. "That's right. But the way I had it figured out, from what Judge Harmer told me, the Devil wasn't interested in real talent. He just wanted to corrrupt everyone's taste, spoil their standards. From then on, he would find it easier to influence their morals. It was all a gigantic plot, and it sounded pretty logical to me. I mean, if the Devil were around today, he'd naturally go into the advertising business, and television, and public relations—"

"Please!" I raised my hand. "I grant you it all sounds logical. And if I were the Devil, I just might encourage people to produce shows like *Damn Yankees* and the rest, simply to be subtle and put the idea into folks' heads that it's possible to cook up a deal. But I'm not the Devil, as you can plainly see."

"Then Judge Harmer is crazy?"

"Like a fox," I told him. "The judge knows what he's doing. He's lined up a great career for you out here. You're going to come on strong. And that's what I want to talk to you about tonight. First, the television series—"

"You really are serious about this? Even though you know I'm lousy?"

"Let the great American public be the ones to decide." I stared at him. "I see you brought your guitar. Good. There's a new number I want you to try—the theme-song for the show." I reached into my desk and brought forth a sheaf of sheet music. "Here it is. Brand new tune, be up there in the Top Ten three weeks after you introduce it. Great title, too. *Strontium-90 Daddy, Don't You Fall Out On Me!*"

He took the music and held it awkwardly.

"Prop it against the bookends here and let's give it a try," I said. "Just run through it cold. I don't expect a finished performance—all I want is a general idea."

Luther Snodgrass nodded and raised his guitar. Then he smiled at me, cleared his throat, and began.

I got a finished performance.

And I do mean *finished.*

Standing there in my office, Luther Snodgrass sang as he'd never sung before—he sang *good.*

I couldn't believe my ears.

Out of his mouth came the pear-shaped tones of a trained vocalist. He sounded like a concert artist, and he played the guitar like Segovia.

"There." He put down the guitar. "How'd you like that?"

I didn't answer. I couldn't, for a moment. Then I whispered, "Try something else. Let me hear your old number—*If I Had To Do It All Over Again*—"

So he sang *that*. And it sounded, so help me, wonderful. He was even pronouncing the words so you could understand them.

"Try another," I muttered.

He did a third selection. It was even better. I didn't wait for him to finish but made him stop in mid-chorus.

* * *

"What's happened?" I demanded. "What's come over you? Why don't you sing the way you always do?"

"Always *did*," he corrected. "I *can't* sing that way any more. I've been trained."

"By whom ?" I snarled, bitterly. Wait until I get my hands on—"

"Mary Jane taught me," Luther said, happily. "Over the week end. From now on, I'm going to be a real singer."

"But how could you change in just one week end? And why can't you change back again?"

"Because she didn't teach me alone." Luther was positively grinning now. "She remembered something Dunn had mentioned."

"Medium Dunn?"

"That's the cat. He said he was also a hypnotist. So she took me to him, and he put me under hypnosis while she coached me. Planted subconscious suggestion, you see? Now I couldn't sing the way I used to, even if I wanted to—"

"Which you don't," I grated, savagely. "Because you know blessed well that with this new voice I can't possibly use you any more. That I'll have to release you from your contract."

"I only did it because I thought you were the Devil," Luther explained. "I just wanted to save my soul."

"You and your square soul! As far as I'm concerned, you can take it and—"

"Then you won't be needing me any longer?"

"Who needs you?" I swivelled away from him. "Look, I'm a businessman. I'm in the entertainment field and what I want is mediocrity. Fortunately, there's plenty of it around, just as awful as you were, too.

I can get myself another boy. So run along. Go back to your Mary Jane. Marry her, settle down, raise six kids and the payments for the mortgage. Sweat out the rest of your days in some lousy factory, rendering chicken-fat."

"Thanks." Luther smiled. "No hard feelings, then?" He moved towards the door, then halted. "Wait until I explain to Mary Jane!" he said. "You know, I almost had *her* convinced you were the Devil, too? I really believed the whole deal about how you had organized to ruin the world with rock-'n-roll and like that. Thanks for relieving my mind."

"Get lost," I said.

* * *

Luther Snodgrass went out. Out of the door, out of my hair. I reached up and touched my hair as Judge Harmer came in.

"Well?" he asked.

"You must have heard his voice," I told him. "I can't use anything like that. Send in this new kid—this Randy Studd."

Judge Harmer hesitated.

"You mean you let Luther Snodgrass go? Just like that?"

"Why not? He's got everything figured out. I'm only a no-talent scout, in business for my wealth. No problem."

Judge Harmer nodded and made his exit.

I continued to touch my hair, brushing my hand over my head carefully, so as not to muss my toupee.

That toupee cost $2,000, but it's worth it.

It hides the horns…

Iron Mask

"Where is she?" demanded Eric Drake, hoarsely. "What have you done with Roselle?"

The tall, bald-headed man shrugged. "Sit down, Eric," he murmured. "There is no need to become excited."

"Tell me where she is," the young man insisted, gray eyes flaring in accusation.

Pierre Charmand met his stare directly. "I have sent Roselle to the Chateau D'Ivers," he answered.

"To the chateau? But you couldn't. Don't you know what they're saying? The Chateau D'Ivers is—"

Pierre Charmand interrupted with a bitter laugh, "I know," he said. "They say the Chateau D'Ivers is haunted. Do you believe it? And do you believe I would send Roselle—my own daughter—to such a place if *I* believed it?"

Eric Drake stared at Pierre Charmand through a veil of candlelight. They were a strange pair, here in the secret quarters of the Underground.

Tall, elderly Pierre Charmand, former Mayor of Dubonne, met the gaze of young Eric Drake, former AP correspondent. A strange pair indeed, and in a strange alliance.

For Pierre Charmand, since the coming of the Nazis to Dubonne, was mayor no longer. He was local head of the Underground movement.

Drake, too, had left his former post with the arrival of the Germans. Now he served the Underground for the sake of two loves—love of Charmand's daughter, Roselle, and love of freedom.

They had been partners together in this movement to free France, but now—

"Why did you send Roselle to the Chateau?" Eric Drake demanded.

Again Pierre Charmand was evasive. "Are you afraid of the ghosts, too?" he mocked.

"Nonsense," Drake snapped. "It's not ghosts she's likely to run into there. It's Germans!"

Charmand chuckled.

"I know," he replied. "And that is precisely why I sent her. The news has come to me that *gauleiter* Hassman plans to visit the Chateau tonight. It is necessary for one of us to arrive before he does."

Both men were silent for a moment, thinking of Hassman. Hassman, the new *gauleiter*, was instituting a reign of terror in the little town of Dubonne. He took French machinery, and French gold, and now he was planning to take French manhood to ship to Germany. His troops, his Gestapo squads, his spies were everywhere. Charmand and his Underground movement had been sadly subdued under the iron rule of Hassman.

"What does Hassman want at the chateau?" Drake asked, breaking the silence.

"Can't you guess?" Charmand replied.

"There's nothing of value there," Drake mused. "The old castle has been deserted since the family was killed in the French Revolution. The peasants say their ghosts still haunt the spot—but I'd guess it's probably filled with dust, cobwebs, and bats. Nobody would care to visit it."

"Exactly." Charmand shrugged "And that is why I thought of it as an ideal hiding-place."

"Hiding-place?"

"Yes. When the Germans came here to Dubonne, my last official act as mayor was to dispose of the state papers. Not the ordinary documents, you understand, but the secret files—just a few sheets of value buried away in the archives at the City Hall.

"These I determined to preserve at any cost, for their historical significance. So I cast about for a suitable hiding-place. While you were so busily sending dispatches on Nazi troop movements to your newspaper, I was scurrying up the hill to conceal those papers at the Chateau D'Ivers."

"You hid them there?"

"Yes, there. I placed them in an iron casket and concealed them in a spot I alone knew—a secret drawer in the mantel over the old fireplace.

"I thought they would be safe. But somehow Hassman must have learned, because I received word today that he is sending a squad to the chateau this evening.

"Naturally, they must not be allowed to find those papers. That is why I sent Roselle this afternoon."

Drake scowled.

"But why did you send your own daughter—a girl—on such a risky mission?"

"Because of the risk," Charmand explained. He rose and went to the window. Drawing aside the blinds he pointed at the streets outside. "Look, my friend," he said. "Look at the streets of Dubonne. Every block patroled by Nazi swine. What one of our people could walk unchallenged through those streets and up to the Chateau in broad daylight? Certainly not you or I, nor Marcel, Antoine, Phillipe, Jean—none of our men. No, only a woman could go forth on such an errand; a woman we can trust. So I sent Roselle."

"But it's twilight now," Drake objected. "She should be back, shouldn't she? And the Nazis will be going up there—"

Pierre Charmand bit his upper lip and turned away.

"You're worried now, aren't you?" Drake accused. "You know it was a foolhardy scheme. That's why you didn't let me in on it. Why, she might be—"

"Don't say it," Charmand whispered.

"Fool!" Drake strode toward the door, fists swinging angrily.

"Where are you going?" muttered the old man.

"I'm going up to the chateau after her," Drake answered.

"But the patrols—"

"Damn the patrols! It's dark, I can slip through them. And I'm going to slip through them. Roselle's up there in that deserted ruin, alone. I'm going to her, now."

* * *

Drake's pace never slackened when he reached the cobbled street outside. He thrust his hand deeply into the pocket of his battered trench-coat and gripped the metal of a gun-butt. Scowling, he tramped down a deserted street in grim haste, his eyes intent on the vistas of the deepening twilight.

A telltale clank of metal warned him to draw back into the shadows beside the trees. A Gestapo man passed in gaunt silhouette.

Drake waited until the German had turned the corner, then hastened on.

The upturned collar of his coat served to hide his face—a face already too well known by the German invaders. For Drake, like all the others in the Underground, was marked for death by the Nazis. It was a dangerous game he played here—a game of hide-and-seek in nighted streets; the stakes, his life itself.

The game went on, quietly; silent as death. And Drake worked his way up the street toward the hill beyond. Every moment of delay, each moment spent in hiding or eluding a patrolman, was torture to the man. For Roselle was up there on the hilltop. He must get to her once.

But a rising moon peered with bloating face over the ruined walls by the time Drake hastened up the pathway that led to the Chateau D'Ivers. The mouldering walls masked a mystery—a mystery shrouded in silence. Drake's ears heard no sound from within. His eyes saw no light save that of the cold and grinning moon above.

Drake pressed through the tangled weeds overrunning an ancient pathway.

He moved warily now, keeping well under the shadows of the gnarled trees.

If the Germans were here—

But there were no Germans.

There was only silence and decay. A fetid stench seemed to emanate palpably from the great, moss-grown stones of the chateau's walls. The ruined spires leered at the moon, and broken windows, like the eyeless sockets of skulls, stared blindly at the night.

Drake neared the doorway, observed with a start that the great carved door swung open on creaking hinges. He caught a glimpse of yawning vistas beyond.

Roselle must be in there, now. Unless—

Drake stifled an oath as he caught the flutter of movement from behind the door.

Something was emerging!

Eric Drake's hand went to his gun. He jerked the muzzle upwards, held it ready, and then—

A cloud of black horror spiraled from the doorway and streamed upwards to the sky.

"Bats!" he muttered.

As the squeaking and chittering column soared aloft, Drake repressed a shudder. He thought of ancient legends, of the monstrous rumors that clustered thicker than the moss about the walls of the chateau.

And Roselle, all alone there in the darkness—

Bat what if she were not *alone?*

The thought was a lash. Drape half-ran up the stone steps, dashed through the open doorway.

"Roselle!" he whispered.

* * *

There was no answer—no answer save for a sibilant echo that slithered from the cold walls of the hallway in which he stood.

Here, in the lair of darkness, Drake pondered which way to turn. There was the room with the fireplace? Where was Roselle? Should he risk calling her?

He hesitated for a moment—and then his doubts were resolved.

For silence shattered in a single scream.

Drake knew the voice. Roselle!

A shot rang out from the left. Its echo boomed through the corridors, and Drake went into action.

He darted toward the doorway to his left, entered the room, and reeled back a step.

Yes, the fireplace was there, and the mantel above it. Faint moonlight revealed the scene—but Drake had eyes only for the slim, alluring body of the girl on the floor. It was Roselle.

And above her a shape hovered in the semi-darkness; such a shape as is born only in the depths of nightmare. Black, cloaked, hooded, it bent over the girl in an attitude of gloating menace. A black paw clutched something to the cloaked breast, and then—the figure was gone.

Even as Drake dashed forward, the shape seemed to melt into the shadows against the farther wall and disappear.

Then Drake was kneeling beside the girl, raising her head, whispering to her.

Roselle opened her eyes. She was unhurt; Drake saw that. The girl was conscious, too—but not wholly so, for she screamed again. "Eric!" she cried. "Eric, you're here!"

"Yes," he whispered. "Everything's all right."

"But where is he?" sobbed the girl. "Where is the thing I saw—*the thing in the Iron Mark?*"

II
The Man without a Face

Moonlight streamed through the ruined windows.

Drake stared deep into the girl's eyes and read her fear. He shook his head. The fear was plain to see, but there was no hysteria.

"He wore an iron mask over his face," Roselle repeated, softly. "I saw him as plainly as I see you. He wasn't a ghost."

Eric Drake nodded thoughtfully.

"That's plain to see," he murmured. "Ghosts don't steal valuable papers. And ghosts don't leave footprints."

He pointed to the floor, where moonbeams glittered upon the silver carpet of the dust. The mouldering motes had been disturbed by footprints—the prints of Roselle's high-heeled slippers and the flat, broader prints of a man's shoes.

Drake saw the incoming tracks, and his gray eyes swerved to observe the prints retreating once more along the castle halls beyond the chamber.

"He went that way," Drake snapped, rising to his feet.

"Eric—you're going to follow?"

"I must." Drake drew Roselle to her feet, placed his hands on her shoulders in a gesture of reassurance.

"You've got to get out of here before Hassman's men show up," he told her. "Go back and report to your father. Tell him what happened—and tell him I'm on the track of those papers. I'll see him at the meeting later tonight."

"But Eric—you're not going to follow him alone?"

"He has the papers. We must get them back. And he can't have gone far in the past five minutes. If I hurry—"

"But you can't go!" There was more than fear in Roselle's dark eyes. Eric laughed.

"He's only a man, no matter what kind of a disguise he's wearing. And I've got a gun."

"Guns won't help you," she whispered.

"What do you mean?"

"I didn't want to tell you this—but I shot at him. And hit him."

"There's no blood," Drake observed.

"Yes, that's right. There's no blood. I shot him in the head—and there was no blood. He didn't stop. He's a monster, I tell you—"

"Stop it, Roselle!" Drake shook her shoulders. "You hit the iron mask, of course. I tell you, nothing supernatural leaves footprints like these. And as long as I see footprints, I'll follow. Now—get out of here, fast."

Along kiss belied the harshness of his command. Then Drake stepped back, wheeled, and plunged into the dark passage beyond the castle chamber. His eyes followed the blurred tracks in the dust.

Ahead was only darkness and silence—deep darkness, deeper silence. Drake never wavered. As he entered the musty corridor the moonlight faded. He snapped on a pencil-flash and groped his way around a turn in the corridor.

The way led down, but the tracks were still plainly visible in the beam of the flash. Drake plodded along.

A winding passageway turned the castle ruins into a veritable maze—a black, forbidding maze that reeked of ancient decay, lurking death. But Drake followed the footprints; footprints that lured him ever deeper into the nighted depths where dwelt the strange silence and the sable shrouds woven by shadows.

Crumbling walls loomed and leered in the heart of the dank inner chambers. The pencil-flash disclosed tunnel mouths and openings on every side, but Drake's eyes were fastened on the plain trail of the fugitive's footprints.

They led him on, they led him down—they might lead him to the gates of hell—but where they went, he could follow. And he must follow.

He increased his pace. Was the attacker hurrying to some chosen spot? Was there a grim purpose in this plainly marked trail?

Would Drake round a bend and be confronted with a waiting presence? Did something lurk in the shadows, crouching to spring?

He strained his ears against silence, but could not read the secret prisoned by the night.

And then—

Abruptly Drake turned the corner at the end of the winding passageway. The footprints led him to a wall and halted; halted against a blank expanse of gray stone.

Drake's pencil-flash swept the flagstones at his feet. Drake's eyes swept the expanse of wall.

Then he fathomed the secret.

"Subterranean exit," he muttered. "Probably another concealed opening."

His surmise proved to be correct. His groping fingers, running swiftly over the surface of the wall above the spot where footprints ended, soon encountered the press-pivot.

A section of wall opened silently—surprisingly, for a mechanism undoubtedly worn by age and rusty with disuse.

Drake stood on the threshold of the tunnel only long enough to play his pencil-flash on the flooring ahead. He saw the footprints, and followed.

Damper, deeper darkness ... secret, sepulchral silence ... and ever the footprints beckoning him on to the brink of unguessable gulfs beyond.

And then, quite suddenly, he emerged. A bend in the tunnel brought him abruptly to a slanting fissure of rock—a fissure through which moonlight streamed. The secret passageway led out of the castle to the lower hillside beyond!

Now there were no footsteps to follow. But. Drake saw something better—a figure!

* * *

There in the bright moon's rays wound the road down the hillside; and on the road Drake discerned the black, grotesquely bobbing shape of the fugitive.

Although the moon was bright, Drake saw no glitter of steel from the head of the fleeing man; at this distance it seemed as though his head, like his entire body, was shrouded in black. Black, crawling like a spiderous shape, the figure moved through moonlight down the road ahead.

Drake reached for his automatic, at the same time pocketing his pocket-flash once more. The action was symbolic. All in a moment the man was transformed from a searcher to a hunter.

He started down the hillside road at a steady trot. The figure didn't turn back. Perhaps the fugitive hadn't heard him. Exulting in his luck, Drake pressed forward, closing the gap between them. His eyes, ever alert for sudden movement, came to abrupt and unexpected focus— not on the fugitive, but on the road far below him.

Other figures were crawling up the hillside from below!

Other figures were swarming purposefully along the hill. Drake, even at this distance, recognized the ugly outlines of military helmets.

Gauleiter Hassman's men—the Gestapo squad was coming to ransack the chateau!

Drake stepped back momentarily.

This was a situation he was not prepared for. The Gestapo would reach the stranger before he could. And perhaps the fugitive was in their employ. He hesitated.

But the black-clad fugitive did not hesitate.

He must have seen the Gestapo squad at the same time Drake glimpsed them. Now he crouched in the center of the road, against a pile of racks. The road slanted steeply down before him, and the Germans were toiling upwards just below. The fugitive tugged at the jumble of rocks, pried a boulder free—

Drake gasped.

With a single gesture, the fugitive lifted the gigantic boulder over his head and sent it crashing down upon the helmets of the Nazis below!

The missile struck with crushing accuracy. A Nazi dropped, pinned and writhing under the gigantic stone.

The rest of the squad glanced up, perceived the solitary figure standing with black silhouette against the sky. The Gestapo men scattered, seeking cover behind crags and between crevices in the path below.

Swiftly, unhesitatingly, the fugitive tore another rock free from the face of the cliff beside the path. Once again he raised it, hurled it crashing toward the head of the nearest Nazi.

It missed, and hurtled down the hillside, striking with a force that sent echoes of doom reverberating through the night.

Now the Nazis had produced revolvers. Flame spat toward the black figure in five angry jets. But the fugitive sought no shelter. He stooped again, deliberately, and lifted another huge chunk of granite.

He dropped it squarely on an iron helmet below. There was a scream. And the shots rang out in redoubled tempo. The fugitive, standing amidst a hail of lead, calmly groped for another rock.

There was something magnificent about his lone fight against these odds—something magnificent and not wholly sane.

But that didn't move Drake to subsequent action. His calculations were shrewd.

The fugitive was one man: the Nazis numbered four. The Nazis had guns, while the fugitive had only the rocks. The fugitive still had the casket—Drake could see it hanging in a knapsack strapped to his black back.

If the Nazis won and took the casket, Drake would be fighting against greater odds. If he sided with the fugitive and helped beat the attackers off, he'd have one man to deal with—if he were an enemy and not a friend.

Besides, enemy or friend, the fugitive was killing Germans. And Drake approved of the idea.

He sent the stamp of his approval crashing through the night as his gun spoke.

Bounding forth from cover, Drake joined the solitary stranger in the road, and as the stranger hurled his rocks, Drake aimed and fired each time an iron helmet was exposed from cover on the roadside below.

The stranger turned. For a moment Brake stared into a black hole where a face should be—then realized that his information was correct. The stranger did wear a mask, but not of iron. His features were covered with a black velvet cloth, with two slits for the eyes. From head to foot the fugitive wore black, and he towered like a gaunt ghost in the moonlight.

Drake was conscious of intent scrutiny, but the mysterious one did not speak. He merely grunted, then turned and pried another rock from the hillside. Again he hurled it down with an incredible display of strength. And Drake aimed at a helmet as a Nazi rose from below and fired at them.

Drake could almost swear he saw the stranger flinch as a bullet struck home, but it could not be. For the fugitive stooped stolidly like an automaton, grasped another boulder, and sent it spinning on its deadly mission. Another Nazi screamed, then fell along the hillside as the boulder bounded over his body.

Drake aimed once more. And his aim was true. Another Nazi fell. And his remaining companion suddenly turned and scuttled back down the road. The stranger rolled another boulder down—Drake fired at the running target—but the solitary surviving Gestapo man vanished below.

Then, and only then, the fugitive turned his fantastically masked visage toward Drake and extended a black-gloved hand.

"*Merci beaucoup,*" he whispered.

Iron Mask

The voice was curiously soft, the French phrasing curiously stilted.

"My thanks, *Monsieur*," whispered the stranger in the mask. "How can I ever repay you?"

In an instant Drake was at his side, the muzzle of his gun pressing into the stranger's back.

"That's simple," Drake grinned. "You can repay me by handing over the casket in your knapsack—the casket you stole from the chateau."

For a moment the stranger stood silent. Then, abruptly, a whispering chuckle rose from the depths behind the black velvet mask.

"What's so amusing?" Drake snapped.

"But this is too incredible!" chuckled the stranger. "Can it be that you also wish to secure this casket?"

"Can be," said Drake, laconically. "Hand it over."

The stranger didn't move.

"It is all right," he whispered. "I know about the papers it contains. I was merely set on rescuing it from the Nazis."

Drake's gun dug deeper, emphasizing his impatience.

"Never mind that," he insisted. "Hand it over. I happen to know that you stole this casket from a girl in the chateau."

"Was she one of our people?" whispered the stranger. "I did not know, or else I should not have interfered. I thought I was the only one who suspected the Nazis were coming."

Drake hesitated only a moment.

"Who are you?" he snapped.

"You know we don't ask fox names," parried the stranger. "But I can give you the password."

"Give it to me, then."

"Silence."

Drake heard the whispered word and lowered his weapon.

He could not doubt the watchword of the Underground.

This stranger was one of the organization, working for the freedom of France. And in accordance to the code of the Underground he need not reveal any compromising information as to his identity.

Still, Drake could not free himself from misgivings. He stared again at the masked features, the gloved hands of the mysterious man in black.

The stranger turned, shrugged.

"Why do I wear a mask? Why do I conceal my hands with gloves?" His whisper came faintly.

"The explanation is simple, if unpleasant. I was a soldier, *Monsieur*. A soldier of France—yes. It happened during the retreat from the Maginot line. The tanks came over and the men with the *flammenwerfers*—the flame-throwers. They burned my face and body.

"When I was found, I was given up for dead. But at the hospital in Paris they worked to save my life. In this they succeeded, but they could not save my face. You understand? That is why I conceal my hands and body, because of the scars. And I must conceal what they gave me in place of a face."

The whispering voice was bitter, harsh, intense.

"They wanted to keep me there, an invalid. But I have work to do. I have a debt to repay to the Nazi horde. I left the hospital, made contact with the Underground. They could not use me in Paris, because of my—deformity. So I have been fighting alone, in my own way.

"I came here. By chance I learned the local *gauleiter* had ordered a raid on the chateau. I did not know his purpose, but I came, thinking to anticipate his search. I found the girl taking this casket. I could not stop to make inquiries. I took the casket, fled—and you know the rest."

Drake nodded. "Ours is a fortunate meeting," he said. "You are mistaken if you think the Underground has no place for you. You have great strength and greater courage. I shall be happy to accompany you to our headquarters tonight—we are holding an important meeting. Let me introduce you to Charmand, our leader. He'll find a place for you."

"But I can't," the stranger whispered. "If they should see me—"

"Perhaps your features are repulsive, Drake answered, cautiously. "But it does not matter, I assure you. No matter what they did to your face—"

"You don't understand," groaned the stranger. "I have no face. They gave me *something else*. You fool, don't you realize what they did to me? Look, then!"

A black-gloved hand rose to the stranger's swathed throat. A single convulsive gesture ripped the black velvet covering from his head.

Drake stared at what leered forth in the gleaming moonlight; stared at the glaring horror that rose from the stranger's shoulders stared at the dreadful reality of what Roselle Charmand had hinted.

Iron Mask

For the stranger had no face. Set in an iron grin, brazen as doom, was a grimacing iron mask!

III
The Gauleiter Strikes

"What is the word?" demanded Pierre Charmand. The tall, bald-headed old Frenchman stared at the masked stranger, a glitter of proud challenge flashing from his stern blue eyes.

"Silence," whispered the voice from behind the black velvet covering.

Dubonne's Underground leader nodded slowly. Then Pierre Charmand turned to Eric Drake, standing at the masked man's side.

"Who is this man and where did you encounter him?" he asked.

Drake told the story, simply and without hesitation. "I think that he can help us," he said. "And he has brought the casket."

Pierre Charmand's eyes sparkled.

"That is well!" he said. "It is very important that we of the Underground retain possession of those documents in the casket. All of the ancient official papers of Dubonne are contained here—some of them were rescued from the days of the Revolution. *Gauleiter* Hassman would give his right arm to possess them."

He rose and extended his hand. It was grasped by the black-gloved hand of the burned soldier in the iron mask.

Drake stood watching the weird tableau—and weird it was.

For the three of them were in the headquarters of Dubonne's Underground—the warehouse of the local brewery.

Surrounded by mountains of barrels, they crouched in a vast chamber; the light of a single candle rising to cast eerie shadows over casks and tuns. It was as though they were met in the great wine-cellar of some fabled ogre—these three incongruous figures; old Frenchman, young American, and creature garbed in the black nightmare of his cloak and hood.

Appreciation of the grotesque scene sounded in a sudden scream.

All three wheeled and faced the doorway.

Roselle Charmand stood there, one hand covering her red lips as she cut short the sound that might betray them to the world outside.

But her blue eyes were wide with horror as she saw her father shaking hands with the creature that had attacked her.

119

"Mon pere," she gasped. "He is here!" Pierre Charmand nodded and stroked his mustache as he gave her a reassuring smile.

"Do not be alarmed, my daughter," he said. "Drake can explain everything."

"Drake—oh, Eric, you're safe! And you've captured the attacker!"

"Well, not exactly," Drake grinned. "Let me tell you what's happened."

He did so, sitting on an overturned cask at the girl's side. She listened, and gradually the fear left her face.

Meanwhile Pierre Charmand conferred with the man wearing the mask. Drake concluded his story just in time to catch the purport of the Underground leader's remarks.

"And so you see," he was concluding, "I have called a meeting for tonight—here. Within the hour all members of the Underground in Dubonne and the surrounding countryside will be assembled.

"We have word that *gauleiter* Hassman is about to issue an order summoning all able-bodied males to forced labor in Germany. Naturally, we must act at once. We must plan an effort to sabotage that campaign."

The iron mask bobbed up and down in agreement.

Pierre Charmand sighed. "There is but one disappointment," he admitted: "I had hoped tonight to have a full report on just when Hassman would strike, and where; how many men he was going to conscript and what method he would use. Two or three of our people have attempted to intercept such a report. But I must confess failure. Now, with the meeting set for midnight—and only an hour to go—I have no report on which to base our plan of campaign."

"Midnight," whispered the man in the mask. "One hour to go."

He rose, suddenly, purposefully.

"Where are you going?" asked Pierre Charmand.

"You say there is an hour," came the whisper. "Perhaps I can do something."

"You mean you can get the report?" breathed Pierre Charmand. "But how?"

The iron-masked man shrugged, heaving his shoulders clumsily. "Do not inquire as to methods," he whispered. "I have developed a certain—technique—in such matters. Rest assured, I shall return with the information you desire."

There was a flurry of black, and the man disappeared from the brewery vault.

Charmand stared at his daughter and Drake and slowly duplicated the departed man's shrug.

"Who knows?" he said. "Perhaps it can be done."

Roselle trembled in Drake's embrace. "He frightens me," she whispered. "Somehow, I have the feeling that he's holding something back—something he hasn't told us."

"We must have faith," Drake reassured her. "But now, there's work to be done."

* * *

The three of them put their heads together in the candlelight; Pierre Charmand's grizzled bald dome, Drake's straight-haired sandy head, and Roselle's cascaded cloud of dark curls all bent forward over the table, and Pierre Charmand began to issue instructions in a low murmur.

As he spoke, the door at the end of the room began to open and close swiftly as Underground members suddenly filtered singly into the room.

They came and came, but always they walked alone. Pious housewives, staid old business men, grinning laborers and gnarled, sunburned farmers appeared and silently took seats on upturned casks in a semi-circle about the table.

Soon a score of them were assembled, waiting for the moment of meeting. Drake lifted his gaze from the papers on the table, glanced at his wristwatch.

Midnight.

"It's time," he told Charmand. "And our friend has not returned."

But even as he spoke the words, the door at the end of the room swung open, and the black cloak of the masked man swirled into the room.

Ignoring the stares of the assemblage, he strode to the table with thundering tread.

A gloved hand swept out, and a white paper fluttered down.

"Here is a report of Hassman's proposed operations," he muttered, in his peculiarly husky voice.

Pierre Charmand raised his eyebrows. "Good work," he said. "Was it—safe?"

"Do you mean, have I been discovered? The answer's no. And I don't think I've been followed, either. The sentry posted outside of the entrance upstairs says that we're all here. You can call the meeting, then. We're safe."

The masked figure sat down awkwardly upon an upturned cask near the table. Drake and Roselle found seats, and Pierre Charmand rose and confronted the meeting of the Underground.

"Comrades," he began. " You all know for what purpose we are met tonight. Ordinarily I'd call for your reports and then take up the matter at hand.

"But I have just received information of vital importance concerning our next plan of operations. A new comrade has succeeded where others have failed—you saw him come in just now.

"Therefore I beg leave of you to examine the information he has just brought in. I should like to be able to pass it on to you immediately, for it concerns our future."

There were nods of assent and murmurs of approval from the audience.

Slowly, Pierre Charmand unfolded the paper the cloaked man had brought to him.

And then—

Hell broke loose.

Without warning came the thundering on the stairs outside the door. Without warning, the rattle of machine-gun fire resounded through the hollow brewery vault.

The door guarding the warehouse crashed in splinters and into the room poured a swarm of gray-clad figures.

"Hassman!" streamed Roselle Charm and.

* * *

A dozen pairs of eyes had recognized the burly figure in the doorway.

The squat, bullet-headed *gauleiter* was a familiar figure in Dubonne—a figure of terror. Terror stood in that doorway now, and his pudgy hands held two spitting Lugers.

A woman's wail of fear died in a spatter of bullets. And then the Underground acted. With a flick of the wrist, Pierre Charmand struck the candle from the table, plunging the vault chamber into total darkness. Men and women ran like rats.

But the darkness was not complete. Red bursts of machine-gun fire spat deadly lightning into the room. The surprised Underground members crouched behind tuns and vats. A few were armed, and they returned the fire of the Nazis as the soldiers swept into the room, raking the walls with their portable machine-gun units.

Over and above the chatter of death rose the screams of the trapped French men and the guttural commands and curses of *gauleiter* Hassman.

The Nazis advanced, groping their way as the Underground defenders rolled beers barrels in their path and toppled casks. Vats pierced by bullets gushed forth amber streams. Soon the Nazis waded ankle-deep on their errand of death.

But they came on. Several fell, crushed by barrels or riddled by the answering bullets of the Underground. Yet they advanced, and it was a ghastly game of hide, and seek played there in the darkness as the machine-guns barked, and their tongues of flame lapped out to lick the bodies of the French in a caress of death.

Drake grasped Roselle by the shoulders, drawing her behind the nearest shelter of barrels. "Stay here," he yelled above the din.

Then he stole forth to the center of the room, groping his way toward the table.

The casket from the chateau rested there; he had seen the masked man place it next to the candle before he sat down.

His hand went out, encountered its cold outlines. He grasped it. An iron grasp encircled his wrist.

Drake lashed out. His fist struck velvet—then iron beneath the velvet.

"Oh, it's you!" he exclaimed. "Had the same idea, eh?"

The hand relaxed its grip on his wrist but did not let go.

"It's me—Drake!" yelled the American.

"Oh." The whisper came and the hand fell away as Drake grasped the casket.

"Come on," Drake said. "Follow me. I think there's another exit. We'd better get out of here fast—there's no hope of resisting."

It was grim truth he spoke.

* * *

The tide of battle was flowing unmistakably in favor of the Nazis. Through the darkness they advanced squad on squad, wading through the spilled liquor in a relentless search for the few remaining Underground members yet alive.

Drake groped his way back to Roselle's side. "Follow me," he commanded. The three of them stole cautiously along a row of tuns against the wall.

"There's an emergency loading chute set somewhere in the wall, as I remember," Drake shouted, above the din of battle. "Wait—I think I've got it."

His outstretched hand rested on an iron handle. He would tug it open and then—

"What about Father," gasped Roselle. "Where is he?"

The answer came grimly.

A sudden hail rattled above their heads. Bullets thudded into the wall. Running feet rounded the corridor of tuns to their left.

Pierre Charmand, panting and exhausted, stumbled blindly into his daughter's arms.

"Mon pere—we're safe! Follow us to escape," the girl shouted.

Drake raised the door by the iron handle set in the wall. "We'll have to crawl through," he warned them.

His admonition was drowned out by the thunder of booted feet thudding down the corridor toward them. Another burst of machine-gun fire swept the air above their crouching figures.

"Now!" whispered Drake.

Quickly, he pushed Roselle Charmand through the doorway. She crawled ahead on hands and knees. Drake bent to follow. Then came the ghastly horror of the light.

Gauleiter Hassman had found a flashlight—and its cold beams swept over the bent bodies of Drake, Charmand, and the iron-masked man.

And with the beam, came bullets. The Nazis behind Hassman opened fire.

"Quick!" Drake warned. He rose and kicked out at the nearest pile of barrels. They fell to barricade the corridor. Pierre Charmand straightened up. His great arms encircled another column of stacked barrels, sent it crashing.

* * *

The iron-masked man also rose. Together he and Charmand heaved against a row of kegs. They began to topple. If they fell, the

124

Nazis would be crushed beneath the kegs. If they fell—

But the bullets fell first.

A red knife cut through Pierre Charmand's waist. A score of slugs tore the grizzled Frenchman almost in two. Sick with horror, Drake saw him fall.

The bullets swerved, and now the iron-masked man was raked by the missiles of death.

But he did not fall!

Drake saw the red line cross his body as the bullets struck—but the man stood like a statue, straining at the row of kegs and casks.

And even as Drake watched, the stranger in the iron mask gave a single massive wrench of his shoulders and sent the entire column of kegs crashing down upon the heads and shoulders of the Nazi gunners.

Then, "Come on," he whispered, and dived through the open loading entrance. Drake followed, before the booming echoes of the fallen barrels had ceased resounding through the vault behind them.

The door clanged shut and they crawled forward in utter darkness. Soon they had overtaken Roselle.

"What happened?" she whispered. "Where is Father?"

"Don't talk," muttered Drake, fiercely. "Keep moving. They may follow."

Through the stifling confines of the loading chute they moved on hands and knees. Drake clutched the casket to his breast. He heard Roselle's strident breathing, heard his own gasps. But the iron-masked stranger was silent.

And then, at last, their bursting lungs knew relief as Drake reached the other end of the chute and cautiously pushed up the hatchway leading to the alley behind the brewery.

He stared out at a moon-drenched, deserted expanse of streets. The Nazi trucks were around the corner in front of the brewery.

"Come on," he urged. "We can get away now."

"Where are we going?" Roselle muttered.

"Follow me—no time to explain," Drake flung over his shoulder as he started down the alley at a steady trot. Girl and stranger joined him.

Wordlessly, Drake led them on; led them surely and unerringly. They toiled up a steep hillside, Drake in the lead.

Suddenly the girl put a hand across her mouth to stifle a gasp of fear. She pointed to the pathway ahead.

"Look there!" she whispered. "A Nazi!"

"A dead Nazi," said Drake, grimly. "We killed him earlier this evening."

"We?"

The masked stranger nodded at the girl. "We're climbing the path where Drake and I fought off the Gestapo squad," he explained.

"There's a cave leading out of the chateau at the top," Drake told her. "I think we'll be safe there for a while."

Only when they reached the cavern did he permit the girl and the masked stranger to halt.. It was several minutes more before they were able to speak.

Slowly, gently, Drake went about the unpleasant task of explaining Pierre Charmand's absence.

"He died for France," Drake said. "And so did the others. We alone are left to carry on the fight. And we should not be here now if our friend had not acted."

Drake turned to the masked stranger.

"That was a heroic stunt of yours," he commented. "Standing there in the direct line of machine-gun fire to pull down those kegs on Hassman's men."

An awkward shrug was his only answer.

But this did not satisfy Drake. His eyes rested on the masked man intently.

"There is just one detail you might explain," Drake drawled.

"And what is that, *Monsieur?*" came the whispering response.

"Just how you pulled that little trick and still managed to remain alive," Drake challenged. "Because—I *saw* at least fifty bullets strike your body!"

There was a moment of tense silence.

Again, an awkward shrug from the stranger. He raised his arms, slowly. Drake and the girl followed his movements. Once again, the masked man removed the black velvet covering from his face. Once again, in the light of the moon streaming through the mouth of the cavern, they gazed on the iron horror of the mask he wore.

Drake noted the silvery surface of the metal, and his keen gaze encompassed many details he hadn't remembered. The. mask was not covering the face alone, but extended like a brazen helmet over his entire head, terminating tightly at the neck where the cloak reached up to cover its edges.

And the iron mask bore—bullet scars. Fully a dozen indentations were visible on the battered surface of the grisly monstrosity.

Drake's gaze never wavered. A deep sigh came from behind the mask.

"Very well," whispered the stranger. "I can no longer conceal the truth from you. I am not human—but immortal."

"Immortal?"

The iron visage bobbed in assent.

"Then—who are you, really?"

"I?" the whisper came. "I am—*The Man in the Iron Mask!*"

IV
Masque de Fer

"You are the Man in the Iron Mask?" gasped Drake.

Incredulity shone in his eyes. Roselle's piquant features contorted in puzzled disbelief.

But the stranger shook his iron visage slowly in assent.

"I am," he whispered.

"But the Iron Mask legend is hundreds of years old," Drake objected.

"So am I," whispered the stranger. "And I can assure you that the story is no legend. While the truth is known to me alone, it is still a matter of historically accepted fact that I lived. All that remains unknown is the fact that I am still alive. Yes, alive—and here to save France in her hour of need!"

"Drake and the girl were silent. The Man in the Iron Mask hunched forward oddly until he squatted directly before them on the floor of the cavern.

"Naturally I couldn't tell you this before, Drake. I told you that I was a soldier with a burned face—because it was more believable. But now that you've guessed part of my secret by seeing bullets strike me without injuring my body, you may as well know the rest. Know that I am immortal—and why."

"Yes—why?" Drake persisted.

"This is my story," whispered the stranger. "But first, I shall help you to recall the accepted historical version.

"In 1679, a man wearing an iron mask—*a masque de fer*—was sent to the fortress of the Isle Ste. Marguerite, off the toast of Provence.

"He arrived in a closely-guarded coach, escorted by the king's men all the way from Paris—and he was imprisoned an royal order.

"The soldiers caught furtive glimpses of his masked face, and marveled at the curiously-wrought ironwork that screened it. Slits for eyes and nostrils and a hinged jaw for a mouth were all that broke the hideous metal prison that held a human head. Naturally they whispered and wondered.

"At the fortress, the Man in the Iron Mask was received by the Governor, Benigne D'Auvergne de Saint-Mars. Saint-Mars had furnished a special room where the Man in the Iron Mask was to be held captive—a room sumptuously appointed with fine furnishings and luxurious hangings.

"He and he alone had charge of the prisoner's welfare, but rumors leaked out—about the fine food provided for this unusual captive, and the plates of silver and pewter that adorned his table.

"It was also rumored that King Louis XIV's minister, Louvois, was a regular visitor; although no one else was allowed to see this prisoner. Saint-Mars guarded his charge well.

"In 1681 the prisoner, accompanied by Saint-Mars, went to Exiles, near Pignerol, traveling in a closed litter. From 1687 to 1698 he was incarcerated at Pignerol. By this time wild stories were whispered, but although many sought to fathom the identity of the captive, little was learned. He was said to pass his time playing the guitar, or pacing in his cell—always wearing this curious mask of iron over his face and head.

"In 1698 he went to the Bastille with Saint-Mars. Here, in 1703, he died. Keepers scraped and whitewashed his prison walls. The doors and window frames were burned. All of the vessels used in his service were melted down. There was nothing left as evidence to show that for 24½ years a prisoner had actually been a captive of Saint-Mars.

"Since that date, the strange story of the Man in the Iron Mask has become a fascinating plaything for historians and theorists; a great mystery, indeed.

"Was the Man in the Iron Mask really Fouquet the disgraced minister of finance under Louis XIV? Was he an obscure Armenian patriarch who preached heresy against the throne? Could he have been Comte de Vermandois, the son of Louis XIV and Mademoiselle de la Valliere?

"Was he the Duc de Beaufort? The English Duke of Monmouth? An Italian adventurer named Count Ercolo Matthioli? Or as Dumas would have it, was the Iron Mask really Louis's twin brother?

"In 1789, with the fall of the Bourbons, the records of the Bastille were opened to the public.

"Every prisoner's name and history was inscribed on a register at the time he entered the prison. Surely the secret of Iron Mask would be revealed here!

"But the page bearing the date of his admittance had been carefully torn out of the register!

`The identity of the Man in the Iron Mask has remained a great mystery.

"And well it might be. For I am the Man in the Iron Mask—and I am immortal."

The whispering voice paused momentarily.

Drake glanced at the brazen horror of that head, but he couldn't read a trace of human emotion in the iron, immovable face.

"But you say that the Iron Mask died, was buried in 1703," he objected.

A low chuckle came from under the mask.

"That was all part of the plot," came the answer. "But now, my friends, you shall learn the truth. Who I am—and what I am."

* * *

Roselle nestled closer to Eric Drake as the Iron Mask again took up his tale.

"My name I shall not reveal, for it was a great one in the annals of France.

"Sufficient to say that I am the son of an alchemist—an alchemist both famous and infamous.

My grandfather was none other than Michel de Notre-Dame."

"Nostradamus!" whispered Eric Drake. "Nostradamus, the prophet!"

"I see you too know history," came the whisper. "Yes, he was indeed the prophet. And my father knew the arts of prophecy which he had learned from Nostradamus. Those arts of divination he taught to me, for I was destined for a brilliant career.

"That was how my father planned it. He was a true seeker of forbidden secrets, a lurker in darkness. But I was to profit from his learning. Young, handsome, equipped with all of his own knowledge and skill, he visioned a great future for me at the court of the Grand Monarch of France.

"Alchemists and prophets were popular; and with my looks I could surely go far.

"I left his home after drinking a toast to the future in mantic brew. And in a short time I arrived in Paris, armed with letters of introduction to those in high places.

"Within a year I was famous. Working only behind the scenes, I gained the confidence and grateful friendship of all the king's ministers. I advised Colbert, the minister of home affairs. Lionne the diplomat sought me out to predict a course of future state policy for France. I knew Louvois, minister of war, and Fouquet the minister of finance.

"In a quiet way, I was really ruling France! It was only a short time until both de la Valliere and later Madame de Maintenon were coming to me for advice on how to rule King Louis himself!

"But the Grand Monarch learned of this somehow. Through the trickery of a rival, a chatlatan, he was told that I had exercised my good looks, youthfulness, and wizard's knowledge to fascinate Madame de Maintenon.

"And Louis, maddened by jealousy, devised this hideous jest of his. I was to be imprisoned, suddenly and quietly—and forced to hide my face behind a mask of iron!

"So it came to pass. I had no trial, no hearing. Although Louvois pleaded for me, the furious Grand Monarch would not heed.

"I was seized, made a captive of Saint-Mars, and condemned to wear the Iron Mask for the rest of my days.

It was a gruesome sentence indeed—but even Louis didn't realize its true meaning. For the rest of my days would constitute a great span indeed—because I was immortal!

"Yes, immortal. The letter from my father reached me secretly; by some tragic irony it arrived only a few hours before I was imprisoned.

"In it my father, who was at the point of death, recalled to me the toast we had drunk together on the day I left for Paris.

"He had given me an alchemic solution—the fabulous goal of his research—an elixir that meant eternal life.

"It sounds fantastic. It did, then. Yet as time went on in that ghastly prison, I realized that I had lost none of my youthful energy. The iron mask was soldered to my face, and I could not remove it to see if my features were aging, but I felt no older after twenty long years than I had on the day I was made a prisoner.

"I shall not dwell on those years—on the frantic, futile efforts I made to escape. Louvois still visited me for advice, and I gave it to him. But King Louis would not hear of my release. He was fanatically determined to keep me under this unnatural punishment until I died.

"Therefore, I determined to die. Saint-Mars, my jailer, had been specially selected by Louis XIV for his unswerving loyalty. He was my only, and constant companion.

"It took me 24 years to wear down his loyalty to the crown. It took me 24 years to persuade him to end this hideous imprisonment of mine, and permit me to escape.

"At last, in the Bastille, he consented. And the opportunity arose. A disgraced Italian secret agent was brought to his care. No one knew that this Matthioli had been made a captive and there was no record. The outside world thought he had disappeared. So I persuaded Saint-Mars not to enter his name on the register. And when Matthiola died, Saint-Mars took word to the king that the Man in the Iron Mask was dead.

"His face was unknown. Louis himself could not be expected to recognize the features of a man shut away for 24 years, his head covered by a mask of iron. The body was accepted, and buried secretly. Then the jailers tore down the room I had occupied and destroyed all evidence of my existence.

"As for me, I was far away.

"I shall never forget that first day of freedom. I bribed a blacksmith with gold, made him remove the hateful mask that hid my features. And then I stared into a mirror—stared and saw the ghastly caricatured lineaments of an old man's face. The face of an ancient madman staring back at me. An old man's face on a young man's body!

"That I was youthful could not he denied. The mysterious elixir was potent in my veins. But my face, concealed by the iron mask, had aged atrociously.

"Then and there I swore to resume the iron mask that had been my badge of secret shame—resume it and wear it until I could bring glory to France; and in bringing that glory, make the Iron Mask a symbol for the ages.

"Again, I shall omit the greater part of my adventures. I left France and bitter memories and traveled far. I became a sort of Wandering Jew. I shall not speak of the long years, for it is not pleasant to remember them. Living for centuries is not a boon—it is a nightmare.

"Money I found, and my art of prophecy had not deserted me. And always I kept to my vow. Always when France was in peril I appeared.

"Secretly I sought out Louis XVI to disclose Marie Antoinette's intrigue with Count Fersen. As an Egyptian priest I talked with Napoleon in the shadow of the Sphinx; helped him plan his conquests.

"Again, I visited Napoleon III when he languished in a foreign prison as a middle-aged failure. I gave him the plans whereby he later triumphed and became master of the Empire

"Secretly, I have made history. And now—in this hour of need—I am in France again. I am here to help the Underground and make France free. I must help in my own way. There are certain things I can do.

"One asset is the fact that I cannot die. On the other hand, I cannot remove this iron mask—for centuries have turned the horror of my face into a mummy's death-grin. I must work silently, and from below. That is why I am in the Underground."

The furtive whisper ceased, and there was a moment of profound silence in the cavern.

Then Roselle sighed.

"But the Underground is dead here in Dubonne," she said. "We are the only ones who escaped. It is true, we are awaiting word from headquarters in Paris—"

"Word from headquarters?" whispered

"Yes," Drake assented. "Charmand told me we could expect an important message shortly. There is to be a general plan of revolt to aid the invasion of the Continent. All Underground units in France and Belgium, Holland, Denmark—everywhere—will be given instructions on a course of procedure."

Drake shrugged. "Of course, that means little now, as Roselle says. Hassman has virtually wiped out our unit. We have no headquarters any more, no means of reorganizing and waiting for this message."

The Iron Mask nodded.

"I think I can solve our problem," he: whispered. "I have taken steps to arrange matters in anticipation of an emergency like this."

Roselle turned to the immortal one, bewilderment in her eyes.

"But where can we go?" she murmured. "Hassman's men are searching for us now. They'll come here soon to find us—and they'll cover any possible future meeting place we might select. Where can we establish the Underground now?"

"Underground," said Iron Mask.

"Underground? Where?"

"Underground," repeated Iron Mask. "From now on we will establish our headquarters—under the offices of *gauleiter* Hassman!"

V
Under the Nazi Heel

Dawn came, and daylight, brilliant noon, and then twilight once again—but Drake and Roselle slept. Iron Mask stolidly declined to rest, but stood guard at the entrance-way until darkness fell.

Only once did he slip away during the day, returning shortly with food.

A meal of sorts awaited man and girl when they awoke. "Help yourselves," came the whisper from behind the mask. "I've already eaten."

"Where did you get the food?" Roselle inquired. Iron Mask shrugged.

"I'm an old hand at this sort of life," he replied. "But come—finish your meal. We've got to move to our new headquarters tonight."

"About that matter," said Drake, "I still don 't see what you mean by saying we can go under the *gauleiter's* offices."

Iron Mask rose awkwardly and waved an arm, stiffly. "Surely you know that Hassman and his men are quartered in the old city hall?"

"Yes," said Roselle. "When my father was mayor, he—" The girl stopped, her voice choking as she remembered the death of Pierre Charmand.

Iron Mask compassionately ignored her distress. "Very well. Beneath the city hall is the cellar regulating the sewerage system installed here back in the 1870 era of the Republic. You must remember? They built the city hall over it; some idea of municipal building with the controls all emanating from a central point.

"Of course, since the Nazis have come, the municipal sewerage system has been abandoned. I doubt very much if they are even aware that there is a sub-cellar under the city hall. Certainly no one ever goes down there.

"I investigated today, and it is quite safe. Of course, the tunnels and pipes aren't very safe any more, but we shall be in the cellar itself."

Drake turned, eyebrows raised in objection.

133

"Just how do you propose we get to the cellar?" he asked. "Are we to march through the city hall under Hassman's nose and ask to be directed to the cellar stairs?"

"We'll get there in the same manner that I did this afternoon," Iron Mask explained. "We'll crawl through the empty pipes. There's an outlet right below this hill. The damned-up sewage still in the pipes is trapped in a second parallel pipe. Our pipe is dry and free—it's fully seven feet in diameter, and we can walk through it."

"Just like Jean Valjean in *Les Miserables!*" exclaimed Roselle.

Iron Mask nodded gravely. "We must be careful, though. The pipe is brittle with age and rust. A sudden shock might cause it to burst and the parallel pipe would discharge its flow and flood us out. I'm afraid, on second thought, that it's no place for a young lady."

"Nonsense!" exclaimed Roselle. "I'm going with you and Drake. There's work to be done. At least we'll have a safe place to wait until we get word from Paris tomorrow. Then we can make other plans."

"Come, then," said Iron Mask.

They left the cavern and descended the hillside cautiously. The moon was bright again, and they clung to the shadowed surface of the rocks lest a passing patrol note their moving figures.

Black-cloaked Iron Mask led them to the forbidding mouth of the pipe, jutting out of the base of the hill above the bank of the river that wound below Dubonne. Once again his great strength came into play as he lifted a huge iron cylinder covering the opening.

"I don't know why they didn't drain the parallel pipe when they shut off the sewerage system," he whispered. "It was probably abandoned very hastily. But this pipe is free. Come on—Drake, use that pencil-flash of yours to guide us. It's dark in here."

It was dark. It was also hot, and unbearably fetid. But somehow, the trio managed to flounder through the long passageway, walking inside a pipe bored in the earth.

Now they were truly "Underground" in every sense of the word!

Relief came at last as they reached the end of the straight span of pipe, rounded a curve that sloped upwards. The going was slow, but they made it. Eventually Iron Mask lifted the huge disk overhead and they clambered up the iron rungs of a ladder.

"The head of the pipe is connected directly with the drainage pool under the streets," Iron Mask explained. "But this exit leads to the floor of the cellar in the city hall."

And so it did. They climbed the iron rungs of the ladder to emerge in the musty cellar.

"Oh!" Roselle exclaimed, "you've prepared for our coming!"

It was true. From somewhere, Iron Mask had unearthed several cots, some blankets, and a few cartons containing a stack of provisions. There was even an old, battered oil lamp which he proceeded to light, his gloved fingers moving clumsily as he struck a match and held it to the wick.

"What's that?" muttered Drake, as an ominous creaking sounded overhead.

* * *

Iron mask uttered a rasping chuckle. "Probably Hassman pacing the floor and worrying over our escape," he whispered. "Don't forget, we're in the cellar directly beneath him."

"Then those stairs must lead to a door in the city hall," Drake decided, pointing to a dusty flight across the cellar.

"True, but the door is barred. They have never come down here and never will," muttered Iron Mask. "We're safe here. And now—"

"And now it's time for me to keep my appointment," Drake snapped, glancing at his watch and re-winding it.

"Drake—do you know where to go?" Roselle asked, anxiously.

"Yes. I have my instructions." From the folds of his trench jacket Drake produced the casket of official papers.

"I am to turn this over to the Paris Underground agent and receive my instructions," he said.

"But Drake, how will you recognize him? Where will you meet?"

"Your father gave me full details," Drake assured her.

"But they must have men out watching for us," Roselle objected., "They know we escaped them the other night. It's broad daylight outside, Eric. They'll hunt you down."

Drake smiled and patted her shoulder.

"Tell you what we'll do," he said. "We'll beat them at their own game and try a bit of spying ourselves.

"My man will be waiting to make contact with me at Antoine's bistro down the street. Roselle, you go through the pipe and come into town from the south. Keep your face down and be sure to step inside the nearest house if you see a Nazi patrol on the streets. But if you can get to Antoine's, just look in and see if you can notice a *curé* carrying a yellow valise. That's my man.

"And you, my friend, can come into town from the north." Drake nodded at Iron Mask. "Naturally, with your cloak and mask you'll be conspicuous. But I'm relying on that. I want the Nazi patrols to spot you—because you can draw them away.

"Owing to your rather peculiar gift of immortality, I don't suppose you fear their bullets. And after witnessing your cleverness and resourcefulness these past hours, I am sure you can elude your pursuers without great danger.

"At any rate, the Nazis will continue to hunt you. If you and Roselle return and Roselle tells me my man is waiting—then I can go up myself to keep the appointment. The Nazis will be off on a wild goose chase in the hills north of town; looking for a man in a mask and a cloak. Right?"

They nodded.

"Then off you go," Drake urged. "Back through the pipe."

They left.

Drake pulled out one of his few remaining cigarettes from a precious package and lit it slowly. Then, quite deliberately, he took out a pack-knife and pried the lid of the metal casket cradled in his lap.

He rummaged through the papers inside until he found a folded yellow sheet. This he read, frowning and muttering to himself as his eyes squinted in the murky lamplight.

Carefully he stuffed the documents back in the casket and lowered the lid.

He doused his cigarette, looked at his watch, frowned again. His head cocked forward as he listened intently for sounds in the city hall above. All was silent. Drake smiled, nodded.

Suddenly he snapped his fingers, sent one hand diving into the pocket of his trench coat and produced a gun.

It cocked with a click.

Drake rose and walked deliberately toward the dusty stairway that led to the city hall above. He climbed the stairs, set his shoulder to the door at the head of the stairway, and stepped into the lair of *gauleiter* Hassman.

Iron Mask

VI
The Sewer

Pure chance had it that Roselle and Iron Mask should meet at the moment both returned to crawl through the sewer pipe.

"Is he waiting?" Iron Mask whispered.

"Yes," said the girl. "I saw him. But the patrols are everywhere. Only a few minutes after I entered town, I saw them swarming down the steps of the city hall. Even Hassman himself came out. I wonder who informed him something was stirring?"

"I did probably," whispered the man in the cloak.

"I let myself be seen very plainly. I've been leading at least three patrols a merry chase across the hills. I managed to dodge down here, but I urge that we hasten out of sight before we're seen."

Again he clumsily lifted the great lid and the two retraced their footsteps through the sewer pipe, moving delicately lest the brittle metal shatter under the impact of their tread.

It was Iron Mask who was the first to emerge in the cellar once again—but it was Roselle who uttered the first gasp of astonishment.

"Eric!" she cried. "Eric's gone!"

Iron Mask whirled in astonishment. "The fool—he must have left while we were away!"

He strode awkwardly toward the room's end where the lamp glowed fitfully, throwing his grotesque shadow across the wall.

"The casket's gone, too," he announced. "There's something queer going on here."

As though stifled by its confining folds, Iron Mask suddenly ripped the black velvet covering from his metal visage and revealed the brazen shield covering his face. His gloved hands went to his iron temples in perplexity.

Roselle, despite her familiarity with the grim mask, couldn't repress a slight tremor of distaste. There was something unnatural about this immortal adventurer. His husky voice, his clumsiness, and his penchant for cloaking his body and features in black—this, coupled with the brazen, leering mask that served to hide his face, caused her to feel a chill of repulsion.

Suddenly, Iron Mask lumbered toward her.

"Where is he?" came the whisper. "It's a conspiracy, isn't it? You and he have something planned. He took the casket and deserted me, didn't he? Admit it."

"No," muttered the girl. "He wouldn't do such a thing! Eric is—"

The reply was cut short by an ominous thudding from overhead. Muffled but audible, a revolver shot echoed through the cellar. And then—

The door at the head of the cellar stairs burst open. Eric raced down the steps, panting.

"Come on," he shouted. "Through the sewer pipe. Hurry! Roselle.

"Tell you later," Drake grunted. "Hassman's back. Get into the pipe, quick!"

One hand grasping the metal casket, the other flourishing a revolver, Drake prodded Roselle and Iron Mask toward the floor opening. They clambered down the iron rungs of the ladder until they stood in the dark tunnel of brittle pipe.

Drake followed, and just in time.

Thunder shook the stairs. Hassman was leading his pack into the cellar!

The fat *gauleiter* caught sight of Eric's head as he descended, and before Drake could pull the iron lid into place, the Nazis were upon him.

No time to descend the ladder—Eric leaped to the bottom of the pipe and began to run forward. Iron Mask and Roselle clambered ahead in the utter darkness.

And behind them came the Nazi horde.

There was a scene ripped from nightmare's darkest depths—the three fugitives groping their way through the black, twisted interior of the slippery iron pipe. They ran lightly, lest their tread shatter the brittle surface. Iron Mask had warned them about the danger of breakthroughs from the parallel pipe over their heads.

Panting, gasping, sobbing for breath, the trio floundered on. And behind them, the Nazis charged.

Hassman at the head, the entire column clambered down the ladder into the pipe.

And then began the race through darkness … the mad, incredible race, punctuated by bursts of flame from Nazi Lugers.

"Hurry!" panted Drake. Roselle clutched his arm as he half-dragged her forward. "They're gaining!" he muttered, as they rounded the bend leading to the end of the pipe.

Iron Mask suddenly stumbled and fell. Drake bit his lip. "Get up!" he hissed. "You're blocking our path—"

He tugged at the fallen figure. Iron Mask rose. But too late.

Iron Mask

For the great figure of Hassman loomed out of the murky twilight as he rounded the bend in the pipe. Behind him came the gray-clad hunters, and their Lugers spoke—

Down!" shouted Drake, tugging at the shoulders of his companions. Flame jetted over their heads and an ear-splitting echo resounded throughout the brittle interior of the pipe. Resounded and magnified.

There was a roar and a rumble; a shuddering convulsion that shook the metal under their feet.

"Earthquake!" screamed Roselle.

"No," Drake muttered. "The pipe's broken!"

His words were hardly spoken before dreadful confirmation came.

Whether caused by weight of their running bodies or by the force of concussion reverberations, the pipe had shattered—and now the parallel pipe poured forth its hideous burden.

With a rush and a roar, a torrent of acrid liquid gushed down upon the heads of the Nazis.

They turned, screaming, but there was no escape. In a moment the entire length of pipe behind them filled with a raging flood of boiling, churning debris.

"Run!" yelled Drake.

There was no need to command. They trio took to their heels and not a moment too soon. They clambered along the pipe as the roaring waters engulfed the Nazis behind them.

And then they were clambering out of the pipe mouth on the hillside, racing up the road toward the cave.

But Hassman and his men did not follow. As they ran up the road, Drake glanced over his shoulder. He saw the torrent surge out of the pipe mouth and spout down in a stream to the river. Gray bodies whirled in its crest and he knew that Hassman and his men would no longer patrol the streets of Dubonne. They had drowned in the sewer, like the rats they were.

Panting with exhaustion, Drake and Roselle entered the safety of the cavern. Iron Mask strode stolidly beside them.

Roselle forced a smile to her lips.

"It's wonderful, Eric," she murmured. "We seem to be spending our entire life just running from one underground hole to another. And all because of this silly casket—"

"I can solve that."

Iron Mask stood in the doorway, blotting out the exit. The whisper came from between metal-shrouded lips.

"What's that?" Drake said.

"I can promise you that this is the last refuge you need ever seek," he whispered. "Just give the casket to me."

"But I'm to turn it over to the Paris representative—"

"Give it to me, now."

Iron Mask's voice was still a whisper, but it was hard—hard as iron.

"Wait a minute, now."

"I wait no longer." The whisper was cold—cold as steel.

The man in the cloak moved down upon the two. The metal mask leered its frozen grin, and there was neither human mirth nor human emotion in its set and steely features.

"Give me that casket."

Drake reached for his revolver.

"Stand back," he warned. "I don't know what you mean by all this, but if you come a step further I'll blast a hole through you.'

A chuckle burbled from beneath the im movable iron lips.

"You forget I am immortal."

"Stand back!"

But Iron Mask came on. His great arms reached forward—and Drake fired. Drake saw the bullet strike the black cloak and rip through the cloth covering the shoulder. But Iron Mask was immortal, and he loomed closer—

* * *

Drake fired again. This time the bullet tore through the cloth above the chest, and Drake saw the shreds part to reveal a patch of skin—of *silver* skin!

A dry, rattling laugh came from the throat of Iron Mask. "You see?" he whispered. "Yes, you see, but don't understand, do you? Then—*look*, you fool!"

Gloved hands raked out awkwardly, sweeping the top of the cloak from Iron Mask's head and revealing his entire skull. It was bare now, rising in a great, silvery dome. And Drake saw that this creature had no iron mask—its entire head was iron!

Drake was stunned into immobility. Chuckling, the creature drew the concealing gloves from gleaming metal hands—hands that now ripped off the black cloak and the garments beneath it.

Iron Mask stood stripped and revealed for what he was; an entity whose head and body were constructed entirely of burnished, deathless metal!

"Robot!" Drake gasped.

Roselle's shriek and Iron Mask's rattling chuckle mingled in mocking reply.

Drake watched the metal monster as it lunged toward him. He fired blindly, wildly; saw the bullets ricochet from the body of the iron robot. He knew then that there was no hope, no solution.

Then the robot was upon him, and its great shaft-like metal arms embraced him. He felt the cold chill of its iron embrace, it crushed him close and squeezed. The world was turning red, spinning madly—

Drake lifted his revolver, brought it down on the robot's shoulders. The chuckling horror bent him back. Agony lanced up Drake's spine. The creature bent its iron head—

Drake struck, then. His eyes focussed on the gleaming expanse of exposed iron skull. And he brought the butt of his revolver down with crushing force on the back of the robot's head.

The blow could not shatter iron—but there was a sudden splintering crash, and the revolver-butt bit deeply into a gaping hole in the ruined cranium.

A whistling scream rose from iron lips and the robot tottered back on its heels. Arms fell, releasing Drake.

He stepped back just in time. With a crash, the robot dropped to the cavern floor. Iron limbs writhed in a last, delirious spasm. Carefully-fashioned jointures were strained and wrenched as though in death-agony as arms and legs twisted convulsively.

And then the ruined head rolled back, and from the opening poured a thin, yellowish ichor.

Drake stooped and peered into the depths of the shattered metal skull. He poked the muzzle of his revolver inside, then stepped back just in time.

A shower of tiny cogs and wires emerged in a writhing tangle, accompanied by the acrid smoke of a miniature explosion.

There was no further movement from the metal body on the floor after that.

Drake stooped and picked up the casket, then joined the sobbing girl.

"Dry your eyes," he said, brusquely. "It's all over now."

"Yes—but—"

"The Nazis are wiped out, the casket is safe, and now the Underground's greatest menace has been removed." Drake's gray eyes stared sombrely at the figure on the cavern floor, but his lips held a tight grin.

"So it's the end," he half-whispered. "The real end of a living legend—the Man in the Iron Mask is no more."

VII
The Final Irony

For a long moment, Drake stood staring down at the gleaming silver body of the robot; then Roselle was in his arms and he was comforting her, whispering.

The girl's eyes never left the twisted inhuman frame of metal that had walked the earth in the guise of man. The cleverly articulated limbs of the metal monster looked oddly grotesque now—Roselle could recall the Iron Mask's clumsy movements.

Here was the explanation, together with the reason for his imperviousness to bullets and great strength.

But there were many other matters not explained. Roselle turned to Drake, and her lips framed questions.

"When did I first suspect?" Drake answered. "Probably at the very start. You fired at his head and the bullet struck. Even a wounded soldier with a steel faceplate would be injured by a bullet. Besides—did you notice he never slept or ate?

"Then, too, the matter of the casket bothered me. Why was he so anxious to find it and keep it on his person? Obviously because it contained something of vital importance—perhaps a clue as to his real identity.

"Even when we heard the story of the Man in the Iron Mask, my suspicions were not allayed. Granting that his story was true, and he was immortal—I still couldn't swallow this business about his being a savior of France.

"It didn't ring true. A savior of France would not counsel Napoleon to conquer. A savior of France would not restore the Empire. A savior of France would certainly be active during World War I.

"Right then and there I reasoned that, immortal or not, he was an enemy. An enemy to watch. And he betrayed us—you see that now, don't you?"

"Yes," said Roselle, slowly. "I think I do."

"He was after the casket from the start," Drake told her. "That's why he attacked you. He wanted to get the casket and the information it contained, before either the Underground or the Nazis would lay hands on it.

So he took it from you and made off with it. He ran into the Gestapo squad on the road, and there was nothing to do but fight. Although he was working for the Nazis, he didn't want them to discover his secret, either. So he fought them. And I helped him.

"Then, when we came to headquarters, he left to secure information before the meeting. Obviously, he had an easy way of securing that information—he merely went to Hassman and asked for it. At the same time he led Hassman back to attack the Underground meeting.

"He meant to wipe us out, but when I got the casket in the darkness he followed me when we escaped. Then we told him there was news coming from Paris regarding future Underground activities.

"That's when he fed us the story about his immortality. He wanted us to believe him. And he wanted us to keep alive until we got the news from Paris. Then we could die, when the information was in his hands.

"Naturally, he selected our new headquarters under the *gauleiter's* offices. Not alone because it was a clever idea from our point of view, but also because he could lead Hassman to us at any time.

"He almost succeeded, but not quite. What he didn't know is that I took advantage of our headquarters to do a little spying on my own.

"When I went out to meet the Underground emissary from Paris, he tipped off Hassman. The whole force went out to wait for me and the Paris Underground agent. They planned to seize us as we met.

"But I didn't go to the rendezvous. Instead, I went upstairs, to Hassman's office. I searched through his papers and found the truth about the Man in the Iron Mask! Who he was and what he was doing!

"I learned then and there that he was a spy of Germany, and an important one.

"Then I opened the casket and read the papers within. One of them was what he was looking for.

"You remember him telling us that the Bastille record of the Man in the Iron Mask was missing? Well, that paper is in the casket. No wonder he wanted it—and didn't want either the French or Germans to find it! For it told the rest of his story, and in it I read the secret of how to destroy him."

* * *

Roselle shook her head. "I still don't understand," she said. "Just who and what was he? Who created him and what was he doing?"

Drake grinned.

"I'll be brief. After putting two and two together—piecing together his story, the papers in Hassman's office, and the Bastille registry, I can tell you this:

"He was a robot, created by Roger Bacon, in the 13th century. The Bastille record says 1287, but we can't be sure."

"Roger Bacon? The English monk?"

"Exactly. He was an alchemist who dabbled in science and what was then called sorcery—though if he created this marvelous mechanism, he was no sorcerer but a genuine savant. There is an old legend about a 'Brazen Head' Bacon made, which could prophecy the future. I never gave the story credit for having any significance—but now I can see. Roger Bacon didn't create a 'Brazen Head' at all; he made this robot. By alchemic means he endowed it with perpetual life, and human intelligence.

"He fashioned it during the years he was imprisoned for heresy—in France. Yes, the French put him in prison, and he languished there nourishing a hatred. A hatred for France.

"So he made the robot, as an instrument of vengeance. The robot was animated by a single purpose—not to save France, but to destroy it.

"That much we know, for the Bastille entry tells us so. What the robot's activities were after Bacon's death we can only surmise. It turned up almost four hundred years later at the court of Louis XIV.

"From that point on, the story roughly corresponds to what he told us when he claimed to be the Man in the Iron Mask. He did appear in court as a prophet and soothsayer, and the king's ministers did seek his advice. Louis XIV did order his imprisonment; but he didn't order that his prisoner wear an iron mask.

"He had always worn the iron mask—for it was his head! No wonder they hid him away in secret. He must have been clever even then, to keep them from finding out that he was an automaton, instead of a man wearing a mask. No one suspected, however.

"And even as a prisoner, no one suspected his advice. He did give advice, but not advice to save France. He plotted her downfall. Historians agree that the actions of Louis XIV were directly responsible for the policies leading to the French Revolution 200 years later. And the robot dictated those policies!

"He escaped just as he said he did, and disappeared again. If he indeed betrayed Marie Antoinette he did so to further the disruption of the king. And if he advised Napoleon he did it maliciously, to injure France.

"When the Bastille fell he came there to find the place in the register where his secret was revealed. Someone—we will never know who it was—got there ahead of him and took the register leaf. He must have searched for it high and low; all we know is that it finally ended up here at Dubonne, buried away in an obscure file of old official papers.

"Now we come to the part of the story pieced together from Hassman's reports.

"The robot had not destroyed France by revolution, or by Napoleonic domination. And yet the deathless urge persisted. Friar Bacon's magic was strong, and although we will never understand why it worked, we can see how it worked.

"The robot was in Germany between 1860 and 1870. We do not know what story he used to account for his disguise—always the robot posed as a man in a mask. But we can guess that he wormed his way into high places. Probably he consulted and advised Bismarck himself. It is not too much to suppose that the robot's advice and cunning led to the Franco-Prussian war!

"Now there comes another gap in history. There is no record of the robot's activities in the following years. France was humbled but not destroyed. Perhaps cunning old Bismarck had imprisoned the robot, just as Louis XI did in the old days. Whatever happened, we know the robot had no connection with World War I that we know of—though it seems highly probable that he was at work, fighting against France. And he almost succeeded, then.

"But Hassman's papers do tell us important thing—they record the meeting of the robot and Adolf Hitler."

Roselle drew back, startled.

"He met Hitler?" she gasped.

* * *

Drake smiled.

"Of course. That is obvious. Think for a moment. Haven't you heard all stories about Hitler consulting with fortune-tellers and soothsayers? Don't you realize all those are blind rumors to disguise the presence of a master plotter? Who but the robot would exercise the cunning and savage hatred necessary to plan the downfall of France?

"And when France fell, who but the robot would exact such a monstrous price? The robot hated France, animated by Roger Bacon's will. And now France had fallen, hence the price."

"What price?" asked the girl.

Drake leaned forward.

"The robot came here to rule France," he whispered.

"Rule?"

"Yes. Hassman's papers reveal that he was taking orders from the robot. That all *gauleiters* took their orders from him. The real gauleiter of France was our robot. That was its price for helping Hitler!"

Again the two humans stared at the twisted metal figure on the floor.

Drake shook his head. "Who knows where it might have ended?" he mused. "Luckily, the robot blundered. Discovering a clue as to the whereabouts of the papers explaining his true origin, the robot came here from Paris. Getting Gestapo information, including Underground passwords, was simple. Then he set out, double-crossing both the Germans and French, in an effort to secure that tell-tale Bastille entry. He fell in with us, and the rest is—history."

Roselle snuggled closer to Drake as they moved past the grisly, gleaming shape on the ground and sought the outer entrance on the hillside.

"I still don't see how you destroyed the robot," the girl murmured. "I saw you strike the iron head, but it wasn't a severe blow."

"The Bastille register entry gave me the secret," said Drake. "It transcribed Roger Bacon's own words—probably discovered by some researcher who had suspected the truth and delved back into ancient chronicles of Bacon's time.

"Bacon hated France, but he was a great scientist and a just man at heart. He never realized what a horror he was unleashing on the world—but he must have suspected that some day the horror would have to be checked. So he wrote down a clue.

"Achilles had a heel—and the iron chain of Tyranny hath always a weak link. That's what Bacon wrote, and what I saw in the register.

"I never guessed the weakness in the Iron Mask until the robot confronted me with bared head. Then I knew that Bacon must have built it with a flaw. My eye caught a subtle difference in the jointures on top of its skull. Bacon had built it so that if need be it could be destroyed.

"When I struck that vital spot on the skull, the head was smashed. For although the Man in the Iron Mask really had an iron head—a narrow strip across the top of the skull was just plain, ordinary *tin!*"

Together, man and girl strode forward into the light streaming across the earth above.

Skeleton in the Closet

When I opened the closet door I saw the skeleton.

He was hanging there on the third hook from the left.

I just shook my head and smiled....

When I came to, I was lying on the floor. The closet door was still open. I raised my eyes timidly. On the floor of the closet I saw a pair of rubbers, some old, dusty tennis shoes, and two ancient house slippers.

I glanced higher and noticed a raincoat, an overcoat, a pair of slacks, and an old hat hanging on the hooks.

Also, the skeleton.

This time I didn't faint. I even managed to get up off the floor. But I couldn't stop looking at the horror.

It dangled there, suspended by its spine from the hook, with bony body swaying to and fro. It was rather large for a skeleton, as skeletons go—and how I wished this one would! I noticed the unusually big bones, and particularly, the face. Or rather, the lack of face. The skull itself grinned a grisly grin. There was mockery in the hollow eye sockets, and menace in the leering teeth.

I wondered wildly how this skeleton had turned up in the closet. Had he been a human being trapped in there and eaten by moths? No—because the door was unlocked.

I sighed. This was just what I might expect to find in my uncle's house.

He had been interested in sorcery—black magic. My uncle was quite an eccentric that way. Every Halloween I used to send him a birthday card. Outside of that we seldom communicated, and all I knew of him was through hearsay. Rumors of what went on in his big house in the country. Rumors about his unusual library of forbidden books, and of the secret societies he was mixed up with. To judge from these reports he was mixed up plenty.

But I'd dismissed all that.

When I received word of his sudden death a little while ago, the lawyer gave me a key to the house and said I'd inherited his estate.

So here I was. And here was the skeleton.

You can't stand looking at a skeleton forever. As for me, I can't stand looking at a skeleton.

So after a moment, I sat down. Sat down and poured myself a nice, stiff drink.

I raise the glass to my lips to shut out the sight of the skeleton hanging in the open closet. I started to gulp.

"Get me down off this damn hook and I'll join you," grunted a voice.

I finished my gulp. The glass fell from my fingers as I stared in startled horror at the closet.

The skeleton was speaking!

"You've spilled your drink," the voice told me.

I spilled another, in a hurry. Right down my throat. And then another:

Talking skeletons! Was it alive?

"Come on," said the skeleton. "Do you think I want to spend the rest of my life in this stuffy closet?"

The skeleton had a deep, sepulchral voice, I noticed. I wondered how he could articulate—though he was a well-articulated skeleton.

"Spend the rest of your *what?*" I answered him, through chattering teeth.

"You've already spent your life, from the looks of you. Tossed it away. Never saw anyone with less looks of life about him. You shouldn't worry about stuffy closets. You need a nice, stuffy grave."

"Well, I can't go to one unless you take me off this hook," argued the skeleton.

* * *

I took another drink—from the bottle, this time. The liquor combined with my fright and worked fast. His argument almost sounded reasonable. Although the clicking of his bones sounded plain ghastly.

"Come on," the skeleton urged. "Lift me down."

"Who's going to hold me up while I'm lifting you down?" I. argued.

Skeleton in the Closet

"What's there to be afraid of?" countered the skeleton.

"If I had a mirror, I'd show you," I told him. "I can't stand the sight of you hanging there."

"Then take me off the hook."

I approached him gingerly and with trembling fingers hooked around his spine, I lifted him down and set him on the floor.

The skeleton ran to the table with amazing and horrifying alacrity. He scrabbled around and poured out a drink. Three fingers. Three bony fingers.

With clicking elbow-sockets; he raised the glass to his lips—or to where his lips once were—and tossed the drink off.

"Where does the stuff go?" I wondered. Aloud, I said, "Where did you come from?"

The skeleton faced me. "What's it to you?" he asked.

"Well how would you like it if you came into a house, opened the closet door, and found a skeleton?"

"I'd like it pretty well," he said. "Then I'd have some company."

I shuddered.

"I'm so lonesome," the skeleton complained. "You don't know how it feels to be a skeleton."

"I don't want to find out, either."

"You will," said the skeleton, with a ghastly leer.. "Some day."

"I still want to know how you got into that closet."

"You might say I used a skeleton key," he told me.

"I might say the hell with you, too," I replied. "In fact, that's just what I do say."

"And I say let's have another drink." The skeleton poured: My hands were shaking, but I managed to drink. We clicked teeth rather than glasses.

"Here's looking at you," said the skeleton.

"Here's not looking at you," I answered. "And speaking of that happy prospect, you've got to get out of here, you know. I can't have you hanging around this way. What would my friends think?"

"Couldn't you tell them I was your family skeleton?" he asked, wistfully. After all, what can I do in my position?"

"You can lie down and play dead."

"This is a bit unusual, I admit," the skeleton acknowledged. "There isn't much precedent for it, is there? Wonder if we could get some help to figure things out."

Robert Bloch

"Well, we could read Thorne Smith's *Skin and Bones*," I suggested. "He had a few remarks to make about a live skeleton. Only his case happened to be a man who turned into a skeleton and back to a man, intermittently. And the man was really there all the time—that is, his flesh was. He just *looked* like a skeleton."

"That wouldn't help me. I not only look like one—I feel like one; and I *am* one." The skeleton took another drink.

* * *

I followed suit. For some reason or other, I was beginning to feel quite tipsy. It couldn't have been the liquor—or was it? At any rate, the skeleton no longer seemed so frightful. He no longer terrified me. I adopted a somewhat haughty attitude when I addressed him next.

"By the way," I observed, "I'm not exactly in the habit of speaking to strange skeletons. Might I ask your name?"

"You might," said the fleshless one. "But you won't get much of an answer." He hiccuped, rattling his lower jaw alarmingly.

"See here," I flared. "Who are you? Or, rather, who *were* you?

"Damned if I know," the skeleton confessed. "That's what's puzzling me. I'm afraid I can't remember. It's amnesia, I guess. Must have been in some kind of an accident."

"It. was a pretty severe accident, judging from the looks of you," I told him.

The skeleton shook his head mournfully.

"You don't know how you got in my closet or why you're still alive, or who you are?" I persisted.

"That's right."

"That's wrong," I corrected. "It's contrary to all the laws of nature. You shouldn't be alive, and you certainly shouldn't be hanging in strange closets."

"It doesn't bother me half as much as not knowing what my name is," the skeleton insisted. "I'm really curious to find that out."

"Maybe I'd better call the morgue," I suggested, "and see if they're missing you."

"Try the funeral parlors, too," the skeleton added.

I picked up the phone and fumbled for the directory.

"Wait a minute," I said. "I can't call these joints and ask if they're

152

minus a live skeleton. The cops would be after me with butterfly nets. We'll have to think of another way."

The skeleton regarded me with a grave look. What other kind of look a skeleton has, I don't know. Or care to know.

"By the way, speaking of names—you haven't told me your name yet, my friend."

I blinked. "So I haven't. I'm Tarleton Fiske. This is the home of my deceased uncle, Magnus Lorry."

"Magnus Lorry? Lorry?" Bony fingers pressed into the skull. "But that's *my* name! It came back to me now. I'm Magnus Lorry—this is my home. And you're my nephew! I'll be a monkey's unc—"

"No insults," I warned him. And gulped.

"You're my uncle," I said. "I can't believe it."

"Why not?"

"Otis Kersen, your lawyer—he said you died of a stroke. You were buried in the family vault at Hopecrest Cemetery. Private funeral, and he handled all the details. There were no mourners present."

"No mourners?"

"I'm the only one left in the family," I explained. "And I was out of town. Otis Kersen wired me. You left me this house and your estate."

"Nobody mourned for me?" repeated the skeleton. "How unfortunate to let a poor man die friendless like that! If I could have been there, I would have mourned."

"You weren't such a friendly fellow when alive," I said, blushing. "You were something of a recluse. Eccentric. You were a—wizard, I believe you called yourself."

"So I was!" exclaimed the skeleton. "I do remember that. I was quite a sorcerer, wasn't I?"

"Yes, I've heard it said."

* * *

"Maybe that's why I'm still alive," the skeleton mused. "I might have had a premonition of death and cast a spell to preserve my consciousness."

"Perhaps."

"But it's funny—there's still a lot I can't seem to recollect. For example, I don't remember having a stroke. I don't recall anything about my death."

"That's not unusual in amnesia cases," I told him. "Often a victim just recovers partial memory. The rest may gradually return."

"Stroke, eh?" said the skeleton.

"Get me a mirror."

"What for?"

"I want to look at myself."

"You're not worth seeing," I argued, honestly.

"Get me a mirror, nephew."

"Very well, Uncle Magnus."

I got him a hand mirror from the dresser in the bedroom. My skeleton uncle grasped it and stared at his reflection, shuddering the while.

"My, I'm gruesome!" he exclaimed.

I nodded.

"Rather repulsive, too?"

"Definitely," I agreed.

"Hate to meet myself up a dark alley."

"Certainly would."

"Hey—"

The skeleton ran a bony phalange across the back of his skull.

"What is it?"

"Look," the skeleton exclaimed. "See this hole in my head?"

"Where?"

"Right here."

"What is it?" I asked, noting the round little opening in his skull.

"It's a bullet hole," gasped the skeleton.

"A bullet hole?"

"Definitely. And you know what?"

"What?"

"I didn't die of a stroke. I've been murdered!"

"No!" I gasped.

"Yes. This bullet must have gone clean through the *medulla oblongata*. Otis Kersen, or somebody, was lying. I tell you, I was murdered!"

"But why—how—?"

"That's not the point," the skeleton rasped. "It's *who?*" I'm going to find out if it takes the rest of my life—I mean, death!"

* * *

Skeleton in the Closet

Magnus Lorry rose to his bony feet and danced up and down excitedly while his vertebrae rattled like castanets.

"I'm going to track down the person who killed me!" he yelled.

"And then what?"

"I haven't forgotten my sorcery," he declared. "I'll cook up a fate for my slayer that he'll never forget as long has he lives—and that won't be long."

My unusual uncle grated his teeth unpleasantly. I averted my eyes in distress.

"Call that fat swine, Otis Kersen! Get that illegal eagle on the wire for me," he ordered.

Obediently, I dialed the attorney's office.

"Mr. Kersen, please," I requested.

"Mr. Kersen is out of town," replied the stenographer's voice on the other end of the wire. "He's gone to Buffalo for a convention."

I reported the news.

"Buffalo? Hell and damnation!" growled the skeleton.

"You suspect him?" I asked.

"I suspect everybody!" the skeleton groaned. "I have no friends. Nobody loves me. Nobody cares. I might as well be dead."

"Don't cry," I said.

"I can't cry," he sighed. "Can't even cry. But I can still act. And I'm going to."

"What do you propose?"

"I think I'm going to do a little sleuthing, A little amateur detective work to find out who murdered me." He stabbed a bony finger in my direction. "And you're going to help me, nephew."

"Glad to. How do we begin?"

"We'll pay a couple of visits."

"Where to?"

"We shall call on some of my rivals."

"Rivals?"

"Rival wizards," my uncle explained. "There are several others in this vicinity who secretly practice the mantic arts. Cheap sorcerers. All of them were jealous of me and my fine collection of incunabula."

"You have incunabula?" I asked.

"Tons of it," he declared."More damned incunabula than you can shake a stick at."

"Doesn't it hurt?"

"Incunabula are books written before 1600," my uncle explained. "I have the finest library on sorcery extant. And some of these scoundrels knew it. I'll bet one of them bumped me off, figuring my estate would be up for sale and he could steal my precious manuscripts and formulæ for a song. That must be it."

"Any idea who might figure such a plot out?" I inquired.

"Well, there's the Mighty Omar," said Magnus Lorry.

"Who is he?"

"A spiritualist, and a fake spiritualistic medium at that. He's just a charlatan who makes a living by holding fraudulent seances, and playing the suckers. He's really interested in the occult, and knowing my real powers, he always hated my guts—when I had them, that is."

"Do you think that he—?"

"I've got a hunch," said the skeleton. "Come on, we'll visit him first." He rose and clanked across the room to the door.

"Wait a minute!" I protested. "You can't go out like that."

"Why not?"

"People will see you walking around—you must be disguised, somehow."

"Useless," he told me. "You can't disguise a face and figure like the one I haven't got."

"But you'll start a riot!"

"Then you'll have to carry me," my uncle said. "That's it! You can carry me in your arms. Say that you're delivering a skeleton to a medical school. I'll play dead."

"That won't be hard for you," I sighed. "But the idea of dragging a skeleton along the street in broad daylight doesn't appeal to me."

"Would you rather wait until after dark, then? Around midnight?"

"Midnight is no time for me to mess with skeletons either. On second thought, we'd better go right now."

I picked him up gingerly by his clavicles.

"Hold still now," I breathed.

* * *

Carrying him down the hall, I kicked open the door, walked down the driveway, and put him in the car. Climbing into the driver's seat, I started the motor.

"Where to?" I asked.

Skeleton in the Closet

He gave me the address, and we were off.

Luckily the streets were not crowded as we drove into city traffic. Soon we moved through the winding streets of the fashionable suburban district where the Mighty Omar had his residence.

Halting for a stop-light, Uncle Magnus turned to me with a leer.

"Step on it," he murmured. "I can't wait to appear before the Mighty Omar. I'll scare him out of a week's growth! The mere sight of me ought to shake a confession out of his guilty mouth."

"Quiet!" I panted. "Do you want somebody to hear you talking? Stop turning your head that way—people will notice."

As a matter of fact, somebody had already noticed. About the most unpleasant somebody I could think of.

A big traffic cop loomed outside the window.

"Hey," he growled. "What you got there?"

"Just a skeleton, officer. I'm taking it over to medical school."

"Did I see it move?" he persisted, eyeing the bony skull with evident distaste.

"Perhaps the car jiggled it a bit," I hazarded.

"Oh, my mistake."

The cop was about to turn away when Uncle Magnus gave vent to an unfortunate impulse. He hiccuped, loudly.

Instantly the cop wheeled.

"What's that?" he said.

"I hiccuped," I told him.

"Drunk, eh? Driving while drunk?" He reached eagerly for his ticket pad.

"Not at all, officer. Just a little sour stomach."

"Oh."

Uncle Magnus couldn't hold it any longer. He hiccuped again, his jaws moving visibly.

"Holy Ike!" barked the officer. "That skeleton moved!"

"How could it move?" I asked, innocently. "You know that such a thing is impossible."

"Oh yeah? Well it did move," said the cop. "And it hiccuped, too! There's something wrong with that skeleton, I'm telling you! Something mighty wrong."

"That's why I'm taking it to medical school."

* * *

The cop wasn't satisfied. His beefy hand came thrusting through the window and he fingered Uncle Magnus's collar-bone.

"What's the matter, officer?" I asked, nervously. "Why are you fingering my skeleton?"

"Is that your skeleton?"

"Of course. Whose else would it be?"

"How can it be your skeleton?" snarled the officer. "Your skeleton must be under your skin."

"Well—"

"Therefore," persisted the cop, with a warning gleam in his eye, "this is not your skeleton. And if it, is not your skeleton, then it must be stolen. What are you doing with a stolen skeleton, you grave-robber?"

It was a horrible moment. And Uncle Magnus chose it for a demonstration.

"Take your pawing hands off me, you big lug," he groaned. "I'm not his skeleton and I'm not your skeleton—I'm my own skeleton, I'll have you know. And if there's any graves robbed, it's likely to be your own—because I'm going to put you in one in a hurry!"

I had never seen a traffic cop run before. It was an enthralling spectacle. How a man could move so fast in those heavy boots, I didn't know. But he was really speedy.

We drove away with equal swiftness. Uncle Magnus chuckled repulsively in my ear.

"Stop that!" I warned him. "And for heaven's sake, cut out this business of frightening strangers."

"Just rehearsing for the Mighty Omar," said my uncle. "I'll really give him the business."

We drove up to the imposingly gaunt frame house that served as residence and place of business for the medium.

I parked and got out.

"Pick me up," whispered my uncle. "Under your arm. And ring the bell. He has a colored butler, but I doubt if he'll trouble us long. We'll go right in and interview our spiritualistic friend. Just let me handle him and everything will be dandy."

Somehow I doubted this last statement.

But there was nothing else to do.

Skeleton in the Closet

Picking up Uncle Magnus, I started up the walk, carrying the skeleton under my arm.

I rang the bell.

The door opened. A bearded negro dressed as a Hindu peered out with rolling eyes. "You wish to have audience with the Mighty Omar?" he intoned, in a sonorous voice.

I nodded.

The door swung wider.

The bearded negro caught sight of my bony burden.

"Lawd save us!" he shrieked, in purest Harlemese. "The haunts are done arriving!"

A moment later I stepped over his prostrate body and stalked down the hall. Uncle Magnus rattled with anticipation under my elbow.

We faced a darkened doorway. "Here," he whispered. "Let me down and we'll sneak in."

We opened the door on pitch blackness. The seance was in full swing.

Moving quietly, we entered the darkened room. My eyes slowly became accustomed to the dimness and soon I could see faint outlines in the gloom.

* * *

Six fat women were seated around a large table with their hands resting on its surface. At the head of the table, like the caller at the Bingo game where these women really belonged, was the Mighty Omar.

The Mighty Omar was a little dried-up man dressed in a turban and an oriental night-gown. He had a face like a prune, and it didn't take long to see that he also had plenty of new wrinkles.

At the moment the Mighty Omar was right in the middle of his act. In fact, he was just going into his trance.

"Oh Mighty Brahm!" he whispered in the darkness. "By the powers of Raja Yoga I command thee—tear aside the veil! Let thy humble servant enter the astral plane and commune with the shades of the departed."

Uncle Magnus rattled angrily at my side, but made no move to interfere just yet.

"Ah!" sighed the Mighty Omar. "I am going now—I am passing through—and who is that I see? Ah yes! It is my psychic guide to the spirit world—Doctor Anabana!"

In a normal voice he confided to the ladies. "Doctor Anabana is a low-plane spirit. He will summon the souls of your dear departed ones and give you their messages. Who wishes to speak to Doctor Anabana?"

The fat lady next to the Mighty Omar cleared her throat nervously.

"Ask him about Grandpa," she quavered. "Grandpa Ike Snodtrotter."

"I will try," moaned the Mighty Omar. "It is hard—so hard." He breathed deeply. "I have a lady, Doctor," he said.

A voice came out of the air. It was shrill, eery.

"What does she desire?"

"She wants to communicate with Ike Snodtrotter. Have you a Mr. Snodtrotter there?"

"I shall see," said the high voice. "If he is here and has a message for the lady, he will communicate with her by knocking the table."

There was a long, ominous silence. Suddenly the table resounded with a furious rapping.

"Grandpa, is that you?" gasped the fat lady.

Again a knocking.

"It is your grandfather," said the high voice of Doctor Anabana, the "spirit guide."

`How are you, Grandpa?" asked the lady, anxiously. "How do you feel?"

"Grandpa says he feels fine," said the high voice. "And to prove it, he will play the tambourine."

Sure enough, from out of nowhere floated a ghostly tambourine, lit by glowing phosphorescence. It sailed above the table in mid-air and suddenly clinked and clanked.

"You see?" said the Mighty Omar, abruptly coming out of his trance. "But we must hurry lest the astral spell be broken. Do any other ladies wish to commune with the departed?"

"I wonder," said a lady at the opposite end of the table. "I would like to see if you couldn't find my Aunt Agatha."

"We can try," said the Mighty Omar. "If Doctor Anabana is willing. What is your Aunt Agatha's full name?"

"Agatha Flug."

* * *

"The Mighty Omar cleared his throat. As he did so, I felt the skeleton moving away from my side in the darkness.

160

"I have a lady, Doctor," intoned the Mighty Omar.

"Ten dollars to that lady!" rasped a voice.

"What?" muttered Omar, in a flustered haste.

"I'm sorry," said the voice. "Thought I was Doctor I.Q."

"Doctor Anabana?" called Omar, in puzzled tones. "Do you hear me?"

"Doctor Anabana had to leave," said the voice—which I now recognized as belonging to my skeleton uncle. "Doctor Gillespie wanted him in the surgery. This is Doctor Banana speaking. I've come to take his place."

"What goes on here?" yelled the Mighty Omar. Then, hastily realizing his position, he recovered dignity. "Will you locate Miss Agatha Flug, please?" he asked.

"To hear is to obey," said my uncle. He raised his voice. "Hey, Aggie!" he bawled. "Company!"

"This is most unusual," fluttered the lady at the end of the table. "Are you sure your spirit control is on the right astral plane?"

"Astral plane?" mocked my uncle. "I'm on an astral dive-bomber, sister! Wait, you wanted to speak to your aunt. Well, here's the old buzzard now. Knock on wood."

Sure enough, the rapping sounded on the table top. But it was a most peculiar rapping—in Conga rhythm.

"One and two and three—kick!" said a high voice, which came from my skeleton uncle, doing his best to imitate a woman.

"How do you feel up there, Aunt Agatha?" breathed the woman at the end of the table.

"I'll show you how I feel," said my uncle, in falsetto. "I'll play you something on the flute."

Incredibly, a silver flute, also phosphorescent, floated out over the heads of the Mighty Omar and the ladies.

"Hit it!" snapped my uncle.

The flute began to play.

"Did you ever hear Pete go tweet-tweet-tweet on his piccolo?"

"What the blue blazes?" screamed the Mighty Omar, forgetting himself.

"That's not my Aunt Agatha!" wailed the lady.

"It's a demon!" yelled the woman beside her. "Ooooh—I felt something tickle me!"

She wasn't the only one. As the hysterical flute tooted on, several of the ladies began to giggle and shriek.

The Mighty Omar rose to his feet.

"What in hell is all this?" he howled. "Turn on the lights!"

It was a bad idea.

The lights went on.

When the ladies saw the live skeleton sitting on the Mighty Omar's lap with the flute in his bony mouth, they didn't wait.

Even as they rose to flee, the skeleton jerked one fleshless arm towards a curtain. He pulled a string. A tambourine and two horns fell on the table, along with a microphone, a loud-speaker, a sheet on a wire, and a midget who had been sitting concealed on a perch near the ceiling.

"I'm from the spirit world!" yelled the skeleton. "Any messages today or would you care to say it with flowers?"

The ladies weren't listening. They were running out of the room.

* * *

The Mighty Omar rose swiftly, dumping the living skeleton to the floor. He tried to dive through the legs of the departing fat women.

A bony hand jerked him back by the collar.

"Come on," said my uncle. "You called up a spirit, now give me a message."

"Let me go," whined Omar. "Go back to hell or wherever you came from."

"Not unless you come with me," grated my uncle.

"Wh—what do you want with me?" The medium was trembling.

"I'm taking you to see an old friend," rasped my uncle. "An old friend named Magnus Lorry."

"B—b—but he's dead."

"I know," growled my uncle. "And you murdered him. Didn't you?"

"N—no—no, I didn't! Let me go!" howled the fake spiritualist. "I'm just a harmless medium—I never murdered Magnus Lorry—I just dabbled a bit in the occult—I never believed—I never knew—"

The skeleton relaxed his grip.

"I ought to take you anyway," he hissed. "But I'll let you go this time if you'll promise me one thing."

"Anything. Anything at all!" sobbed the not-so-Mighty Omar.

"Give up this vile racket," said the skeleton. "Get a job in the war industries or something useful."

"Yes—I will—right away."

The skeleton released him and stalked off. I followed.

As we went down the hall, somebody rang the front door. It opened abruptly as we neared it, and to my consternation I recognized the figure standing there in the twilight.

It was the traffic cop who had halted us at the corner.

"Here you are!" he snorted. "I've tracked you down at last!"

"Here we aren't!" said my skeletonic uncle, turning and taking to his bony heels down the hall. I followed with some speed as I noted the revolver in the cop's pudgy hand.

"Back door," wheezed my uncle.

The cop thundered behind us. "Halt or I'll shoot!" he bawled.

We didn't and he did—but by the time the bullet buried itself in the back door we had slammed it behind us. At a dead run we made for the car in the twilight.

"Where to?" I gasped.

"To hell out of this place," directed my uncle. "Gas rationing be damned!"

We whizzed into the street. The cop appeared and in the rear-view mirror I noted that he was mounting a motorcycle.

I turned a corner quickly.

"Guess the Mighty Omar wasn't guilty," said Uncle Magnus.

"I'm not so sure," I told him.

"He was too frightened to lie out of it," argued the living skeleton. "How did you like my act?"

"It frightened me," I admitted.

"Good. If we can dodge this cop, I'll try it again."

"Who have you in mind?"

"Dr. Eggkopf. He's a psychiatrist at the army induction center."

"A psychiatrist?"

"Yes, but his hobby is collecting demonolatry—books on sorcery. He used to grab off items at the book dealers' shops and he hated me."

"You want to go to the army induction center now?" I asked, whizzing through an arterial as I noted the cop on the motorcycle behind us.

"Afraid I can't," panted Uncle Magnus.

"Why not?"

"Isn't safe to get myself involved there," said the skeleton. "Doctor Eggkopf is pretty nearsighted and a tough customer. If I visit him at the army induction center he's liable to draft me."

* * *

I tried to answer, but by this time the wailing of the siren on the motorcycle drowned out my reply.

"He's gaining on us!" screamed my uncle. "Nosey fool!"

I twisted and turned. We were now in the heart of the downtown area. The siren blasted and we drove hell-for-leather. The skeleton bounced around in the back seat.

"Stop that!" he begged. "Do you want to get us both killed?"

"I'm the only one who can be killed," I muttered.

"Do something—lose him!"

"I'm doing my best!"

The glaring face of the cop was clearly distinguishable despite the darkness. The siren screeched in our ears.

I skidded around the corner on a wheel and a half.

"Listen!" yelled Uncle Magnus.

I listened. Another wail rose to drown out the siren. A great, piercing wail.

At the same moment, the lights on the street abruptly blinked and went out. In the office buildings around us, the windows winked into darkness.

"Don't you understand?" I shouted. "It's a blackout!"

"Blackout?"

"Yes. I'll have to pull to the curb and run for it with you."

"Where to?"

"Must be a downtown air-raid shelter nearby. If we hide on the street, the wardens will pick us up."

"There's a subway entrance," panted Uncle Magnus. "Now!"

We ground to a halt as the sirens wailed. Leaping from the car, we streaked down the street. Behind us the bewildered cop groped in darkness.

"Halt there!" he bellowed.

"This way," I gasped. I saw the black mouth of a subway entrance loom out of the lesser darkness.

We clattered down the stairs—I with my heels and the skeleton with his bony metatarsae.

"We're safe now," I whispered, pausing on the landing.

"It was dark all around us. Somewhere below the crowd stood in dimly-lighted safety.

"Can't go down further," grunted the skeleton. "I don't want to be seen."

"I'm sure nobody would want to look at you," I assured him. "But we're all right here."

Somebody else came racing down the steps and we froze into silence.

From the heavy footsteps I deduced the presence of a stout man.

I nudged the skeleton, who stood close to the wall.

In a moment several pairs of high heels clicked down the stairs. Two girls, I judged, from the tread.

"You all right, Mamie?" giggled the first.

"Okie-dokie by me," her companion replied.

"Gee, ain't blackouts thrilling?" observed the first girl.

"Me, I'd like it better if I had me a sailor," Mamie answered, snapping her gum.

"Any sailors down here?" the other girl tittered.

* * *

The stout man and myself were silent. Uncle Magnus rattled his bones slightly but made no other sign.

"What's the matter, nobody sociable?" complained Mamie. She moved closer in the darkness. Unluckily for her, she moved closer to Uncle Magnus.

"Eeek!" she murmured. "What was that?"

"What?" inquired the other girl.

"I felt something cold."

"Cold?"

"Cold, and—bony," explained the girl, in puzzled tones. Then, "Oh Gawd!"

"What is it?"

"I don't know—it's all bony—like a skeleton!"

"You're screwy!" her companion diagnosed.

"No kidding, I did!" Mamie insisted.

"This is a subway, not a graveyard," scoffed the other girl. "Wait, I'll light a match and see who's getting fresh around here."

"Don't—" I began. But too late.

The match flared up. Uncle Magnus's leering skull stood out.

With a scream duet, the two girls clattered down the stairs to the safety of the subway proper.

In the darkness I heard the stout man chuckle.

"Cute trick," he laughed. "A mask, huh?"

Uncle Magnus was silent at my side. I answered. "Yes, sir. It's a mask. I was on my way to a costume party when the blackout caught us."

The stout man moved closer.

"Say," he boomed. "I know you. You're Tarleton, aren't you?"

"What?" I muttered.

"Sure. Don't you recognize me?"

"Otis Kersen," I muttered."I thought you were out of town."

"You told me to get out," he said. "But I didn't. Just left word at the office, that's all. After all, there's nothing to be afraid of, you know. Old Magnus Lorry is safe in his grave, nobody knows anything, you have the estate and we divvy up—"

I turned, but too late. Uncle Magnus had found matches in my pocket.

Otis Kersen saw the full skeleton this time. He screamed.

"In my grave, am I?" groaned Magnus Lorry. "You forget that wizards have power."

"Lorry!" wailed Otis Kersen. "You're back from the dead!"

"Yes," said the skeleton, through clenched teeth. "This young scoundrel was humoring me, dragging me around on a wild goose chase. But I've found my goose and now I'll cook it."

"I'm innocent!" Otis Kersen gasped. "Utterly innocent! He thought up the idea—remember—he came to town secretly and slipped into your house while you slept—he brought a gun—shot you right through the head—we buried you secretly and I faked a medical certificate—he made me do it—"

* * *

I tripped on the lower step. That was my biggest mistake. When the skeleton's fingers closed around my throat I knew the end had come.

"All right," he snarled in my ear. "Up we go to the car before the lights turn on." He turned. "You too, Kersen."

"Where are you taking us?" I whispered.

"Home," said the skeleton. "Home. Where my books are. My books with their spells, their incantations. I'm going to show you two a little practical experiment in sorcery."

"What do you mean?"

Skeleton in the Closet

"You'll see," gloated my skeletonic uncle. "You'll see. Turn about is fair play."

Then I passed out.

When I came to, I was in this bedroom. I'm still here, writing this. Somewhere outside in the great house, a skeleton stalks amidst strange circles, muttering chants. He will be coming for me soon, and for Otis Kersen.

I think I know what he intends.

That's why I'm writing this. To toss it through the window.

If you on the outside find and read this, come to my uncle's house. Magnus Lorry is the name. He probably won't be here—he must have some wizard's plan for a getaway.

Never mind that. Just go to the bedroom closet and open the door. I have a hunch you'll see a skeleton hanging there. That skeleton will be Otis Kersen.

Never mind that, either. But please do something about the other skeleton right next to it. Because—

It's probably me!

The Tchen-lam's Vengeance

Never mind how I got to Lhassa. I did a lot more than shaving my head, learning six dialects and studying up on Tantric Buddhism as formulated by Padrasam Ghava. I spent three years in Manning, and before I reached the city of pantheons I had passed as a Buriat, a round-hatted Chakhar, a Khalka, and a half-dozen incarnations of disguise. I drank thick tea in a hundred *yurts* before I got into the particular temple I had my eye on. The lamas are wise and cruel and relentless, and they have spies everywhere.

But finally I succeeded, and then aimed my three camels into the desert on the endless trek through the Gobi. The most evil city in the world lay behind me, and the malign sands stretched before me—the desert staring up like a great yellow face.

But it was worth it.

I had stolen the Lotus of Lhassa.

The Supreme Emerald, the sacred stone of Gautama, rested in my belt. It was worth a quarter of a million—and my life.

Now I must pass through the desert and reach the coast if I valued safety. I drove the camels on.

It wasn't so bad the first week. Exultation buoyed me up, triumph was a cloak to shield me from the scorching sun. But then loneliness came, and thirst, and exhaustion. I wandered through the eternal dust of a demon's graveyard.

I began imagining things.

The mountains were all around me, and they grinned against the horizon, their jagged edges like the teeth in the mouth of a mad dog. At dusk a wind would bay from the black throat of the night, and I could feel those teeth yawning for me.

But it was worse by day, when I trudged through a sea of ochre flame that was the desert, and the sun blazed down like a finger-ring stone on the hand of an angry god.

Sometimes the rocks were black dwarfs that danced around me; sometimes the dust was a yellow dragon that coiled across my path.

I slept under boulders white as the sun-bleached bones of giants, and I huddled in the Cyclopean ruins of cities dead five thousand years.

After a while there were no more cities nor boulders nor mountains, and nothing was left which I could compare to humanity. The buzzards had stopped following me, and the beetles were gone. I walked under a burning sun that filled the sky and hissed down in molten rays upon the empty, endless sand. Then I got that terrible feeling of *aloneness*. There was nothing in the world but torture of sun and sand, with me between. The sand burned my feet and the sun burned my head, and then little rays of fire lanced through my body, and I walked on and on and on.

My body was covered with horrible sores, and my blood was black as it ran from my nose and mouth. My feet were swollen into shapeless blobs of agony. The skin rolled from my face like mummy-flesh exposed to the outer air. My head was an iron bowl filled with the venomous stewing juice of fever.

But I still had the Lotus...

I didn't rave or curse or mumble or sing. It was worse than that. I didn't think about water, or food, or sleep. The expression on my face never altered. I just tottered on, like some ghastly marionette. When the camels blackened and died, I left them where they fell, without taking up the knapsack or water-skins. When I thought I was going to die I dropped in my tracks, but I always got up again.

This was it. This was what I had expected. And it was worth the horror. I had the Lotus. I'd make it.

The desert was a vast, lonely room I had to cross—a single great room a million miles long. I was all alone in that room, and I kept plodding.

* * *

Then one day I sensed the presence of another in the room. It was just like that. If somebody comes into a room you know it, even if the room is a million miles long. Another had come in. Perhaps he was a hundred thousand miles away, but I felt him.

The Tchen-lam's Vengeance

And I knew fear. From that moment on I didn't mind sun or fever or the cancer of weariness which gnawed at my heart. I had a great dread.

The *tchen-lam*. The *tchen-lam* are the Guardians of the Lotus. They are the spies of the temples of Lhasa and they are the most evil men in the world. They are the Hunters and at the twilight Hour of Mutation they set forth on missions of vengeance.

All Tibet fears the *tchen-lam*, the magic ones. They know the Black and the Red and the White Secrets and they control winds and water and desert sand. Offenders against the faith are marked for doom in the secret temples, and then the *tchen-lam* go forth to bring that doom.

If my theft had been discovered and they were on my trail, I could never escape. This I knew, and this is why I was afraid.

The *tchen-lam* are cruel.

Khalka Mongols will hang you up by the nose on iron hoops, and tie weights to your legs. Chakhars are slightly more imaginative. They will stake you out under the desert sun, cut off your eyelids, and set beetles on you. The Torgots flay you alive and thrust you into a sack filled with wild dogs. The subtle Soyots may amputate your arms and legs, and then place you in a pit with the rats.

But the *tchen-lam* are worse.

I heard of a man who was captured for blasphemous profanation of a temple. There are aver a hundred bones in the human body, and the *tchen-lam* broke every one, slowly, and kept him alive. Then he was skinned, and his bones were removed, one by one. He lived until he had nothing left but two ribs, a pelvis, and a spine. It took months.

This was only one of their punishments.

And the *tchen-lam* crept behind me as I fled.

At last one day fell, like a molten tear-drop from the eyes of agony. I had crouched in the sand all night, burrowed deep, and when I tried to rise with the coming of the sun I could not stir. I sensed the presence of the other close behind me, but I could not stir. Could not stir, even with the ghastly inspiration of approaching doom.

I lay there shuddering, and the presence stole closer, and then I felt it upon me hours later.

A shadow stained the searing sand. I rolled over and looked up into a yellow face.

I blinked. There was nothing else to do. The face bent closer. Thin lips nibbled at my ear and a voice rustled.

"You are the American?"

I tried to nod.

"I have been seeking you."

I blinked again.

"I have heard much of you and you are the man I want."

I couldn't move. The face smiled, and then the whispering came again.

"You must not die, you know."

There was enough left in me for irony. "Why not?" I gasped.

"Because you and I are going back to America to start a beauty parlor."

Because you and I are going back to America to start a beauty parlor.

Never in fact, fiction, or fancy were words as mad as these.

I had stolen the Lotus of Lhassa, I was pursued over a desert hell by the cruelest beings in the world, I lay dying of exhaustion, in the middle of the Gobi—and a yellow face bends over me and whispers, "You and I are going back to America to start a beauty parlor."

Of course I must be mad. I had to be. I began to laugh and laugh and laugh.

* * *

The yellow-faced man thrust a jug of water into my mouth and stopped my laughter, and he stroked the papyrus of my forehead and he propped me up in his arms. I became sufficiently revived to gaze up into his skeletal visage. His head was like a rotten, wrinkled apricot, and only his eyes were alive. The man was further gone than myself, and I sensed that indomitable will alone kept him on his feet. Those eyes blazed at me more forcefully than the sun, and they filled me with a peculiar power. I stood up.

"Who are you?" I whispered. "A *tchen-lam*?"

He shook his bead slowly. "No. I am called Dagur. I come from the Deccan, and my mission in Lhassa can be spoken of later. I heard of you there and followed you through the desert."

"Heard of me?" I gasped. "Then it was known—"

Again he shook his rotten, wrinkled head. "I gain my wisdom in stranger ways," he said. "But I know you are the man I am seeking—international adventurer, grave-robber, treasure-thief. I want to take you with me when we go to America and start a beauty parlor."

I was getting used to this by now, and didn't reel at the weird state-ment. But I was still afraid.

"The *tchen-lam*," I muttered. "Did you see them?"

"One follows us now," answered Dagur, calmly. "He wants the Lotus of Lhassa, which you stole."

I sank to the ground again. "What shall we do?" I whispered.

"Wait for him, of course," answered Dagur. "And when he comes we will give him the Lotus."

"What?"

"It will be for the best. The *tchen-lam* cannot be avoided. He will seek you to the ends of the earth. We might as well face him here and strike a bargain."

"A bargain? But he'll kill me, I'll lose the jewel—"

"The Lotus of Lhassa cannot be profaned," Dagur answered. "It must not be taken by force, the priests believe. Therefore he will not kill you for it. It would be sacrilege. You must give it to him outright."

"It's worth a quarter-million," I protested. "I spent three years plan-ning this, and I've gone through hell here on the desert. Why should I give it to him?"

"Because a quarter-million is nothing. Because it is a mite com-pared to the fortune you and I will make together—if we live. And be-cause you'll die here on the desert with the jewel unless we bargain."

"What kind of bargain will you strike?"

"Listen. You are weak, dying. So am I. But the *tchen-lam* will be a strong man, with a body trained to withstand the rigors of the desert. So I will bargain with him in this wise—I shall take his body in ex-change for the jewel and give him my body in return. Then we shall have strength enough, between us, to reach the coast."

"You're mad," I mumbled, but I thought *I* was. "You cannot ex-change bodies with another."

"I am Dagur. I have studied in the secret places, and I have a magic. By concentration my astral can invade the body of another, and I can place men in new bodies at will, if they be submissive. Extended hypno-sis, your science calls it. So if the emissary from Lhassa agrees, so be it."

"You can change bodies," I repeated.

"Of course. That is how we will make our fortune," insisted Dagur.

I lay back for good. I knew I was delirious. There was no Dagur, no mad scheme. I was dying alone. N o reality. There couldn't be anything so fantastic. And yet—

Far down the shimmering way I saw the figure approaching. It plodded leadenly, like a wound-up doll. I recognized the tall yellow hat, the great otter collar, the huge skirt. It was a *tchen-lam*!

* * *

The figure headed straight for us, unerring and relentless. I made out the features; the ivory mask of cruelty in which emerald eyes were set.

But Dagur did not flinch. The man approached, never hastening. Dagur raised a hand in greeting.

"We will bargain," he said.

The *tchen-lam* turned his basilisk-gaze toward me and nodded. "It is the one," he said, in clipped English. "And you speak for him?"

"I do," Dagur replied.

"So. Your bargain?"

"He will give you the Lotus of Lhassa in exchange for your body."

I expected the Tibetan to strike Dagur dead. His expression didn't alter, but there was a heightening intensity in his stare.

"Think," argued Dagur. "You could follow him until he dies on the desert, this is true, and then take the jewel. But this way it is easier, simpler. You take the jewel, give your body, and use my weak form to return to Lhassa. Time counts; every moment the Lotus of Lhassa is away from its shrine is an affront in the eyes of the gods. Give your body and take the jewel.'"

"Thieves must be punished," said the *tchen-lam*. He said it softly, but I thought of my bones being broken and torn out, and trembled.

"Natural death is no punishment," insisted Dagur. "Perhaps there is another way."

"Yes, another way!" The Tibetan's voice trembled with exultation. "I shall accept, yes, I shall accept your offer. My brothers in Lhassa will think it a capital jest, a capital jest."

Dagur looked puzzled, and so did I. But my new friend persisted. "Very well, then. It is done. You must submit your will to mine. Then our spirits will mingle, and each seek the other's flesh. We will use the veritable Lotus of Lhassa for our focal point. Give it to me."

I gave him the jewel. The sparkling drop of emerald brilliance shone in the sunlight. The grotesque Hindu knelt, and the yellow monk knelt facing him. The jewel lay on the sand between. Both bowed their heads and stared.

And I lay there, racked with fever, dying in the desert as I watched two magicians, or two madmen, sealing an unholy bargain which was to decide my fate.

"Submit," whispered Dagur. "Your will is strong, friend, and you must submit to aid me." The *tchen-lam* nodded. Suddenly both men became motionless. Rigid as puppets, eyes closed, they knelt in the sand. The jewel flamed. Then both bodies shuddered.

This was horror from High Asia, I knew. I was either dying or crazy. But I stared as the men fell and writhed on the ground; stared as they opened their eyes and blinked, sat up.

"Done!" The high-pitched voice of the *tchen-lam* came from Dagur's withered throat.

"Yes, done," whispered Dagur—from the body of the *tchen-lam*. It was unbelievable, but unmistakable.

I was too weak, too sick, to realize the fall import of what I had just seen; the substantiation of the East's oldest myth. Transference of souls, the original and most ancient of all beliefs, just accomplished before my fevered eyes.

"Now I am strong enough to reach the coast with my friend," announced Dagur, rising and shaking himself—for all the world like a poodle emerging from water. "And you, is your withered body capable of dragging itself back to Lhassa?"

The wrinkled face reared up and I got a shock as I saw the *tchen-lam*'s blazing eyes. "It is my will, not my body, which shall take me," he announced. "But now, the bargain. Give me the jewel. No—you hand it to me." And he pointed at me.

I picked up the jewel dumbly and held it out to him. A claw grasped it.

"A bargain is a bargain," said the *tchen-lam*, gravely. "But I have also sworn to my brothers that you shall know our vengeance. No one, from the dawn of time, be he beggar or Khan, has ever escaped us once he is marked for doom."

"You cannot harm him," Dagur reminded. "Your promise."

"I know. But my personal vengeance shall overtake him just the same, though I shall never raise a hand to strike him. He shall suffer at my hands nonetheless, as was sworn. That is why I consented to the bargain, because I know I can make him suffer in spite of it. I am a *tchen-lam*, and the *tchen-lam* are the greatest wizards in all Asia." He held up the jewel, and his eyes blazed through its fire, mingled with it in an emerald haze. I stared, and cold crept up my spine. "The greatest wizards in all Asia," muttered the *tchen-lam*.

"The greatest fools in all Asia," hissed Dagur. I never even saw the knife flash down, but suddenly the Tibetan crumpled to the ground and lay still. Dagur rose, wiped the blade, and pocketed the jewel.

"I am the greatest wizard," he laughed. "I have cheated him, gained life, and the Lotus of Lhassa is still ours."

"But you told me you couldn't—" I began.

"I did not dare say otherwise, or when our souls met and mingled he would have known the thought," Dagur replied. "But now we are free, and you shall have no curse on you. He is dead, though I still have his body. And we go to the coast, to make our fortunes in a beauty parlor."

* * *

At that moment I myself crumpled. It had all been too much. Desert nightmare, ending in incredible horror. I went out, and stayed out. He must have carried me. I don't know. How he fed us, kept me alive, went on—these things I cannot say. I awoke weeks later in a Canton hospital. Dagur was beside me, and he thrust a fortune into my hands. He'd sold the jewel, of course.

We were rich, and I was going to get well. It was all over. Dagur was in the yellow body of a Tibetan monk, and I nearly went out again when I saw that horrid reminder of reality I longed to forget. But I was well, and rich.

Dagur smiled.

"Up in a week," he said. "Then we book passage to America. My entrance is all arranged, thanks to the money. We shall make fortunes."

"How? What?"

"Why, as I told you. We shall go to America and start a beauty parlor."

I was sick of mystery.

"Let's have it straight," I began, sitting up. "Who are you, and where did you hear of me?"

Dagur smiled. Or rather Dagur smiled with the face of the *tchen-lam*.

"I am Dagur, as I told you. I was born in India. My father was Rajput, exiled by the British Raj. He studied ceremonial magics in the temples. I grew up with priests. I learned many things—levitation, hypnotism, things Western science still calls magic. *Sakhyati*, the tree of teachings from which *Yogi* springs as the merest branch, I have mastered. One of the powers I gained is that of transferring bodies."

Now I've met *fakirs* before, and fanatics, and charlatans doing rope tricks. But I could not scoff at Dagur, because of what I'd seen in the desert. Because of what I saw now—Dagur's eyes in the hatefully yellow face of the *tchen-lam*. He was a wizard.

"I went to Lhassa on your errand," Dagur continued. "I too meant to have the Lotus for my own. I must have followed your trail, because when I camped I heard stories of a lone Khalka pilgrim, a Buriat wanderer, and a Chakhar. Each place saw only one man, never all three. Therefore I reasoned that someone was travelling in disguise. At first I meant to overtake you and kill you. Then, my friend, as time went on I began to marvel at your cleverness. When my idea came, I saw that you would make a living ally instead of a dead rival. So I allowed you to steal the Lotus and followed you into the desert. The rest you know."

"You saved my life," I mumbled.

"Nothing." Dagur raised a yellow claw of deprecation.

"But this mumbling about a beauty parlor?"

"Simple. In India I am a holy man, yes. I can perform small magics, I can steal. But I want my heritage. My father, the Rajput, once lived in palaces. I want those riches. I can never earn them by petty thievery. I cannot become wealthy exercising my powers for fools. But in America, with your aid—ah!"

"Beauty parlor?" I persisted.

"I have studied your Western culture, as you call it—a culture of decadence, a woman's civilization, founded on outward deception and falsehood. The beauty parlor is a symbol of occidental deceit; a mask of loveliness over rotten decay."

"The devil with your sophomore philosophy," I countered. "Facts."

"Here they are, then. Every year American women spend billions, yes, billions of dollars on beauty culture. They go to be massaged and marcelled and manicured, to be kneaded and sweated and pounded into youthfulness. Thousands of wealthy women spend fortunes endeavoring to recapture their lost charms. Do they succeed?"

"Well—no. I suppose not. But they still go, still pay."

"Exactly. And don't you think more of them would go, and pay greater sums if they did succeed, turning their ugly bodies into young, attractive forms once more?"

"Yes."

"That is where we come in, my friend. Oh, I could start out as a fortune-teller, a *swami,* a cult-leader. My knowledge would be of service there. But there isn't enough in it. I want riches, quickly. And I shall have them, making old women young again."

"But how? By giving them some of *yogi* treatment or exercise? Have you got a philtre, or a rejuvenating secret?"

Dagur smiled, and again that yellow face was creased.

"No. Simpler than that. You saw my secret on the desert.. If the subjects be willing, I can hypnotize them and change bodies."

I sat bolt upright in bed.

"Yes, change bodies. Instead of pounding some foolish old woman into a tight corset and charging her exorbitant fees, I shall give her the real boon she craves—a young, fresh body of her own."

"How? With whom shall these old women exchange their worn-out frames? Where do the young women come from?"

Dagur's creased smile grew evilly insinuating.

"Come now, my friend; I picked you because you are cleverer than that. You are something of a rogue yourself, I have reason to believe. And surely the answer to the question is easy."

I almost sickened. "You mean we abduct young girls and force them into such an unholy exchange?" I asked.

"Force? No—I have told you I cannot force anyone into hypnotic surrender without their mental consent. But in beauty salons, there are machines, surely? For fixing the ladies' hair, perhaps? Metal clamps on the head, I believe."

"Yes."

"And in western scientific classrooms there are machines on which a subject gazes at lights or colored objects until his will surrenders."

"I guess so."

"We merely combine the two. Adjust the clamps on the two women. The young girl surrenders her will after a time; so does the unbeautiful lady. They fall asleep—quite sound asleep. Then I concentrate. Their astrals are pliant. The exchange is made, and it is done. Simple?"

"Fantastic!" I muttered. "We'll never get away with it!"

But we did.

The Tchen-lam's Vengeance

* * *

The last week in bed I spent in planning. We figured it all out. We had money enough to splurge at the start. Rent an exclusive salon. Advertise discreetly. Build up an atmosphere of scented refinement like an ordinary beauty and health parlor. Curious women would come. Then, after procuring the girls, the first experiment. If it succeeded, the news would spread like wildfire. We could charge ten, twenty, fifty thousand dollars for a genuine rejuvenation.

Of course, there would be difficulties. An old friend of mine, never mind his name, would handle the girl angle for me. That was no problem. But the difficulties lay in making the sudden change plausible.

Dagur and I worked out our scheme quite carefully.

Dagur was to be a Hindu. Of course his skin was yellow, but that wouldn't matter. All Orientals with "new" discoveries are Hindus as far as Americans are concerned. Dagur was to be a Hindu with a new "thought rejuvenation" process, supplemented by the use of "secret oils and formulas known to the *devi-dasi* of Hindu temples." The old come-on stuff. We'd get the women, give them a few preliminary treatments in the old style, make them think that oils and perfumes and exercises were aiding their rejuvenescence. Then we'd work up to the big moment; put them under a machine and go to work.

That's where the subtle part came in. It might be difficult for an old battle-axe to fall asleep under a dryer and wake up an hour later in an entirely new body. If she was a brunette and woke up with blonde hair it might be doubly hard to convince her. I had a secret hunch most of the old girls weren't so confident in their treatments anyway; just wanted to be flattered and pampered. Actual changes in their unlovely figures might shock rather than please them—unless it was worked properly.

Well, I figured out a way to work it properly. To begin with, we wouldn't exchange bodies with just any young and fairly pretty girl we might get hold of. During the preliminary treatments we'd study our case. Try to visualize what the middle-aged dowager looked like twenty years ago. Was her hair brown, or black, or red, or a certain shade of blondness? Was it straight or curly? How tall was she? What was her weight? The color of her eyes? Yes, and what kind of a voice did she have? Get all the actual details.

And then, go out and find the right young woman to fill the bill. Perhaps we couldn't always get an exact duplicate. But we could come close. Then we might do a little adjustment work; plastic surgery on the nose, for example. Removing a mole, or adding one as the case might be. Then our plan might well be foolproof.

"I've got it—the final touch!" I yelled, the last day. "We keep the old dames on the premises during their entire course of treatments and never show them a mirror for a week. Keep at them every day during the fake preliminary treatments, kidding them along that they're getting younger gradually. Psychological suggestion, that they are losing five years a day. Naturally, they can't see themselves. A little dope might do wonders, too. Lead them up to the final phase, effect the transfer, and there they are. Fully convinced. Young, beautiful, and satisfied. Why, it's a humanitarian business, Dagur! We'll really be doing a great good!"

Dagur smiled, and I didn't care for his wolfish leer. I knew that he was thinking of the young girls for whom we would *not* be doing good; kidnapping them, forcing them into old, withered bodies, and then disposing of them once and for all.

But why quibble? Thousands of girls disappear every year, and suffer worse fates. Perhaps. And at any rate, why bother? There was millions in this idea, millions.

There was. We sailed, made New York, established connections. It was all easy—and I could use ease after my gruelling experience in the land of nightmares.

No more *tchen-lam* to fear. No more desert. Sitting in a penthouse and calling up this party about the girls; renting an elegant suite of offices, arranging with soft-voiced secretaries about advertising and rates. It was a picnic.

Dagur wore a turban, and a satisfied smile. We were ready to open. I was surprised at the roguery rampant in fine professions; we hired some broken-down quacks who could spout about "hormone injections" and the "rejuvenatory function of glands" who lent excellent pseudo-scientific atmosphere.

There was no hitch of any kind. Our first client was quite a wealthy woman—I shall not mention names, for she is still prominent. At this time, she was prominent only about the hips. A distinct matron type, on the verge of matriarchy.

* * *

The Tchen-lam's Vengeance

For the first time we put our scheme into operation. It clicked. We had no trouble getting data on her appearance in 1923. We decided that a reduction to the age of 28 would be spectacular enough without bringing too much suspicion and incredulity into play. We got our data, and I arranged for the right girl.

My party brought the girl over, and we kept her locked up in the special rooms downstairs. We didn't treat her badly; just held her. Meanwhile, the staff went to work on our client, planted the build-up. Finally the afternoon arrived and it was all up to Dagur. Sink or swim, success or failure—Dagur must make good his boast or we were lost.

We brought the bewildered, half-drugged old woman into the room of mirrors we'd chosen. Dagur made a very impressive speech— it was truly a masterpiece. I know, because I wrote it for him. She was credulous. She was more than willing to submit to a trance.

Dagur had her out in the chair in five minutes. Then we brought in the girl. She was hysterical, a little, but Dagur injected morphine and then got her under the dryer. I hadn't inspected the apparatus he used, but it was only a matter of moments after he snapped the switch before her eyes closed.

Dagur turned out the lights and only a flame behind the mirrors blazed up. His yellow eyes closed. He rocked back and forth. I sat quietly. The sleeping old face and the sleeping young face contorted in agony as though both women suffered nightmares.

I felt the silence, felt what stole through the silence. Waves beat down in darkness. I stared at Dagur's face, thought of the *tchen-lam*, his curse on me which would never be fulfilled. I shuddered. Perhaps we'd fail; that was the curse the monk had meant. I began to perspire. And still the three silent figures sat in darkness. Then the lights clicked up, Dagur opened his eyes wearily, clapped his hands. The two women stirred. I got the old one out of there, into the locked room adjoining. Then we went back. The young brunette was stretching herself lazily.

This was the moment. Suppose nothing had happened? Suppose it was the same girl, after all?

She spoke.

Then I knew. Even before Dagur handed her the mirror and she gasped in incredulous joy, I knew we had done it.

I went into the room where the trembling, half-crazed old woman lay; the kidnapped young woman who awoke bewildered in a strange

181

body. I felt a certain pity for her, but then she was obviously suffering this way; so I did what had to be done.

Afterward I came out in time to hear our newly rejuvenated patient raving with joy. I saw her hand over the check. Fifteen thousand.

Right there I got clever on my own hook. I told Dagur about the restrictions on banking laws which applied to aliens. I deposited the money under my own name. All money would hereafter be deposited.

There was plenty of money. The woman went out. She told her story to her friends—but her new body fairly shrieked the news for her. We had a flood of clients.

We didn't take them all. It was too great a risk. A few each week, ones we could duplicate easily with young girls. Our fees rose and rose. In six months we cleared three hundred thousand, profit exclusively. There was never a hitch, never a bit of trouble.

So it was. Success at last, success with the maddest scheme of all. I should have been the happiest man in the world—but I wasn't.

No, my conscience didn't bother me. I've never had one, I suppose. I got qualms, occasionally, when I had to dispose of old bodies; but then it came to be a routine thing. Like changing a window display in a department store, and throwing out the old dummies.

I didn't have compunctions about how we got the girls, either. I'm no sentimentalist. But there were other things bothering me—more subtle disturbances.

They say the desert does something to you. Perhaps that was it. I'd been three years in the East on my mission. I'd gone to the most fearful city in the world and bearded the demons in their lair. I'd nearly died in the worst inferno on the face of the globe. It might have done something queer to my mind.

Because in the middle of the night I'd wake up and think about the *tchen-lam's* curse. Foolish? Of course; the man was dead.

But then again, he wasn't dead. Dagur's body was dead, and the *tchen-lam's* spirit. Still, the body of the *tchen-lam* lived, and I saw it every day, with Dagur's eyes peering out at me.

The modern beauty salon, the cooing women attendants, all served as a pitiful mask for secret sorcery for the mysteries of High Asia. I walked in the Twentieth Century atmosphere of high-geared business, but I looked into the face of a Mongol priest who had cursed me. I beheld the most incredible of all magic—the transference of souls. And it got me.

182

The Tchen-lam's Vengeance

I'd think more and more about Tibet; dream of the lame, goitred women in their brocaded shirts, of the green-coated Torgots, of the diseased beggars in the streets of Lhassa. That was it. I ran a beauty parlor, but I dreamed of filth, squalor disease, vermin. The Tibetans are a filthy race, and I'd remember their pitted faces, their scrofulous bald heads. Looking into the yellow face of Dagur I saw horrid markings.

* * *

One day I read a squib in the paper. About the death of an antique merchant in Canton. I thought of the Lotus of Lhassa, and shuddered. Had the *tchen-lam* taken it back? If so, why didn't they learn where I had gone? Why hadn't they followed me to exact the vengeance the priest had sworn on me?

Perhaps they had followed me. Perhaps they were coming now. I got to sneaking into my apartment at night, peering behind me on the street, eyeing everyone who came into our reception room at the beauty salon.

But there was no one. There was only Dagur, with his hateful yellow face—the face of the man who cursed me; the man who was a member of the cruelest sect in the world.

When my fears about the *tchen-lam* coming after me abated, I began to center my hatred on Dagur and his face. I didn't like it, or him. We never quarreled openly; too busy making money, but I fancy he disliked me as much as I did him.

Now we rarely met save at the salon, when there was work to be done or planned. I couldn't stand that yellow face, reminding me of my ancient guilt and my prophesied doom. If it weren't for that I would have been able to forget; to think of myself merely as a successful business man. But the face haunted me.

Maybe I could get rid of it. Dagur was clever, I knew that. He was an evil man, and a wise one. He'd defied the masters of Asia. But in picking me for a partner he'd unwittingly acknowledged that I was his equal if not his peer.

I was his peer. The money was all in my name.

I thought about this a lot lately. I could get the money and get rid of the *tchen-lam*s face with one quick stroke—a stroke to Dagur's heart. Perhaps my friends who brought the women could arrange it. Perhaps I could do it myself.

No. Dagur was famous now, because of the business. His sudden disappearance would stir up trouble. But—if the business fell....

Four hundred thousand dollars was enough for me. Dagur wasn't needed any more.

I could wreck the business, perhaps, and expose Dagur. He'd take the rap. As a mere partner, not implicated in the actual transference, I'd be safe. And the money was mine.

Then I wouldn't see the *tchen-lam*'s face, or worry about a ridiculous curse. Why did that savage's silly threat haunt me? He couldn't hurt me, dead, even though his body lived. He couldn't...

But he made me sweat at night in dreams. And I had to stop that.

Dagur stopped it for me. I guess I under-rated the wisdom of the East, which is indeed the wisdom of ageless serpents. *He* must have planned, too, and his mind was subtle. I never suspected the trap.

One day he called me into conference.

* * *

We met in the room where the soul-transference was effected. It was private there, and quiet. We sat down. Dagur began to talk to me about quitting the business.

"Oho," I thought. "He wants money."

But Dagur never mentioned money. He just talked on and on about how he was sick of the racket, and now that we were both wealthy we might retire. He talked like a friend, like a brother. He talked until it grew dark and the room became dim.

He snapped on the lights behind the mirrors and I saw his yellow face; the *tchen-lam*'s face that I had grown to hate and fear. It unnerved me, that grim reminder of unbelievable days, but I could not help staring at it. Staring at Dagur's eyes in that yellow face; staring as he talked on and on in a gentle drone and his eyes got bigger, and I saw that face loom up. It came to me across a burning desert, that face stalked me over the Gobi once more. But I didn't resist. I was caught in the mirror light and the voice-drone and the staring eyes. I was lost in Dagur's eyes.

The face was big as the desert now. I was lost in the face. I was lost. The *tchen-lam* was all about me, and I couldn't resist. I felt myself sinking.

Myself. What was myself? A dark blur, a liquid blur that could flow. Flow out of my body, into that face. Flow out, because all my being was concentrated on that face. Flow out into mirror-gleam and voice-drone and yellow face. I was ooze in darkness, I was flowing, flowing…

Then the chuckling laughter woke me, shook me into sanity. I open my eyes, shocked to realize they been closed. Dagttr was laughing me. He snapped up the lights and he was laughing. Dagur was laughing.

No—*I* was laughing!

But how could I be? I was sitting here, and the laughter came from my *face* across the room.

Then I knew. Dagur had tricked me. Like he tricked the old women. He'd put me into a receptive state, subtly hypnotized me—and changed bodies. Changed bodies. The body he stole from the *tchen-lam* he now gave to me, and stole my own.

Dagur laughed. I could only tremble as he mocked.

"I know your mind, my friend. I know what you were planning for me. But I beat you to the draw, as you would say. The money is all in your name—well it is in *my* name now. I am you. It was written from the first that this must happen, and you didn't know, of course."

I stood up. Or my body did. The *tchen-lam's* body. I couldn't think, or hear, or feel. I staggered to a mirror. I stared down at the lean, emaciated form. I stared into the hateful yellow face I feared and dreaded—the face that was now my own for all time.

I began to laugh, uncontrollably. Within a week, staring at the face, I should go completely mad. Was this the *tchen-lam's* vengeance?

"I shall leave you now," Dagur was saying. "Of course, there is nothing you can do. I am glad of your assistance. I thank you for the money, and for ridding me of a body I was beginning to dislike for certain obvious reasons. The Tibetans are so filthy, you know?"

What did he mean?

"Yes." Dagur was opening the door. "It is all in the stars, my friend. In giving you the body I am unwittingly carrying out the curse of the *tchen-lam*, I suppose. He is dead, but remember what he said about making you suffer by his own hands? It seemed impossible for him to fulfill that threat, but I fancy he has. Yes, you are going to suffer at his hands."

Dagur left. I was standing in the twilight, brain reeling. It was too sudden, too mad; the climax of a nightmare.

But the real climax was yet to come. "You will suffer at his hands," Dagur said. Filthy Tibetans? Glad to get rid of the *tchen-lam's* body? How could that body harm me when I was in it?

Then I glanced down at the strange yellow claws that were now my own and I understood everything, quite completely and quite horribly. I was going to suffer at the *tchen-lam*'s hands, truly so. For I stared at those hands, and knew the truth, knew the dead man's vengeance.

I was in the body of the *tchen-lam*. And the *tchen-lam* had leprosy!

Fairy Tale

"There is fairies in the bottom of my garden," said the guy.

"The hell you say!" yelled Tim Booker

"No. I don't say 'the hell.' I alla time say there is fairies in the bottom of my garden."

Tim Booker blew up completely and almost dropped the telephone from his hand.

This was the last straw. For five years Booker had been sitting at the phone in his rental agency office, listening to insults from tenants. That was his job at the agency—to take insults, note them down, and refer them to the boss. His not to reason why, his but to listen and lie.

During these five years, Tim Booker prided himself that he had heard everything. He knew the story of leaky plumbing by heart. The tales of noisy radiators, no heat, dripping faucets and loud neighbors were old stuff to Mr. Booker. He could handle anything from a squawk about the rent ceiling to a plea for redecorating a bathroom.

But now his nerves gave way. When the loud voice over the telephone said, "There is fairies in the bottom of my garden," Tim Booker just couldn't stand it any longer.

He lost his temper. Somebody was kidding him. Fairies in the bottom of his garden, were there?

"What am I supposed to do about it?" snarled Mr. Booker. "Do you want me to come down and wave a magic wand at them? You're drunk—get off the wire!"

"I'm not drunk," insisted the soft voice at the other end. "I'm Tom Rowland of 711 Honeysuckle Drive. And if you don't come out here right away, I'm gonna tell the Rent Control Board on you."

Tim Booker felt an icy chill take liberties with his spine.

"No," he gasped. "Not that—anything but *that!* I'll be right out, Mr. Rowland."

He hung up, trembling. His natural subservience returned. Through long habit he was once again a servant of the rental agency, and like a good servant he cringed at the very mention of the Rent Control Board.

Even fairy-befuddled drunks were easier to handle. Tim Booker sighed, reached for his hat, and left the office. Shuddering at the vibrating needle on his gas gauge, Mr. Booker swung his car out into the traffic and guided its squeaky chassis towards 711 Honeysuckle Drive and Mr. Thomas Lowland.

711 Honeysuckle Drive proved to be a most imposing mansion set back on a wide, tree-bordered lawn. Spacious grounds stretched out in back, and Thomas Rowland stretched out on the spacious grounds.

At least, he guessed it was Mr. Rowland who lay on the back lawn with a bottle resting against his chin.

As Tim Booker turned in the drive, the recumbent gentleman rolled out of the way and waved his bottle in greeting.

"Welcome to Honeysuckle Drive," he called, wobbling to his feet unsteadily. "Have a drink. Place's yours. All yours! You're my pal, real lifesaver!" He halted and assumed a look of grim belligerency. "Say, who the hell are you?" he sneered.

Tim Booker climbed out of the car. "I'm the man from the agency. I've come to see about those fairies in the bottom of your garden."

Mr. Rowland's sneer deepened.

"Who told you?" he demanded truculently. "Who alla time told you?"

"Why, you did!"

"Oh!" The smile returned to Rowland's flushed face. "Then you're alla time my pal. I remember, now."

Tim Booker sighed. He *had* been right. Little Mr. Rowland was very drunk indeed. And this affair was just another wild goose chase.

* * *

Mr. Rowland floundered around exactly like a wild goose as he led Tim Booker down the path towards the garden back of the house.

There really was a garden—a large and pretty area with trellises and a swing, and a pebbled pathway leading to a rock garden at the rear of the place. Flowers bloomed in luxuriant profusion. Tim Booker noted one incongruity. The grass needed cutting badly.

"Don't you mow your lawn?" he asked. Mr. Rowland swung around and blinked blearily.

"O'Driscoll mowed it. He was alla time mowing it."

"O'Driscoll? Who's O'Driscoll?"

"Emmett O'Driscoll. He was my gardener. He got drafted last month. Now I alla time got nobody to mow my lawn."

"Too bad."

"He brought the fairies with him, see? They alla time come with his family, he said. And now he's drafted. They took him away and left me with the fairies all alone. Alla time alone."

Mr. Rowland sobbed a little.

"I wish to Gawd the army would alla time draft them, too. What's happening to me shouldn't happen to Hitler!"

He tapped Tim Booker on the chest with a trembling finger.

"You ever see snakes?" he demanded. "Pink elephants?"

"No," Booker admitted.

"Well I have, brother. I alla time see such things. They aren't pretty. But I'd a damned sight well rather see a zoo-full of them than these fairies. Fairies! Gawd—alla time fairies!"

Abruptly he recovered himself and sighed. "You wanna know why I'm drunk?" he asked, sorrowfully. "You wanna know why I'm alla time drunk?"

Mr. Booker didn't want to know, but he couldn't help it, so he nodded weakly.

"All right, if you gotta be nosey," said Rowland, triumphantly. "I'll tell you why I'm alla time drunk. On account of I'm alla time drinking, see?"

This startling explanation would have held Tim Booker for a while, but Mr. Rowland insisted on continuing.

"And why am I alla time drinking? Because I alla time see those blasted fairies. That's why I drink! Jeez, I wish I was drunk now!" exclaimed Mr. Rowland, falling down.

Tim Booker, wondering how he would end this maudlin session and get out of the place, helped little Mr. Rowland to his feet.

"Why don't you go inside and lie down for a while?" he suggested.

"Because I alla time want to show you these fairies first," Rowland mutttered. "Then we'll both go inside and lie down."

"Very well," said Tim Booker. "Where are these fairies?"

Mr. Rowland reeled down the pebbled pathway towards the rock garden. He paused before a cluster of rocks, his red-rimmed eyes revolving woozily as he scanned the underbrush.

"Here," he exclaimed. "Here are the little stinkers now!"

Smiling superciliously, Tim Booker joined Mr. Rowland and peered down at the shrubbery.

"I don't see any—" he began.

"Holy jumping smokes!" be yelled, leaping backwards across the path. "What are those?"

"Fairies," chanted Mr. Rowland patiently. "Alla time fairies!"

Fairies, they were.

* * *

Tim Booker stared down at a cluster of tiny faces, rising impudently from the bushes at his feet. Marvelously, incredibly tiny faces unmistakably human in features barely six inches from the ground!

Bright, beady eyes twinkled from shrewd, wrinkled countenances. Tim Booker caught a glimpse of ragged garments clothing arms and legs thin as pretzel sticks. For one unbelievable moment he saw the pattern of a minute hand, no bigger than a single cornflake, as it rested against a leaf.

There was a shrill tinkle of high-pitched laughter, a sudden scurry, and the figures and faces disappeared.

The fairies were no longer "alla time." They were gone.

Tim Booker blinked.

"I—I can't believe it," he whispered.

"Why don't you alla time write to Ripley?" suggested Mr. Rowland, taking a hasty swig from his almost empty bottle. "Me, I'm getting out of here."

"What?"

"I'm leaving," said Mr. Rowland, wobbling back up the path. "I'm alla time through with fairies."

"But that means breaking your lease," gasped Tim Booker.

"I don't care if my lease smashes to bits," replied Rowland.

"You can't do such a thing!" Tim Booker shouted, horrified by such blasphemy against all landlords.

Fairy Tale

"All right, so we'll alla time take it to court. Or the Rent Control Board. You want I should tell those guys about how you have alla time fairies in your garden?"

"No," whispered Booker. "No, we don't want that."

Triumphantly, Mr. Rowland rounded the corner of the house on one leg and disappeared.

Tim Booker climbed wearily into his car and fumbled with keys and clutch.

Suddenly, from the depths of the garden, he heard the sound of shrill, mocking laughter.

He zoomed down the drive in high, but the laughter followed him to the street, and clung to him that night in dreams.

* * *

Tim Booker would gladly have forgotten about the fairies at 711 Honeysuckle Drive, but Desmond Goudger wouldn't let him.

Desmond Goudger was Tim Booker's Boss—with a capital "B." He was the kind of an employer who will always be thought of with a capital "B"—even though the "B" doesn't necessarily stand for "Boss."

It was his Boss who started all the trouble.

"What's this about 711 Honeysuckle Drive?" he demanded harshly, pausing at Tim Booker's desk the next morning. "You let a tenant go without holding him to the lease?"

"He was drafted," Booker lied, nervously watching the telephone tremble in its cradle as the Boss's voice boomed.

"Well, hurry up and rent that dump," ordered Desmond Goudger. "With the housing shortage, you ought to have a client ready to move in tomorrow."

But Tim Booker didn't have a client the next day, nor the next. He hoped to heaven he never would. Explaining those fairies would cost him his job.

On the third day, the Boss stalked out of his office and chewed his cigar against Tim Booker's ear.

"What's the matter with you, Booker?" he growled. "Haven't you got a sucker for that 711 property yet?"

"I don't think so—you see, that is—"

"Listen, Booker," grunted Desmond Goudger. "I'm going to give you a piece of my mind."

"I don't see how you can spare it," Tim Booker *almost* said. What he really did was cringe and listen. For five minutes, the Boss distributed a portion of his mentality gratis. His conclusion was masterly, but Tim Booker didn't appreciate it.

"You'll damned well have that joint rented by tomorrow," he snapped, "or else."

With a final bite on his frayed cigar, Desmond Goudger strode off.

Tim Booker sat at his desk for a long moment. Twice his hand went out towards the volume of rental applicants. It would be so easy to pick a name from the list and call. He didn't try.

It was no use. He couldn't.

Suddenly Tim Booker straightened up. Resolution kindled, flamed in his eyes.

He got up, grabbed his hat, left the office, climbed into his car, and drove to 711 Honeysuckle Drive. In the grip of his determination, all these actions seemed part of a single resolute gesture.

It was not until he was actually walking down the pebbled pathway of that deserted back yard that Tim Booker realized what he was actually going to do.

He, Tim Booker, fully (if sloppily) dressed and in his right (if slightly vacillating) mind—he, Tim Booker, was actually going to talk to the fairies!

Booker glanced nervously over his shoulder. There was nobody around. The garden gleamed in the afternoon sunlight. It looked peaceful, placid. The long, uncut grass at his feet rustled in a gentle breeze.

Everything was the way it should be. Normal. There were no fairies. It was all a mistake. There were no—

"Ouch! It's stepping on me yez are, gossoon!"

* * *

Tim Booker jumped like a kangaroo.

Peering up from between his turned-in toes was an incredible little figure. He drew his shoes back in dismay. The tiny mannikin stared up at him, squinting as though trying to focus his vision on something far distant.

"Och, and it's you again," said the mannikin, petulantly.

"Why not?" Tim Booker recovered a little of his composure. After all, there was nothing to fear from a creature six inches tall. He bent down, crouching on his knees, and scrutinized the tiny being before him.

The fairy was certainly no more than six inches in height, and yet there was nothing dwarfed or misshapen about his perfectly proportioned little body. Tiny, tight brown ringlets covered a head the size of an apricot. A face scarcely bigger than the circumference of a walnut regarded Tim Booker gravely, as Booker gazed in fascination at the truly pipe-stem limbs, covered with minute pinpoint freckles. The fairy, save for a sort of apron around the waist, was naked.

Booker didn't know why the fairy's woolen apron attracted his attention, but there was something familiar about it.

"And what may yez be starin' at with yer saucer eyes?" demanded the fairy, in a shrill, exasperated tone. "If it's the breach I'm after wearin' to cover me nakedness, why then 'tis but an ould sock of Emmett Driscoll's. He knitted it for me, fine gentleman that he was. Sure, and as for the hole in the toe, it's sewed up it is entirely, so the wind doesn't whistle up the small of me back."

Tim Booker remembered the story of the drafted gardener who had been responsible for the presence of the fairies. He began to formulate an argument.

"O'Driscoll was a pretty nice guy, I hear," he observed.

The mannikin nodded. "Sure and he was that. 'Twas O'Driscoll who built us the rock garden. Kind he was, and understandin' of the needs of the wee folk. He chased the accursed dogs and cats away. He was forever seein' to it that we got the dew fresh from the lawn.

"Many's the bit of clothing he's fashioned for us, to ward off the damp. As for Rowland, and may a blight rest forever on his name, he never bothered his head about the garden when Emmett O'Driscoll was here.

"Yes, O'Driscoll served us well—and why shouldn't he, I'm askin'? Have not the wee folk served the O'Driscolls for generations past on the Ould Sod? Sure and I can be after rememberin' Rory O'Driscoll, his grandsire, and a fine strappin' bucko—"

Tim Booker cut through this flood of stage-Irish brogue and planted his planned suggestion.

"There's just one thing I don't understand," he said, naively. "Why did you folk desert O'Driscoll? Why didn't you go with him when he was drafted?"

* * *

The fairy laughed, making a sound like a Crackerjack prize whistle.

"Sure, and what would we be doin' in the military, I'm askin'? We'd be forever racin' about at the blast of a bugle … sleepin' on a parade ground where there's no dew, and a great lumberin' tank forever about to roll over yez! No, we stay here until O'Driscoll is back from the wars."

Booker took this statement impatiently. Then he hit on another argument.

"But isn't it bad for you to be here all alone? Who'll make your clothes now? What about this Rowland fellow?"

"Och!" The fairy looked doleful for a moment. "Rowland alone is a different matter entirely, that he is! After O'Driscoll left, he took to comin' out into the garden to sleep off his rampages. He trampled down the flowers and murthered them."

"So maybe you'd better leave," Booker suggested.

"Why? It's gone he is now entirely, thanks to yez," chirped the fairy, making a little bow. "We're free to stay here and wait for O'Driscoll to polish off the haythens and come back to us. It's the run of the place we have here now."

"But that's just it," said Tim Booker, in exasperation.

The fairy paid no attention to him whatsoever. He had turned, and was now beckoning in the direction of the shrubbery.

"Come out," he called. "Come out and meet the fine, grand gentleman to whom we are bespoken for his kindness."

With florid gesticulations, he ushered forth five more tiny figures. Bowing and curtseying, the fairies presented their grinning faces to Tim Booker.

"I'm Nubbin," said the first fairy, before introducing his companions. "And this, sir, is Sib."

Sib was quite elderly for a fairy, in Tim Booker's opinion—a little wizened, monkey-like figure with white hair and a wrinkled face the size and texture of a prune.

"And Slip."

Slip, by virtue of a ragged handkerchief cut like a dress, proved to be a lady. Her age was evidently equal to Sib's, and she greeted Tim Booker in a piping squeak. "Sure, it's a plasure to meet up with yer worship, that it is."

Nubbin introduced the others.

"Here's Gandy, sir."

Gandy was a snub-nosed youngster with an impudent smirk. Booker, gazing at him, was reminded of a miniature Mickey Rooney.

"How's tricks?" asked Gandy, in a surprisingly blase voice with but a trace of brogue.

"Yeah. What's buzzin', cousin?" drawled a new voice—if you can imagine a flute drawling.

Tim Booker stared down at a saucy, pert, girlish face. The female fairy had red hair. With a shock, be realized that the obliging Emmett O'Driscoll had give her a pair of improvised slacks to wear.

"This is Dunnie," said Nubbin. "And a wild colleen she is."

The five fairies crowded about Booker's knees, gazing at his face and limbs with open curiosity and whispering behind their petal-like hands.

"You're after fergettin' me," squealed a small voice from the bushes. A sixth fairy emerged.

"Oh, Thomakin!"Nubbin exclaimed. "I did forget, truly."

"It's a noble pleasure to be beholdin' yer august and illustrious countenance, that is a fact," said fat little Thomakin. He bustled forward, wearing his bandana handkerchief toga with pompous dignity. He halted at Booker's side and lifted a hand.

* * *

Tim Booker, with equal gravity, made an attempt to shake hands. He could scarcely feel the tiny paw lost in the immensity of his own great palm.

"We're that grateful to you," said Thomakin, "for providin' us with this great, grand house."

Booker bit his lip.

"I'm glad to hear that." He hesitated, then plunged on. "But that's just what I've come out here to tell you, folks. You can't have this great, grand house."

"What?"

"I'd like you to have it, sure. If it were mine, I'd give it to you. But it isn't mine, don't you see? It's owned by my boss, Desmond Goudger. And I'm going to have to rent it to a new tenant right away. He sent me out here to tell you to vacate the premises."

"Vacate the premises?"

"Get off the property?"

"Leave?"

Tim Booker nodded.

Dunnie faced him, tossing her carrot-curls. "And what if we don't choose to leave?" she asked, mockingly. "What then?"

"Then we'll sue you," said Booker, weakly. He realized how meaningless the threat was as soon as he uttered it.

"Very well," said Gandy, suddenly impudence itself. "Sue and be damned to yez, says I."

"We'll not get off, and that's final," added Dunnie.

It was then that desperate Tim Booker made an unforeseen decision.

He rose to his feet and scowled.

"So you won't get off?" be muttered. "All right, to hell with you! I'll move into this place myself!"

* * *

Three days later, Tim Booker and his wife, Mildred, moved into the house at 711 Honeysuckle Drive.

Tim had no trouble with Mildred when she heard the news. A single mention of that exclusive suburban address more than persuaded her the house must be ideal. Her flying visit was unnecessary—she had scarcely bothered to look at the place. 'Tim didn't show her the garden and she didn't bother to look for herself. Mildred was too busy making the kind of squeals women always make when confronted with something expensive.

"Oh, it's wonderful, Timmie dear," she gurgled.

Tim Booker didn't even frown at his nickname when it fell from her lips. He was too happy about the whole thing.

Now Desmond Goudger wouldn't be on his neck about renting the place. Mildred wouldn't be nagging at him because she wanted to get a better address and crash society.

Whatever the financial sacrifice, Tim Booker wanted to keep his boss and his wife happy. Only when they were happy were they quiet. Tim Booker needed quiet after his experiences.

He only hoped to heaven, that Mildred wouldn't find out about the fairies in the garden.

Fairy Tale

During the first three days she was completely engrossed in unpacking household belongings and putting them in the wrong places. On the fourth day she rearranged everything, and on the fifth she switched the rearranged furniture around again. Tim Booker buried himself in work at the rental agency and waited.

It wasn't until the weekend that Mildred got out into the back yard at all. Tim Booker reluctantly guided her down the path, keeping a wary eye peeled for sudden movements in the long grass.

Nothing happened. The fairies had discreetly retreated to their rock-garden grottoes.

Emboldened, Booker steered Mildred over to the rock garden itself arid beamed as his wife gasped in the sort of ecstasy women can summon up at will.

"How perfectly wonderful, Timmie!" she cooed. "A rock garden! The whole place is charming. We must buy some of those deck chairs and lawn umbrellas at once!"

"Timmie" groaned, but inwardly.

"And you must mow the lawn right away," said Mildred, cocking her head and critically surveying the tall grass. "Then we'll be all set."

"All set for what?"

"It's a surprise," said Mildred, happily. "Now why don't you just run in and get the lawn mower and start cutting the grass right now?"

Tim Booker, who had at least eight good reasons why he didn't want to mow the lawn this particular afternoon, obediently went in and got the lawn mower and started cutting the grass.

Mildred watched him for quite a while. She hummed gaily. Tim sweated and looked for the fairies. Not a one emerged. They were probably hiding from his wife—and in a way, he envied them.

For a brief moment he held a wild hope that perhaps the wee folk had vanished, after all.

That hope was dispelled the following morning, replaced by gloom.

* * *

Tim Booker, coming out to the back doorstep for the Sunday paper and the cream, found that his milk had curdled.

He said nothing. Later that morning he ran down to the shopping district and bought fresh milk.

But on Monday morning, Mildred secured the milk and opened the bottle at breakfast.

"Timmie, this milk is sour!" she announced.

"Mummph—is it?" Tim Booker played dumb.

"I'll speak to the milkman about it," Mildred announced.

Tim Booker had other ideas. That morning he tiptoed down the path and halted beside the rock garden.

"Hey, there!" he hissed, in a loud stage-whisper. "Hey, you guys!"

Fat little Thomakin peered around a rock.

"Good morning to yez," he said. "And what can we be after doin' for yer honor this morning?"

"You can damned well be after not tampering with my milk," said Tim Booker, tactlessly.

Thomakin frowned.

"Oh, and it's the curdled milk that's bothering yez?" he commented.

"You did do it, didn't you?" Tim Booker accused.

"Of course we did that," answered Thomakin. "And beggin' your pardon, sir, we'll be after doin' it again unless yez heed the warnin'."

"What warning?"

"Don't use the lawn-mower," said the fairy.

"Don't use the lawn-mower?" Tim Booker echoed.

"Absolutely not! The wee folk do detest the livin' presence of iron."

"Oh." Snatches of ancient legend returned to Booker. "You don't like iron, do you? I suppose that's the real reason you wouldn't hang around an army camp."

"Correct yez are entirely," said Thomakin. He studied Tim Booker's face, hanging high above him, and a shrewd gleam came into the fairy's pinpoint eyes.

"Sure, and it's readin' your mind I am,'" accused Thomakin. "And you'd best be droppin' such daft notions. If yez think to clear us out of here with iron, then badly mistaken yez are. For we'll curdle your milk and sour your preserves and plague yez in a hundred ways."

"No lawn-mower?" sighed Tim Booker. "I must let the grass run wild?"

"Precisely," answered the fairy.

Booker shrugged and walked back up the path. He didn't say anything to Mildred and hoped she wouldn't bring the subject up.

Fairy Tale

That evening, when he came home from the office, Mildred met him at the door.

"Timmie, dear," she chortled. "It's been *such* a hot day! I do wish you'd sprinkle the lawn before you came into the house."

Tim Booker didn't need any bulletins on the weather. He had spent a sweltering day at work, and what he wanted most right now was a good cold shower for himself.

Instead, he obediently trotted out to sprinkle the lawn. He dragged the hose up from the basement, connected it, and stalked out into the back yard.

Muttering grimly under his breath, he angrily yanked the nozzle of the hose and let the spray fly. He turned the water up full force and spattered the walk, the grass, and then the pebbled pathway.

Just when the hose hit the rock-garden, Tim Booker didn't know.

A startled squeal brought the matter to his attention.

"Oouueee!" piped the voice.

Tim Booker glanced down just in time to see Nubbin run across the pathway, vainly trying to dodge the stream from the hose.

"Turn it off, man!" yelled Nubbin. "It's drenchin' me, yez are!"

For the first time that day, Tim Booker's spirits soared. Deliberately, he played the hose on the spluttering Nubbin. The little fairy was literally swept off his feet by the force of the water.

"So you won't clear out?" grinned Booker. "Well, then, stay here and take it."

Relentlessly, the hose pursued the fleeing Nubbin, hunted him out between the rocks. Tim Booker lost all sense of dignity and decency. He'd show these fairies! It was bad enough to have a wife and a boss to order him around, but when supernatural midges, six inches tall, tried to do the trick—

"What the—?"

Booker glanced down. The water had suddenly ceased to flow from the hose. A few drops dribbled weakly towards the soggy ground.

He turned quickly, and beheld a horrid sight.

Far up the pathway, five tiny forms crouched over the length of rubber hose.

He recognized the five other fairies. They were bending down to the hose, pressing their faces to it, and—

"By heaven!" yelled Tim Booker, *"you've bitten my hose in two!"*

He charged towards the wee folk furiously. They scampered off with derisive hoots and made for the tall grass along the fence.

"Don't you know there's a rubber shortage?" Booker screamed.

As they reached protection, the rearmost figure turned. It was Gandy. Incredulously, Tim Booker halted and stared as Gandy paused and deliberately thumbed his nose at him.

* * *

It was a declaration of war. Tim Booker found that out when he returned home again the following evening.

An angry Mildred met him at the door.

"Somebody's been breaking in and stealing my preserves!" she chattered. "Some vandals are loose in the neighborhood, Timmie. Five jars of my best cranberries are gone. I want you to call the police, immediately."

Tim Booker winced.

"Now wait a minute" he temporized hastily.

"And another thing," Mildred shrilled. "Come here a minute. I want you to take a look at this!"

She marched Booker down the pathway into the back yard.

"Look at these flower beds," she exclaimed. "All trampled down. I tell you, some hooligans have been at work here."

Booker nodded. He knew exactly what she meant, even if she didn't. The war had started.

"You don't seem very upset," Mildred declared. "One would think you would be, after the rascals had nerve enough to write about you."

"Write about me?"

"Look there."

Booker followed his wife's frantic finger as it pointed off in the direction of the board fence. His eyes goggled with disbelief.

There were legends on the fence—legends scrawled in chalk, written in wavering letters close to the ground. Tim Booker read the legends and reddened.

"TIM BOOKER IS A LYING SCOUNDREL"
"BOOKER BEATS HIS WIFE"
"A FOUL MURRAIN ON TIM BOOKER AND ALL HIS ILK"
"THE BACK OF ME HAND TO BOOKER"

Fairy Tale

"BOOKER HAS HOLES IN HIS SOCKS AND WE CAN SEE THEM"
"BOOKER HAS FLAT FEET"

"What in blazes!" Tim Booker inquired, dancing up and down in the intensity of his emotion. "I haven't got flat feet or holes in my socks! Why it's—"

Mildred giggled.

"I think they're kind of funny," she admitted. "I don't see why you have to fly into a rage over a little thing like that when some thieves have been stealing my preserves and doing something really dreadful."

Booker stared at her, open-mouthed.

"Just get a rag and wipe off those chalk-marks," she commanded. "We don't want them up there tomorrow afternoon."

"Why not?"

"Because of the garden party, stupid."

"Garden party?" groaned Booker.

"Of course. I had meant it as a surprise, but yon might as well know now. I've ordered some nice lawn chairs and tables—those lovely metal ones—and some beach umbrellas and games and everything. And there'll be special entertainment and oodles and gobs of people and—"

"Garden party," said Booker, dully.

"And guess what, Timmie? Oh, I'm so excited! I've even persuaded Mr. and Mrs. Goudger to come. And some of their fine society friends! This is our big chance, Timmie. They've already accepted the invitations, and seeing tomorrow is Saturday we'll start out at noon. It's' so wonderful!"

"Garden party," whispered Tim Booker. "That's all I needed!"

"I'm going in now and phone the society editor," gushed Mildred, happily.

She skipped up the pathway.

* * *

Booker stood there with his hands in his pockets. With a hollow groan, he edged over to the rock garden and bent down to whisper.

"Come on out," he pleaded to the empty air. "I want to talk to you."

There was no response.

"You must listen to me," he begged. "Please—please—whatever you do, behave yourselves tomorrow afternoon! I've got to hold this

201

garden party here in the back yard. For heaven's sake, don't start anything!"

No reply came from the empty twilight.

"I'll do anything you want if you'll help me out," Booker panted. "Anything at all. I'll never mow the lawn or sprinkle the grass again. I'll even sell my car so the exhaust fumes won't bother you. I'll—I'll build you a swimming pool, that's what I'll do! Anything, just so you keep out of the way while my guests are here. Please, please cooperate!"

Silence greeted his implorations in the dusk.

It was only as he started back up the path that Tim Booker heard, faintly borne on the twilight air, the faint, mysterious sound of an elfin razzberry.

* * *

The garden party was in full swing. Tables and chairs were set all over the lawn, and colorful, striped awnings had been hoisted, with much painful grunting, by Tim Booker early that morning.

It had taken him until noon to get everything in place, and served as an excuse for not cutting the long grass—though Mildred had given him a good tongue-lashing about that little matter.

Now, sweating freely in his new gabardine sports suit, Tim Booker wandered around and watched Dinah mix drinks at a table set up near the rock-garden. Dinah was very large, very black, and very busy. Mildred had hired her for this affair, and she plunged into her duties with gusto—particularly when it came to mixing drinks with gin in them.

Booker was in the very act of snatching a glass for himself when Mildred came up and yanked him by the arm.

"Come on, Timmie," she commanded gaily, pushing his drink away. "I want you to meet some of the guests."

Under her breath she muttered, "Quit mooching drinks, and for heaven's sake, smile! "

So Tim Booker smiled, as Mildred dragged him around by the elbow and introduced him to his new and aristocratic neighbors—a prime bunch of stinkers, if you asked him.

But nobody asked him.

"Oooh!" squeaked Mildred a moment later. "The Goudgers are arriving!"

Sure enough, Desmond Goudger and his wife, Mimi—a fat, gushing woman, with dyed hair—were waddling down the pebbled pathway.

Mr. Goudger came with the inevitable half-chewed cigar working between his lips, and Mrs. Goudger—to Tim Booker's horror—came with her poodle.

It was a horrid little beast, that poodle; round and fat, with frizzy fur that bore signs of artificial curling. Tim Booker was certain Mrs. Goudger had used her own curling iron on its hair.

Introductions were effected, and Mrs. Goudger, simpering, included her poodle. "And this is Fluffy," she said, giggling.

Tim Booker forced a smile. "Hello, Fluffy," he said, bending down to pet the beast.

Fluffy smiled, wrinkled her nose, and promptly nipped at his ankle.

Booker jumped a foot backwards and sat down, rubbing his leg, as Fluffy yapped hysterically from between Mrs. Goudger's fat calves.

"Playful, isn't she?" grated Tim Booker, with a ghastly leer. He wondered if you could stuff dog-biscuits with dynamite.

Mildred took charge of the situation.

"Get up and stop clowning, Timmie dear," she cooed. "Let's all sit down at a table. Dinah will be here with some drinks directly."

Dinah brought the drinks. Booker could hardly wait to grab his highball. He needed it. While Mr. and Mrs. Goudger sipped, Booker gulped and glanced nervously about the garden. He was looking for the fairies.

They had kept out of sight, so far. Tim Booker hoped to goodness they would continue to do so.

Handling these guests was going to be enough of a problem. Booker saw them sitting at the other tables, drinking and gabbling away. The men, for the most part, seemed a decent sort—confining their activities to drinking. But their wives spent the time criticizing the chairs, the colored awnings, the garden in general, and Mildred's lawn dress.

* * *

"Nice place you have here." Goudger thrust his smouldering cigar in Booker's face.

"Oh—yeah, we like it a lot," Booker answered.

"I don't see how you can afford it on your salary," said Desmond Goudger.

Mildred promptly nudged Booker. She wanted him to ask for a raise—he knew it. Tim Booker gulped and dutifully opened his mouth. But Goudger beat him to it.

"No, I don't see how you manage it," he smiled. "And it's going to be harder after I cut your salary next month as I've planned."

Tim Booker gulped again.

"Thought I'd let you know," chuckled Goudger. "We've got to pare down expenses—it's wartime, you understand."

"But, Mr. Goudger—"

"Eeeeeek!"

Mimi Goudger made the sound, and a face.

"What is it, darling?" snapped Desmond Goudger.

"Oh—nothing." Mrs. Goudger subsided, squirming uncomfortably.

"About that salary proposition—" said Tim Booker.

"Eeeeyow!"

This time Mimi Goudger rose completely from her chair. Her face crimson, she turned to Booker.

"You pinched me!" she accused.

"I—what?" gasped Tim Booker.

"You deliberately pinched me," said Mrs. Goudger. "At first I thought you were only trying to be playful, but this is too much."

"But you must be mistaken," spluttered Booker. "I haven't let my hands leave my lap."

Mildred and Mr. Goudger glared at him. The unhappy Booker cast an imploring glance at his accuser.

"Where did you get pinched?" he inquired.

"What a question to ask a lady!" cried Mrs. Goudger. "But if you must know, it was between the second and third rung of my seat."

Tim Booker cast a quick glance underneath the lady's chair—just in time to see the tiny figure of Nubbin disappear in the rustling grass.

The fairies were at work again!

With a muttered, "Pardon me—explain it all later," Tim Booker rose and fled.

It was useless to try and pursue the malicious sprite. He was going for a drink.

At the liquor table, Dinah confronted him with a bewildered flutter of her ham-like hands.

"Lawsy, Mistah Bookah," she said. "You-all is got some mighty peeculyah guestses! Somebody done stole a whole quaht of Irish whiskey from this heah table."

"Oh gosh!" said Tim Booker, snatching the nearest bottle and draining a great gulp of the fiery liquor.

* * *

With tears in his eyes, he turned to face a strange spectacle. A brawny man in a leopard-skin and a thin, earnest-looking blonde girl in a bedsheet stood at a corner of the lawn.

Mildred was talking to them as Booker stumbled over.

"What kind of a freak show is this?" he demanded.

Mildred flashed him a scornful glance. "Lady-pincher!" she sneered.

"Never mind that—who are these people?" .

"Haven't you ever heard of Valour and Chrystis, the celebrated Grecian dancers?" she asked him.

"Is that some kind of a trick question?" Booker shot back. "I assume you are trying to tell me that these two are Valour and Chrystis, the celebrated whatever-they-are. What I want to know is—what are they doing on our lawn?"

"They're going to dance, stupid!" said Mildred. "Greeks always danced on the lawn."

"Not on my lawn they didn't."

"But this is my biggest surprise, Timmie. Mimi Goudger is just crazy about artistic things. She's a patron of the dance."

Tim Booker eyed the muscular man, and his lanky feminine partner with illy-concealed distaste.

"Mean they're going to clodhop around barefoot?"

A blast from the portable phonograph on the back porch settled the question. Dinah had put on a record, and now Mildred stepped to the center of the lawn, clapping her hands. Hastily she introduced the two celebrated devotees of Terpsichore, and the leopard-skinned giant and his agile partner scampered to the center of the greensward.

Helplessly shrugging his shoulders, Tim Booker floundered back to the table and joined the Goudgers.

They were staring at the dance team as they cavorted in a semi-adagio over the lawn.

Absent-mindedly, Desmond Goudger's hand fumbled for his drink and the cigar he had placed on the edge of the table.

Then he poked Tim Booker.

"Did you steal my drink, Booker?" he demanded, in a thunderous whisper.

"Of course not," Booker replied. "I've one of my own here."

But when he looked, his own drink was gone.

"But I did have," he protested. "Just a—"

"Quiet!" snapped Mildred, digging him in the ribs.

Booker cast a quick glance at the grass beyond his feet. Sure enough, bobbing across the lawn, apparently moving of its own volition, was a whiskey-glass. Following it came a tall highball glass. Bringing up the rear like a miniature torch, was Goudger's smudging cigar.

"Those damned fairies," muttered Tim Booker. "They stole the whiskey—they're drunk, that's what they are! Drunk!"

"Who's drunk?" yelled Desmond Goudger. "I tell you you stole my glass and you accuse me of being drunk. Listen here, Booker—"

Booker didn't listen. He stared in rapt horror at the dancers on the lawn.

Something was going wrong with their routine. Something was going very much wrong. The two dancers were giggling and lifting their feet in awkward haste.

Grass rippled at their feet. Only Booker saw the tiny scurrying figures, hidden by the tall grass-blades, who tickled the bare toes of the pair.

* * *

And as the babble of audience comment rose, only Booker could detect shrill voices, grumbling a few audible words.

"Trampling down the grass … it's fixing them we are…"

The dancers were rapidly being "fixed."

But the fairies had further plans. Tim Booker suddenly was aware of movement under his very feet. Fluffy, the poodle, was jumping around, uttering hysterical yaps.

Tim Booker shot a glance beneath the table, just in time to see Dunnie, her red hair flaming, rise from the grass and stick Fluffy in an exposed flank with Mrs. Goudger's hat-pin.

Then Dunnie disappeared. So did Fluffy.

With a shrill yelp, the poodle charged across the lawn. Goaded by pain and indignation, Fluffy swept forward, yapping and yipping, straight for the dancers.

Leopard-skin had his partner balanced on his back at the very moment that Fluffy bore down on them.

He began to yap a little himself, and ran around through the grass. Then Fluffy caught up with him and it was all over.

The three disappeared in a whirling ball that struck the ground.

It was a sublime spectacle, but nobody even noticed it.

For at that moment, the gay, striped umbrella awning over the table suddenly collapsed and fell down upon Desmond Goudger, his wife, Mildred, and Tim Booker.

Pandemonium, true to tradition, reigned.

Floundering, gasping, choking beneath the canopy, Tim Booker fought his way free. Twice he was bitten by somebody as he was bending over struggling to his feet. He thought at the time that it was probably Mrs. Goudger, but decided not to mention it.

It was bad enough to face her and her irate husband when the awning was finally thrown aside.

Mildred saved the day. Laughing merrily, she smiled at the bewildered assemblage.

"Just a little accident," she giggled. "Wasn't it, Timmie?"

"Timmie" rubbed his shins and choked up a fearful smile.

"Let's all have a drink," Mildred suggested. "Then I've got something else on the program."

For once she had come out with the right suggestion. Booker noted that she was diplomatically putting a double shot of whiskey in each drink she mixed. Within a few minutes the drinks were distributed and peace was restored.

By this time the liquor was actually taking hold of the crowd. The peaceful mood was usurped by a sudden gaiety. Everybody began laughing too loudly or shrilly.

Mildred, pleased at the change, quickly served another round of refreshments.

Booker drank both drinks and sneaked a few more. The warm glow was all he had to fortify him. He kept glancing around, waiting for the next move on the part of his tiny tormentors.

It didn't take a second glance at the nibbled ropes to tell him who was responsible for the fallen awning. He watched the grass, but saw no movements. Maybe they were all so drunk by this time that they'd crawled into the rock-garden to sleep it off. Booker felt like crawling in with them.

He didn't have a chance.

Because at that very moment, Mildred announced, "Now everybody's going to play croquet."

* * *

Sure enough, Dinah was coming down from the porch with an armful of mallets, balls and wire wickets. She set them up from a hastily-scrutinized map in her hand. Meanwhile Mildred laughingly recruited the men to push tables and chairs out of the way.

"Croquet!" muttered Tim Booker, savagely downing another drink. "That does it!"

Everything got blurry, then. The trouble was, it wouldn't stay that way.

Booker was perfectly conscious when his wife grabbed him by one hand, thrust a croquet mallet into the other, and simpered, "We're playing partners, dear. Against the Goudgers."

"On this lawn?" moaned Booker.

"Must we?" He glanced helplessly about as he saw the other couples gathering. The fairies wouldn't like their lawn trampled down—they wouldn't approve of all these wickets and pegs. And they were liable to do something about it.

"Let's have another drink first," Booker suggested, sparring for time.

"You've had enough," Mildred snapped. "Come on. Grab your mallet and let's go to work—or play."

Then everything got mercifully blurry again for Mr. Booker. He saw his wife and the Goudgers doing things with mallets and large wooden balls that rolled through wire wickets.

But he also saw something else.

The grass at the edge of the lawn was moving. Moving and bending! Bobbing above the tops of the blades he saw heads—small heads that wobbled in drunken rage. Over the click of the mallets and the squeals of the guests, Booker's alcohol-attuned ears heard the high, shrill whispering.

"It's abusin' our lawn they are, with their iron wickets."

"Begorra, and we'd best be after takin' matters in hand."

"Dunnie, dear, and did ye bring the whiskey?"

"Whist! We'd be up and at 'em."

Booker knew he was drunk. He tried to imagine that he had hallucinations, and didn't succeed very well. He knew those fairies! Slip and Sib and Gandy and Dunnie, Thomakin and Nubbin were crouching there in the grass—

"Watch this one now!"

Desmond Goudger's great voice boomed in his ears. The red-faced man mangled a cigar between his molars as he stepped up and swung his mallet.

"I used to be a champion at this sort of thing," he asserted. "I played polo for a while, too."

"Who rode you?" squeaked a voice.

"What's that?" yelled Goudger, glaring at Tim Booker.

But Tim Booker hadn't said a word. The voice came from somewhere behind his knees. He wheeled around, but the fairy was gone.

"Huh!" Goudger grasped his mallet and bent down to hit the ball. He jumped as if stung.

"What's the matter, dear?" asked Mrs. Goudger bewilderedly.

Goudger got redder, but said nothing. He shifted his legs and prepared to fake a swing.

"What in perdition?" Goudger straightened up, glowering.

"What is it?" insisted Mimi Goudger.

Goudger looked very embarrassed. "I don't like to say it," he blurted, "but somebody seems to be pulling my socks down on me."

"Don't look at me," said Tim Booker, hastily. "Why should I pull down your socks?"

"To spoil my stroke," Goudger answered.

"I wouldn't spoil your stroke. Go ahead and have it—I hope it's apoplexy."

"What?" roared Goudger.

* * *

Tim Booker wheeled again. He hadn't said anything. The shrill voice came from his side, on the ground.

"Timmie, that isn't funny," whined Mildred, simpering at Desmond Goudger. "Go ahead, Mr. Goudger."

The boss put his foot on the ball for a tight croquet stance. Then he started to swing.

"Oooooh!" gasped his wife. "Something bit my ankle."

"Mosquitoes," said Tim Booker.

"Nuts!" yelled Desmond Goudger. "You've put me off again."

Desperately, he swung. The wooden ball rolled for the wicket. They stood watching it.

"Perfect," said Mildred.

At the last minute something happened. The ball did not swerve through the thick grass—but suddenly the wicket seemed to jump to one side.

Open-mouthed, they saw the ball continue, while the wicket turned on one end and swung away from its path.

"How in the—"

Goudger's question was never finished. From all around them came a series of simultaneous gasps, oaths, and startled cries.

Tim Booker, through blurry eyes, saw that the rest of his guests were having the same odd difficulties. All over the lawn, wickets were moving and turning. Men and women were pulling up their socks and stockings.

To Booker's horror, a fat man suddenly tripped over a wicket and sprawled on the turf. A moment before there had been no wicket in his path.

"What kind of a circus is this?" Goudger exclaimed. "My drinks are stolen, my wife is pinched, awnings fall down, and now your croquet game goes whacky. Damn it all, I'm not licked yet. I don't know how you're managing to cheat me, Booker, but I'll show you."

He swung at the ball madly. His mallet came down with a sharp click. At the last second it swerved chide and hit Goudger's ankle.

"Ouch!" thundered Desmond Goudger.

From behind him, out of nowhere, a new croquet ball came sailing through the air. As Booker watched, it rose and smacked Goudger smartly on the back of the head.

"Ooooof!" Goudger gasped.

Booker stared at Gandy in the grass behind. He had thrown the croquet ball.

He was still staring as Desmond Goudger, bellowing like a bull, charged down on him.

"Curse you, Booker!" yelled the baffled man. "You threw that ball at me."

"I saw him, too!" added Mimi Goudger, glibly.

"Brute!" sobbed Mildred.

* * *

The blur faded from Booker's brain. Suddenly he saw them all as his mortal enemies. He crouched, waiting for Goudger's spring, and gripped the mallet in his hand.

"I hit you, eh?" he shouted. "All right, I'll do it again, too!"

Raising the mallet, he swung it outward.

Desmond Goudger ran right into it, stomach first.

Right then and there the riot started.

Mimi picked up a croquet ball and hit Mildred. Mildred tripped Mimi. A man fell over Mimi's legs and promptly lashed out at his neighbor.

And Tim Booker, yelling like an Irish banshee, charged on the mob, waving his mallet like a shillelagh.

"Out of my garden!" he screeched. "Out of here, all of you! You worthless, lily-livered bunch of croquet-playing fools! I'd rather have a hundred fairies on my hands than an ill-tempered gang of mortals like you!"

Behind him came the high, squeaking battle cry of the wee folk.

A shower of croquet balls rose from the grass to pelt the fleeing guests. Wickets rose out of nowhere to trip their flying feet. Mallets launched themselves miraculously from the grass and thudded into backsides.

And with oaths and imprecations, Tim Booker whirled his weapon and drove them from his garden. They ran for their cars, they ran for their lives—and Mildred and the Goudgers led all the rest.

Only when the last car whirled out of the driveway bearing the final group of frightened guests and Mildred as well, did Tim Booker check his rage.

He stood slumped in the twilight, sick with the realization of what he'd done. He'd lost his reputation, his job, and his wife, all in one fell swoop.

Panic gripped him.

"I've got to get out of here," he muttered. Without a backward glance, he turned and ran towards the house to pack his trunk.

* * *

The panic was gone from Tim Booker's soul when he dumped his grips and trunk on the bed in the YMCA.

There was no frown on Booker's face. Surprisingly enough, he was grinning cheerfully as he sat down on a chair and removed his shoes.

This was the life, after all. For the first time he realized he hadn't lost anything that really mattered. He spoke aloud, sorting his random thoughts.

"Mildred and I were through a long time ago, I guess. I just didn't dare admit it to myself, that's all. Now I'm free, and she can find somebody else to nag.

"And I haven't got an old tyrant like Goudger on my neck, either. I'll find a better job right away."

He opened his suitcases, humming under his breath.

"Guess I owe those fairies a debt of gratitude after all. Good little people, those fairies. Hope they enjoy themselves there with the house to themselves."

He unstrapped his trunk and fumbled for a key.

"Come to think of it," he breathed, "I'm rid of them, too. Not that I don't appreciate what they've done for me. But spending my whole life with that crew of leprechauns would be pretty wearing. I'm glad *that* adventure is over."

He opened his trunk, began to take out his clothing. Then he stepped back, stiffened.

The drawers of the trunk were slowly opening outward. Booker's eyes popped.

From each of the six drawers a tiny face peered up at him with an elfin grin.

"You!" whispered Booker. "Here!"

"That's right," squeaked Nubbin; gaily. "It's here we are, my fine sir! After the fine way you protected us from those guests, did you ever for a minute think we'd be desertin' you? Ah no, me dear man—we've switched allegiance. From now on we're not Emmett O'Driscoll's wee folk any longer—we were after playing stowaway in yer trunk—and now we belong to you."

"You belong to me," said Booker, dully.

"For life!" answered Nubbin.

Fairy Tale

Booker held his head in his hands as he watched the six fairies scamper from the trunk and dance down across his bed.

This was the end. He'd have the fairies on his hands for the rest of his days now. How could he get a fresh start? How could he hope to carry out his plans—get a job in an airplane factory, for example.

An airplane factory!

Suddenly Tim Booker sat up and grinned.

"You're mine for life," he said. "You'll serve me faithfully?"

The six tiny heads nodded.

"Then listen here," said Booker. "I've got some orders."

For ten minutes the wee folk clustered about Tim Booker, climbing across his lap and nodding as he spoke.

Only once was there an interruption.

"But the iron—" said Thomakin.

"It's for your country!" snapped Tim Booker. "Remember that. We're all making sacrifices. And you'll stand contact with iron for such a cause."

They nodded again.

So Tim Booker, smiling happily, went to the telephone and called Washington, long distance. He waited for his connection, got his party, gave his name and address, and stated his business. It was a long conversation, but Booker got to the point.

"That's what I thought, sir," he said. "I'd read you were using midgets to crawl up inside and weld those tiny airplane parts. But I think I've got some workers who will do even better for you."

He glanced happily at the fairies on the bed.

"No, sir," said Tim Booker. "They're not exactly midgets. But you'd better hire them anyway. I can tell you one thing—I'd rather have them fighting for me than against me. And that's no fairy tale."

The Red Swimmer

Luke Treach bowed and smirked in the Spanish sunlight as his distinguished passengers came up the gangplank. His curled and scented hair rippled most elegantly in the Caribbean breeze; a breeze that lifted the dainty ruffles at the wrists and throat of his rich velvet coat.

He made a fine figure of a Spanish gentleman, did English Luke Treach that merry morning, as he stood stroking his spade beard to hide the malicious smile which he had managed to erase from his lean, browned face, but which still persisted about his cruelly thin lips.

Captain Luke Treach bowed then, as the old grandee and his daughter ascended, bowed low a second time when the white-bearded gentleman addressed him as "Captain Obispo." Treach gazed covertly into the aged, aristocratic face of his passenger, then allowed his glance to embrace the figure of the woman. Abruptly he started, jerked erect.

Now Captain Treach had gazed on the fine ladies of old England, yes, and the plump, rosy-cheeked barmaids, too; he had seen the dusky Caribs that danced upon the beach; in Cuba and Barbados and the Antilles there were dark-eyed Spanish girls that lured with sly laughter, and mulatto or mestizo maidens savage in the charm of their delight. Captain Treach had known many women, but there was none to compare with the girl who now stood before him.

Her hair was ebony over ivory forehead, her eyes dark diamonds and lips warm ruby red. These comparisons came naturally to the Captain, for his covetous nature was ever ruling. But never had it ruled him as it did at this moment; he wanted this girl, with her maiden beauty of face and her slim, young, untaught body curved and lissome for delight. Young, dark, smiling—Body of Christ! The captain swore inwardly as his lips shaped their polite greeting.

215

Courteously he welcomed Señor Montelupe and his daughter to the ship. Yes, their cabins were in readiness, and he trusted that they would be comfortable. But certainly, they would cast off at once, and might the Blessed Savior speed them on a prosperous, untroubled voyage to Mother Spain.

Guns and men here? Yes, for there were pirates—cursed scoundrels, these buccaneers; and if they attacked, it was best to be ready—though Gracious God forbid!

* * *

Captain Treach escorted Señor Montelupe and his daughter to their cabins, then returned to watch his bullies bring up the chests and bags his passengers brought with them; chests and bags—silk, satin, gold, jewels.

It made Treach smile. He smiled again as he thought of pirates. This second smile made his wolfish face assume an almost beneficent aspect, for it was the charitable smile of one well pleased with himself. And Captain Luke Treach, now known as Captain Obispo, but more famous as "English Luke," had good reason to respect his cleverness.

First, he had taken the galleon. Few men had been lost, much wealth gained. After efficiently disposing of the crew and their captain, he had hit upon a brilliant idea. Instead of careening off some inlet and waiting until intermediaries reached him to buy and dispose of his loot, he would seek a regular port.

The galleon *Golden Crest* had been bound for Vera Cruz. Very well, he would sail for Vera Cruz, rig himself out in the captain's garb, and dress his men according to Spanish style. He and his mates spoke the tongue well—with a little careful disguise they would pass as Spaniards. On reaching port they could dispose of their cargo, cash in the booty, and sail away again swiftly with no one the wiser. Better still, the appearance of the ship would preclude any fuss such as might be occasioned by its disappearance; there would be no reprisal, no scouring of the seas by Spanish fleets in search of English Luke the buccaneer.

A noble idea, Luke Treach thought at the time. And it had worked. With the common seamen kept on shipboard against any betrayal, he and his lieutenants had entered town. Officials had even been permitted to land on the ship and inspect it. Trade had been accomplished without suspicion, and Luke was ready to sail.

The Red Swimmer

Then Commandante Portiz had asked him to take passengers. At first Luke had demurred, until he had learned that Señor Montelupe and his daughter were returning to Spain with all their wealth. They wanted to leave at once; he had been an official and there was some scandal.

Wealthy? Scandal meant money—it would be brought aboard ship. Luke Treach agreed, and the affair was settled.

Now they were ready to set sail, and more luck had befallen the clever captain. This daughter of Montelupe—she was a new treasure, another prize.

So Treach smiled indulgently when he thought of his cunning and what it had gained for him.

But ever business-like, his musing abruptly ceased and his thoughts turned to the exigencies of the moment. He gave the orders to lift anchor in the clarion voice for which he was justly famous.

A moment later he proved that his English erudition in the matter of cursing, as he loosed a fine volley of oaths at the half-naked seamen straining at the ropes on deck.

Then Captain Treach sauntered below, gentleman-like, pausing merely to kick aside the sailor who chanced to stray across his path carrying a sparpiece. He rapped discreetly on the cabin door, surreptitiously spat out his plug of tobacco and entered the Montelupe quarters.

* * *

The old man greeted him, but Captain Treach had eyes only for the appointments he found therein; for the piles of brocaded and jeweled cloth now removed from their wrappings and stacked against the wall; for the jewel-caskets and the ingots in the rough sea-bags.

And then he stared at Ynez Montelupe, stared with the selfsame avidity. All the while he spoke graciously enough to the old fool, but his gaze burned a blush into the girl's cheeks, and he thought of the night—not tonight, but the next, when they would be past hail or chance of pursuit.

He chatted for perhaps an hour. Yes, he had an excellent voyage out. No, his passage had been free of storm or danger from freebooters, though that cursed Blackbeard was reputed to be in these waters. He fabricated news from Spain, glibly explained the death at sea of the ship's *padre*. He was forced to do most of the talking, for the doltish old man merely stared at him with his liquid, curiously youthful brown eyes. Treach didn't like that stare; it held a faint tinge of contempt or amusement; but then, he would not have to put up with it for long. On this thought he took his departure, after graciously asking their attendance at dinner in his own quarters.

Upstairs the gentlemanly mood left him, and he called for rum and his lieutenant, Roger Groat. Groat shambled into his cabin, mouthing oaths and damnation because the lace frippery at his wrists dangled into his tankard while he was drinking. The red-bearded lieutenant made it known that he was sick of wearing these thrice-damned Spanish spangles, and the men were tired of the masquerade as well. They grumbled because they weren't put ashore to amuse themselves with the proceeds of the plunder.

To this information Captain Treach listened with occasional frowns. Then he told Croat that they would sail on only another day; dispose of the old fool, and head in for the nearest island a few hours off their position at that time.

"Rich, isn't he?" muttered Croat. "Blackie and Tom swore he had bullion in those bags o' his."

He chuckled, then snickered as he brought a hairy paw down on the table at which they sat.

"And the girl's a beauty. A beauty, by God, and there'll be rare sport—"

Captain Treach raised his hand. A slight gesture, but the accompanying frown was enough to quell the big man into silence.

"The girl is mine," he snapped. "Mine alone. The swag we'll divide according to our articles, but the girl is mine.

"You and the others will have your fill of wenching when we put in, but she's mine."

Croat could not restrain a hoarse chuckle.

"I don't envy her, at that. Remember Lucy, on that English ship we took? When you finished with her and Salvatore tried to take her, you flayed the lass. And I warrant this one would prefer the crew's sport to the other end."

Captain Treach smiled. "Tell Salvatore I want wine for dinner. Amontillado. I want my guests to eat, drink and be merry tonight."

They both laughed.

II

They both laughed. This Captain Obispo was certainly a witty man. And tonight he was out-doing himself. Señorita Ynez found her first instinctive dislike fading, though she still felt a tinge of strange panic whenever his beady eyes rested too intently upon her face or bosom.

As for Señor Montelupe, his taciturnity waned under the brandy and the mellow amontillado sherry. His reserve down, he proceeded to let his host guide the conversation into personal channels.

Captain Treach asked him about his duties in Vera Cruz; learned that the old man had held a secretarial post for years and owned several lucrative mines. There had been a scandal of sorts....

Money, the captain presumed. No, not exactly money. The old man's reticence held him silent for a moment, but the wine, the courtesy, the mood urged him on. His bright eyes grew shadowy as he spoke.

There was—was the captain a church-goer?

Something in the shadowed eyes cued Treach to ignore the natural lie and speak truly. No, he was not a son of the Mother Church.

That was well, said Señor Montelupe. For there was a charge against him, a charge of sorcery.

Yes, the Black Arts, as ignorant fools called them—the mantic arts. He had studied with the Moorish masters in Spain as a youth; not wizardry or witchcraft, but the true magics that lie in nature; aeromancy, the controlling of winds; hydromancy, divination and command of waters; pyromancy, the lore of fire. It was science, not sorcery, which he sought to rule, and the ancient Moors held secrets of natural wisdom known to seers before Solomon.

Here in this new world he had availed himself of his governmental position to study certain things; it would be wise for one so old to take heed of the Elixir Vitæ, the Elixir of Life.

And native blood was cheap; slaves and peons died by the dozens in the mines each day, perished by flogging and torture. He had meant no harm; he wanted to kill no one, but merely to study the blood of a few slaves, to experiment with revivification of the dead—that did no harm. And he *had* discovered things—marvelous secrets, gathered from the wisdom of Egyptis, the Orient, the Arab sages. In his hands he would use his knowledge for good, not evil.

But the natives complained, the people whispered, and the *alcalde* told the *padre*, who in turn brought tidings to the Commandante. And so Señor Montelupe had given up his post, taken his daughter—his wife was dead these many years, alas!—and departed for home.

Luke listened, with a polite show of interest. No need to antagonize the old duffer. He and his talk of magic—but then, what could one expect from a bloody Spaniard?—those fools were all alike with their Inquisition, and witch-burning, and alchemy.

Alchemy! The thought crossed his mind even as he nodded in polite assent to the grandee's words. Alchemy—the transmutation of base metals into gold, wasn't it? Perhaps this stupid Southern dog knew something. Best to draw him out.

* * *

Luke drew him out, aided by further drafts of wine. He politely hinted that a man of Señor Montelupe's wisdom must have uncovered secrets in his quest of baleful knowledge.

Señor Montelupe stroked his gray beard as he replied that he had uncovered secrets. His eyes flamed with a bright gleam of fanaticism as he leaned across the great cabin-table.

He, Montelupe, had succeeded in his experiments. Men had sought the Elixir of Life in ancient lands for centuries untold, without avail. Charm, incantation, invocation—all methods had failed. But he had come to a new world, and there his efforts had been crowned with triumph. It was a great discovery; much toil and study had gone into it, and not a little blood. It was not generally known, but his wife had died from an injection of a spurious Elixir he had compounded in earlier studies. Since then the tragic failure had spurred him on, and many slaves had been sacrificed to the attainment of perfection. But he had done it—there was a vial filled with a golden liquid; not the mythical water of poor Ponce de Leon's Fountain of Youth, but the veritable *Elixir Vitæ*. Its compoundment had cost Señor Montelupe many years of his life, but now when he returned to Spain with his wealth, he and his daughter would be insured eternity—eternity in which to study, to seek further wisdom.

Luke Treach frowned and swore damnation to himself. The blasted idiot was mad! No alchemical secrets here, no Philosopher's Stone, or anything real; only this demented gibberish about some crazy scheme of perpetual life. The Spanish dog bored him; for that he would pay on the morrow. And she would pay, too—Ynez, listening with a cryptic smile that implied belief in her father's words, and a covert glimmer in her eyes which proclaimed that she thought the captain an ignorant fool, incapable of understanding the magnitude of her sire's secrets.

Yes, he would pay, and she would pay—though in sweeter coinage.

With that thought hidden in his politely-phrased adieu, Luke Treach strode up on deck for a breath of fresh air; air untainted by this fool's talk of wizardry and enchantment.

He checked the position, oversaw the change of watch at the wheel, and retired to sleep against the morrow's sport.

* * *

Night clouds had scudded before the dawn, and the sun ruled azure southern heavens ere he awoke. The cabin window showed him beauty of sea and sky, but his ears heard sounds most unlovely.

This was the day, and the men were drunk. Groat had evidently broken out the rum.

Cursing, Treach ran up on deck, and found shambles. The *Golden Crest* drifted, unpiloted. Laughing, gleeful men overran the ship, moving about at will or clustering before the broached casks that stood upon the after-deck. The English sea-dogs had abandoned their Spanish costumes in favor of pirate regalia, or utter nakedness.

Treach saw his steward, Salvatore, slopping rum over his maroon coat with the white piping, then wiping his red mouth with the lacy sleeve that had once graced the arm of a Portuguese admiral of war. He saw Roger Groat slapping his naked, tattooed thighs with the flat of a cutlass as he danced about "One-Light" Samuel Slew, whose black eye-patch was the sole incongruous note in the ensemble he wore—the grotesque finery of some silken lady whose denuded body had long since passed to the mercies of the sharks. The rest roared and bellowed forth crude gibes, or shouted toasts over the swilling of their tankards.

Treach paused. The men had broken discipline, but they were in a jovial mood and order could be restored. But what matter? Their drinking could have waited until night, as planned, but a few hours made no difference now. Let them have their sport. And he—now he could go below and seek Ynez.

He went, smiling.

Ynez and her father were staring out of the cabin window, their eyes veiled with perplexity.

"What does this mean, Captain?" asked the old man, as Treach entered. Then his face betrayed that he knew the answer.

For Treach had entered without knocking, and he had entered not as Captain Obispo, but as English Luke—swaggering, his smile a sneer.

"What does this mean?" Ynez echoed, in a faint voice that trailed away beneath the intensity of Treach's stare.

Treach laughed.

"Mean? It means a lot, I fancy. Firstly, that you've made a mistake in taking passage with us. Ye see, we've changed our colors—we're an English crew, not Spanish, and we fly still a third flag today, I fancy. Have ye heard of the Jolly Roger?"

He grinned. His bow was a mockery of previous courtliness.

"So it's English Luke Treach at yer service today, my friends."

"Buccaneer!" The old Spaniard scowled, then drew Ynez close to his side. She trembled in her father's arms, but her terror invested her with a weird enhancing of beauty; the beauty of a frightened fawn. Luke stared at the softness of her black eyes, at the trembling of her fear-taut body.

He stared so closely that he did not see the sudden gesture of the old man—did not observe his hand slip a tiny golden vial from his pocket to the bodice of his daughter.

He stared at the girl, and then he began to laugh. The laugh told all. It told Señor Montelupe that he need not waste words in threats or pleas. It told Ynez Montelupe that which made her crimson with shame.

Laughing, the pirate advanced. This time he saw the second movement of the old man—saw the silver dagger slid from the sleeve and raised on high. But his laughter did not cease as he tore the cutlass from its scabbard at his side. The blade slashed down upon the Spaniard's wrist. When it struck it seemed as though the steel had sent sparks flying, but it was only blood, spurting forth in tiny gouts as the hand fell severed to the cabin floor.

The old man cried out; then Luke was upon him, lifting the graybeard bodily and carrying him from the cabin. On deck he collared Roger Groat and kicked the form of the fainting grandee to indicate his prize.

"Amuse yourself," he instructed the lieutenant. "I go below again."

"Amuse *yourself*," parroted Groat, leering.

Treach good-naturedly pushed the man in the face with the flat of his wet blade, and went down the stairs again.

The Red Swimmer

* * *

Once more he entered the cabin, and saw that Ynez still stood there. She faced him now and she did not cringe. Her features held no fear, for they were set in the immobility of death. Only her eyes were alive—so dreadfully, so intently alive that Luke Treach stood staring aghast into their black depths. His own face twisted as though seared by the black flame that leapt forth from her burning orbs. Then he mastered himself and advanced.

"Ye'd best pull no tricks with me, girl," he muttered.

Her dead face smiled a dead smile—the mirthless smile of a corpse that crawls to feed. And her voice spoke, muffled as though it came from the under-earth.

"I fear ye not," said Ynez. "I fear no man, and no thing. Ye had best fear *me.*"

Her tone was leaden, and the words were heavy against Luke Treach's ears. He grimaced, shrugged in a bravado he did not feel.

"Enough of this!" he growled. "Come, lass—"

"Wait."

Luke paused.

"Ye shall have will over me, if ye must. But dog though thou art, I warn thee still. My father gave me this."

She held up the little golden vial. It was empty.

"Ye heard what it contained—the precious distillation which insures eternal life. I drank of it. And so I warn thee. I cannot die, and the hatred within me cannot die. Use me as thou wilt; yea, cast me into the sea"—her eyes flamed—"but I shall return, Luke Treach. I shall return. And there will be reckoning."

For a moment the buccaneer trembled with instinctive horror. Then the wine mounted to his brain, and as the light faded from the girl's eyes he stepped across the cabin with a hoarse laugh. Ynez threw the empty vial in his face, but he only grinned.

III

Luke Treach stumbled from the cabin with a curse—stumbled with the body of the swooning girl across his shoulder. Lurching figures moved in the dusk, snarling and laughing in drunken animation.

Treach cursed savagely as he sought the deck and made for a group

223

of huddling men that clustered about the mast.

He was rather surprised to see that old Señor Montelupe was still alive, considering what had been done to him.

The old grandee was nailed to the mast most painfully, by his remaining hand.

The men turned to Treach and regarded him with bleary eyes.

"What'll we do, Cap'n?" demanded Groat, moving to the pirate's side. "A tough old bird, this vulture. He'll not die and he'll not be still. He hangs there and curses and prays in his Spanish, damme if he don't."

Treach smiled wolfishly.

"Perhaps I can devise a new diversion," he said.

There was snickering, for the buckos knew their captain. They watched as he threw the swooning Ynez to the deck, and the mangled head of Montelupe turned to follow Treach's movements.

The captain's knife flashed, and the anguished old man moaned aloud as he cast the terribly altered form over the vessel's side. Then Treach faced the father. The gray Spaniard stared from tortured eyes until Luke's face fell in shame.

"Fool!" The voice rang faint, but vibrant with hatred. "Fool!"

Luke wished to turn away, but those eyes, that voice, held him prisoner before the victim.

"There is vengeance for fools," hissed the old man. "I've prayed to Powers while your dogs tormented me; prayed to Powers over wind and water. You and your currish crew are doomed, I swear—and *your* torment shall not end there."

Was this death-racked horror really smiling?

Luke shuddered. He stepped forward, blenching before the madman's eyes. For the old man was mumbling.

To the crew, it appeared as if Montelupe were whispering in confidence to Treach, for the captain bent his head close to the ravaged face, and the Spaniard's lips moved. It was hard to hear what he was saying.

"Vengeance ... my daughter ... elixir ... nothing can stop life that will flow eternally through veins ... nothing can stop hate ... vengeance for you ... return."

In the gathering shadow it was difficult for the men to see the expression on their captain's face. Could it be fear at the dying man's whispers?

But a moment later everyone witnessed their captain's rage. For suddenly the horrid head writhed as the old Spaniard spat full in Treach's face.

Then a sword flashed out, and a red-daubed head rolled across the deck. At that moment the sky bled, and crimson waters bubbled against the sunset. When the maimed body went over the side, the waters stirred with a new turbulence, and a wind sprang up from the flaming western sky.

Treach shuddered even as he cursed, noting the silence of his companions, their furtive looks and gesturings. The imbecile had awed them with his curses—faith, but it was lucky they had not heard what the old devil had said there at the last! Still, his wizard babbling was working on these superstitious fools.

With an effort, Luke met the mood and mastered it. He shouted for fresh rum, roundly cuffed the nearest members of the crew, and swaggered forward.

After a time his mates followed, and the warm bite of the liquor soon banished morbid melancholy.

They drank as sunset smoldered into dusk, drank as the dark clouds of night fled before the rise of wailing winds; drank even as the waters lashed the ship through trough and swell. For now white waves raced and reared, and the sea began to boil and bubble as though heated at some devil's cauldron from below.

* * *

Near midnight the storm broke, and the rain lashed the drunken roisterers from the deck. It was then that several awoke from their bemusement, but it was too late.

The *Golden Crest* whirled in an angry sea amidst a wind that shrieked and tore at sail and spar. Treach roared futile orders to the scant dozen of his crew that he could muster, but these did not avail. No one dared go aloft or brave the gale above the deck. Even when the mast fell, the panic-crazed. men were helpless to forestall further disaster.

The black night howled about them, and the sea surged over the decks as the ship heeled against the storm. Floundering figures were tossed screaming over the side as the waters retreated; cursing sailors blundered in the darkness as the yard-arms crashed about them to splinter the deck and cabins into a shambles.

Some there were who made a break for the boats. Five or six lifted one over the side and clambered in, just as a new wave struck. They dashed to death against the bows as the craft smashed to bits before the flooding impact of the water.

The ship lurched madly. It was leaking, foundering—that was a certainty. Treach collared Roger Groat, Salvatore, Samuel Slew, and as many others as he could shake into consciousness. His orders were curt; oath-weighted. They dashed below, returning with rations, water-jugs. A great combing wave crashed over the deck, then subsided as the men dashed for another boat.

They made it, lowered the ropes and floundered in, casting off just in time to escape the flooding fury that spent itself against the vessel's side.

Rowing was madness in these swirling waters, but they pushed away in time.

Already the great vessel was rearing and plunging in the throes of final surrender. It rose and sank, and above the storm came the sound of faint shrieks as those left behind realized the imminence of their doom.

Then, with a geyser-burst, the waters boiled above the ship, poising against the ruined mast-stumps before they hurled down to smash the vessel to ruins.

With a rumble, they fell and claimed their own. The craft rose up, tilted at the bow, and fell into the gigantic trough as the wave crashed down upon it. There was a single mighty roar of triumph as the ship slid into the sea; then foaming waters closed about it, and a terrible circle spread and widened from the point of its disappearance.

Treach and the men met the shock, though two yammering forms disappeared under the drenching violence of the inundation and were sucked down by the hungry depths.

Then they tossed all alone in the black storm amidst the sound of gigantic laughter, and the booming wind mocked them through the night.

IV

It was calm as death the next morning; and the waves purred against the side of the boat as though in satisfaction at the appeasement of their hunger.

The Red Swimmer

The weary men slept as the sun rose; Treach huddled forward over the provisions, Roger Groat bent over his oar, Salvatore stretched across his seat, Sam Slew and Gorlac lying supine in the dampness at the bottom of the craft.

It was Gorlac who woke first; Gorlac, the gigantic Krooman. His brutal negroid face wrinkled into a frown as he surveyed his sleeping companions and the empty sea in which they drifted. Then his eyes fell upon the two water-casks, the oiled sea-bag of provisions at the captain's side. He stretched black ape-arms forward, ate and drank noisily.

Treach chose this moment to awake, and for a second. he stared at the giant Negro, who sat obliviously munching a slab of bully-beef. Then he snarled an oath and drew his knife. In a moment he had flung himself forward on the startled black and buried his blade in the gleaming ebon column of the corded neck.

Gorlac grunted in pain, and crushed the captain's body in a terrible embrace. His arms tightened as Treach tore the knife from the wound in the neck and stabbed again and again at the dark back.

The Negro, grimacing with mad pain, locked his great hands about the pirate's neck and squeezed—squeezed terribly, with sobs of agony as he sought to throttle his foe. Then Treach slid the knife around to the ribs, arched upward in a silver slash, and disemboweled his antagonist. The ape-paws relaxed their grip, and the captain slid the twitching body over the side.

It fell with a splash, and disappeared. The captain crawled back to his place, feeling his throat experimentally to make sure that all was well; then polishing his knife carefully on his breeches. He looked up to face the stares of his awakened companions. The scuffle had taken place so quickly that the men were still rubbing their eyes and grumbling their bewilderment.

"Gorlac's gone," announced Treach, in. a harsh voice. "And damn my lights and liver, the rest of ye curs will go too if I catch ye tampering with the provisions."

He took out a small stone from his blouse and began to sharpen his knife, gazing meaningly at his audience. They sat stolid, each man looking off into the empty sea and thinking his own thoughts.

Luke mused with the rest. His mind was teeming in turmoil. First thoughts were pangs of regret as he remembered the fine ship, the fine crew he had lost—and more tragic still, the stores of bullion and silver ingots; the money-chests gleaned from trading off loot for gold doubloons and pieces-of-eight. And there had been a small fortune in the silks and jewels and moneys left by his two passengers as well. It was all lost.

Further reflection was brought to bear on his own plight; adrift here in the boundless sea with three men, an open boat, and water and provisions for perhaps two days.

From these ponderings his thoughts strayed off into darker considerations. Luke Treach was a practical man and an all-round materialistic scoundrel to boot, but he could not help but remember the strange dying words of the Spaniard—he who claimed mantic powers. The wretch may have been raving, but he spoke of aeromancy, power over wind and water, and of conjuring up a storm. The storm had come. And the seer had cursed him with other things....

But enough! A little food, a little water, a few attempts at formulating a plan; these were the things he needed to drive such foolishness from his brain.

He apportioned a meager fare of beef and hard-tack to the three survivors of his crew, and snapped orders for rowing assignments and night watches. Dark grinning Salvatore, big dour Groat and the leanly sinister "Dead-Light" Slew listened stolidly to his commands and set to.

But rowing is onerous, and the broiling sun of the mid-Caribbean no kindly overseer. The sea is a lonely place, and last night these men had glimpsed Death with jaws agape to swallow. Now they feared that those jaws would close about them again, not to engulf but to gnaw slowly with the sharp teeth of thirst and hunger.

* * *

The day passed in sullen, apprehensive silence; Groat and Slew, then Treach and Salvatore, taking the oars while the alternate pair rested and tried to shield their eyes from the eternal glare.

Row—but where? There was no compass, and until the stars shone guidance was missing. Treach hoped to put south to the islands, and the sun's deceptive shimmer showed him the way none too truly.

Nevertheless the labor kept the men from thinking too much; kept them from remembering little things that now carne to slyly torment Treach. There had been a little golden vial, and the wizard had sworn a vengeance. What was that about Eternal Life? Couldn't torture kill? What did it mean?

Sunset again—flaming sunset, like that in which Montelupe had died. He had died; the dead harm no one. She too could harm no one, now.

But it was night. Captain Treach apportioned the food in darkness, watched his companions at the water to insure that they were not overgreedy.

Treach snapped commands, set the course by the stars. The men hauled at the oars in silence, and the boat glided through black waters.

Groat and Slew labored. Salvatore dropped off to sleep, his swarthy face buried in his hands as he huddled up against the forward seat. Treach kept awake by sheer will, cursing mechanically at the oarsmen, so that the sound of his voice might drown out the greater sound of the Silence—the empty Silence of rolling waters. The very rustle and lap of the waves seemed to become a part of a maddening stillness that sapped the mind. The night sea was an entity that crawled about them. Treach felt this, although no concrete thought was formulated. But his instinct awakened him to fear; fear which the silent sea now personified. Here, drifting alone in black infinitude, the Powers of which the dead wizard had spoken assumed new reality. It was easy for the tired imagination to conceive of vast pulsing shapes, embodiments of the night and the wind and the water.

Treach felt his burning forehead, drew the back of his hand over lips cracked with fever.

He fell asleep while the waters murmured. In his dreams the water was whispering. From far away it whispered—from behind the boat. The whispering grew louder. It was right behind the boat now. He could almost hear words floating up out of the water. The whispering was trying to tell him something—something about vengeance, and a curse—right under the boat now....

There was a scream of utter agony.

* * *

Treach wrenched himself from sleep, sat bolt-upright as the scream trailed off into a gurgling noise in the blackness.

"What's that?" he shouted to his companions.

For a moment there was no answer. Groat's face was buried in trembling hands.

Salvatore heard him, but when he opened his mouth it merely hung loosely, without moving in speech. And Slew was gone.

"Where's Sam?" shouted Treach.

Salvatore managed to regain partial control of his jaws.

"He—gone," the swarthy man spluttered. "It came over the side and took him—it was kissing him and then it pulled him into the water—it took him—*santo Dios*—"

Then Treach was upon Salvatore, shaking his shoulders and shrieking into his very face.

"What took him, damme? Speak up, man, for the love of heaven!"

"I not know," whimpered the other. "I not know. We row here, and then Slew, he stop rowing. I take the oar. He just sit there at end of boat. All at once he say, 'Listen.' I listen, hear nothing. 'Listen,' he say. 'I hear whisper.' I tell him he crazy. But he just sit and look at water and say, 'It getting louder.' All at once he lean down, and then—*sacramento!*—two arms come up out of water and go around his neck. He just scream once and then over side he go. No splash, no bubbles. He go, and I see arms—all red arms. *All red!*"

As the big man slumped down in the boat Treach peered wildly at the black waters about him. They were still, unruffled. No body, no rippling.

"You're daft, man," he whispered, but there was no conviction in his voice.

"Those red arms," Groat muttered, from behind. "I never believed in mermaids or sea-monsters, but—"

"Shut up, both of you! You're crazy! Slew fell overboard, that's all. Fever's got you. There's nothing in the water but sharks. And they have no arms."

"You threw something in water with arms," Salvatore mumbled.

Treach struck the man across the mouth. "Shut up!" he screamed. "Let me alone."

Silently, he sat there until dawn arose, and when he saw its redness, he shuddered.

* * *

They were all mad now, food and water gone, Slew gone. And the sun, searing down, cooked the madness into their brains until thoughts writhed and twisted amidst flames.

Salvatore wouldn't row any more. He kept staring at the water behind the boat while Treach and Groat worked the oars. Treach watched him.

Toward midday Salvatore turned.

"There," he whispered. "I know. I know it come. I see it. There in the water. It following us. Swimming in water. Oh, Cap'n, look there."

"Shut up!" But Treach looked. It was only sunlight glinting on the waves behind.

"Look. It move again!"

Something *was* moving, away back.

"Sharks, you fool!"

"Sharks are not red."

"Shut up!"

They pulled the oars, but Salvatore gazed back as sunset dripped blood upon the waves. He was trembling and his face was soaking with perspiration not born of heat alone.

"Let us all stay awake tonight," he whispered. "Maybe we pray and it go away. Otherwise—"

"Quiet!" Treach snapped the command with his old authority.

But the authority was in his voice alone now. Inside, Luke Treach was afraid.

When the sun went down he heard the whispering at once. It welled out of the black waters, and he prayed that the moon might rise at once. Hearing that whispering in the blackness was too much. He turned toward the back of the boat. He'd talk to Salvatore, anything, just drown out that growing whisper. He turned—and saw.

The big man was on his knees. He was leaning over the gunwale. His arms were outstretched and he was staring down into the black water, his face icy with horror.

And two arms were rising out of the water—two long, red arms. They were pinkly phosphorescent in the darkness. They glowed like— like stepped flesh.

The arms reached out, twin serpents that embraced. Treach tried to call out, to motion to Groat. He was frozen, frozen as the arms rose, embraced Salvatore. And silently, the big man toppled over the side. The splash broke the spell.

"Quick!" Treach screamed. Groat followed him on his hands and knees as they thrashed their oars in the blackness of the waves. Nothing moved.

"Sharks move a lot," Groat muttered, in a hoarse voice. "Sharks move, and octopus move. But this—you saw?"

"I didn't see anything," Treach lied. "He was mad. Threw himself over."

"Drowning men move," Groat croaked.

Treach mastered himself. "Row," he commanded. "For God's sake, row, man! We must reach land before tomorrow night."

They rowed as though Death were at their heels. And in their hearts it was this they feared. They rowed past midnight; tired, feverish, aflame with thirst and hunger. But Fear called their strokes, and Fear drove the boat on through the inky, whispering waters.

Treach was nearly mad now. There *was* something out there! He could no longer keep from thinking of the curse—of what Ynez had said about not being able to die. Yet he had killed her; what he did would kill anyone. She must be dead.

"What's that?" Groat had stopped rowing.

"Where?"

"Back there in the water—see, where the moonlight hits the wave."

"I don't see—" Treach stopped, eyes wide with dread.

"Yes, you do. You see it. That head, coming toward us."

They sat there while the bobbing thing approached. And the whispering rose about them in a great murmur as of winds rising from ocean depths, and the whispering was clear this time so that they heard.

"Where are you, Luke Treach? I come for you. You have taken my eyes, Luke Treach, and I cannot see. But you are there, and I come for you."

Groat began to laugh. A low chuckling rose from his throat until it drowned out the sound of the whispering. Groat raised his head to the moon and bayed his laughter. He sat there quaking with mirth.

And Treach watched him, then watched the bobbing head that circled the boat. It went around once, twice. It stopped for a moment on his side, and he saw a dark, seal-like outline that might or might not have been human. It hesitated in the water, and Treach drew his knife. Then it circled the boat again and came to rest on the side where Groat sat laughing. Two arms rose out of the water in the moonlight—two red arms, glistening and wet. And Groat went over, still laughing. His laughter rose, then bubbled away as the arms dragged him down.

It was then that Treach himself began to laugh. All alone in the boat he sat, laughing up to the moon. He laughed because he knew he was mad—what he had seen could not be true.

The Red Swimmer

He was mad, and yet he would escape. Luke Treach seized an oar and began to row with demented fury.

* * *

The sun was high when he ceased. Madness passed, and the events of the night were a dream. Treach leaned back, rubbed his eyes, and looked around in amazement.

"Groat? Salvatore? Slew? Where are you?"

They were gone—but they couldn't be gone, or it would be true.

"Groat? Salvatore? Slew?"

And then the waves around the boat parted, and three heads appeared in the water. Sam Slew's one-eyed stare came from a blue, bloated face. Salvatore's eyes were closed and his mouth was sealed with seaweed. The drowned visage of Groat, smiling through a tangle of kelp, bobbed horridly on the waves. All three heads came to the side of the boat. They shimmered there through the haze of heat from the sun.

Treach had been screaming for a long time in a high shrill voice when they disappeared.

"Fever," he muttered. "Just one day more."

He clawed at the oars.

But now he couldn't keep his eyes off the water. And as noon approached, he could begin to see the swimmer behind—far off, crawling through the trough of the waves. It was keeping distance; but a few strokes and it would be upon him.

The delirious pirate redoubled his efforts with every ounce of remaining strength. And still the gap between boat and swimmer narrowed. Now Treach could see long red arms in the water. He could not quite make out a head or face, but he saw the arms. Remembering what he had done he shuddered. *Red arms!*

But the breeze was changing. Offshore?

He faced the sunset. A black bulk loomed from the water to his west. Dominica, he guessed. If he could make it before nightfall he would be safe.

He rowed on, faster.

The swimmer was fast, too. The gap narrowed, just as the red band of sunset narrowed.

"How can she follow?" Treach muttered. "She's blind. I know that. She took the others, searching for me. How can she follow? Wizard

233

tricks—that vial! Why didn't I believe it would keep her alive, even after *that!* I must row—harder."

Panting, the wrecked body of Luke Treach tugged at the oars. His bloodshot eyes stared now at the bobbing head just behind the boat. His ears buzzed, but he heard the whisperings.

"I swore it, Luke Treach. Now I come for you."

There was no use to row, but Treach rowed; no use to scream, but Treach screamed; screamed and rowed as the red thing swam around the boat. Then it was crawling over the side, and Luke Treach avoided the pinkish-red arms as they reached out. Laughing, he drew his knife. But then it crawled into the boat so that Treach saw it, drowned, yet livid red all over. And he pointed the knife, but it came on, eyeless and groping. One hand grasped the knife and then both arms went around Luke Treach so that he fell back. The hand grasping the knife came down and a voice that was not a voice whispered:

"I came a long way—from death itself. And now I shall do to you what you did to me before you cast me over the side. You shall be as red as I am."

And the knife sang down as Luke Treach's knife had sung down when he killed Ynez before her father and cast her into the sea. It sang down, and when it ceased the red swimmer went over the side of the drifting boat and disappeared.

Night fell, and still the boat drifted.

At dawn it bumped the shore.

Two men found it there some hours later.

They peered into it and shuddered at the sight of the figure lying on the bottom of the boat.

"Dead?" whispered one.

"Of course he's dead."

"Wrecked, doubtlessly, in an open boat."

"Yes." His voice was vibrant with horror. "But what could have done *this* to him?"

"Just what was done?—I cannot understand it yet."

The first man stared again at the red thing in the boat. "You fool," he said, "can't you see that this man was *flayed alive?"*

Unheavenly Twin

This may not be such a good story, but at least it's a novel one, when you come to think of how it's being written. You see, I'm writing it with my feet.

No, I'm not trying to be funny. I'm what they call an Armless Wonder, you know. I don't particularly care for the word "freak," understand, but I travel with a tent show during the season and one of my biggest stunts is this writing with my toes. It's probably as easy for me as it is for you to write in a normal way, but circus crowds eat it up all summer. Winters I stay at Malone's Boarding House.

That is, I did stay there. But not any more, thank you. That's where the story comes in. We sideshow people are a queer enough crowd, and I've run up against some mighty strange yarns in my time, but nothing to beat the story I saw unfolded with my own eyes. I think about it all the time, and I don't like that.

Perhaps if I write it out, I'll be able to get a little peace again. Now I have nightmares, and I dream about Count Vomar and his secret; dream about the *thing* I saw the last night I stayed at Malone's Boarding House. But I'm getting ahead of my story.

Malone's Boarding House was unique—possibly the only "freak" hotel in the world. All the performers with the show put up there for the winter season, and I suppose to an outsider the dinner table would look mighty queer.

There was General Atom, the midget. Only twenty-eight inches tall he was, sitting in his own special high-chair, and smoking that crummy pipe of his. Señorita Linda, his wife, always hated that pipe. She was the Bearded Lady in professional life, and she claimed that the smoke smelled up her whiskers. She had a beautiful beard; the only

235

red-haired Bearded Lady I've ever seen. Of course, she might have used henna.

Besides these two there was Tom Gallor, the Cowboy Giant. He generally sat at the head of the table, and it was certainly convenient when he stretched out his long ape-arm to pass the sugar down the line. Ordo, the Dog-faced Boy, was another character. He looked frightful as sin, but he was really a mild chap. It was amusing to think that our "ferocious hound-faced monster" could scarcely touch meat because of his false teeth.

There were perhaps a dozen more; the Fat Lady, the usual human skeleton, a tattooed woman named Daisy O'Connor, who had drifted somehow into the profession; Rameses, the India-rubber Man, who had to be served a special diet; a sword-swallower whom I never did meet, and Leela, the Leopard Woman.

We were a pretty jolly lot around the dinner table, and I guess we had as much fun as any bunch of boarders could have. You'd be amazed at the hobbies and avocations some of these sideshow people cultivated, but they were a happy crowd at the supper table.

Malone, who owned the house, used to be with a show himself; a barker he was, until he retired and bought out the rooming house. It was still his custom to stand before the dining room door at supper time and beat the gong, chanting some barker's doggerel as though urging the rubes to "gather 'round for the *big* show." Yes, it was a merry enough gang for dinner.

* * *

All but Count Vomar. He ate in his room. Aloof he was, and very eccentric. He didn't play bridge in the parlor of an evening; never got into our poker games upstairs. He seldom went out; and, as I say, he even ate alone.

Of course, he had a reason. For Count Vomar was a unique freak. He was twins.

It sounds silly, but I'm not up on my technical lingo. Vomar was an ordinary man, at first glance, but he had a tremendous paunch. He never wore anything but a bathrobe, slitted at the waist; and it was sometimes disturbing to meet him in the hallway and be conscious of two beady little eyes peering at you from the opening above his belly.

Unheavenly Twin

That was the twin—a monster. It grew out of his body at the waist; a sort of undeveloped Siamese twin. It had arms and legs, but very tiny ones, and a head about the size of an infant's. But the real oddity of the creature was that it was *alive.*

It was attached to Vomar by a big tube of flesh, and it apparently had organs of its own; enough to make it move and react, anyway. It ate, too—and that was why Vomar did not dine with the rest of us…

He was a young, good-looking chap, this Count Vomar. But there was something about his bulging waist that made him look old; his face was grave, too. I've seen him work on the platform when the show was on, and the way he stared at the crowds was disturbing.

He would watch the boobs standing before his couch, and see the dizzy dames exclaim over the shriveled little creature that writhed on his stomach. And the more they "oohed" and looked disgusted, the more cynically he smiled. How he must have hated people! And himself, too, I suppose.

That's what first attracted me, I guess. I'd worked with him a season on the road, and when we hit winter quarters we both put up at Malone's. The rest of the gang sort of avoided Vomar, and I followed suit. They sensed that he felt "different," and most of us put him down as a crab and a sorehead. "Temperamental" was the kindest thing they said.

But I felt a little curious about it all. You see, most of our kind don't sulk much because we're different. It's a sort of pride we have, I suppose. Take me, for instance—what if I'd been born with hands, like all the rest? I'd be just another guy, that's all; probably working in a factory if I wasn't standing in the breadline. As it is, I have a swell berth with the show, and I like it. And most of the sideshow folk feel just as satisfied.

Vomar was different. I knew he hated the name "freak," and I rather fancied that he felt terribly alone at times, but was too shy to mix with us. How he passed his time all winter I could not imagine.

That's why when I met him in the hall one afternoon I invited him in. I had a rather nice place fixed up; I'm a great one for reading. So I asked him if he'd care to borrow a few books.

And do you know that man was grateful? Here the gang had been ripping him up the back for a wet blanket, and when I actually gave him a kind word he was friendly as the devil. He came in, sat on the bed in his dressing gown, and talked books with me until supper. He knew literature, too—all kinds of classics and artistic things. Some of it was way over my head, and I told him so. He invited me to his quarters; he had a library there, he said. I might find something I liked.

So that evening I went to visit Count Vomar, and our friendship began.

He was very frank after his reserve was down. I found out that his name was Harry Reesten; that he had been born in Ohio and grew up alone with his folks. They had money, but lost it later. So Harry became Count Vomar and went out with the show.

Naturally, we had to discuss—it. I felt embarrassed, but he was perfectly candid. He said that at birth the doctors had not thought he would live; that for several years it was nip and tuck all around. Then he began telling me about the operations and consultations he had gone through as a child.

* * *

I could see that he had studied his case a lot; he talked about "monsters" and "teratology," which is the science of such things, I guess. His case wasn't very much different from that of a two-headed calf, I guess, or real Siamese twins. All kinds of freaks can be born, he said, and neither man nor animal is immune. But I can't explain it like he did to me.

Anyhow, he spoke of those early days, and how the surgeons didn't dare to operate on the thing because it fed partly through his own body; a "parasite" or "vampire," it was, with some organs that depended on his own blood-stream.

His folks had kept him away from other kids when he was a child. They had money and gave him a tutor. Then came the '29 crash, and he was forced into the sideshows for a living.

He was very bitter about it all. I guess that came from his always being alone, as much as anything else. But he hated appearing in front of strangers, and he hated to feel *different.* I could hardly blame him for that, because he was educated, and liked good things.

We talked, and I looked over his library. I've never seen such a collection of books in my life; half of them I'd never heard of before. A lot of them were on philosophy and psychology. I looked over a bunch of medical books, too; most of them had something to do with this "teratology"—studies of monsters. And he had other things in the classical line; I guess he had enough reading there to keep him busy most of the time.

But he seemed to like talking to me, and we arranged to visit. After a few weeks I really got to know him quite well.

Then he began to tell me things. He showed *it* to me—one night. I had seen it on the platform, of course, but never close up. And I got a terrible shock. It was—*human.* A great big baby with crinkly skin; there was hair on its head growing quite naturally, and it had dimpled little hands and feet.

I could see its chest move when it breathed, in a sort of rhythm with Count Vomar's own breathing; and every once in a while it waved its arms and legs around a little—just like a small child. But its face was not a baby's. It was like the face of Count Vomar, but even older, somehow. Small and dark it was, but there were wrinkles around the mouth, and when it drew back its lips I was amazed to find full-grown second teeth.

The eyelids were closed at first, I remember, but as I watched they opened. I stared into those eyes and all at once I was sick. Because they were big, and black—and *intelligent!*

They knew things.

Vomar was watching me and saw my face, I guess. But he didn't look at me when he whispered what he did.

"You've seen it, too," he said. "You must have guessed. It's not only alive as an animal is alive, you know. It eats like a man, and when I'm—when *we're* alone—it moves a great deal. He *is* my brother, after all...."

Vomar flushed. "I don't like to tell you this, but you're my friend and I'll feel better if I get this off my chest. I want to tell you the real reason why I stay alone. It's because my brother won't let me go out."

I began to get curious ideas about Vomar's sanity then. But he was hurrying on.

"I never knew, at first, just how much the thing knew. But one day—and I swear to God it's true—*he spoke to me.* Words, mind you; he can talk, think! I never told the doctors, and he's too cunning to show many signs of life except when we're alone. But he feeds on my brain. What I know, he knows. I can't explain it, except that there is a psychic connection. He is nourished at my blood-stream, as I've already informed you.

"Now, you can understand what I go through. I've tried everything, I tell you—I want to be separated, and he does, too. But no doctor in the world can do it. Lately he has suggested other ways. Do you believe in sorcery, or witchcraft? The legends about demons and familiars? Never mind—that's wild talk. I must be getting silly."

* * *

Vomar looked so unhappy that I was at a loss what to say. Presently he went on.

"Sometimes I think I'm going mad, if I'm not already. He says such strange things; terrible things he whispers at night, before we go to sleep. And I think he tries to—get hold of me then. Hypnotize me, make me do things. That's why I bought those books of magic; he told me where to find them and what he proposed I should do with them. And he whispered:

"'If men cannot help us, there are Others who will make bargains....'"

He shuddered. "Please—forget that. I'm not feeling so well tonight, and— No, I'll tell you the rest. He's sleeping now, and I want someone to know in case—in case anything should go wrong—

'I'll tell you what I've noticed lately. *He's growing!* It's very hard for me to walk, because he's getting heavy. I feel weaker myself. He's taking more blood, just as he threatened to do, if I didn't call up those Others the books tell of. He wants to grow, to dominate me; he's jealous.

"Do you believe in an Evil Personality? I'm beginning to think about it a lot, lately. The books say such things can grow, like vampires they are. I'm getting to be afraid. He's told me—"

I. heard all this, and a lot more. I didn't like the look on Vomar's pale face, and I didn't like the looks of—*it,* sleeping at his waist. And I most certainly didn't care for Vomar's strange way of talking; it was too convincing. He actually seemed to believe it, and I wondered if he were a mental case.

I excused myself and left. I never went back, except that once. Somehow I felt frightened, and I almost knew what was going to come. I spoke to nobody about Vomar, and they didn't ask. But there was a lot of outside gossip starting up about the Count.

* * *

None of the gang ever saw him in the halls; or in his room, either, for that matter. Malone talked about raising his room rent, because it seems Vomar asked for more food; had special meat dishes sent up, and all that. They were left at the door. Count Vomar talked about feeling anaemic and run-down, but would not let Malone send for a doctor.

<u>Unheavenly Twin</u>

Several weeks went by and I heard all the gossip. But I knew. Then came the day that Señorita Linda, the Bearded Lady, started her scandal. She said she had passed Count Vomar's room one night and heard somebody talking inside; somebody with a high, shrill voice that was not the Count's. There were snickers … *But I knew.*

And I was a coward. I didn't dare tell anyone, or do anything about it. And I did not dare go up to that room again, after what I had heard. So the days slipped by, and the nights went slowly onward, although I couldn't sleep. And then one evening the food placed at Vomar's door was left untouched: And the next morning Señorita Linda heard the whispering and started her story again.

Malone investigated, called through the locked door to Count Vomar. There was no answer, but the landlord could hear that shrill whispering or chattering going on inside the room.

Then I rallied my courage and told Malone enough so that we both went up to the room and he used his skeleton key. I don't know what I expected to see, but I almost knew we were too late. And when we went in—

Count Vomar was lying on the bed—what was left of him, that is. He had been dead for several days and had apparently died in his sleep, for there were no signs of death agony. We told the gang, and had a private funeral in a hurry….

They never did learn any more, or understand why I left so hurriedly the next day. They never learned the truth about Count Vomar, nor heard about the rest of the things we saw in his room.

Cancer, tumor, parasite—but it's a vampire, they say, that really *shrivels* a man so that he shrinks to skin and bones and his bloodless body turns yellow. It's a vampire that feeds on blood and grows.

And it was a vampire that sat on Count Vomar's chest when we found him; a great bulging body almost three feet tall that had fed horribly on Vomar in his sleep. A great, loathsome child-thing that Malone killed with a knife while it whispered and chattered and chuckled as it squatted on Count Vomar's chest.

The little twin horror had done what Vomar said it threatened to do; and now I'm not sure of anything in this world any more. Not since I saw dead, shriveled Count Vomar, and crawling on his chest the living, feeding, bloated monster that was his brother.

The Strange Island of Doctor Nork

I

Between the Greater Antilles and the Lesser Antilles rises a little group of islands generally known as the Medium-Sized Antilles.

Mere pimples on the smiling face of the Caribbean, they remain unsqueezed by the hands of man.

Far off the usual trade routes, their shores are only infrequently desecrated by a banana peeling washed off a United Fruit Lines boat.

It eras here that I came on the fateful day in August, my monoplane circling until it descended upon the broad, sandy beach of the central island—the strange island of Doctor Nork.

II

How Sidney Dearborn ever heard of Doctor Nork, I cannot say. The old dingbat, doddering around the confines of his palatial estate, seldom pays much attention to his news magazine, let alone interesting himself in the doings of a mere individual.

But probably even a man like Dearborn, who is devoting most of his time to becoming an octogenarian—has been for the past eighty years—occasionally pauses and reads the papers.

Quite possibly, Dearborn read an article about Doctor Nork in one of his own magazines. I can see him calling my editor in New York.

"Hello—this is Dearborn. Get me an exclusive feature interview on Nork.

"Nork. Nork! No, I'm not sick. Fella's name. N-o-r-k. Big scientist. Lives all alone on an island someplace, doing experiments.

"How do I know what kind of experiments? Find out for me. Tell our readers. That's what I'm paying you fifty grand a year for—to find out facts.

"This story on Nork is drivel. Pure drivel. No facts. It says he's endowed by a lot of foundations. Endowed for what? Can he split an atom? Get me all the dope.

"Know what I think? I smell Communism, that's what I smell. What would a big scientist want to hide out on an island for if he wasn't afraid? The American people deserve to know.

"Well, send a man down to see him. Interview him. I want a complete writeup on Nork within ten days, And say—hello, hello—I want you to be sure and find out where he stands on the oleomargarine tax!"

That's the way the conversation probably went. I can only guess. All I know is that the managing editor called me into the front office and gave me the assignment.

"Charter a plane," he said. "Get there, get the yarn, and get back. Get it?"

I got it, but good.

III

The smooth yellow beach on which my monoplane had landed evidently girdled the island, which was approximately a mile in diameter. Inland, palmettos clustered thickly in a dense jungle that ended abruptly at the foot of a gigantic cliff occupying the island's center. Monkeys, macaws, toucans and parakeets set up a Disney-like clatter as I toted my suitcase and portable typewriter across the sands, but there was no evidence of human life—not even a Burma-Shave sign.

For a moment I wondered if I had made a mistake. I felt like Robinson Crusoe, and remembered the stirring episode where he discovers in the sand the imprint of a naked human foot.

Then I gasped. I *was* Robinson Crusoe. For there, before me in the golden sand, was the symbol of life itself! Not the raw imprint of savage life, but the very essence of civilization.

It was an old Pepsi-Cola bottle.

I stooped down to pick it up and then noted, with a sudden shock, that the bottle was not empty.

* * *

The Strange Island of Doctor Nork

A soggy, crumpled sheet of paper had been stuffed down the neck, which was sealed with a battered cap. I pried it loose, then fished out the parchment and unfolded the sheet. The message was written in a childish scrawl.

> *To Whom It May Concern*
> *Doctor Nork is a mean, nasty old thing,*
> *so there!*
> *(Signed) A True Friend*

So I *was* on the right island, after all.

My elation subsided as I realized "A True Friend's" warning about my future host. Well, it was no concern of mine. For all I knew, "A True Friend" might be a far meaner and nastier old thing than Doctor Nork.

At any rate, I wasn't here to sit in judgment; I was here to get a story on the mysterious medico.

Resealing the message in the bottle, I tossed it into the water. Apparently that had been "A True Friend's" intention, but his aim was bad.

I toted my luggage towards the palmetto forest as the macaws formed a screaming rainbow round my head.

Oh, those living flames of beauty! Oh, those lovely, lambent—

"Oh, for crying out loud!"

I muttered.

Apparently it was safer to walk under the shelter of the trees.

IV

I was still wiping my pith helmet when I felt a hand tap my shoulder. I wheeled, then recoiled in horror. It hadn't been a hand on my shoulder, after all. I beheld a paw.

Crouching, confronting me, was the shaggy, shambling figure of a gigantic great ape. Gorilla-eyes glared, and a tusked maw gaped wide in slavering dread. A growl rumbled up into the threatening throat.

"You want handkerchief?" said the ape.

The intonation was bestial, but the words were human, intelligible. I stared, gulped, and shook my head in amazement.

"Who you fella?" the ape demanded. "You fella come safari?"

I shook my head again, but the hallucination didn't disappear.

"You come in jungle hunt for diamonds, gold, no? You seek Elephant's Graveyard, maybe, heap much ivory?"

I could only goggle.

"You *bwana* search for White Goddess?" I shrugged my heart back out of my mouth and down to where it belonged. Then I found my voice again. "You—you can actually talk!" I gasped. "I-I- never thought I'd live to hear a gorilla talk like that."

The ape grimaced dreadfully.

"Sounds pretty corny, eh, Jack? I think so, too—all that pidgin English and fake native lingo. Strictly from hunger. But you know how it is with the Doc—he makes me talk that way, says it's what they want to hear.

"Sometimes I get pretty ashamed when I think that an anthropoid of my education has to go around making like a *schmoe*, but I got my orders. Like I say, you know the Doc."

"But I don't know the Doc," I answered. "That's just what I came down here for; I want to meet him."

"You from the publishers?" asked the gorilla.

"News magazine," I replied. "I'm here for an interview."

"Might have known it," the ape muttered. "You don't have a mustache. Thought you were a villain at first; but the villains all have mustaches, don't they?"

I was getting confused again.

The anthropoid ignored my bewilderment and courteously relieved me of my luggage. "Come on," he growled. "Follow me."

He led a path through the palmettos. "Reporter, eh?" he mused. "What do you do evenings?"

"How do you mean?"

"Fly, hurtle sail, batter, flame, or blast?"

"I don't understand," I confessed. "You must have me mixed up with somebody else. Evenings, I go home. Sometimes I look up a friend and play a little Gin Rummy."

"Tell you what you do," the gorilla suggested. "When you get done with the Doc, look me up and I'll take you on for a few hands."

V

The cliff-top was a broad, flat plateau overlooking the beach and sea below. The wind blew cold and clear across the treeless expanse, and borne upon its eddies the seagulls wheeled and circled.

Remembering the macaws I made an instinctive grab for my solar topee and jammed it down over my forehead. Then I peered out under its brim at the domicile of Doctor Nork.

Nork's residence sprawled across the plateau like some gigantic concrete wheel. A white-domed central structure acted as the hub, from which extended a half-dozen radii in the shape of wings attached to the main building. The outer circumference was rimmed by a high stone fence, broken by a single gate. The ape led me towards it while I stared up and marveled at the elaborate structure set upon a lonely tropical isle.

Then we were standing before the gate, which apparently served as a front door. I noted a neatly lettered sign reading:

ERASMUS NORK, M.D.
Doctor is in—Please be Seated

I had nothing to sit on but my valise. The gorilla opened the front door and bid me enter. He shambled onto a spacious white hallway, its antiseptic decor reminiscent of an old Doctor Kildare movie. I followed him as we walked along the corridor, passing half a dozen closed doors in succession. Finally we paused before a large double-door at the end of the hall.

"I'll announce you," the ape suggested. "Doctor Nork is conducting an experiment."

He slipped through the half-open doorway and disappeared. I stood in the hall and listened to the drone of a faraway dynamo. It accented the eeriness of this white palace set in the heart of a tropical jungle. Weird scientific experiments and talking apes—

"Come right in, my friend!" The booming voice resounded from the room behind the door. "Welcome to the Island!" I stepped forward into the laboratory of Doctor Nork.

A great arc-light glared from the domed roof, glared down upon a scene of horror. A huge steel operating table occupied the center of the room, and it was in use. Strapped securely to its surface was a half-clad girl, hair streaming, mouth contorted, eyes wide with terror.

Towering above her was a tall, thin, red-bearded man with a beaked nose and slanted eyes. Like a surgeon, he wore a white gown. Like a surgeon, he brandished a glittering knife. Even as I watched, he raised the cruel blade and his arm swooped down to the girl's bare white bosom.

The red-bearded man grinned exultantly.

"How's tricks?" he whispered. The knife came down—

"Stop!"

I plunged forward frantically. Hairy arms pinioned me from behind. The ape held me fast.

"Hold it!" snarled the red-bearded man. "There—got it?"

"Swell, Boss!" squeaked an unfamiliar voice from the corner of the room. I twisted my head and saw a little man with a smock standing before an easel. Even as I watched, he did things to the tripod stand, folding it under his arm, and gathering the board up, scuttled from the room.

The tall man dropped the knife and fumbled with the cords binding the girl.

"Curse these knots!" he grumbled. "Ought to use the disintegrator. There you are, Toots."

The girl stood up and fluffed out her hair. She smiled at me—no, past me, over my shoulder where the ape stood.

"How's for a little Gin?" she said.

The gorilla nodded and released me. Linked arm in arm, girl and gorilla ambled from the room. And the tall, red-bearded man gestured towards me with his knife.

"Sit down, my friend," he said. "You must be tired after your trip. Maybe you'd prefer to lie down—how about right here, on the operating table?"

"No thanks, I gulped. "You're Doctor Nork, I presume?"

"Of course. Glad to see you. It isn't often we get a chance to converse with a representative of civilization. You must tell me all that's happening in the world. Has the atomic bomb blown up any continents lately?"

"I don't know—I left New York yesterday," I answered.

Nork shrugged. "So you came all the way down here just for an interview, eh? I suppose you want to discuss the new slants we worked out?"

"Slants?" I fumbled for his meaning. "I was sent here to find out something about your experiments. I hear you are conducting some mysterious investigations."

"Mysterious investigations? Experiments? My dear sir, you've been badly misled. I'm a business man. This is a business office." Doctor

Nork took out a strop and began to sharpen his knife splitting hairs from his beard to test the keen edge of the blade.

"But I heard—"

"You were mistaken." Nork spoke curtly.

At that moment the door opened and the gorilla entered.

"Hey, Doc, those guys are here for the experiments," he announced.

Nork blushed and avoided my accusing stare.

"Tell them I'm busy," he barked. "Tell them they'll have to wait."

"But the subject is already strapped down. The stenographer is ready. Everything is set up."

"Confound it!" muttered the Doctor. "Oh, very well!"

"You don't have to come down, Doc," the ape said. "Just give me the equipment and I'll take it to them."

Doctor Nork shrugged and stepped over to one of the blank, gleaming white laboratory walls. He pressed a tile and something clicked. A section of the wall slid back and revealed a long rack. Objects hung from thongs, dangled from hooks.

I stared at the display. There were long black whips, short cats-of-nine-tails, blackjacks, bludgeons, truncheons, clubs, assegais, knobkerries, shillelaghs.

The gorilla lumbered over and selected an armful at random.

"This oughta do the trick, eh, Doc?"

Nork nodded. Another click and the wall slid back into place. He pressed a second tile. A grating wheeze echoed through the room as a portion of the floor moved to disclose a secret stairway descending into black depths below. The ape clambered down the steps, bearing his homicidal burden.. With a loud clang, the floor closed behind him.

I reeled, bewildered. Whips, weapons, concealed passages, and a nameless experiment—what did it mean?

Nork feigned nonchalance as he faced me.

"Come on," I said. "Quit stalling. My editor sent me down here for a feature story and I intend to get it. Now I—"

My words were cut short, then drowned out by a ghastly shriek. It came from beneath my very feet; rising in a weird wail, an ululation of utter agony.

"What's that?" I gasped.

"I didn't hear anything," purred Nork.

Again the dreadful scream tore the air to ribbons.

"Whats going on here?" I panted. "What does it all mean? What kind of experiment needs whips and bludgeons? What are they doing down there?"

"Oh all right, I suppose I'll have to tell you," Nork sighed. "But it's really nothing at all. They're just beating the living hell out of a guy."

VI

I made a dive for the Doctor's bearded throat. "You fiend!" I shrieked. "Now I know what you are—a mad scientist!"

"Hey, cut it out!" yelled Nork. "You're tearing my beard!"

Indeed, the red beard came loose in my hands, revealing a smaller black beard beneath it.

"Don't touch the black beard—that's genuine!" warned the scientist. "I just wear the red for sketches. Red seems to be all the thing this season. Wait, let me explain things to you."

"Explain things? While you're torturing that poor devil down there in the cellar?"

"What poor devil? He's a volunteer. Also a confirmed masochist; he likes to be beaten up. Besides, I'm paying him five hundred dollars for his trouble."

"You're paying him five hundred dollars—?"

"Didn't I tell you this was business? Come on, I'll let you see for yourself."

The Doctor pressed the wall, the steps below were revealed, and I followed him down into the noisome darkness. As we passed into the nighted depths, the screams and groans rose hideously. The hair on my scalp followed suit.

We groped along a damp stone corridor until we reached a dimly lit room. It was a sight I never expected to see—a sight no man of the twentieth century should see—a medieval dungeon.

Torchlight flared on rack and strappado on boot and Iron Maiden and wheel. Torchlight flickered down on the table where the groaning man writhed beneath the blows of two gigantic blackamoors.

The ape stood by silently, hand resting on the shoulders of a small man who sat perched on a high stool. Head cocked attentively as though listening, the little man was frantically scribbling down shorthand jottings.

Thuds, curses, screeches, blows, moans and gasps filled the air—but they faded into a sort of background noise as the little man beamed ecstatically and babbled at each fresh sound.

"WHUUP!" he yelled. "OOFFLE!"

"Huh?" I murmured.

"GUTCH! Boy, didja hear dat one, hey! GUTCH; Tha's a new one, huh Doc?" He peered over his spectacles and addressed the blackamoors. "Hey, how's fer usin' the brass knucks now? We ain't had no brass knucks lately."

"OK," grunted the biggest of the Negroes. "Dat is, if'n it's OK wid de victim."

"OK, don't mind me," piped the man on the table, grinning up through the black-and-blue blur of his ravaged face. "I can take it." Surprisingly, he giggled. "Lay on, MacDuff!"

The Negroes began to assail his midriff with brass knuckles. He howled and grunted at every blow.

"SPLATT!" yapped the stenographer on the stool. "Oh, Boy, lissen to him! URRK! BLIPP! WHIZZLE! Hey, you witha lead pipe—rap him onna noggin again, I did'n catch it the firs' time: There! SPOOOIIINNNGGG!!!"

Doctor Nork tapped me on the shoulder. "Had enough?" he whispered. I nodded.

"Let's go." He led the way back to the stairs, calling over his shoulder, "Don't overdo it, boys, and be careful how you hit him. Last time you broke three whips and a truncheon. Those things cost money, you know."

"BOING!" yelled the stenographer. "BOINGA-BOINGA-BOINGA!"

As we plodded up the steps, Nork sighed. "There's so much to worry about," he confided. "So much to do. It isn't easy, being the mastermind of all the comic books."

VII

We sat in another chamber, now—Doctor Nork's spacious and imposing library. A hundred shelves, rising to the dizzying height of the ceiling, encircled us on all sides. Every shelf was packed, crammed, jammed full of paperbound books with lurid covers. Nork reached over to an end-table and selected one at random, riffling the pages as he spoke.

"Of course, you can understand what we're doing down there, now," he said. "Just getting our blurbs that's all. Filling the old balloons."

"Filling the what?"

"The balloons. You know—the things coming out of the characters' mouths in comic books. When a crook gets hit by the hero, he makes a noise. Or the weapon makes a noise. Sometimes they both make noises."

"Like BANG and OUCH?"

"There—you see?" Doctor Nork beamed. "We can't use BANG and OUCH all the time. Or WHAM and ZOWIE and POW. They're corny. Besides, the Flushing Chain of Comic Books covers about twenty titles a month—that means roughly five thousand separate panels or drawings. Now you figure that at least four thousand of those panels in every comic book represent somebody getting hit, lashed, flayed, burned, punched, beaten, shot, stabbed, or run over with a steamroller—that takes a lot of different noises and sounds for balloons.

"We strive for variety, understand? But variety alone is not enough. My boss, the publisher, Bloodengore Flushing, is a stickler for realism. He wants accurate sounds. So that's why we hold experiments. We beat up a victim and take down the noises for our balloons. Get it?"

I got it, but couldn't handle it. "You mean to say your comic books are drawn from real life?"

"More or less. That's where I come in. Mr. Flushing pays me a fortune, my dear sir, to mastermind the Flushing Chain. He endowed this laboratory, set up a fund for research, took me under contract for that purpose alone—to make sure that the sixty million readers of such famous comics as *Captain Torture* and *Hatchet Man* get only the finest and most realistic literature.

"Why, would you believe it, when I took over he only published three comic books and two of them were actually funny?

"It was ridiculous, and I told him so. Everybody knows that there's no point in a comic book that's funny! Why, people will laugh at it! What they want is thrills; girls with big busts and men with big muscles."

"I don't know much about comic books," I confessed. "I had rather a sketchy education. I thought people just wrote and drew them into some kind of an office."

"'That's the old-fashioned way," Nork laughed. "Since I went to work for Flushing, we've changed all that. Ours is a great humanitarian enterprise; catering to sixty million readers as we do, bringing them romance, adventure, murder, arson, insanity, fratricide, bestiality. That's a great responsibility, my boy, and I am keenly aware of it.

"When I went to work for the Chain, I was just a broken-down old Nobel Prize winner, puttering around in a laboratory. I smashed a few atoms, that's just about all I did. Now I am engaged in a great crusade to bring comic-book culture to the masses.

"That's why Flushing hired me. Up to the time I came here, comic books were put out just about the way you said they were: in offices, by artists and writers who worked solely with their imaginations. They kept thinking up new variants of Superman and that's about all they could do—occasionally they did a sort of Tarzan takeoff or a Dick Tracy imitation. But it was stale, flat, repetitious.

"You see, the trouble was that they lacked *facts* to go by. They went stale because they didn't know anything about their subject matter. None of them had ever been to the jungle, let alone lived with gorillas. None of them had ever used a ray-gun or split a Jap spy's head open with a butcher's cleaver. None of them could walk through walls, or put on a suit of red underwear and fly through the air.

"That's where I came in. I brought the scientific method to bear, the experimental approach. Now all the artists and writers work from rough sketches and material supplied by me, here in my laboratory. Everything you see in Flushing Comics has been pre-tested and is guaranteed accurate."

"You mean you've created a comic book world?" I gasped.

"More or less. Who do you think taught that gorilla to talk? I worked with him ever since he was a tiny rhesus; made him listen to Linguaphone records, everything. And why do you think our drawings are so accurate? Because I have an artist here sketching night and day; you saw me posing as the Mad Doctor with that girl when you came in. That's why I wore the false red beard—it looks better in color reproduction. Many people have been kind enough to tell me that I make the best and most convincing Mad Doctor they've ever seen."

"I'm sure you do," I said, politely.

"Take those fellows downstairs—they're working on the sound effects, as I told you. All over this great laboratory experiments are going on concurrently, and trained observers are noting the results; roughing out sketches, transcribing bits of dialogue, thinking up plots. The result is obvious—Flushing Comics today are beyond all doubt the most realistically gruesome, hideous, ghastly, sanguinary and horrible comics is the world."

"But what about all those super-characters?" I asked. "You can teach gorillas to talk and pose for pictures and beat people up, but where do you get the ideas for those invincible heroes with the wonderful powers?"

"I give them the powers," purred Doc, for Nork. "My experiments in nuclear physics, chemo-biology, endocrinology and mopery have borne fruit. Strange fruit. As you shall presently see. Speaking of fruit, it's time for luncheon. And now you'll have an opportunity to meet some of the actual characters I have created for Flushing Comics."

VIII

Doctor Nork and I dined in palatial splendor. For the first few minutes after our entry into the huge hall, we were alone, save for the silent servants; tall, white- faced men who stared straight ahead it impassive obeisance as they offered us our choice of delicacies.

"How well trained they are," I whispered, as one of the black-liveried footman served me with a helping of jugged flamingo and pickled eland tongues. "They never say a word do they?"

"Not remarkable at all," said Doctor Nork, as he carved the *piece de resistance*—a huge baked wildebeeste head with an enormous apple in its mouth. "How can they say anything? Some of them are zombies and the rest of them are dead. I reanimated them myself, you know."

"I didn't know," I gulped. "And I'm not so sure I want to. You actually raised corpses up to be your servants?"

"Sure. Don't you read the comics? Scientists are always going into their laboratories and shooting a lot of electrical arcs through bodies. Had to try it myself just for the sake of accuracy. It worked. And after I had these cadavers animated again, and I had no other use for them except as serve ants. Still it worries me."

"Worried me, too," I agreed. "I don't like their looks."

"Oh, that doesn't matter," Nork replied. "I just don't want the Waiter's Union to find out." He gnawed a yak-leg and offered me some jellied eel.

"Where are the other I was supposed to meet?" I asked.

"Others? They'll be along, I'm sure. Matter of fact, here they come now."

The Strange Island of Doctor Nork

His remark was unnecessary. My bursting eardrums and bulging eyes attested to the arrival of some exceedingly strange strangers.

The first one to enter wasn't so bad—he was obviously human, despite his red cloak and the helmet he wore, which resembled an inverted *commode*. The only thing that disconcerted me in the least was the fact that he didn't walk in. He *flew*.

Behind him was a hopping figure. It might have been a gigantic frog with a human face. It might have been a gigantic human with a frog's body. Whatever it was, I didn't care for it.

Right behind the batrachian being stalked a tall man who displayed remarkable stoicism, in so far ashes hair seemed to be on fire.

Even as I stared, my attention was arrested, tried, and condemned by another gentleman whose exceedingly long neck seemed to be made of wood. This neck was surmounted by a most unconventional head—flat on top, hooked in the rear, and round in front. There were no features visible in the round surface, which was shiny and metallic.

My eyes were still fighting the battle of the bulge when the girl came in. She was tall, slim, alluring; her body a pale shaft of moonlight and her hair a shimmering simulacrum of the sun. She wore a combination of leopard-skin bra and shorts that was very pretty, in spots.

I saw no reason why she needed to also wear a large boa-constrictor for a scarf—but she did. One would also assume that a wench with such long, lithe, lovely limbs might be satisfied to walk; but no, she had to ride on the back of a lion.

"Greetings!" said the girl, as the lion halted before us and begin to slaver over my shoes.

"Hi," chirped Doctor Nork. He beamed at me. "Meet my daughter, Albino—the White Goddess of the Jungle."

"Your daughter?"

"Brought her up among the animals to be useful in my work. Decided to make a female Tarzan out of her at an early age, when she showed signs of inheriting my own fondness for wild game. You may not know it, but I used to be quite a sportsman myself. Earned quite a reputation as a deer-hunter in my youth—I was a fast man with a buck."

Albino sat down, unwound her snake, and replaced it with a napkin. She began to feed her lion from my plate.

"Pass the salt," she said.

I did so, trembling—a human saltshaker. She noticed my tremor and sniffed disdainfully.

"Where'd you find this jerk, Pa?" she asked. "You know I don't like sissies."

I was all set to give her a snappy comeback, but something choked off my flow of conversation. That something was the boa-constrictor, which now began to twine around my neck. I removed it hastily and wiped my hands on what I thought was a napkin. But napkins don't roar.

I took my hands out of the lion's mane and turned to Doctor Nork. "What an aggregation," I murmured.

"All normal people," he assured me. "At least, they were until I got to work on them. You see before you, my dear sir, the results of years of experiments. My daughter was just a plain, ordinary little girl until I taught her how to behave like a monkey. In her case, all that was required was a little child psychology. Instead of giving her a doll to play with, I gave her a talking gorilla. The rest followed easily.

"In some of the other cases, surgery was necessary. Take Water Boy, for example."

"Who?"

* * *

He indicated the frog-man. "One of Flushing Comics' most popular characters. I made him; raised him from a tadpole, as it were. As a result of a unique series of experiments, he's now more frog than human. It was a risky business to turn a man into a frog—more than once I thought he'd croak. But you can see for yourself how successful I've been."

Nork pointed at the man with the flaming hair. "That's Fire-Bug," he told me. "The Human Torch. Goes around give criminals the hotfoot. I developed his metabolism to the point where he can actually live on fire."

"That's why he's eating coal, eh?"

"Precisely. And as for our flying man, Rogers—"

"Buck Rogers?"

"No. Two-Dollar Rogers, we call him. He's twice as good as Buck."

I turned away in bewilderment. "Let me get this straight once and for all," I said. "You experiment on people and develop superhuman or unusual characteristics. Then you watch their actions and use what you see as the basis for plot-material in comic books."

"Right. Now—"

The Strange Island of Doctor Nork

A violent pounding interrupted him. The strange being with the long wooden neck and the metallic head was using the blank spot where his face should be—using it as a walnut-cracker.

"Hammerhead," explained the Doctor. "Our readers get a bang out of him." He giggled. "Did you see our last issue featuring him? Had a sequence where he uses his head as an atom-smasher."

I tried to ignore the scientist's remarks and make a little time with Albino. But she obviously despised me for a weakling; just a poor coward who was probably secretly afraid of rhinocerii.

"Ow!"

* * *

The shout came from down at the end of the table. Hammerhead had accidentally banged the fingers of Fire-Bug.

"Look what you're doing, clumsy!" he yelled.

"Don't get hot under the collar," retorted Hammerhead.

For answer Fire-Bug opened his mouth, but no remarks came out. Instead, a six-foot tongue of living flame belched forth. Hammerhead ducked just in time, but Two-Dollar Rogers got smoke in his eyes. Rising, cloak whirling about him in red fury, the superhuman flier whipped out a strange, gleaming weapon and leveled it at the human torch.

"I'll blast you!" he yelled. Lightning crackled from the muzzle, and Fire-Bug ducked as an atomic beam disintegrated the chair in which he had been sitting. At the same time, he let go with another burst of flame.

Water Boy opened his frog-mouth and extinguished the blaze, inelegantly but effectively.

"Wet smack!" screamed Rogers, leveling his weapon. Fire-Bug turned toward him, ready to blaze away. Hammerhead poised himself to pound him down.

"*Quiet!*" screamed Doctor Nork. "Cut it out—get out of here, all of you. If you can't learn to behave and get along with one another, I'll—I'll turn the Faceless Fiend loose on you!"

There was a deathly silence.

"There," said the Doctor. "That's telling them, eh? But where are you?"

"Here," I gasped. "Right here—under the table."

Albino sniffed.

"I—uh—dropped my fork," I said.

"You're scared," she accused. "I can tell by the way your hand trembles."

"What hand?"

"The one on my ankle. Take it off."

* * *

I rose and took my place again. "All right," I said. "I *am* scared. Who wouldn't be with all this blasting and firing and pounding going on?"

"If you think these characters are bad, you ought to see the Faceless Fiend," she told me.

"Who is he? I noticed everybody shut up when his name was mentioned."

Nork's face clouded. He sighed heavily and reached for a platter of breaded horse-kidneys. "One of my few failures," he murmured. "Some of my agents spirited away a mass-murderer from the penal colony in French Guiana. That's where I get most of my subjects—you'll find that comic book characters are best when they have criminal minds.

"Anyhow, this time I intended to create a super-criminal for a new book. The man was frightfully disfigured, and as a first step I attempted to remedy his condition with plastic surgery. At the same time, I began psychiatric treatment with deep hypnosis; my aim was to uncondition all fits reflexes and hibit all his inhibitions. This I did, while working on his face to remove the scars.

* * *

"Alas, I did my work too well. I had him in a state of complete abandon, psychically, long before his features were rebuilt by plastic surgery. As a matter of fact, I had just finished removing his old features and hadn't gotten around to building new ones when he— escaped. Ran away.

"Of course, when the poor fellow removed the bandages, he found that he had no face left at all. This, coupled with his mental unbalance, resulted in the creation of the perfect super-criminal: the Faceless Fiend.

"Nobody knows what he looks like, because he doesn't look like anyone. He has no scruples—just hatred of society. Gifted with superhuman cunning, he has managed to evade capture and even now is lurking somewhere on this island. I've sent my staff out time and time again to comb the jungles for him. I imported several beachcombers just to comb the beaches. But he eludes me.

"Meanwhile he swears vengeance on me and all my work. He threatens me in a million ways. I am convinced it is he who writes letters to the press denouncing comic books."

"Say, wait a minute," I said. "I wonder if he wrote that note?"

I told him about the message I'd found in a bottle on the beach.

"That's his work," Norlc nodded. "A dangerous adversary, my friend."

The gorilla shined into the room and taped the Doctor on the shoulder.

"Sorry to interrupt," he said, "but it's time for you to come down to the crocodile pits.

"We're getting ready to draw that sequence where Wonder Child ties their tails into Boy Scout knots. If we get that out of the way this afternoon, we can go right on to the scene where he strangles his grandmother—right?"

"Right." Nork rose. "Excuse me," he said. "The press of business affairs. Perhaps you're tired. I'll ask Albino to see you to your room."

"Follow me," the girl urged. "Do you want to ride my lion?'

"No thanks, I'll walk."

We left the banquet hall and ascended a spiral staircase. The blonde girl led me into a handsomely furnished bedroom.

"Maybe a little sleep will quiet your nerves," she observed. The scorn in her voice was evident.

"I'll be all right, thanks," I said. "Oh—what's that?"

A rumbling rose, and the air was suddenly suffused with blue flame.

"Nothing at all, scaredy-cat," she snickered. "Just a little hurricane coming up, I suppose."

"Hurricane?"

I stared out of the window and saw that she spoke the truth.

IX

The storm was gathering over the tropical isle. Water boiled like lava across the beach. The palmettos prostrated themselves before the fury of the storm. Wind roared from all points of the compass, and the currents clashed overhead to tear the very air to ribbons.

A kaleidoscopic cloud of macaws blew across the island, followed by a white cumulus of seagulls—borne ruthlessly away by the violence of the elements.

"Quit shaking, you coward!" taunted the girl. "I'll turn on the the lights." She did so. I collapsed across the bed, watching the onslaught of the storm. The walls trembled and I followed suit.

"Oh, you're impossible," she told me. "Just like all the other men I've ever met—afraid of everything."

"You can't blame me," I replied. "After all, not everybody has had your advantages. Being brought up by a gorilla, and all that."

"Never mind the excuses," Albino said. "It doesn't matter. I've been the White Goddess of the jungle here for five years, and I'm getting pretty darn sick of it, too. Always waiting for some strong, handsome, virile he-man to come along and woo me, like they do in the comic books. And what do I get? A bunch of weaklings, namby-pamby characters who are afraid of everything—lions, snakes, hurricanes."

"And you're not afraid of anything?"

"Of course not."

"You're sure?"

There was a crash overhead and suddenly the lights went out. The room was black—an inky vacuum in the dark womb of storm.

I winced, but the girl's voice rose strong and clear in the darkness.

"I fear nothing," she told me. "Not even the Faceless Fiend himself."

"That's very good to hear. I'd hate to have caused you any discomfort."

"What's that?" I yelled. "Who said that?"

"Me. The Faceless Fiend."

"You're here—in this room?"

"Just came in through a secret staircase," the slow voice hissed. "I've been waiting to get my hands on you ever since you arrived."

"You don't say," I answered, hurling myself in the direction of the door. Thunder boomed and wind howled.

"Don't try to escape," chuckled the unseen presence. "You can't see in the dark, but I can. And I'm going to get you."

"Help!" I yelled. Albino—save me!"

"Stay where you are," the girl commanded. "I'm coming."

"So am I!" cackled the menacing voice.

I whirled, then cried out.

"Ouch!" I yelled. Something hit me in the back of my neck.

It was the ceiling.

X

When I opened my eyes, I was lying strapped to a table in a long, narrow underground chamber. Blue light flickered in mephitic gloom. Crouching above me was a cloaked figure. I stared up and was rewarded only by a blank look. This creature, this monster, this being with an empty gap between neck and hairline, was something not to be countenanced. It was beyond all doubt the Faceless Fiend. His chuckle sounded out of emptiness, slithering off the slimy walls.

"Don't look so unhappy, my friend," he purred. "You ought to thank me for rescuing you. Here you are, safe and sound in a nice, comfortable sewer, while above us the entire laboratory has collapsed."

"Collapsed? Was it lightning?"

"No, just rain. The place just melted away."

"How could that be?"

"Simple," explained my captor, "Doctor Nork built it all out of guano. Apparently he didn't feed the seagulls enough cement. At any rate, the entire structure has been demolished—and your friends have all perished. No one is left but the two of us."

"Dead?" I cried. "All of them—you're sure?"

"Beyond a doubt. It's an end to the whole insane scheme; the comic books will go out of existence, and Doctor Nork will no longer be free to perpetrate his wicked experiments in the name of science."

"But the girl," I persisted. "Albino, she was in the room with us—"

"I snatched you through the trapdoor and down the secret staircase just in time. I'm afraid you'll have to face it. We're alone. And now, speaking of facing it—"

The cloaked figure stooped to the side of the table and rose again. One hand clutched a small saw. "Speaking of facing it," he continued, "I am about to perform a small experiment of my own. Ever since I lost my face, I've waited for a chance to find another. I hid down here in the sewers under the laboratory and bided my time. I didn't want to take a stupid mug like Nork's and I certainly wouldn't appropriate the visage of any of his monsters.

"But when you flew in to the island this morning, I knew my long vigil was over. Sorry, I cannot offer you any anesthetic, but time is short."

"You—you mean you're going to steal my face?" I screamed.

"I prefer to think of it as a little facelifting job," answered my captor. "Please now; just relax."

The Faceless Fiend bent forward, saw in hand. It was a typical scene from a comic story—as such, it probably would have delighted ten million dear little kiddies throughout the land. But it didn't amuse me in the least.

The saw grazed my neck—

A roar shattered the walls. A tawny blur bore the cloaked figure backwards into the shadows. There were screams, and growls, and other less pleasant noises generally heard only at presidential conventions or in zoos.

"Good work!"

Albino was at my side, using the saw on the ropes that bound me. She gestured towards the shadows of the sewer beyond, where the lion was now creating a Bodiless Fiend.

"We got through the trapdoor in time, just behind you. Then part of the walls gave, and we were delayed—but not too long."

"Then it's true," I said. "The laboratory is destroyed?"

"Everything's gone," she sighed. "Even this sewer isn't safe much longer. Let's get out of here."

A crash accented her words. Turning, I saw that the shadowed portion of the sewer had disappeared, hiding both the lion and the Faceless Fiend from view forever beneath fresh debris.

"This way," Albino urged, pulling me along the corridor. "There should be a sewer outlet to the beach."

"Thanks for rescuing me," I panted.

"Think nothing of it," the girl answered. "That's just a reflex action, you know. Been rescuing people for years now for the comics."

The damp walls of the sewer twisted and turned. We raced along, Albino taking a lithe-limbed lead. She rounded a curve ahead of me and I blundered forward.

Suddenly she screamed.

I turned the corner and grasped her arm.

"What's the matter?" I said.

The girl stood there shaking in a frenzy of fear.

"Eeeeeh!" she shrieked. "Take it away!"

"Huh?" I said.

For answer, she clung to me and threw herself forward and upward into my arms. I held her close.

"Look!" she sobbed. "Down there—make it go away!"

"Where?" I asked.

"There."

'But—it's only a mouse," I said.

She began to cry. I stepped, forward, carrying her in my arms, and the mouse retreated to its burrow with a shrill squeak.

Albino was weeping hysterically, and the more she cried the more I grinned.

"There, there," I said. "Don't you worry. I'll protect you."

There isn't much more to tell. By the time we emerged upon the broad expanse of the beach, the hurricane had blown away and only a gentle rain fell upon the ruins of the big laboratory on the cliff.

Despite my fears, I found the plane quite undamaged, save for a minor accident that had crumpled part of the landing gear. As it was, I managed a takeoff and a subsequent landing some hours later in the airport at Jamaica.

Within a day Albino and I were back in civilization. I managed to sell her on the notion, while *en route*, that her brand of courage was of no value in New York.

"People seldom encounter lions and tigers in the city," I told her, "but the place is simply lousy with mice. What you need is someone like me to protect you."

She agreed, meekly enough. And that's why we were married, even before I reported to my editor with the story.

That episode is still painful in my memory. Being called a liar and a drunkard is bad enough, but when he accused me of opium-smoking, there was only one course left open to me.

"I resign!" I shouted, as he booted me down the stairs.

Still, it's all over now, and Albino doesn't mind. I have a new job— bought a little newsstand over on Seventh Avenue. I don't make much money selling newspapers, but there's always enough to buy a few mousetraps for the house.

Besides, I manage to sell quite a lot of comic books....

Lilies

The Colorado Apartments is a substantial building, its red-brick walls rising to a four-story eminence that sets it definitely apart from the squalid sordidness of the surrounding neighborhood. Its tenants are likewise removed from the general wretched run of tenement scum that dwells in the ramshackle pest-holes adjoining the dignified brick edifice.

Most of these tenants have been in the building since its construction twenty three years ago; they are solid, middle-aged and infinitely respectable—the men white collar clerks or accounts, the women plump, comfortable and childless, filling lonely hours with parential ministration to pet canaries. There are widowers, too—grey old men, and widows—grey old women; a very solid, conservative group of tenants indeed. They are a clannish group, the women exchanging gossip and recipes across the back porch of a morning; the men greeting each other from behind their evening papers on the front porch. They would visit one another perhaps, were it not for the unseen barrier of an apartment, the alien sense of espionage that is implied in the phrase, "across the hall". Apartment dwellers love privacy. Still, they do exchange foods—a cut of pie or pudding or perhaps a cool drink in the spring or summer.

There was, for example, Mrs. Hahn and her flowers.

Mrs. Hahn was an elderly widow who dwelt directly below our 3rd floor apartment in number 13. She was German, a motherly soul much given to puttering around in her kitchen. She never left her house save on a Saturday afternoon when her married son called for her in his car and they spent the rest of the afternoon in the country. Invariably on Saturday evening she would laboriously mount the stairs to our apartment and present my mother with an armful of wild flowers gathered in the country by "me and my son Willie".

Her pathetic pleasure in this humble task and her reward in our thanks she enjoyed with wistful pride. She was grateful for this, her one weekly rite, the one chance she still had to be giving and doing in a world that had passed her by.

This weekly incident was repeated regularly for nearly a year. Every Saturday the old woman and her flowers came in the midnight dust—the floral tributes varying with the season; violets, sweet peas, marigolds, gladiolas, nasturtiums, poppies, roses.

Finally there came a Saturday late in October when the expected visitor did not materialize. Night deepened, and still no familiar ring upon our doorbell. We had not seen the old woman all week, and my mother was greatly relieved when at eight o'clock the bell finally rang and she opened the door to find the bent, familiar figure of the old woman standing outside in the darkness of the shadowed hall.

"Good evening." The usual greeting, cheerful yet hesitant.

"Why, good evening, Mrs. Hahn. Been out in the country again this week?"

"Well, no, not exactly., Anyway, my son Willie come and bring me these flowers—what a thoughtful boy he is, my son! and I thought if you might like a few—"

She proffered the bouquet. My mother thanked her; she turned and slowly descended the stairs once more. We heard the door of her apartment close softly, and closed our own.

My Mother snapped on the light. Then she gasped—for the flowers in her arms were white calla lilies. She held them, staring oddly at the waxen blooms; was still holding them, in fact, when she looked through the window. A big car pulled up—black it was and shiny, with a closed back, and very long—and two men stepped out. One of them was Willie Hahn, and he was crying. Mother stepped over to the window. Hahn and the stranger were coming up the steps. They were outside our door now, on the way upstairs, and I heard a flash of their conversation.

"Yes, I brought some flowers—lilies, of course. Left them here about an hour ago on the—"

Mother looked out of the window at the funeral car: Then she glanced down at the flowers again, and for the first time noticed the tag around the stems.

Lilies

"In memory of my dear mother, Mrs. Ludwig Hahn."

Upstairs they were moving the coffin, and nobody noticed that the flowers on her breast were gone.

The Hound of Pedro

They said he was a wizard, that he could never die. Men whispered that he held traffic with the undead and that his swarthy servants were not of human kind. The Indians murmured their fears of his incredibly wrinkled face in which, they averred, blazed two green eyes that flamed in a manner alien to men. The padres muttered too, and hinted that no mortal could exercise the powers he controlled.

But nobody knew who Black Pedro Dominguez was, or where he had come from. Even today the peons tell their tales of the Spanish oppressor, and mumble fearfully that monstrous climax which has become a legend throughout all Sonora.

It was a spring day in Novorros; that morning of April fifth, 1717. The hot sun beat upon the adobes, the wind whirled dust amidst the cacti. The bells were tolling noontide in the little stone chapel of the mission. Almost it seemed as though they pealed in welcome to the little band of men that rode up through the canyon to Novorros town that noon. Indeed they might, for the shaman's drums had boomed over the western hills the night before, spreading the story of the caballero who rode with his beast of black.

The Yaqui tribesmen filled the streets, their sullen faces illumined by the light of curiosity. The padre and his two brothers of the cloth watched discreetly from the steps of the mission as Black Pedro Dominguez rode into town.

* * *

Forty men and fifty horses smoked through the dust at a gallop. Strange, shining men, faceless in iron armor, straddling snorting steeds—the Indians were curiously impressed. They knew of the *conquistadores* from tales their fathers told; they had seen horses before. But the sight of the burnished steel corselets, the sun-tipped lances, the grilled masks—these things impressed them.

The padre and his brethren were impressed, too, but by more subtle details. They noted the man that rode behind the leader, the tall, lean figure on the white pony whose garb differed curiously from the war-like raiment of his fellows. This thin rider's face was hidden not by steel but by a silken mask; he wore no helmet, but a curious turban. By this and by his light Saracenic armor the priests knew him for a Moor. A Moor of Granada—here!

Then there was the heavy figure on the bay mare, the man who sat uneasily astride as though unused to riding. He wore no helmet, but about his head was wound a scarlet neckerchief. The glitter of his squinting eyes was matched by the sparkle of the gold earrings that dangled at either side of his bearded visage. He carried neither sword nor spear, but in his bloused belt reposed a hilted cutlass, in a scabbard that shone with jewels. The padre recognized him, for he had crossed the Caribbean in a galleon long years ago. This man was a buccaneer.

There were other unusual features which the white men observed while the Yaquis remained in ignorance, but there were two things which both groups noticed, two objects which impressed: Black Pedro Dominguez and his hound.

Had anyone present known of the legend, the comparison would have been irresistible, for Pedro Dominguez was seated on his horse like a malignant Buddha. He was a hog in armor, a swarthy, bearded hog whose porcine jowls were surmounted by a splayed nose and the skull-shadowed eyes of a more carnivorous beast. His forehead was a livid scar; he had been branded there by slave-irons, it seemed. There was something impressive about the man's very obscene ugliness; he *was* Buddha, but Buddha turned demon.

The natives felt it, the priests felt it. Here was evil in man.

Then they saw the hound. A great black shape loped at the heels of Pedro's horse. Huge as a cougar, supple as a panther, black as the velvet of midnight; this was the hound of Pedro. Yellow claws gleamed in the ink of great splayed paws; dark muscles rippled across the enormous belly. The lion-head was jeweled with ruby eyes, and the great slavering jaws opened on a fanged red maw that gaped in hideous hunger.

The natives felt it, the priests felt it. Here was evil in beast.

The Hound of Pedro

Black Pedro Dominguez and his hound rode through the town. The cavalcade halted at the mission steps. The priest raised his hands in benediction as Pedro dismounted and stood before him.

The band had traveled far. There was foam on the horses' flanks and dust upon the armor of their riders. Sweat oozed across Black Pedro's scarred forehead. The hound cowered at his feet, moaning, with its tongue lolling like a red serpent.

Therefore as Pedro approached, the padre opened his mouth to invite him into the mission; rest, food, water might be provided.

*   *   *

Before he could speak, Black Pedro growled a greeting. He, he informed the padre, was Pedro Dominguez of Mexico City. He wished nothing from the good father save that he should immediately pronounce the prayers for the dead.

"What is this, sir?" the padre asked. "Can it be that you carry with you the body of some poor man who died unshriven in the desert?"

"No," said Pedro, curtly. "But get along with the prayer." His dark eyes smoldered.

"But I do not understand," the priest continued. "Who is this prayer for?"

"For you—you fool!" Pedro smiled, grim mirth flaming in his eyes. "For you!"

It happened very quickly then. Even as he spoke, Pedro's saber had leaped from the scabbard, risen in Pedro's hand, and descended in flashing fury on the priest's neck. There was a thud and the padre's body lay in red dust. There was a puddle in the little space between head and neck.

Others had seized the two brethren. Daggers flashed in silver sunlight. The black-gowned men dropped beside their superior.

The Yaquis stood silent. Then a vast murmuring arose, a muffled drone of anger. These strangers had killed the white brothers. Knives and bows appeared in brown hands. The tall natures closed in on the mission steps, converging in a red wave.

As if by premeditated signal the little band of whites grouped themselves in a semicircle. Pistols appeared. And as the tribesmen closed m, flame burst upon them. A score dropped, screaming. Another belch of fire. Brown bodies writhed in agony on the dusty ground. The natives turned and fled up the adobe-lined street. The whites remounted, wheeled their steeds, and leveled their lances. Steel shivered through the retreating backs. Swords hacked at heads and shoulders. There were screams and imprecations; horses whinnied and armor clanged. But above all was the sound of grisly laughter as Black Pedro sat quaking on the mission steps. Beside him was the great hound. As the beast began to worry the bodies of the young tribesmen, Pedro laughed anew.

II

The truce came soon. The Yaquis dragged away the bodies of their slain. Gomez, the mestizo chieftain, parleyed in the mission chapel with Pedro that evening. When he heard Pedro's terms—his command—the old Indian's gray face turned pale with sick rage. He muttered to himself of Yaztan, the great Yaqui leader to the south. Even now a messenger to Yaztan was on his way, and that champion would raise an army of thousands to march against this invader.

Pedro listened, chuckled. He beckoned to the turbaned figure of the Moor behind him. Smiling with cryptic relish, the Arab bowed and left the room. In a moment he returned, bearing a leathern saddle-bag.

Pedro placed it on the table before him. Then he faced the silent Indian.

"Yaztan," he said. "I have heard of this Yaztan, the mighty chief. Is it not true that he is said to have a ring of gold set within his nose, and has pierced his cheeks with golden bracelets?"

The Indian nodded in assent.

Pedro smiled, looked at the Yaqui without comment, and opened the bag on the table.

* * *

Something shriveled and dry rolled out—something that held the glitter of gold about a crumbled nose and sparkled yellowly in bloodless cheeks. There were no eyes in this—the head of Yaztan.

"I have already visited your chief," Pedro purred. "Before he died he told me of this place; of its mission, and of your tribe's mines. He spoke of your gold, and by the nature of your people's ornaments I see that he spoke truly. Now, as I have said, you will mine this gold for us. You have heard my terms; think them over. Or perhaps you might join Yaztan—"

The Hound of Pedro

Thus began the tyranny of Black Pedro; the dreadful days of bondage about which men still whisper.

They tell how Pedro visited the crude native mines, and how he ordered them enlarged and changed so that the labors of his servants might be increased. They speak of the manner in which he conscripted all the able-bodied males of the tribe, so that the women were forced to hunt while their men-folk toiled in the mines, guarded over by the bearded white men with their flame-rods that dealt death to the disobedient and their whips that bloodied the backs of the laggard and weary. They tell also of the gold that was piled in the mission towers, of the ingot-lined chamber at the church where now Black Pedro dwelt.

They speak with shame about the usage accorded their women by Pedro and his men, of Maquila the chieftain's daughter who danced to the stroke of whips in the courtyard when she failed to please the strange dark man who rode behind Black Pedro. They whisper of young virgins who disappeared each month; for with every moon Pedro exacted the tribute of a maiden.

The dark man would come at dusk to the village and demand the girl; then she would ride away to the mission house and disappear. No one dared approach that night, though the screaming sometimes would be borne afar on the lonely wind; no one dared ask next day why the girl did not return.

There was asking at first; the chief's son came, with ten young men. And Pedro scowled at them, while his hirelings seized the youths in sight of the entire tribe. They were stripped and carried to the desert. Here Black Pedro caused holes to be dug in the sand and in these holes were lowered the bodies of the young tribesmen, and earth was heaped around so that they stood buried up to the neck.

Only their heads stood silhouetted against the sand; only their faces wreathed in wonderment and vague fear. They could not know, dared not guess their fate. Did Pedro mean to leave them here to starve and die? Would they suffer hunger, thirst, the torment of heat? Would the wheeling vultures come to feast?

* * *

The tribe watched, impassive, held in check by Pedro's crew. They saw Pedro conversing with the dark man, and the swarthy squint-eyed one with the rings in his ears. They heard Pedro whisper

273

to the squint-eyed one, and he laughed terribly and cursed in his outlandish tongue.

Then Black Pedro motioned to his soldiers, and they forced the throng away. There were fathers, mothers, wives, children of the ten young braves in that group; they were herded back with the rest.

Ten pairs of eyes followed them—ten pairs of eyes from heads set in the sand. Hopeless, helpless eyes.

The men escorted the savages back to the village. Pedro, the dark man, and the squint-eyed lieutenant remained all alone with the buried, living heads.

What occurred in the next few hours could never be rightly known. But the Yaquis could guess. For there were terrible hintings.

Several soldiers went into the convent and presently returned carrying great wooden balls of hardened fiber. These they carried back into the desert.

The savages had seen Pedro roll these balls along the inner lawn of the convent garden at times; he and the dark man were adept at bowling.

The balls were carried with them into the desert. Perhaps that was what Pedro had whispered to make the others laugh. He might have conceived a jest.

Ten-pins. Ten heads.

The heavy wooden balls rumbled thunderously as they rolled across the flat sands. The sound of human screams rose unmistakably over the booming.

When Pedro and his companions returned it was already dark. Their faces were flushed as though from exertion. When the released tribesmen hastened out to the desert, they could find no trace of heads in the sand. The men had vanished. But in the twilight when Black Pedro returned, they had seen ominous stains on the wooden bowling-balls.

The natives asked no questions, but their scowls deepened to the impassive malignity of the savage enraged. They dared not search the spot or linger to dig up that which they suspected lay beneath the sands; dared not search because it was night.

At night, Pedro's hound was abroad. It roamed their village at will, descended even to the mines where they toiled under the lash by day. When hungry, the beast sprang on the native nearest—unless an alert white guard beat it off in time. Sometimes the guard would not bother to repulse the hound if the attacked native was old and feeble.

The Hound of Pedro

That hound....

The Yaquis feared it more than they did their vicious but human master. They began to conceive queer fancies connected with both of these oppressors. These fancies were based on their scanty knowledge of what went on behind the convent walls where Pedro and his men lived in guarded seclusion. No one entered the place save to be conducted into dungeons and torture chambers below, but rumors spread. It was guessed that Pedro's band had come from Mexico, lured by tales of mines and yellow metal. How long he would stay here none could say, but the gold was piling up daily in the chapel rooms. A few old natives had been detailed to tend it there, and they started the disturbing rumors of life within the walls.

The dark man, they said, was a shaman—a wizard. It was he who advised Pedro, the old natives whispered; and it was he who tended the torture vaults in the abandoned cellars below the former mission. Victims came from the mines; disobedient natives were taken here and "punished" before their reward of death.

But (so hinted the oldsters) they were "punished" as a wizard would chastize; they were sacrificed, and their bodies rended in terrible ways.

It was the dark man, too, that demanded the virgin every moon. She was led into the cellars, the old Indians averred, and given in sacrifice where none could see. The dark man and Black Pedro and the hound went down into those depths with her, and there would be the sound of chanting and praying, the screams of the girl mingled with the baying of that sable beast.

The old ones cautiously spoke of how the hound would re-emerge after this and slink off into outer darkness, but they said Pedro and the dark man remained below for several days. When the hound returned they ventured abroad once more, to hear tales of new atrocities committed without the mission walls.

Some of the tribe believed these old ones in their mutterings. Certainly they came to fear Black Pedro and his great dog increasingly as the months went by. And the secret messengers they had sent to the south gave no word.

But even the most credulous refused to believe the wilder stories of Pedro speaking to the dog, and the animal replying in human tongue. Nevertheless a growing panic manifested itself in tribal ranks. There was talk of fleeing, but this was impossible. Uprising was out of the question; in truth, the men with the flame-rods were not over-cruel—it was Pedro, the dark man, and the strange beast that reveled in brutality.

* * *

Panic increased the rumors so that Pedro and his hound became almost legendary figures of evil. The two were almost alike in their animal lusts; dreadful things were hinted as to the fate of the maiden taken each month—tales of bestial passion and the old shaman stories of the uses accorded virgin blood. These stories drew added color from the almost human attributes displayed at times by the hound. If it could not talk to its master as the wildest stories reputed, it could at least understand human speech and make itself understood.

The Yaquis began to realize that on nights following the monthly ceremonies the great black hound prowled about their adobes; that it listened below windows and lurked amidst the shadows beyond their campfires.

For whenever there was midnight talk of rebellion and discontent Black Pedro knew of it, and summoned the speaker to the mission. Could it be that the beast actually *reported* these things? Or was it the wizardry of the strange dark man?

None knew the truth, but each passing day the shadow of Pedro and his hound loomed larger over all their lives. And far away the messengers sped south to spread the tale.

III

Don Manuel Digron halted his march at the head of the canyon. Signal fires smoked in the dusk, and the three emissaries were waiting as the messengers had said.

They held a secret parley in the darkness, while Don Manuel listened to the natives' story. He scowled deeply as he heard, then broached his plan of action. The Yaquis nodded, then faded away in the gloom of the twilight canyons.

The men-at-arms dismounted, encamped. Don Manuel Digron kept counsel with his aide, Diego.

"Sure it is the same man," he growled. "This is Black Pedro Dominguez of whom they speak. Friar Orspito tells me that this Pedro is long wedded to the Devil, for the Holy Inquisition seeks him even now in Mother Spain. He fled from there with the Moor, Abouri—a black wizard of Granada; men tell of their exploits. The hound Pedro rules is not an earthly thing, I warrant, if tales I've heard are true."

"What does such a man here?" Diego inquired. A frown crossed Don Manuel's lean face.

"I know not. He left Mexico City—he and his band of freebooters and gutter-rats—no doubt the smell of gold lured him across the plains to Sonora. It is always so. With gold he and his damned sorcerer can command an empire."

"Are we to turn him over to Mother Church or the civil authorities?" asked Diego.

"Neither," Manuel drawled. "We have no horses to convey forty captives across the desert, nor water and provisions to sustain them. They must be disposed of here—and if half the tales of evil magic be true, it is God's work to do this."

The Don stared at the fire for a moment, then continued.

"We may taste of necromancy tonight, Diego. The chieftains inform me that this is the eve appointed for sacrifice. A living maiden is delivered to him once each moon. I trust our arrival is timely; I do not care to ponder on the usage accorded a woman by these sorcerous swine."

The two men ate and drank.

IV

Two men ate and drank within the mission walls. Black Pedro dined tonight with Abouri, the Moor; they toasted gold and goety alike from amber goblets.

There was little of speech between them, but many a glance of dark understanding. The Moor smiled after a long silence, and lifted his glass.

"Fortune!" he pledged.

Pedro sneered, his little pig-eyes sullen with discontent.

"When shall we leave this cursed hole, Abouri? I long for cities where there is no sun to dry the juices from my body; we've gold enough to ransom the kings of all the world. Why tarry?"

The Moor pursed his lips urbanely as he stroked his graying beard, and his smile was placating.

"Patience," he counseled. "Be guided. by my wisdom, O brother. Was it not I who led you from the galleys to riches beyond all dreams? Did we not pledge a pact before Ahriman, your Sathanas; has not He guided us on our way?"

"True." Pedro was thoughtful.

"I have brought you wealth," pursued the Moor. "And I must have my due, as our bond with your Lucifer demands. Here we have found the blood of maidens and other useful things, and I may carry out my bargain undisturbed. That was our agreement with the Master before the Altar—wealth for you, and mantic power for me, and souls for Him."

Strange fear flooded Pedro's face.

"'Tis a dreadful pledge," he half whispered. "Souls for Him! And at what price! For the hound frightens me, and I am afraid when the exchange is made; should anything go amiss—"

The Moor raised his hand in a gesture of restraint. "That was the bond. The hound is His; He gave it to us as an instrument to secure souls for His Devil's bondage. A few days each month is little enough to ask in return for wealth. And yours is a nature to delight in the shedding of blood."

"As a man, yes—I warrant I find pleasure enough in slaying," Pedro admitted, with utter candor. "But as the other—"

Again the Moor checked his companion's speech. "Here is the maiden now, and we must prepare for this night's work."

Two trembling natives had entered the room, pushing a bound and frightened girl before them. She struggled in her bonds once they freed her legs, but they took no heed. Bowing low, they averted their faces and ran out. The Moor rose and approached the dark, lithe figure of the Indian maiden. As his hands grasped her pinioned arms she closed her eyes in utter fear.

Black Pedro leered, laughing.

"A fine wench, indeed!" he chuckled. "Could I but—"

"No," declared the Moor, sensing his purpose. "She must remain immaculate for the sacrifice. Come."

All mirth, all desire, vanished from Pedro's face as he followed the Moor and his captive down the winding stairs to the cellar crypts below. He knew what was to happen, and he was afraid.

There was nothing to reassure him in the dungeon itself. A vast, gloomy chamber, taper-litten, it was an oddly terrifying place.

The Hound of Pedro

Corridors stretched off into further gloom. Here were to be found the cages and the racks for prisoners, but the Moor did not go on. Instead he proceeded down the center of the main chamber to the further wall, where stood a great table and two flat rocks. There had been an altar here once, but it had since been removed and the crucifix above it inverted. An inverted crescent was emblazoned against it.

The girl was placed on the table. Braziers and flares were lit; alembics lifted to the light. Bubble-glass jars were hung over the fires, and a tripod sent pungent incense through the room in swirls of spiced smoke.

Tightly the girl was bound. Strongly the basin was held. Swiftly the knife was plunged. And a shriek, a moan, then bubble, bubble, bubble, as the basin filled.

Incense added, red and yellow powders filled the basin as it hung over the tripod. Black Pedro's swarthy face was pale, and sweat spurted across his gashed brows. The Moor ignored him as he worked over the flames.

Black horror loped into the room as the great dark hound slunk purposefully down the stairs. With prescient intelligence it stalked to the further of the two stone slabs and took its place upon it. Pedro reluctantly followed suit, mounting the second slab.

And then the Moor took up the basin, filled with red and silver bubbles that glistened in the light. And the tapers were snuffed out so that darkness fell upon the crypt, and only a strange red light flamed forth from the basin in the wizard's hands. That, and the emberous glow from the hound's deep eyes....

The hound lapped at the basin's contents with a long red tongue. Pedro sipped, his lips ashen with terror. The Moor stood beneath the cross and crescent in the pulsing darkness. He raised his arms in a gesture of invocation as man and beast sank into coma deep as death. Sibilantly came the wizard's prayer.

"Ahriman, Lord of Beasts and men—"

V

His sword was crimson when Manuel Digron raced down the darkened stairs. Behind him lay nightmare; nightmare and screaming death in the black reaches of the mission walls. The men-at-arms slew swiftly, but the Yaquis remained to mangle and maim in bloody attack.

The surprise attack had been successful. The Indians and the Spaniards had converged on the mission, and the forty were slain— murdered in their beds, for the most part; though a few had put up stout resistance under the leadership of the buccaneer.

Now Don Manuel Digron sought the cellar, with Diego and his lieutenants at his heels. The torches brought light as they rounded the curve in the stairs, and for a moment Manuel stared aghast.

The dead, bloodless thing lay on the table. Before it stood a tur- baned figure, rapt in prayer; and behind it the two dreadful slabs of stone, on which lay a man and a gigantic hound. The lips of the hound and the lips of the man were alike bloody. And the hound squatted in a dreadfully man-like fashion, while the man crouched. It was un- natural, that tableau.

At Manuel's descent, turmoil came. The Moor looked up and wheeled about, snatching a dagger from his scarved waist. Manuel dodged the descending weapon and thrust his sword upward so that it pierced the dark man's belly.

Then it ripped upward dreadfully, so that a crimson-gray tor- rent gushed forth from the side, and the Moor dropped writhing into death.

Then Manuel advanced to the slab where Black Pedro Dominguez lay. The great swarthy man cringed and gibbered, but drew no weap- on. Instead he cowered, whimpering like a beast when Manuel's sword ran him through.

Manuel turned upon the hound, but the great beast had already sprung. Two men-at-arms stood on the stairs, and it leaped for the first one's throat. He fell, and beast-jaws crunched. The mighty creature turned as the other soldier raised his lance. A great paw brushed spear and shield aside; then talons ripped into the man's face and left behind only a furrow of bleeding horror.

The hound was silent, ghastly silent; it did not growl or bay. Instead it turned and rose. On two hind legs it stood, in monstrous simulation of humanity; then it turned and raced up the stairs in frantic flight. Manuel stumbled, recovered a moment later.

The rest was never quite real to him. He lay still for but a moment, listening to the groans of the dying wizard on the crypt floor, but what he heard haunted him forever.

Babblings of black delirium … hints of a monstrous exchange the wizard made monthly after a blood sacrifice to Ahriman … tales of a lycanthropic pact whereby the bodies of Black Pedro and the Devil's hound held alien souls for days following the sacrifice, when the hound that was not a hound ravened forth for souls given to Satan in return for gold and gifts ... the cracked voice of the sorcerer, telling of a rite just concluded ... the monthly exchange just made through blood and prayers, and a werewolf serving Evil loosed upon the world once more to seek souls for the Master ... delirium or truth?

It was then that Manuel understood and screamed aloud as he jerked erect, glaring with horrified eyes at the feebly writhing body of the Moor. Shuddering; he whirled and sprang up the stairs in pursuit of the hound.

His soldiers met him. The Indians, they said, had captured the black beast as it raced into view from the depths. A Yaqui lay dead on the floor, his throat ribboned in mute testimony to the hound's ferocity. And now Manuel could hear, drums dinning in the hills, throbbing blood-lust.

He was muttering long-forgotten prayers as he ran toward where the red glare flickered, muttering prayers as he whipped the sword from his scabbard. A Yaqui death-chant, grim and relentless, boomed out into the savage night. Then Manuel plunged over the brow of the hill—and saw.

He saw that the Yaquis had remembered the deaths of their ten young men; they had remembered the ghastly jest of Black Pedro. And since he was dead, they were repeating that jest with Pedro's hound. He saw the dark head buried in sand to its shaggy throat; heard the thunder of wooden balls as they bowled along the sand, as they plunged unerringly at the screaming horror that was their target.

Manuel fell upon the natives. Snarling curses that somehow kept him sane, he and his men drove them back with the flats of their swords. And at last, alone, Manuel dared to approach the thing in the sand—the black, jutting head that lifted its foaming muzzle to the skies as it moaned in that last agony.

But Manuel, knowing what he did, dared not look at it. The wizard's dying whispers had been too much.

He gave only a swift, furtive glance as in mercy he thrust his sword through the ruined beast-skull. And as he stabbed, his heart went icy cold. He had seen the smashed jaws move feebly in one final effort as the dazed, eyes glared into his own. Then, above the muffled, triumphant thunder of the distant drums, Don Manuel heard that which confirmed all the legends and rumors of which the wizard had hinted.

Don Miguel heard the incredible voice, then collapsed beside the dying beast-head with the sound still dinning in his ears.

The hound of horror spoke.

And it moaned, *"Mercy—a prayer for the dead—for me—Black Pedro."*

The Bat Is My Brother

It began in twilight—a twilight I could not see.

My eyes opened on darkness, and for a moment I wondered if I were still asleep and dreaming. Then I slid my hands down and felt the cheap lining of the casket, and I knew that this nightmare was real.

I wanted to scream, but who can hear screams through six feet of earth above a grave?

Better to save my breath and try to save my sanity. I fell back, and the darkness rose all around me. The darkness, the cold, clammy darkness of death.

I could not remember how I had come here, or what hideous error had brought about my premature interment. All I knew was that I lived—but unless I managed to escape, I would soon be in a condition horribly appropriate to my surroundings.

Then began that which I dare not remember in detail. The splintering of wood, the burrowing struggle through loosely-packed grave earth; the gasping hysteria accompanying my clawing, suffocated progress to the sane surface of the world above.

It is enough that I finally emerged. I can only thank poverty for my deliverance—the poverty which had placed me in a flimsy, unsealed coffin and a pauper's shallow grave.

Clotted with sticky clay, drenched with cold perspiration, racked by utter revulsion, I crawled forth from betwixt the gaping jaws of death.

Dusk crept between the tombstones, and somewhere to my left the moon leered down to watch the shadowy legions that conquered in the name of Night.

The moon saw me, and a wind whispered furtively to brooding

trees, and the trees bent low to mumble a message to all those sleeping below their shade.

I grew restless beneath the moon's glaring eye, and I wanted to leave this spot before the trees had told my secret to the nameless, numberless dead.

Despite my desire, several minutes passed before I summoned strength to stand erect, without trembling.

Then I breathed deeply of fog and faint putridity; breathed, and turned away along the path.

It was at that moment the figure appeared.

It glided like a shadow from the deeper shadows haunting the trees, and as the moonlight fell upon a human face I felt my heart surge in exultation.

I raced towards the waiting figure, words choking in my throat as they fought for prior utterance.

"You'll help me, won't you?" I babbled. "You can see … they buried me down there … I was trapped … alive in the grave … out now … you'll understand … I can't remember how it began, but … you'll help me?"

A head moved in silent assent.

I halted, regaining composure, striving for coherency.

"This is awkward," I said, more quietly. "I've really no right to ask you for assistance. I don't even know who you are."

The voice from the shadows was only a whisper, but each word thundered in my brain.

"I am a vampire," said the stranger.

Madness. I turned to flee, but the voice pursued me.

"Yes, I am a vampire," he said. "And … *so are you.*"

II

I must have fainted, then. I must have fainted, and he must have carried me out of the cemetery, for when I opened my eyes once more I lay on a sofa in his house.

The panelled walls loomed high, and shadows crawled across the ceiling beyond the candlelight. I sat up, blinked, and stared at the stranger who bent over me.

I could see him now, and I wondered. He was of medium height, gray-haired, clean-shaven, and clad discreetly in a dark business suit. At first glance he appeared normal enough.

The Bat Is My Brother

As his face glided towards me, I stared closer, trying to pierce the veil of his seeming sanity, striving to see the madness beneath the prosaic exterior of dress and flesh.

I stared and saw that which was worse than any madness.

At close glance his countenance was cruelly illumined by the light. I saw the waxen pallor of his skin, and what was worse than that, the peculiar corrugation. For his entire face and throat was covered by a web of tiny wrinkles, and when he smiled it was with a mummy's grin.

Yes, his face was white and wrinkled; white, wrinkled, and long dead. Only his lips and eyes were alive, and they were red ... *too* red. A face as white as corpse-flesh, holding lips and eyes as red as blood.

He smelled *musty*.

All these impressions came to me before he spoke. His voice was like the rustle of the wind through a mortuary wreath.

"You are awake? It is well."

"Where am I? And who are you?" I asked the questions but dreaded an answer. The answer came.

"You are in my house. You will be safe here, I think. As for me, I am your guardian."

"Guardian?"

He smiled. I saw his teeth. Such teeth I had never seen save in the maw of a carnivorous beast. And yet—wasn't *that* the answer?

"You are bewildered, my friend. Understandably so. And that is why you need a guardian. Until you learn the ways of your new life, I shall protect you." He nodded. "Yes Graham Keene, I shall protect you."

"Graham Keene."

It was my name. I knew it *now*. But how did *he* know it?

"In the name of mercy," I groaned, "tell me what has happened to me!"

He patted my shoulder. Even through the cloth I could feel the icy weight of his pallid fingers. They crawled across my neck like worms, like wriggling white worms—

"You must be calm," he told me. "This is a great shock, I know. Your confusion is understandable. If you will just relax a bit and listen, I think I can explain everything."

I listened.

"To begin with, you must accept certain obvious facts. The first being—that you are a vampire."

"But—"

He pursed his lips, his *too* red lips, and nodded.

"There is no doubt about it, unfortunately. Can you tell me how you happened to be emerging from a grave?"

"No. I don't remember. I must have suffered a cataleptic seizure. The shock gave me partial amnesia. But it will come back to me. I'm all right, I must be."

The words rang hollowly even as they gushed from my throat.

"Perhaps. But I think not." He sighed and pointed.

"I can prove your condition to you easily enough. Would you be so good as to tell me what you see behind you, Graham Keene?"

"Behind me?"

"Yes, on the wall."

I stared.

"I don't see anything."

"Exactly."

"But—"

"Where is your shadow?"

* * *

I looked again. There was no shadow, no silhouette. Far a moment my sanity wavered. Then I stared at him. "You have no shadow either," I exclaimed, triumphantly. "What does that prove?"

"That I am a vampire," he said, easily. "And so are you."

"Nonsense. It's just a trick of the light," I scoffed.

"Still skeptical? Then explain this optical illusion." A bony hand proffered a shining object.

I took it, held it. It was a simple pocket mirror.

"Look."

I looked.

The mirror dropped from my fingers and splintered on the floor.

"There's no reflection!" I murmured.

"Vampires have no reflections." His voice was soft. He might have been reasoning with a child.

"If you still doubt," he persisted, "I advise you to feel your pulse. Try to detect a heartbeat."

Have you ever listened for the faint voice of hope to sound within you … knowing that it alone can save you? Have you ever listened and heard nothing? Nothing but the silence of *death?*

The Bat Is My Brother

I knew it then, past all doubt. I was of the Undead ... the Undead who cast no shadows, whose images do not reflect in mirrors, whose hearts are forever stilled, but whose bodies live on—live, and walk abroad, and take nourishment.

Nourishment!

I thought of my companion's red lips and his pointed teeth. I thought of the light blazing in his eyes. A light of hunger. Hunger for what?

How soon must I share that hunger?

He must have sensed the question, for he began to speak once more.

"You are satisfied that I speak the truth, I see. That is well. You must accept your condition and then prepare to make the necessary adjustments. For there is much you have to learn in order to face the centuries to come.

"To begin with, I will tell you that many of the common superstitions about—people like us—are false."

He might have been discussing the weather, for all the emotion his face betrayed. But I could not restrain a shudder of revulsion at his words.

"They say we canna abide garlic. That is a lie. They say we cannot cross running water. Another lie. They say that we must lie by day in the earth of our own graves. That's picturesque nonsense.

"These things, and these alone, are true. Remember them, for they are important to your future. We must sleep by day and rise only at sunset. At dawn an overpowering lethargy bedrugs our senses, and we fall into coma until dusk. We need not sleep in coffins—that is sheer melodrama, I assure you!—but it is best to sleep in darkness, and away from any chance of discovery by men.

"I do not know why this is so, any more than I can account for other phenomena relative to the disease. For vampirism is a disease, you know."

* * *

He smiled when he said it. I didn't smile. I groaned.

"Yes, it is a disease. Contagious, of course, and transmissible in the classic manner, through a bite. Like rabies. What reanimates the body after death no one can say. And why it is necessary to take certain forms of nourishment to sustain existence, I do not know. The daylight coma is a more easily classified medical phenomenon. Perhaps an allergy to the direct actinic rays of the sun.

287

"I am interested in these matters, and I have studied them.

"In the centuries to come I shall endeavor to do some intensive research on the problem. It will prove valuable in perpetuating my existence, and yours."

The voice was harsher now. The slim fingers clawed the air in excitement.

"Think of that, for a moment, Graham Keene," he whispered. "Forget your morbid superstitious dread of this condition and look at the reality.

"Picture yourself as you were before you awoke at sunset. Suppose you had remained there, inside that coffin, nevermore to awaken! Dead—dead for all eternity!"

He shook his head. "You can thank your condition for an escape. It gives you a new life, not just for a few paltry years, but for centuries. Perhaps—forever!

"Yes, think and give thanks! You need never die, now. Weapons cannot harm you, nor disease, nor the workings of age. You are immortal—and I shall show you how to live like a god!"

He sobered. "But that can wait. First we must attend to our needs. I want you to listen carefully now. Put aside your silly prejudices and hear me out. I will tell you that which needs be told regarding our nourishment.

"It isn't easy, you know.

"There aren't any schools you can attend to learn what to do. There are no correspondence courses or books of helpful information. You must learn everything through your own efforts. Everything.

"Even so simple and vital a matter as biting the neck—using the incisors properly—is entirely a matter of personal judgment.

"Take that little detail just as an example. You must choose the classic trinity to begin with—the time, the place, and the girl.

"When you are ready, you must pretend that you are about to kiss her. Both hands go under her ears. That is important, to hold her neck steady, and at the proper angle.

You must keep smiling all the while, without allowing a betrayal of intent to creep into your features or your eyes. Then you bend your head. You kiss her throat. If she relaxes, you turn your mouth to the base of her neck, open it swiftly and place the incisors in position.

"Simultaneously—it *must* be simultaneously—you bring your left hand up to cover her mouth. The right hand must find, seize, and pinion her hands behind her back. No need to hold her throat now. The teeth are doing that. Then, and only then, will instinct come to your aid. It must come then, because once you begin, all else is swept away in the red, swirling blur of fulfillment."

I cannot describe his intonation as he spoke, or the unconscious pantomime which accompanied the incredible instructions. But it is simple to name the look that came into his eyes.

Hunger.

"Come, Graham Keene," he whispered. "We must go now."

"Go? Where?"

"To dine," he told me. "To dine!"

III

He led me from the house, and down a garden pathway through a hedge.

The moon was high, and as we walked along a windswept bluff, flying figures spun a moving web across the moon's bright face.

My companion shrugged.

"Bats," he said. And smiled.

"They say that—we—have the power of changing shape. That we become bats, or wolves. Alas, it's only another superstition. Would that it were true? For then our life would be easy. As it is, the search for sustenance in mortal form is hard. But you will soon understand."

I drew back. His hand rested on my shoulder in cold command.

"Where are you taking me?" I asked.

"To food."

Irresolution left me. I emerged from nightmare, shook myself into sanity.

"No—I won't!" I murmured. "I can't—"

"You must," he told me. "Do you want to go back to the grave?"

"I'd rather," I whispered. "Yes, I'd rather die."

His teeth gleamed in the moonlight.

"That's the pity of it," he said. "You can't die. You'll weaken without sustenance, yes. And you will appear to be dead. Then, whoever finds you will put you in the grave.

"But you'll be alive down there. How would you like to lie there undying in the darkness … writhing as you decay … suffering the torments of red hunger as you suffer the pangs of dissolution?

"How long do you think that goes on? How long before the brain itself is rotted away? How long must one endure the charnal consciousness of the devouring worm? Does the very dust still billow in agony?"

His voice held horror.

"That is the fate you escaped. But it still the fate that awaits you unless you dine with me.

"Besides, it isn't something to avoid, believe me. And I am sure, my friend, that you already feel the pangs of—appetite."

I could not, dared not answer.

For it was true. Even as he spoke, I felt hunger. A hunger greater than any I had ever known. Call it a craving, call it a desire—call it lust. I felt it, gnawing deep within me. Repugnance was nibbled away by the terrible teeth of growing need.

"Follow me," he said, and I followed. Followed along the bluff and down a lonely country road.

We halted abruptly on the highway. A blazing neon sign winked incongruously ahead.

I read the absurd legend.

"DANNY'S DRIVE-IN."

Even as I watched, the sign blinked out.

"Right," whispered my guardian. "It's closing time. They will be leaving now."

"Who?"

"Mr. Danny and his waitress. She serves customers in their cars. They always leave together, I know. They are locking up for the night now. Come along and do as you are told."

I followed him down the road. His feet crunched gravel as he stalked towards the now darkened drive-in stand. My stride quickened in excitement. I moved forward as though pushed by a gigantic hand. The hand of hunger—

He reached the side door of the shack. His fingers rasped the screen.

An irritable voice sounded.

"What do you want? We're closing."

"Can't you serve any more customers?"

"Nah. Too late. Go away."

"But we're very hungry."

I almost grinned. Yes, we were *very* hungry.

"Beat it!" Danny was in no mood for hospitality.

The Bat Is My Brother

"Can't we get anything?"

Danny was silent for a moment. He was evidently debating the point. Then he called to someone inside the stand.

"Marie! Couple customers outside. Think we can fix 'em up in a hurry?"

"Oh, I guess so." The girl's voice was soft, complaisant. Would she be soft and complaisant, too?

"Open up. You guys mind eating outside?"

"Not at all."

"Open the door, Marie."

Marie's high heels clattered across the wooden floor. She opened the screen door, blinked out into the darkness.

My companion stepped inside the doorway. Abruptly, he pushed the girl forward.

"Now!" he rasped.

I lunged at her in darkness. I didn't remember his instructions about smiling at her, or placing my hands beneath her ears. All I knew was that her throat was white, and smooth, except where a tiny vein Throbbed in her neck.

I wanted to touch her neck there with my fingers—with my mouth—with my teeth. So I dragged her into the darkness, and my hands were over her mouth, and I could hear her heels scraping through the gravel as I pulled her along. From inside the shack I heard a single long moan, and then nothing.

Nothing … except the rushing white blur of her neck, as my face swooped towards the throbbing vein….

IV

It was cold in the cellar—cold, and dark. I stirred uneasily on my couch and my eyes blinked open on blackness. I strained to see, raising myself to a sitting position as the chill slowly faded from my bones.

I felt sluggish, heavy with reptilian contentment. I yawned, trying to grasp a thread of memory from the red haze cloaking my thoughts.

Where was I? How had I come here? What had I been doing?

I yawned. One hand went to my mouth. My lips were caked with a dry, flaking substance.

I felt it—and then remembrance flooded me.

Last night, at the drive-in, I had feasted. And then—

"No!" I gasped.

"You have slept? Good."

My host stood before me. I arose hastily and confronted him.

"Tell me it isn't true," I pleaded. "Tell me I was dreaming."

"You were," he answered. "When I came out of the shack you lay under the trees, unconscious. I carried you home before dawn and placed you here to rest. You have been dreaming from sunrise to sunset, Graham Keene."

"But last night—?"

"Was real."

"You mean I took that girl and—?"

"Exactly." He nodded. "But come, we must go upstairs and talk. There are certain questions I must ask."

We climbed the stairs slowly and emerged on ground level. Now I could observe my surroundings with a more objective eye. This house was large, and old. Although completely furnished, it looked somehow untenanted. It was as though nobody had lived here for a long time.

Then I remembered who my host was, and what he was. I smiled grimly. It was true. Nobody was *living* in this house now.

Dust lay thickly everywhere, and the spiders had spun patterns of decay in the corners. Shades were drawn against the darkness, but still it crept in through the cracked walls. For darkness and decay belonged here.

We entered the study where I had awakened last night, and as I was seated, my guardian cocked his head towards me in an attitude of inquiry.

"Let us speak frankly," he began. "I want you to answer an important question."

"Yes?"

"What did you do with her?"

"Her?"

"That girl—last night. What did you do with her body?"

I put my hands to my temples. "It was all a blur. I can't seem to remember."

His head darted towards me eyes blazing. "I'll tell you what you did with her," he rasped. "You threw her body down the well. I saw it floating there."

"Yes," I groaned. "I remember now."

"You fool—why did you do that?"

"I wanted to hide it….I thought they'd never know—"

"You *thought!*" Scorn weighted his voice. "You didn't think for an instant. Don't you see, now she will never rise?"

"Rise?"

"Yes, as you rose. Rise to become one of us."

"But I don't understand."

"That is painfully evident." He paced the floor, then wheeled towards me.

"I see that I shall have to explain certain things to you. Perhaps you are not to blame, because you don't realize the situation. Come with me."

He beckoned. I followed. We walked down the hall, entered a large, shelf-lined room. It was obviously a library. He lit a lamp, halted.

"Take a look around," he invited. "See what you make of it, my friend."

* * *

I scanned the titles on the shelves—titles stamped in gold on thick, handsome bindings; titles worn to illegibility on ancient, raddled leather. The latest in scientific and medical treatises stood on these shelves, flanked by age-encrusted incunabula.

Modern volumes dealt with psychopathology. The ancient lore was frankly concerned with black magic.

"Here is the collection," he whispered. "Here is gathered together all that is known, all that has ever been written about—us."

"A library on vampirism?"

"Yes. It took me decades to assemble it completely."

"But why?"

"Because knowledge is power. And it is power I seek."

Suddenly a resurgent sanity impelled me. I shook off the nightmare enveloping me and sought an objective viewpoint. A question crept into my mind, and I did not try to hold it back.

"Just who are you, anyway?" I demanded. "What is your name?"

My host smiled.

"I have no name," he answered.

"No name?"

"Unfortunate, is it not? When I was buried, there were no loving friends, apparently, to erect a tombstone. And when I arose from the grave, I had no mentor to guide me back to a memory of the past. Those were barbaric times in the East Prussia of 1777."

"You died in 1777?" I muttered.

"To the best of my knowledge," he retorted, bowing slightly in mock deprecation. "And so it is that my real name is unknown. Apparently I perished far from my native heath, for diligent research on my part has failed to uncover my paternity, or any contemporaries who recognized me at the time of my—er—resurrection.

"And so it is that I have no name; or rather, I have many pseudonyms. During the past sixteen decades I have traveled far, and have been all things to all men. I shall not endeavor to recite my history.

"It is enough to say that slowly, gradually, I have grown wise in the ways of the world. And I have evolved a plan. To this end I have amassed wealth, and brought together a library as a basis for my operations.

"Those operations I propose will interest you. And they will explain my anger when I think of you throwing the girl's body into the well."

He sat down. I followed suit. I felt anticipation crawling along my spine. He was about to reveal something—something I wanted to hear, yet dreaded. The revelation came, slyly, slowly.

"Have you ever wondered," he began, "why there are not more vampires in the world?"

"What do you mean?"

"Consider. It is said, and it is true, that every victim of a vampire becomes a vampire in turn. The new vampire finds other victims. Isn't it reasonable to suppose, therefore, that in a short time—through sheer mathematical progression—the virus of vampirism would run epidemic throughout the world? In other words, have you ever wondered why the world is not filled with vampires by this time?"

"Well, yes—I never thought of it that way. What is the reason?" I asked.

He glared and raised a white finger. It stabbed forward at my chest—a rapier of accusation.

"Because of fools like you. Fools who cast their victims into wells; fools whose victims are buried in sealed coffins, who hide the bodies or dismember them so no one would suspect their work.

The Bat Is My Brother

"As a result, few new recruits join the ranks. And the old ones—myself included—are constantly subject to the ravages of the centuries. We eventually disintegrate, you know. To my knowledge, there are only a few hundred vampires today. And yet, if new victims all were given the opportunity to rise—we would have a vampire army within a year. Within three years there would be millions of vampires! Within ten years we could rule earth!

"Can't you see that? If there was no cremation, no careless disposal of bodies, no bungling, we could end our hunted existence as creatures of the night—brothers of the bat! No longer would we be a legendary, cowering minority, living each a law unto himself!

"All that is needed is a plan. And I—I have evolved that plan!"

His voice rose. So did the hairs upon my neck. I was beginning to comprehend, now—

"Suppose we started with the humble instruments of destiny," he suggested. "Those forlorn, unnoticed, ignorant little old men—night watchmen of graveyards and cemeteries."

* * *

A smile creased his corpse-like countenance. "Suppose we eliminated them? Took over their jobs? Put vampires in their places—men who would go to the fresh graves and dig up the bodies of each victim they had bitten while those bodies were still warm and pulsing and undecayed?

"We could save the lives of most of the recruits we make. Reasonable, is it not?"

To me it was madness but I nodded.

"Suppose that we made victims of those attendants? Then carried them off, nursed them back to reanimation, and allowed them to resume their posts as our allies? They work only at night—no one would knew.

"Just a little suggestion, but so obvious! And it world mean so much!" His smile broadened.

"All that it takes is organization on our part. I know many of my brethren. It is my desire soon to call them together and present this plan. Never before have we worked cooperatively, but when I show them the possibilities, they cannot fail to respond.

"Can you imagine it? An earth which we could control and terrorize—a world in which human beings become our property, our cattle?

295

"It is so simple, really. Sweep aside your foolish concepts of *Dracula* and the other superstitious confectionery that masquerades in the public mind as an authentic picture. I admit that we are—unearthly. But there is no reason for us to be stupid, impractical figures of fantasy. There is more for us than crawling around in black cloaks and recoiling at the sight of crucifixes!

"After all we are a life-form, a race of our own. Biology has not yet recognized us, but we exist. Our morphology and metabolism has not been evaluated or charted; our actions and reactions never studied. But we exist. And we are superior to ordinary mortals. Let us assert this superiority! Plain human cunning, coupled with our super-normal powers, can create for us a mastery over all living things. For we are greater than Life—we are Life-in-Death!"

I half-rose. He waved me back, breathlessly.

"Suppose we band together and make plans? Suppose we go about, first of all, selecting our victims on the basis of value to our ranks? Instead of regarding them as sources of easy nourishment, let's think in terms of an army seeking recruits. Let us select keen brains, youthfully strong bodies. Let us prey upon the best earth has to offer. Then we shall wax strong and no man shall stay our hand—or teeth!"

He crouched like a black spider, spinning his web of words to enmesh my sanity. His eyes glittered. It was absurd somehow to see this creature of superstitious terror calmly creating a super-dictatorship of the dead.

And yet, I was one of them. It was real. The nameless one would do it, too.

"Have you ever stopped to wonder why I tell you this? Have you ever stopped to wonder why you are my confidant in this venture?" he purred.

I shook my head.

"It is because you are young. I am old. For years I have labored only to this end. Now that my plans are perfected, I need assistance. Youth, a modern viewpoint. I knew of you, Graham Keene. I watched you before ... you became one of us. You were selected for this purpose."

"Selected?" Suddenly it hit home. I fought down a stranglehold gasp as I asked the question. "Then you know who—did this to me? *You know who bit me?*"

Rotting fangs gaped in a smile. He nodded slowly.

"Of course," he whispered. "Why—*I* did!"

The Bat Is My Brother

V

He was probably prepared for anything except the calmness with which I accepted this revelation.

Certainly he was pleased. And the rest of that night, and all the next night, were spent in going over the plans, in detail. I learned that he had not yet communicated with—others—in regard to his ideas.

A meeting would be arranged soon. Then we would begin the campaign. As he said, the times were ripe. War, a world in unrest—we would be able to move unchallenged and find unusual opportunities.

I agreed. I was even able to add certain suggestions as to detail. He was pleased with my cooperation.

Then, on the third night, came hunger.

He offered to serve as my guide, but I brushed him aside.

"Let me try my own wings," I smiled. "After all, I must learn sooner or later. And I promise you, I shall be very careful. This time I will see to it that the body remains intact. Then I shall discover the place of burial and we can perform an experiment. I will select a likely recruit, we shall go forth to open the grave, and thus will we test our plan in miniature."

He fairly beamed at that. And I went forth that night, alone.

I returned only as dawn welled out of the eastern sky—returned to slumber through the day.

That night we spoke, and I confided my success to his eager ears.

"Sidney J. Garrat is the name," I said. "A college professor, about 45. I found him wandering along a path near the campus. The trees form a dark, deserted avenue. He offered no resistance. I left him there. I don't think they'll bother with an autopsy—for the marks on his throat are invisible and he is known to have a weak heart.

"He lived alone without relatives. He had no money. That means a wooden coffin and quick burial at Everest tomorrow. Tomorrow night we can go there."

My companion nodded.

"You have done well," he said.

We spent the remainder of the night in perfecting our plans. We would go to Everest, locate the night watchman and put him out of the way, then seek the new grave of Professor Garrat.

And so it was that we re-entered the cemetery on the following evening.

Once again a midnight moon glared from the Cyclopean socket of the sky. Once more the wind whispered to us on our way, and the trees bowed in black obeisance along the path.

We crept up to the shanty of the graveyard watchman and peered through the window at his stooping figure.

"I'll knock," I suggested. "Then when he comes to the door—"

My companion shook his gray head. "No teeth," he whispered. "The man is old, useless to us. I shall resort to more mundane weapons."

I shrugged. Then I knocked. The old man opened the door, blinked out at me with rheumy eyes.

"What is it?" he wheezed, querulously. "Ain't nobuddy suppose' tuh be in uh cemetery this time uh night—"

Lean fingers closed around his windpipe. My companion dragged him forth towards nearby shrubbery. His free arm rose and fell, and a silver arc stabbed down. He had used a knife.

Then we made haste along the path, before the scent of blood could divert us from our mission—and far ahead, on the hillside dedicated to the last slumbers of Poverty, I saw the raw, gaping edges of a new-made grave.

He ran back to the hut, then, and procured the spades we had neglected in our haste. The moon was our lantern and the grisly work began amidst a whistling wind.

No one saw us, no one heard us, for only empty eyes and shattered ears lay far beneath the earth.

We toiled, and then we stooped and tugged. The grave was deep, very deep. At the bottom the coffin lay, and we dragged forth the pine box.

"Terrible job," confided my companion. "Not a professionally dug grave at all, in my opinion. Wasn't filled in right. And this coffin is pine, but very thick. He'd never claw his own way out. Couldn't break through the boards. And the earth was packed too tightly. Why would they waste so much time on a pauper's grave?"

"Doesn't matter," I whispered. "Let's open it up. If he's revived, we must hurry."

We'd brought a hammer from the caretaker's shanty, too, and he went down into the pit itself to pry the rails free. I heard the board covering move, and peered down over the edge of the grave.

He bent forward, stooping to peer into the coffin, his face a mask of livid death in the moonlight. I heard him hiss.

"Why—the coffin is empty!" he gasped.

The Bat Is My Brother

"Not for long!"

I drew the wrench from my pocket, raised it, brought it down with every ounce of strength I possessed until it shattered through his skull.

* * *

And then I leaped down into the pit and pressed the writhing, mewing shape down into the coffin, slammed the lid on, and drove the heavy nails into place. I could hear his whimperings rise to muffled screams, but the screams grew faint as I began to heap the clods of earth upon the coffin-lid.

I worked and panted there until no sound came from the coffin below. I packed the earth down hard—harder than I had last night when I dug the grave in the first place.

And then, at last, the task was over.

He lay there, the nameless one, the deathless one; lay six feet underground in a stout wooden coffin.

He could not claw his way free, I knew. And even if he did, I'd pressed him into his wooden prison face down. He'd claw his way to hell, not to earth.

But he was past escape. Let him lie there, as he had described it to me—not dead, not alive. Let him be conscious as he decayed, and as the wood decayed and the worms crawled in to feast. Let him suffer until the maggots at last reached his corrupt brain and ate away his evil consciousness.

I could have driven a stake through his heart. But his ghastly desire deserved defeat in this harsher fate.

Thus it was ended, and I could return now before discovery and the coming of dawn—return to his great house which was the only home I knew on the face of the earth.

Return I did, and for the past hours I have been writing this that all might know the truth.

I am not skilled with words, and what I read here smacks of mawkish melodrama. For the world is superstitious and yet cynical—and this account will be deemed. the ravings of a fool or madman; worse still, a practical joke.

So I must implore you; if you seek to test the truth of what I've set down, go to Everest tomorrow and search out the newly-dug grave on the hillside. Talk to the police when they find the dead watchman, make them go to the well near Danny's roadside stand.

Then, if you must, dig up the grave and find that which must still writhe and crawl within. When you see it, you'll believe—and in justice, you will not relieve the torment of that monstrous being by driving a stake through his heart.

For that stake represents release and peace.

I wish you'd come here, after that—and bring a stake for me....

Black Lotus

This is the story of Genghir the Dreamer, and of the curious fate that overtook him in his dreams; a story old men whisper in the souks of Ispahan as other old men once whispered it in fabled Teraz, five thousand years ago. What portion of it is truth and what portion only fantasy, I leave unto your judgment. There are strange sayings in the banned books, and Alhazred had reasons for his madness; but as I have said, the judgment rests with you. I but relate the tale.

Know then that Genghir was lord over a distant kingdom in the days of the unicorn and the fleet-winged griffin. Rich and powerful was his domain, and peaceful and well-ruled withal, so that its sovereign need occupy himself only with his pleasures.

Handsome was Genghir, but formed as a woman is formed, so that he cared not for the chase or manly combat. His days were spent in rest and study, and his nights in revelry amongst the women. The functions of government rested upon the shoulders of Hassim el Wadir, the Vizier, whilst the true sultan dallied at his pleasures.

Grievous was the life he led, and soon the land was torn by dissension and corruption. But this Genghir heeded not at all, and Hassim he ordered flayed for misuse of his office. And there was revolution and killing throughout the land; and then a fearful plague arose; but all this Genghir minded not, even though two-thirds of his people died. For his thoughts were alien and far away, and the weight of his rule he felt as but a feather. His eyes knew only the musty pages of ensorcelled books and the soft white flesh of women. The witchery of words and wine and wenches cast a spell upon his senses. There was dark magic in the black-bound books his father had brought from ancient conquered realms, and there was enchantment in the old wines and

301

the young bodies that his desires knew; so that he lived in a land of un-reality and dreams. Surely he would have died were it not that those left in the land, after the plague, had fled to other kingdoms, leaving him in an empty city. The report of their going never reached his ears, for well his courtiers knew that those who brought displeasing news were beheaded. But one by one they slipped away, taking with them gold and precious jewels, until the palace lay deserted under a sun that shone upon a barren land.

No longer did the women rest within the zenana, or disport as nymphs beside the amber pools. The sultan turned to other pleasures from the realms of Cathay, and in robes of velvet black he lay and toyed with the juices of the poppy. Then did life become indeed but a dream, and the opium-visioned nightmares took on the semblances of events and places mentioned in the eldritch volumes that he read by day. Time became but as the lengthening of a monstrous dream. Genghir ventured forth into his gardens no more, and less and less did he partake of food or wine. Even his books he forgot, and lay for all the time in a drugged sleep, nor heeded the coming and going of the few followers that remained within his retinue. And a silence of desolation fell upon the land.

Now it came to pass that opium and other drugs were not enough, so that Genghir was forced to seek recourse in other and more potent distillations. And in one of the curious evil books he read of a subtle potion brewed from the juices of the Black Lotus that grows beneath the waning moon. Dire and dreadful were the warnings of the scribe regarding the concoction of this forbidden preparation, for its genesis was deemed unholy, and the dangers surrounding its use by a novice were couched in trenchant terms. But Genghir thirsted for the lurid magic of its dreams and for the promise of its delight, nor would he be content until he should taste of its forbidden ecstasy.

His palace stood dim and deserted, for in the latter days the rem-nant of his sycophants and houris had departed from the dusky halls, whose cheap splendours had long since been bartered for the true de-lights found only in the land of opiate dreams. There now remained but three faithful servitors to guard Genghir on his couch of visions, and these he called unto his side and commanded them to journey forth and seek the venom-distilled beauty of the Black Lotus, in the hidden swamps afar of which the cryptic book had told. And they were much afraid, both for him and for themselves, because they had heard curious legends; with one accord they beseeched him to recall his words. But he grew angered, and his eyes were seen to flame like opals, whereat they departed.

A fortnight passed ere one of them returned—a fortnight during which the dreamer tried in vain to beguile his satiated senses with the common reek of the white flower. Overjoyed was he when the slave returned with his precious burden and brewed from it the blissful juices of nepenthe, following the injunctions set forth in the curious book. But he did not speak of his journey, or venture aught concerning the fate of his two companions; and even the dazed dreamer wondered why he kept his features veiled. In his eagerness he did not inquire, but was content to see the philtre carefully compounded and the pearly-hued liquor inserted in the nargileh. Immediately upon the completion of this task, the servitor departed, and no man knows the manner of his going, save that he lashed his camel far across the desert, riding as though possessed by demons. Genghir did not note his genii-beset progress, for already he was enraptured at the thought of what was to come. Indeed he had not stirred from his divan in the palace chambers, and in his brain was naught but the thirsty dement of desire for the strange new thrill foretold in the elder lore. Queer dreams were promised to him who durst inhale the fumes, dreams of which the old book dare not even hint—"Dreams which surpass Reality, or blend with it in new and unhallowed ways." So spake the scribes, but Genghir was not afraid, and heeded only the promise of delights it was said to hold.

And so it was that he lay on his couch that evening and smoked his hookah alone in the deepening darkness, a dream king in a land where all but dreams was dead. His divan overlooked the balcony high above the empty city, and as the moon rose, its crescent-given rays glistened upon the iridescent bublings of the white fluid in the great bowl through which the smoke was drawn. Sweet indeed was the essence's taste, sweeter than the honeycombs of Kashmir or the kisses of the chosen brides of Paradise. Slowly there came stealing over his senses a new and delightful languor—it was as if he were a creature free-born, a being of the boundless air. He gazed half-seeing at the bubbles, and suddenly they bubbled up, up, up, until they bathed the room in a veil of shimmering beauty, and he felt all identity vanish in their crystalline depths.

Now ensued a period of profound and mystic sadness. He seemed to lie within the graven walls of a tomb, upon a slab of pale-white marble. Shrill funereal pipings seemed to echo from afar, and his nostrils were titillated by the distilled aromatic incense of the sepulchral lily. He knew himself to be dead, and yet he retained the consciousness that was his own in life. The timelessness of common dreams was not his lot; centuries passed on leadenly, and he knew every second of their length as he lay within the tomb of his fathers; enmausoleumed upon a slab covered with stone that was carven with demon-given basilisks.

Long after the odors and the music had faded from the darkness in which he lay came the advent of corruption. He felt his body grow bloatedly purulenscent; felt his features coagulate and his limbs slough off into charnel, oozing slime. And even that was as an instant in the weary, dragging hours of his eternity there. So much longer did he lie bodiless that he lost all conscious recollection of ever having possessed one, and even the dust that had been his bones lost all significance to him. The past, present, and future were as naught; and thus unconsciously Genghir had revealed unto him the basic mystery of life.

Years later the crumbling walls clove thunderously asunder, and shards of debris covered over the decaying slab that now housed naught but an undying consciousness. And even they were overcast by dust and earth, until there was but nothingness to mark the site of the proud tomb where once lay the lords of the house of Genghir. And the soul of Genghir was as nothingness alone amongst nothingness.

Such was the substance of the first dream. As the flicker of his soul expired into everlasting darkness within the earth, Genghir awoke, and he was sweat-bathed, trembling with fear, and as pale as the death he feared. And anon he turned the pages of his book to where it spoke of the Lotus and its prophecies thereof and this he read:

"The first dream shall foretell that which is to come."

Whereat Genghir grew much afraid, and closed the book in the ensilvered moonlight, then lay back upon his couch to sleep, and to forget. But then there came stealing upon his senses the subtly sweet odor of the essence, and its magic englamoured and engulfed, till he grew frantic with the insidious craving for its sinister soothing. Forgotten was fear and prophetic warning; all dissolved peace.

But not for long. Once again the opaque mists of roseate, sweet voluptuousness parted and dissolved, and the enchantment of rapturous, ineffable bliss faded as a new vision supervened.

He saw himself awaken and rise from the couch in the light of dawn, to gaze haggardly upon a new day. He saw the wretched agony of his being as the drug wore off its potency and left his body racked with spasms of exquisite pain. His head seemed to swell as if about to burst; his rotting, benightmared brain seemed to grow inside his skull and split his head asunder. He beheld his frantic gropings about the deserted chamber, the mad capers of grotesque agony that made him tear his hair and foam epileptically at the mouth and gibber terribly as he clawed with twitching fingers at his temples. The white-hot mist of searing anguish sent him reeling to the floor, and then it seemed as though in his dream-consciousness there came to him a horrible longing to be rid of his torment at any cost, and to escape from a living hell to a dead one. In his madness he cursed the book and the warning; cursed the ghastly lotus flower and its essence; cursed himself and his pain. And as the stark biting teeth of his torture bored still closer to the roots of his sanity, he saw himself drag his rigid, paralytic body to the outer balcony of his deserted palace, and with a grimace of agony greater than can be sensed by sanity, he raised himself slowly to the rail. Meanwhile, as he stood there, his head swelled and bloated to monstrous, unbelievable proportions, then burst rottenly asunder in a ghastly blob of gray and scarlet putrefaction, from which arose the stupefying scent of black lotuses. Then, with a single inarticulate cry of horror and despair, he crumpled and toppled from the balcony, to spatter himself in red madness upon the court below.

At this instant he awoke, and his teeth shook inside his mouth as he gagged and retched in terrible repulsion. He felt old and decrepit, and the tide of life ebbed in his veins. He would have fainted were it not for the revivifying fumes of the nargileh that still smoldered beside him. Then unto himself he swore a mighty oath to abandon the ways of the dreamer forever, and rose to his feet and took unto himself the book and turned the pages to the passage of warning, wherein he read this rune:

"The second dream shall show what might have been."

Then there descended upon him a resignation and a black despair. All of his life unrolled before him once again and he knew himself for what he was—a deluded fool. And he knew also that if he did not go back to his drugged slumber there would come to pass the horror of his second dream, as it foretold. So, wearily, and with queer wonder in his heart, he clasped the book to his bosom and betook himself once again to his couch in the moonlight. And his pale fingers lifted the hookah to his ashen lips once again and he once more knew the bliss of Nirvana. He was under the compulsion of a sorcerous thrall.

...O night-black lotus flower, that groweth beneath the River Nile! O poisoned perfumer of all darkness, waving and weaving in the spells of moonlight! O cryptic magic that worketh only evils...

Genghir the Dreamer slept. But there was brooding ecstasy and mystic wonder in his dreams, and he knew the beauty that lies in twilight grottoes on the dark side of the moon, and his brow was fanned and his slumbers lulled by the pale wind that is the little gods who dance in paradise. And he stood alone in a sea of endless infinity, before a monstrous flower that beckoned great, hypnotic petals before his dream-dazed eyes, and whispered unto him a command. In his vision he glanced down to where a dagger hung by his side, in his jeweled stomacher of sultanship.

And there came to him a sudden gleam of understanding. This before him was the Black Lotus, symbol of the evil that waits for men in sleep. It was casting a spell upon him that would lure him to death. He knew now the way of atonement for the past and the release of his enchantment—he must strike!

But even as he moved, the great flower shot out one velvet petal steeped in the cloying scent that was a wind from the gate of heaven. And the black petal entwined itself about his neck like a loathsome and beautiful serpent, and with its succubi-like embrace sought to drown his senses in a sea of scented bliss.

But Genghir would not be frustrated. The allurement of delight left him cold, but his numbing brain commanded him. He raised the silver dagger from his side and with a single blow, slashed off the twining coiler from his neck...

Then Genghir saw the flowers and the petals vanish, and he was left alone in a universe of mocking laughter: a dim world that rocked with leering mirth of idiotic gods. For an instant he awoke to see a ruby necklace encircling his bare throat; to realize monstrously that in his dream he had cut his own throat. Then, on a bed of moonlight, he died, and there was silence in the deserted roam, while from the dead throat of Genghir the Dreamer little drops of blood fell upon an open page of a curious book; upon a curious sentence in oddly underlined letters:

"The third dream brings reality."

Nothing more remained, save the all-pervading scent of lotus flowers that filled the nighted room.